"YOU ARE SO ARROGANT."

Bones came closer until only a few feet separated us. "I'm very powerful. More than you're aware of. That is truth, not arrogance. Every member of your team couldn't protect you as well as I can, and you know it. Whether you want my help or not, Kitten, you're getting it."

"Don't worry about me, I can take care of myself."

I was suddenly gripped in Bones's arms with my head tilted back. Maybe that was my own fault. I'd been so busy keeping up my emotional shields, I'd forgotten about my physical ones. And truth be told, I never expected him to bite me.

Yeah, I'd let my usual vampire guards down all the way with Bones.

His fangs buried deep into my neck. The strangest kind of heat flooded through me.

Stop it, I wanted to say, but couldn't seem to form the words. What came out was a primitive groan instead. He tightened his arms around me, tilting me back, and li̲c̲k̲i̲n̲g̲ ̲m̲y̲ ̲n̲e̲c̲k̲ before sinking his t̲e̲e̲t̲h̲ ̲i̲n̲ ̲a̲g̲a̲i̲n̲.

I found m̲y̲s̲e̲l̲f̲ ̲t̲h̲i̲n̲k̲i̲n̲g̲ ̲i̲f̲ ̲I̲ ̲h̲a̲d̲ ̲t̲o̲ die, at least I'd d̲i̲e̲ ̲h̲a̲p̲p̲y̲.

By Jeaniene Frost

DESTINED FOR AN EARLY GRAVE
AT GRAVE'S END
ONE FOOT IN THE GRAVE
HALFWAY TO THE GRAVE

One Foot in the Grave

in the Grave

A Night Huntress Novel

Jeaniene Frost

AVON

An Imprint of HarperCollinsPublishers

This is a work of fiction. Names, characters, places, and incidents are products of the author's imagination or are used fictitiously and are not to be construed as real. Any resemblance to actual events, locales, organizations, or persons, living or dead, is entirely coincidental.

AVON BOOKS
An Imprint of HarperCollins*Publishers*
10 East 53rd Street
New York, New York 10022–5299

Copyright © 2008 by Jeaniene Frost
Excerpts from *One Foot in the Grave* copyright © 2008 by Jeaniene Frost; *Your Scandalous Ways* copyright © 2008 by Loretta Chekani; *After the Kiss* copyright © 2008 by Suzanne Enoch; *Before the Scandal* copyright © 2008 by Suzanne Enoch
ISBN: 978-0-06-124509-1
www.avonromance.com

First Avon Books paperback printing: May 2008

Avon Trademark Reg. U.S. Pat. Off. and in Other Countries, Marca Registrada, Hecho en U.S.A.
HarperCollins® is a registered trademark of HarperCollins Publishers.

Printed in the U.S.A.

10 9 8 7

To my father.
You are now,
and will always be,
my hero.

Acknowledgments

This past year has really driven home why books have an acknowledgments page. Writing an initial draft might be done in solitude, but everything after that isn't.

First, I want to thank God, for granting me what I hadn't even dared to pray for.

Next, I want to thank my husband, Matthew, for giving me the love and support that made me believe I could pursue my dreams, and for accepting me as I am, which has made all the difference.

I want to thank the fans of the Night Huntress series. Your enthusiasm for my characters means more to me than I can ever express.

I owe a huge thank you to my editor, Erika Tsang, who really rolled up her sleeves with me on this one. Aside from her outstanding feedback on what was and wasn't needed to get this story told, she also spent an hour with me discussing the varied potentials for a ghoul's diet (hope your appetite has finally recovered!). You're the best, Erika.

Thanks go to my agent, Rachel Vater. I can't imagine anyone else helping me along this journey.

Immense gratitude goes to Tom Egner, for my gorgeous covers. Further thanks go to the wonderful people at Avon Books, who've made my experience with the publishing world such a pleasant one.

Sincerest thanks go to Melissa Marr, Jordan Summers, Mark Del Franco, and Rhona Westbrook, for beta-reading OFITG and keeping me on track. Also thanks to Vicki Pettersson, for enough hours of encouragement to warrant therapy payments.

Of course, I'm grateful to my family, especially my parents and sisters. Your unconditional support has meant the world to me.

Last but not least, I want to again thank Melissa Marr. You'll never know how important your friendship has been along this strange, bumpy road. I'd try to articulate, but we both know you're better with words than I am.

Oпe

I WAITED OUTSIDE THE LARGE, FOUR-STORY home in Manhasset that was owned by a Mr. Liam Flannery. This wasn't a social call, as anyone looking at me could tell. The long jacket I wore was open, leaving my gun and shoulder holster clearly visible, as was my FBI badge. My pants were loose-fitting and so was my blouse, to hide the twenty pounds of silver weapons strapped to my arms and legs.

My knock was answered by an older man in a business suit. "Special Agent Catrina Arthur," I said. "Here to see Mr. Flannery."

Catrina wasn't my real name, but it's what was on my doctored badge. The doorman gave me an insincere smile.

"I'll see if Mr. Flannery is in. Wait here."

I already knew Liam Flannery was in. What I also knew was that Mr. Flannery wasn't human, and neither was the doorman.

Well, neither was I, even though I was the only one out of the three of us with a heartbeat.

A few minutes later, the door reopened. "Mr. Flannery has agreed to see you."

That was his first mistake. If I had anything to say about it, it would also be his last.

My first thought as I entered Liam Flannery's house was, *Wow*. Hand-carved wood adorned all the walls, the floor was some kind of really expensive-looking marble, and antiques were tastefully littered everywhere the eye could see. Being dead sure didn't mean you couldn't live it up.

The hairs on the back of my neck stood on end as power filled the room. Flannery wouldn't know I could feel it, just like I'd felt it from his ghoul doorman. I might look as average as the next person, but I had a few secrets up my sleeve. And lots of knives, of course.

"Agent Arthur," Flannery said. "This must be about my two employees, but I've already been questioned by the police."

His accent was English, which was at odds with his Irish name. Just hearing that intonation made a shiver run up my spine. English accents held memories for me.

I turned around. Flannery looked even better than the picture in his FBI file. His pale crystal flesh almost shimmered against the tan color of his shirt. I'll say one thing for vampires—they all had gorgeous skin. Liam's eyes were a clear turquoise, and his chestnut hair fell past his collar.

Yep, he was pretty. He probably had no trouble scaring up dinner. But the most impressive thing about him was his aura. It flowed off him in tingling, power-filled waves. A Master vampire without a doubt.

"Yes, this is about Thomas Stillwell and Jerome Hawthorn. The Bureau would appreciate your cooperation."

My polite stalling was to gauge how many other people were in the house. I strained my ears, but so far came up with no one but Flannery, the ghoul doorman, and myself.

"Of course. Anything to assist law and order," he said with an undercurrent of amusement.

"And you're comfortable speaking here?" I asked, trying to get more of a look around. "Or is there somewhere private you'd prefer?"

He sauntered over. "Agent Arthur, if you want to have a private word with me, call me Liam. And I do hope you want to talk about something other than boring Jerome and Thomas."

Oh, I had little intention of talking as soon as I got Liam in private. Since he'd been implicated in the deaths of his employees, Flannery had made my to-do list, though I wasn't here to arrest him. The average person didn't believe in vampires or ghouls, so there wasn't a legal process for dealing with murdering ones. No, there was a covert branch of Homeland Security instead, and my boss, Don, would send me. There were rumors about me in the undead world, true. Ones that had grown during my tenure at this job, but only one vampire knew who I really was. And I hadn't seen him in over four years.

"Liam, you're not flirting with a federal agent who's investigating you in a double homicide, are you?"

"Catrina, an innocent man doesn't fret over the wheels of law whenever they rumble in the distance. At least I commend the feds on sending *you* to speak with me, beautiful woman that you are. You also look a bit familiar, though I'm sure I would have remembered meeting you before."

"You haven't," I said immediately. "Trust me, I would have remembered."

I didn't mean it as a compliment, but it caused him to chuckle in a way that was too insinuating for my liking.

"I'll bet."

You smug son of a bitch. Let's see how long you'll keep that smirk.

"Back to business, Liam. Are we talking here, or somewhere private?"

He made a noise of defeat. "If you insist on traveling this path, we may as well be comfortable in the library. Come with me."

I followed him past more lavish, empty rooms to the library. It was magnificent, with hundreds of new and old books. There were even scrolls preserved in a glass display case, but it was the large piece of artwork on the wall that caught my attention.

"This looks . . . primitive."

At first glance it appeared to be wood or ivory, but on closer inspection, it looked like bones. Human ones.

"Aborigine, nearly three hundred years old. Given to me by some mates of mine in Australia."

Liam came nearer, his turquoise eyes starting to glint with emerald. I knew the pinpoints of green in his gaze for what they were. Lust and feeding looked the same on a vampire. Both made the eyes glow emerald and the fangs pop out. Liam was either hungry or horny, but I wasn't going to satisfy any of his cravings.

My cell phone rang. "Hello," I answered.

"Agent Arthur, are you still questioning Mr. Flannery?" my second-in-command, Tate, asked.

"Yes. This should be wrapped up in thirty minutes."

Translation: If I didn't answer again in half an hour, Tate and my team would come in after me.

Tate hung up without further comment. He hated it when I handled things alone, but too bad. Flannery's house was as quiet as a tomb, apropos as that may be, and it had been a long time since I'd battled with a Master vampire.

"I believe the police told you that the bodies of Thomas Stillwell and Jerome Hawthorn were found with most of their blood missing. And not any visible wounds on them to account for it," I said, jumping right in.

Liam shrugged. "Does the Bureau have a theory?"

Oh, we had more than a theory. I knew Liam would have just closed the telltale holes on Thomas and Jerome's necks with a drop of his own blood before they died. Boom, two bodies drained, no vampire calling card to rally the villagers—unless you knew what tricks to look for.

Flatly I shot back, "*You* do, though, don't you?"

"You know what I have a theory on, Catrina? That you taste as sweet as you look. In fact, I haven't thought about anything else since you walked in."

I didn't resist when Liam closed the distance between us and lifted my chin. After all, this would distract him better than anything I came up with.

His lips were cool on mine and vibrating with energy, giving my mouth pleasant tingles. He was a very good kisser, sensing when to deepen it and when to *really* deepen it. For a minute, I actually allowed myself to enjoy it—God, four years of celibacy must be taking its toll!—and then I got down to business.

My arms went around him, concealing me pulling a dagger from my sleeve. At the same time, he slid his hands down to my hips and felt the hard outlines under my pants.

"What the hell—?" he muttered, pulling back.

I smiled. "Surprise!" And then I struck.

It would have been a killing blow, but Liam was faster than I anticipated. He swept my feet out from under me just as I jabbed, so my silver missed his heart by inches. Instead of attempting to regain my stability, I let myself drop, rolling away from the kick he aimed at my head. Liam moved in a streak to try it again, but then jerked back when three of my throwing knives landed in his chest. Dammit, I'd missed his heart *again*.

"Sweet bleedin' Christ!" Liam exclaimed. He quit pretending to be human and let his eyes turn glowing emerald while fangs popped out in his upper teeth. "*You* must be the fabled Red Reaper. What brings the vampire bogeyman to my home?"

He sounded intrigued, but not afraid. He was more wary, however, and circled around me as I sprang to my feet, throwing off my jacket to better access my weapons.

"The usual," I said. "You murdered humans. I'm here to settle the score."

Liam actually rolled his eyes. "Believe me, poppet, Jerome and Thomas had it coming. Those thieving bastards stole from me. It's so hard to find good help these days."

"Keep talking, pretty boy. I don't care."

I rolled my head around on my shoulders and palmed more knives. Neither of us blinked as we waited for the other to make a move. What Liam didn't know was that I was aware he'd summoned for help. I could hear the ghoul creep quietly closer toward us, barely disturbing the air around him. Liam's chattering was just to buy time.

He shook his head in apparent self-recrimination.

"Your appearance should have warned me. The Red Reaper is said to have hair as red as blood, gray eyes like smoke, and your skin . . . mmm, now there's the real distinction. I've never seen such beautiful flesh on a human before. Christ, girl, I wasn't even going to bite you. Well, not the way you're thinking."

"I'm flattered you want to fuck me as well as murder me. Really, Liam, that's sweet."

He grinned. "Valentine's Day was just last month, after all."

He was forcing me toward the door and I let him. Deliberately I pulled my longest knife from my pants leg, the one that was practically a small sword, and switched it with my throwing knives in my right hand.

Liam grinned wider when he saw it. "Impressive, but you haven't seen *my* lance yet. Drop your trappings and I'll show you. You can even keep a few knives on, if you'd like. Would only make it more interesting."

He lunged forward, but I didn't take the bait. Instead I flung the five knives in my left hand at him and whirled to avoid the blow from the ghoul behind me. With a single swipe that reverberated through my arm, I sent the blade into the ghoul's neck with all my strength.

It came out on the other side. The ghoul's head rotated on its axis for a moment, wide eyes fixed on mine, before it plopped to the ground. There was only one way to kill a ghoul, and that was it.

Liam yanked my silver knives out of him as if they were merely toothpicks.

"You nasty bitch, *now* I'm going to hurt you! Magnus has been my friend for over forty years!"

That signaled the end to the bantering. Liam came at me with incredible speed. He had no weapons except his body and his teeth, but those were formidable. Liam pounded his fists into me, and I retaliated with punishing blows. For several minutes, we just hammered at each other, knocking over every table and lamp in our path. Finally he threw me across the room, and I crashed near the unusual art piece I'd admired. When he came after me, I kicked out and knocked him backward into the display case. Then I tore the sculpture off the wall and chucked it at his head.

Liam ducked, cursing when the intricate artwork broke into pieces behind him.

"Don't you have any bleedin' respect for artifacts? That piece was older than I am! And how in the *blazes* did you get eyes like that?"

I didn't need to look to know what he was talking

about. My formerly gray gaze would now be glowing as green as Liam's. Fighting brought out the proof of my mixed heritage that my unknown vampire father had left me.

"That bone puzzle was older than you are, huh? So you're what, two hundred? Two fifty? You're strong then. I've skewered vamps as old as seven hundred who didn't hit as hard as you do. You're going to be fun to kill."

God help me, but I wasn't kidding. There was no sport when I just staked a vampire and let my team sweep up the remains.

Liam grinned at me. "Two hundred and twenty, poppet. In pulseless years, that is. The other ones weren't good for anything but poverty and misery. London was a sewage back then. Looks much better now."

"Too bad you won't be seeing it again."

"I doubt that, poppet. You think you'll enjoy killing me? I know I'll *love* fucking you."

"Let's see what you've got," I taunted.

He flew across the room—too swiftly for me to avoid him—and delivered a brutal blow to my head. It made light explode in my brain and would have put a normal person right into the grave. Me, I'd never been normal, so while I fought nausea, I also reacted quickly.

I went limp, letting my mouth hang open and my eyes roll back as I dropped to the ground with my throat temptingly tilted upward. Near my relaxed hand was one of the throwing knives he'd pulled from his chest. Would Liam kick me while I was down, or see how badly I was hurt?

My gamble paid off. "That's better," Liam muttered, and knelt next to me. He let his hands travel over my body, and then he grunted in amusement.

"Talk about an army of one. Woman's wearing a whole bloody arsenal."

He unzipped my pants in a businesslike manner. Probably he was going to strip me of my knives; that would be the smart thing. When he pulled my pants past my hips, however, he paused. His fingers traced over the tattoo on my hip that I'd gotten four years ago, right after I left my old life in Ohio behind for this new one.

Seizing my chance, I closed my hand over the nearby dagger and drove the knife into his heart. Liam's shocked eyes met mine as he froze.

"I thought if the *Alexander* didn't kill me, nothing would . . ."

I was just about to deliver that final, fatal twist when the last piece clicked. *A ship named the* Alexander. *He was from London, and he'd been dead about two hundred and twenty years. He had Aborigine artwork, given to him from a friend in Australia* . . .

"Which one are you?" I asked, holding the knife still. If he moved, it would shred his heart. If he stayed motionless, it wouldn't kill him. Yet.

"What?"

"In 1788, four convicts sailed to South Wales penal colonies on a ship named the *Alexander*. One escaped soon after arriving. A year later, that runaway convict returned and killed everyone but his three friends. One of them was turned into a vampire by choice, two by force. I know who you're not, so tell me who you are."

If it were possible, he looked even more astonished

than he had when I stabbed him in the heart. "Only a few people in the world know that story."

I gave the blade a menacing flick that edged it fractions deeper. He got the point, all right.

"Ian. I am Ian."

Mother*fucker!* On top of me was the man who'd turned the love of my life into a vampire almost two hundred and twenty years ago. Talk about irony.

Liam, or Ian, was a murderer by his own admission. Granted, his employees may or may not have stolen from him; the world never lacked for fools. Vampires played by a different set of rules when it came to their possessions. They were territorial to a fantastic degree. If Thomas and Jerome knew what he was and stole from him, they'd have known the consequences. But that wasn't what stayed my hand. Eventually it boiled down to one simple truth—I might have left Bones, but I couldn't kill the person responsible for bringing him into my life.

Yeah, call me sentimental.

"Liam, or Ian, if you prefer, listen to me very carefully. You and I are going to stand up. I'm going to pull this knife out, and then you're going to run away. Your heart's been punctured, but you'll heal. I owed someone a life and I'm making it yours."

He stared at me. The glowing lights of our eyes merged.

"Crispin." Bones's real name hung between us, but I didn't react. Ian let out a pained laugh. "It could only be Crispin. Should have known from the way you fought, not to mention your tattoo that's identical to his. Nasty trick, faking to be unconscious. He would have never fallen for it. He'd have kicked you until you quit pretending."

"You're right," I agreed mildly. "That's the first thing Bones taught me. Always kick someone when they're down. I paid attention. You didn't."

"Well, well, little Red Reaper. So you're the reason he's been in such a foul mood the past few years."

At once my heart constricted with joy. Ian had just confirmed what I hadn't allowed myself to wonder. Bones was alive. Even if he hated me for leaving him, he was alive.

Ian pressed his advantage. "You and Crispin, hmm? I haven't spoken to him in a few months, but I can find him. I could take you to him, if you'd like."

The thought of seeing Bones again caused a shattering of emotions in me. To cover them, I laughed derisively.

"Not for gold. Bones found me and turned me out as bait for the marks he was paid to kill. Even talked me into that tattoo. Speaking of gold, when you see Bones again, you can tell him he still owes me money. He never paid me my share of the jobs like he promised. The only reason it's *your* lucky day is he helped rescue my mother once, so I owe him for that, and you're my payment. But if I ever see Bones again, it'll be at the end of my knife."

Each word hurt, but they were necessary. I wouldn't hang a target around Bones's neck by admitting I still loved him. If Ian repeated what I said, Bones would know it wasn't true. He hadn't refused to pay me on the jobs I'd done with him—I'd refused to take the money. Nor had he talked me into my tattoo. I'd gotten the crossbones matching his out of useless longing after I left him.

"You're part vampire. You have to be with those glowing eyes. Tell me—how?"

I almost didn't, but figured, what the hell. Ian already knew my secret. The *how* was anticlimactic.

"Some newly dead vampire raped my mother, and unluckily for her, his sperm still swam. I don't know who he is, but one day I'll find him and kill him. Until then, I'll settle for deadbeats just like him."

Somewhere on the far side of the room, my cell phone rang. I didn't move to answer it, but spoke hurriedly.

"That's my backup. When I don't answer, they come in with force. More force than you can take on right now. Move slowly; stand up. When I take this knife out, you run like hell and don't stop. You'll get your life, but you're leaving this house and you're not coming back. Do we have a deal? Think before you answer, because I don't bluff."

Ian smiled tightly. "Oh, I believe you. You've got a knife in my heart. That gives you little reason to lie."

I didn't blink. "Then let's do this."

Without another comment, Ian began to pull himself to his knees. Each movement was agony for him, I could tell, but he thinned his lips and didn't make a sound. When we both stood, I carefully drew the blade out of his back and held the bloody knife in front of me.

"Goodbye, Ian. Get lost."

He crashed through a window to my left in a blur of speed that was slower than before, but still impressive. Out in front, I heard my men rushing up to the door. There was one last thing I had to do.

I plunged the same dagger into my belly, deep enough to make me drop to my knees, but high enough to avoid mortal injury. When my second officer, Tate, came running into the room, I was gasping and bent double, blood pouring out onto the lovely thick carpet.

"Jesus, Cat!" he exclaimed. "Someone get the Brams!"

My other two captains, Dave and Juan, fanned out to comply. Tate picked me up and carried me out of the house. With jagged breaths I gave my instructions.

"One got away but don't chase him. He's too strong. No one else is in the house, but do a quick check and then pull back. We have to leave in case he comes back with reinforcements. They'd slaughter us."

"One sweep and then fall back, fall back!" Dave ordered, shutting the doors of the van I'd been taken to. Tate pulled the knife out and pressed bandages to the wound, giving me several pills to swallow that no regular pharmacy carried.

After four years and a team of brilliant scientists, my boss, Don, had managed to filter through the components in undead blood to come up with a wonder drug. On regular humans, it repaired injuries such as broken bones and internal bleeding like magic. We'd named it Brams, in honor of the writer who'd made vampires famous.

"You shouldn't have gone in alone," Tate berated me. "Goddammit, Cat, next time listen to me!"

I gave a faint chuckle. "Whatever you say. I'm not in the mood to argue."

Then I passed out.

Two

MY HOUSE WAS A SMALL TWO-STORY STRUC-
ture at the end of a cul-de-sac. The interior was
almost spartan in its bareness. A single couch downstairs, bookshelves, some lamps, and a minibar loaded
with gin and tonic. If my liver wasn't half vampire, I'd
have expired from cirrhosis already. Certainly Tate,
Juan, and Dave never complained about all my booze. A
steady supply of liquor and a deck of cards was enough
to keep them coming back. Too bad none of them were
great poker players, even when sober. Get them drunk
and it was funny to watch their card skills drop by the
second.

So, how does one sign on for this life of luxury? My
boss, Don, found me at twenty-two when I got into a
little trouble with the law. You know, the usual youth-
ful stuff. Killed the governor of Ohio and several of
his staff, but they'd been modern-day slavers who sold
women to the undead for food and fun. Yeah, they de-

served to die, especially since I was one of the women they'd tried to sell. Me and my vampire boyfriend, Bones, had delivered our own brand of justice to them, which left a lot of bodies.

After I was arrested, my funky pathology reports tattled on me for not being totally human. Don snapped me up to lead his secret "Homeland Security" unit by giving me the quintessential offer I couldn't refuse. Or death threat, to be more accurate. I'd taken the job. What choice did I have?

But despite his many flaws, Don truly cared about defending those the normal law could never protect. I cared about that as well. It was why I risked my life, because I felt this was the reason I'd been born half dead but looking all human. I could be both bait and hook to what prowled in the night. It wasn't a happily-ever-after, true, but at least I'd made a positive difference for some people.

My phone rang as I changed into my pajamas. Since it was almost midnight, it had to be either one of the guys or Denise, because my mother was never up this late.

"Hey, Cat. Just get in?"

Denise knew what I did, and she knew what I was. One night while minding my own business, I'd come across a vamp trying to turn her neck into a Big Gulp. By the time I killed him, she'd already seen enough to know he wasn't human. To her credit, she hadn't screamed, fainted, or done any of the things a normal person would. She'd simply blinked and said, "Wow. I owe you a beer, at least."

"Yeah," I answered. "Just got in now."

"Uh, bad day?" she asked.

But she didn't know I'd spent most of the day healing from a self-inflicted stab wound with the help of Brams and the dubious benefit of having gutted myself with a knife coated in vampire blood. That in itself had probably done more to heal me than Don's magic pills. Nothing but nothing healed like vampire blood.

"Um, the usual. How about you? How was your date?"

She laughed. "I'm on the phone with you; what does that say? In fact, I was just about to defrost a cheesecake. Want to come over?"

"Sure, but I'm in my pajamas."

"Don't forget the fluffy slippers." I could almost see Denise's grin. "You wouldn't look right without them."

"See you soon."

We hung up and I smiled. Loneliness was put on hold. At least until the cheesecake ran out.

At this time of night, the Virginia roads were mostly deserted, but my eyes were peeled because this was prime undead foraging hour. Usually it was just a vamp taking a snack. They used the power in their gaze and the hallucinogenic in their fangs to drink and run, leaving their meals with a false memory and a lower iron count. Bones had been the one to reveal that to me. He'd taught me all about vampires: their strengths (many!), weaknesses (few, and sunlight, crosses, and wooden stakes weren't among them), their beliefs (that Cain was the first vampire, created when God punished him for murdering Abel by changing him into something that must forever drink blood as a reminder that he'd spilled his brother's), and how they lived in pyramidlike societies where the top vampire ruled over all the "children" they created. Yeah, Bones had taught me everything I knew.

And then I'd left him.

I swerved and hit the brakes as a cat darted in front of my tires. I climbed out to find it lying near my car. It tried to run, but I caught it and looked it over. There was blood on its nose, some scratches, and it let out a cry when I moved its leg. Broken, without a doubt.

Mumbling soothing nonsense, I got out my cell phone. "I just hit a kitten," I told Denise. "Can you find a vet for me? I can't just leave it."

She made a cooing sound of sympathy and went to fetch the phone book. After a moment, she was back.

"This one is open all night and they're not far from you. Let me know how the kitty does, okay? I'll put the cheesecake back in the freezer."

I hung up, then called the vet to get directions. In ten minutes, I pulled up to Noah's Furry Ark.

Over my pajamas I had on my coat, but instead of boots, yes, I was wearing blue fuzzy slippers. I probably looked like a housewife from hell.

The man behind the desk smiled when I entered. "Are you the lady that just called? With the cat?"

"That's me."

"And you are Mrs. . . . . ?"

"Miss. Cristine Russell." That was the name I went under now, another tribute to my lost love, since Bones's human name had been Crispin Russell. My sentimental curse would be the end of me.

That friendly smile widened. "I'm Dr. Noah Rose."

Noah. That explained the corny name of the place.

He took the kitty for X-rays and returned after a few minutes.

"One broken leg, some abrasions, and malnutrition. He should be fine in a couple weeks. This was a stray?"

"As far as I know, Dr. Rose."

"Noah, please. Cute little kitten; are you going to keep him?"

The word *kitten* made me flinch, but I covered it and answered without thinking.

"Yes."

The kitten's wide eyes fixed on me, as though he knew his fate had been settled. With his tiny leg in a cast and ointment in his scratches, he looked truly pitiful.

"With food and rest, this kitty will be good as new."

"That's great. How much do I owe you?"

He smiled in an abashed way. "No charge. You did a nice thing. You'll have to bring him back in two weeks for me to remove that cast. When is good for you?"

"Anything late. I, er, work strange hours."

"Evenings aren't a problem."

He gave me another shy smile, and something told me he wasn't as accommodating with every client. Still, he seemed harmless. That was a rarity in the men I met.

"What about eight on Thursday in two weeks?"

"Fine."

"Thanks for the help, Noah. I owe you one." With the cat in tow, I started toward the door.

"Wait!" He came around the desk and then stopped. "This is entirely unprofessional, but if you think you owe me, not that you *do*, of course, but . . . I'm new in

town, and . . . well, I don't know many people. Most of
my clients are older or married and . . . what I'm trying
to say is . . ."

I raised a questioning brow at this ramble, and he
actually flushed. "Never mind. If you don't show up for
your appointment, I'll understand. I'm sorry."

The poor guy was a sweetheart. I gave him a
quick feminine perusal, far different from the danger-
assessment one I'd done when I first came in. Noah
was tall, dark, and boyishly handsome. Maybe I'd
hook him up with Denise—she just said her other date
hadn't impressed her.

"Okay, Noah, the answer's yes. In fact, my friend
Denise and I were going to catch dinner Monday night.
You're welcome to join us."

He let out a breath. "Monday is perfect. I'll call you
Sunday to confirm. I don't normally do things like this.
God, that sounds like a line. Let me ask for your num-
ber, before I talk you out of it."

With a smile I wrote down my cell number. If Noah
and Denise hit it off, I'd quietly leave before dessert.
If he turned out to be a jerk, then I'd make sure he
was sent on his way without bothering her further. Hey,
what were friends for?

"Please don't change your mind," he said when I
handed him my number.

Instead of responding, I merely waved good night.

THREE

At ten to six the following Monday, my phone rang. I glanced at the number that flashed up and frowned. Why was Denise calling me from her house? She was supposed to have gotten here fifteen minutes ago.

"What's up?" I answered. "You're running late."

It sounded like she took a deep breath. "Cat, don't be mad at me, but . . . I'm not coming."

"Are you sick?" I asked worriedly.

There was the sound of another deep breath. "No, I'm not coming because I want *you* to go out with Noah. Alone. You said he seemed like a really nice guy."

"But I don't want to go on a date!" I protested. "I was only doing this so you could meet him, but then have a graceful way out if he wasn't your type."

"For God's sake, Cat, I don't need another date, but you do! I mean, my *grandmother* gets more action than you. Look, I know you don't talk about the other guy, whoever he was, but we've been friends for over three years and you've got to start to live. Dazzle Noah with your drinking skills, burn his ears with your language, but *try* to have a little fun with a guy you're not intending to kill by the end of the night. At least once. Maybe then you won't be so sad all the time."

She'd hit a nerve. Even though I'd never mentioned specifics about Bones, especially the one about him being a vampire, she knew I'd loved someone and then lost him. And she knew how alone I felt, more than I'd ever admit to.

I sighed. "I don't think it's a good idea—"

"I do," she cut me off at once. "You're not dead, so you need to stop acting like you are. It's just dinner, not eloping to Vegas. No one says you even have to see Noah again. But just go out this once. Come on."

I looked at my new kitty. He blinked, which I took as a yes as well.

"All right. Noah's due here in five minutes. I'll go, but I'll probably say something completely inappropriate and be home in an hour."

Denise laughed. "It doesn't matter; at least you'd have given it a shot. Call me when you get in."

I said goodbye and hung up. Apparently I was going on a date. Ready or not.

As I passed by a mirror, I did a double take at my reflection. My newly brown hair was cut shoulder-length and looked foreign, but that was the idea, in case Ian decided to confirm the rumors about my appearance. I didn't need any vampires or ghouls getting a heads-up as to who I was because of my hair color. Blondes might have more fun, but I was hoping for a higher body count. The Red Reaper had been laid to rest. Long live the Brunette Reaper!

When Noah knocked on the door, I was as prepared as I was going to be. His smile froze when he saw me.

"You were a redhead before, right? I didn't just imagine it in my anxiety?"

I raised a brow, no longer red but honey-colored. "I wanted a change. Been a redhead all my life, and I felt like something different."

He backpedaled at once. "Well, it's beautiful. *You're* beautiful. I mean, you were beautiful before and you still are now. Let's go, before you change your mind."

I already had, but that had nothing to do with Noah. Still, much as I hated to admit it, Denise was right. I could spend another night tormenting myself over someone I could never have, or I could go out and try to have a nice evening for a change.

"Bad news," I told him. "My friend, um, got held up and she couldn't make it. Sorry. If you want to cancel I'll completely understand."

"No," Noah said at once, smiling. "I'm hungry. Let's eat."

It's just one date, I reminded myself as I walked to his car. What harm could there be?

Noah and I went to Renardo's, an Italian bistro. Out of courtesy I drank only red wine, not wanting to reveal my penchant for vast quantities of gin and tonic.

"What do you do for a living, Cristine?" he asked.

"Field research and recruitment for the Bureau."

It was sorta true, if you called hunting down and killing creatures of the night *research*. Or defined going across the country rounding up the best men the military, law enforcement, FBI, or even the criminal justice system had to offer as *recruitment*. Hey, far be it for an operation that killed the undead to discriminate in who we hired, right? Some of our best team members had once worn an orange jersey. Juan was a penal code graduate who chose working for Don over twenty years behind bars. The mishmash might not make for the most traditionally behaved fighting unit, but it sure was a deadly one.

Noah's eyes widened. "The Bureau? You're an FBI agent?"

"Not technically. Our department is more of an extension of Homeland Security."

"Oh, so you have one of those jobs where you could tell me what you did, but then you'd have to kill me?" he teased.

I almost choked on my wine. *You said it, buddy.* "Uh, nothing that exciting. Just recruitment and research. I'm on call constantly, though, and I work strange hours. That's why Denise would be a better person to introduce you around Richmond than me."

This I said directly to put out any illusions. Noah was sweet, but anything more wouldn't happen.

"I understand strange hours and being on call. I get paged at any hour for an emergency. Nothing as serious as your line of work, but still. Even the littlest things in life deserve attention. I've always felt how you treated something weaker than you showed your true character."

Well, well. He had just raised a notch in my opinion.

"Sorry Denise couldn't make it," I said for probably the fifth time. "I think you'd really like her."

Noah leaned forward. "I'm sure I would, but I'm not sorry she couldn't make it. I only used meeting people as an excuse to ask you out. I really just wanted to go on a date with you. It must have been those fuzzy slippers."

I laughed, which startled me. Truthfully, I'd expected to have a miserable time, but this was . . . nice.

"I'll bear that in mind."

I studied him over my wineglass. Noah wore a crewneck gray shirt and a sports coat, with charcoal slacks. His black hair was freshly cut, but that one lock kept falling over his forehead. Noah certainly had no reason to lack for dates. Even if his skin didn't have that creamy crystal luminescence that glittered in the moonlight . . .

I shook my head. Dammit, I had to stop haunting myself with Bones! There was no hope for the two of us. Even if we did manage to conquer the insurmountable obstacles of my job killing the undead, or my mother's seething hatred of anything with fangs, we *still* wouldn't work. Bones was a vampire. He'd stay forever young while I'd inevitably grow old and die. The only way around my mortality was if I changed over, and I refused to do that. No matter how it broke my heart, I'd made the only decision I could by leaving him. Hell, Bones might not even think about me anymore. He'd probably moved on; it had been over four years since we'd seen each other. Maybe it was time for me to move on, too.

"Do you want to skip dessert and go for a walk?" I impulsively asked.

Noah didn't hesitate. "I'd love to."

We drove forty minutes to get to the beach. Being March, it was still frigid, and I wrapped my coat around me in the cold ocean breeze. Noah walked closely next to me, his hands inside his pockets.

"I love the ocean. It's why I moved from Pittsburgh to Virginia. Ever since I first saw it, I knew I wanted to live near it. There's something about it that makes me feel small, but like I'm still part of the bigger picture. That sounds cheesy, but it's true."

Wistfully I smiled. "It's not cheesy. I feel the same way about the mountains. I still go back there, whenever I get a chance . . ."

My voice trailed off, because I was remembering who I'd been with when I first saw the mountains. This had to stop.

In a burst of longing to forget, I grabbed Noah and almost yanked his head down to mine. He hesitated a fraction before responding, wrapping his arms around me, his pulse tripling as I kissed him.

Just as suddenly as I began, I pulled away. "I'm sorry. That was rude of me."

A shaky chuckle escaped him. "That kind of rudeness I'd been hoping for. In fact, I was planning a smooth maneuver with asking you to sit, maybe putting my arm around you . . . but I like your way better."

God, his lip was bleeding. Stupid me forgot to check my strength. Poor Noah was apparently a glutton for abuse. At least I didn't knock his teeth down his throat; he might have objected more strongly to that.

Noah grasped my shoulders, and this time he lowered his head under his own power. I restrained my normal force, kissing him gently and letting his tongue dip past my lips. His heart rate shot up higher and his blood traveled south. It was almost funny to hear his body's reaction.

I pushed Noah back. "That's all I'm willing to give."

"I'm very happy with that, Cristine. The only other thing I want is to see you again. I *really* want to see you again."

His face was earnest and so honest. Completely unlike mine with all my secrets.

I sighed again. "Noah, I lead a very . . . odd life. My job has me traveling frequently, leaving without notice, and having to cancel almost every plan I make. Does that sound like something you want to get involved in?"

He nodded. "It sounds great, because it's *your* life. I would love to get involved in it."

The sensible part of my brain sent me a clear warning. *Don't do it.* My loneliness slapped it down.

"Then I'd like to see you again, too."

Four

A KNOCK BOOMED AT MY DOOR, CAUSING ME
to bolt up in bed. It was only nine in the morning.
No one came by this early; they all knew my sleeping habits. Even Noah, who I'd been dating now for a
month, knew better than to call or come over at such
an ungodly hour.

I went downstairs, habit making me put a silver knife
in my robe pocket, and looked through the peephole.

Tate was on the other side, and he also appeared as
though he'd been freshly woken up.

"What's wrong?" I said as I opened the door.

"We need to get to the compound. Don's waiting for
us, and he's calling in Juan and Dave as well."

I left the door open and went back upstairs to throw
on some clothes. No way was I showing up in my
Tweety Bird pajamas; that would hardly inspire respect
among my men.

After changing and doing a quick brush of my teeth,

I climbed into Tate's car, blinking at the bright morning sunlight.

"Do you know why we're being hauled in? Why didn't Don call me first?"

Tate grunted. "He wanted to ask my opinion of the situation before speaking to you. There were some murders last night in Ohio. Pretty graphic, no attempt made to hide the bodies. In fact, they were displayed."

"What's so unusual about that? Terrible, I give you, but not out of the ordinary."

I was confused. We didn't jet around to every nasty crime scene, or we'd never be able to cover them all. There was more than he was telling me.

"We're almost there. I'll let Don fill you in on the rest. My job was just to pick you up."

Tate had been a sergeant in Special Forces before joining Don, and his years in the military showed. *Follow orders, don't question command decisions.* It was what Don loved about him—and why I frustrated my boss so much, because my credo seemed to be the exact opposite.

In twenty minutes, we were at the compound. The armed guards waved us through the gates as usual. Tate and I were such a common sight, we didn't even show identification anymore. We practically knew all the guards by name, rank, and serial number.

Don was in his office, pacing by his desk, and my brows shot up. My boss was normally cool and collected. This was only the second time I'd seen him pace in the four years since he recruited me. The first was when he found out that Ian, or Liam Flannery, as Don still thought of him, had gotten away. Don had wanted me to bring the vampire in to keep as a pet, so we could siphon blood from him to make more Brams. When I came back without Ian, I thought Don would pop a seam. Or wear a trench in his carpet. My being stabbed was barely an afterthought. Don really had a mixed-up set of priorities, in my opinion.

On his desk were photos that looked downloaded. He gestured to them as we came in.

"I have a friend at the Franklin County Police Department who scanned these two hours ago and sent them to me. He's already contained the area and barred any more police or medical examiners from the scene. You're leaving as soon as the team is assembled. Pick your best men, because you're going to need them. We'll have additional personnel standing by to deploy at your command. This has to be put to bed immediately."

Franklin County. My old hometown. "Cut the mystery, Don. You have my attention."

In reply he handed me one of the photographs. It was of a small room, with a pile of fresh body parts strewn on the carpet. I recognized it at once, because it used to be my bedroom at my grandparents' house. The writing on the wall froze me, and I knew at once why Don was freaked.

here kitty kitty

That wasn't good. Not fucking good at all. The fact that this deliberate taunt was clearly addressed to me, *and* in the house I grew up in, showed two terrifying things. Someone knew my stage name—and my real one.

"Where's my mother?" She was my first thought. Perhaps they only knew about Catherine Crawfield, or maybe they knew about Cristine Russell, too.

Don held up a hand. "We've sent men to her house with instructions to bring her here. We're doing that as a precaution, because I think if they knew who and where you were now, they wouldn't have bothered with your birthplace."

Yes, that was true. I was so upset I wasn't thinking clearly. That had to stop, because there was no time to be stupid.

"Do you have any idea who this could be, Cat?"

"Of course not! Why would I?"

Don pondered that for a minute, pulling the hairs on his eyebrow.

"It's coincidental that you've been dating Noah Rose for a month now, and suddenly someone's found you out? Have you told him what you are? What you do?"

I gave Don a nasty glare. "You ran a full background check on Noah the minute you discovered I was dating him. Without my permission, I might add, and no, Noah doesn't know anything about vampires, what I do, or what I am. This better be the last time I have to assure you of that."

Don gave a concurring nod, then went on to speculate again. "Do you think this could be Liam Flannery? Did you tell him *anything* before that he could have used to trace you?"

A cold chill went through me. Ian had connections to my past, all right. Through Bones. Bones knew my family's old address, my real name, and he used to only call me Kitten. Could this be Bones? Would he have done something this extreme to draw me out of hiding? After over four years, did he still even think about me?

"No, I didn't tell Flannery anything. I don't see how he could be responsible."

The lie tripped off my tongue without pause. If it was Bones, directly or indirectly, I'd deal with him myself. Don and Tate thought his body was packed away on ice in the basement freezer. I wasn't about to change that.

Juan and Dave arrived. Both of them also looked like they'd been freshly woken. Briefly Don filled them in on the situation and its implication.

"Cat, I will leave you four to it," he concluded. "Pick your team and plug this leak. The planes will be ready when you are. And don't worry about bringing me back any stragglers this time. Just eliminate whoever knows about you."

Grimly I nodded, and prayed my suspicions were wrong.

"Have you been home since you started with this Death Squad from Hell? Think anyone will recognize you?"

Dave had kept up a stream of steady chatter as we circled over the air base before landing.

"No, I haven't been back since my grandparents died. I only had one friend"—and I was definitely *not* referring to a certain horny, alcoholic ghost—"and he graduated from college and moved to Santa Monica years ago."

That had been Timmie, my old neighbor. Last I checked, he was a reporter for one of those "the truth is out there" independent magazines. You know, the kind that every once in a while hit on an incredible, factual story and then made Don's life hell while he tried to find ways to discredit it. Timmie believed I had been killed in a shootout with the police after murdering my grandparents, some police officers, and the governor. What a way to be thought of. Don hadn't spared my reputation in making me disappear. I even had a headstone and fake autopsy reports.

"Besides . . ." I shook off the past like a wet raincoat. "With my hair shorter and brown, I look very different. No one would recognize me now."

Except Bones. He'd know me a mile away by scent alone. The thought of seeing him again, even under such murderous circumstances, made my heart pound. How low I'd fallen.

"You're sure about bringing Cooper?" Dave nudged me and glanced toward the back of the plane. We had our own little area up front. Weren't we the special ones?

"I know it's only been two months since we brought Cooper on, but he's smart, fast, and ruthless. His years as an undercover narcotics officer probably helped there. He's performed well in training operations, so it's time to see how he does in the field."

Dave frowned. "He doesn't like you, Cat. He thinks you'll turn on us one day because you're a half-breed. I think he should be put under the juice and have the last two months wiped from his mind."

"Put under the juice" referred to the brainwashing techniques Don had perfected over the last years. Our in-house vampires had their fangs milked like snakes. The hallucinogenic drops they produced were then refined and harvested. When combined with the usual mind-fuck method the military used, it left the participant happily unaware of any details regarding our operation. That was how we weeded through the recruits and didn't worry about one blabbing about a chick with superhuman powers. All they remembered was a day of hard training.

"Cooper doesn't have to like me—he only has to follow orders. If he can't do that, then he's out. Or dead, if he gets himself killed first. He's the least of our concerns now."

The plane touched down with a jar. Dave smiled at me.

"Welcome home, Cat."

FIVE

THE HOUSE I GREW UP IN WAS ON A CHERRY orchard that looked like it hadn't been harvested in years. Maybe not since my grandparents were murdered. Licking Falls, Ohio, was a place I hadn't thought I'd see again, and the scary thing was that it seemed like time had stood still in this small town. God, this house would get a sick sort of notoriety. Four people had been killed inside these walls. Two supposedly by their own granddaughter, who'd then gone on a senseless murder spree, and now this couple.

It was ironic that the last time I'd walked up to my front porch, it had also been to a double murder. Pain blasted through me at the mental image of my grandfather slumped on the kitchen floor and my grandmother's red handprints staining the stairs where she'd tried to crawl away.

Dave and I circled around the kitchen, careful not to disturb anything more than necessary.

"Were the bodies checked? Was anything found?"

Tate coughed. "The bodies are still here, Cat. Don ordered they not be moved until you looked at them. Nothing has been confiscated."

Great. Don was too smart for his own good. "Have they been photographed? Documented? We can rip through them to look?"

Juan winced at my choice of words, but Tate nodded. The house was surrounded by exterior troops in case this was a trap. It was just before noon, so we were somewhat safer. Vampires hated to be up early. No, I had been brought here specifically, and I was betting whoever did this was getting their beauty rest.

"Okay then. Let's get started."

An hour later, Cooper was at his breaking point.

"I'm going to be sick."

I glanced past the remains of what used to be a happy couple. Yep, Cooper's mocha face was positively green.

"You throw up and you'll eat it off the floor, soldier."

He cursed, and I returned to examining the torso in front of me. Occasionally I heard his stomach heave, but he swallowed back the bile and kept working. I held out hope for his abilities yet.

My hand struck something odd in the chest cavity of the female. Something hard that wasn't bone. Carefully I pulled it out, ignoring the squishy suction sounds it made as I drew it free.

Tate and Juan leaned over me intently. "Looks like a rock of some kind," Tate noted.

"What's that supposed to mean?" Juan wondered.

I felt as hard as the stone in my hand. Silently I screamed inside.

"It's not a rock. It's a piece of limestone. From a cave."

"Stay back five miles from all sides. Any closer and they'll hear your heartbeats. No overhead air support, no radio. Hand signals only; we don't want to give away our numbers. I'll enter the cave from the mouth, and you will give me exactly thirty minutes. If I don't come out, you use the rockets and blast it, then contain the perimeter and watch your backs. Anything comes out of that cave except me, you shoot it until you're sure it's really dead. And then you shoot it some more."

Tate angrily rounded on me. "This is a bullshit plan! That missile would only kill you, but the vampires would just dig themselves out later. If you don't come out, we're coming in after you. Period."

"Tate is right. We're not blowing you up before I get a chance to show you my sausage." Even Juan sounded worried. His innuendo was halfhearted at best.

"No way, Cat," Dave agreed. "You've saved my ass too many times for me to flip that switch."

"This isn't a democracy." Ice edged my words. "I make the decisions. You follow them. Don't you get it? If I'm not out in thirty minutes, then I'm *dead*."

We spoke while flying in the chopper to thwart any undead eavesdroppers. I was paranoid to a fantastic degree after finding that rock. I hated to believe it, but I couldn't imagine who else could have left it except Bones. That memento from the cave was too personal for it to have been Ian. Bones was the only one who knew about the cave, and everything else. The thought of him tearing apart those people sickened me. What could have happened in four years to change him so much, that he'd do such a gruesome thing? That's why I needed only thirty minutes. Either I would kill him or he'd kill me, but it would be fast regardless. Bones always did get straight down to business, and he wouldn't expect a romantic reunion. Not when he just sent me a bouquet of body parts.

The helicopter landed twenty miles away. We would drive the next fifteen and I would walk the last five. The three of them argued with me the entire time, but I ignored them. My mind was numb. I'd wanted desperately to see Bones again, but never had I imagined it would be like this. *Why?* I wondered again. *Why would Bones do something so horrible, so extreme, after all this time?*

"Don't do it, Cat."

Tate tried one last time as I wrapped my jacket around me. It was lined with silver weapons, useful for much more than warmth. Winter was slow to release its grip this year. Tate gripped my arm, but I yanked free.

"If I go down, lead the team. Keep them alive. That's your job. This is mine."

Before he could say anything more, I broke into a run.

The last mile I slowed to a walk, dreading the confrontation. My ears were pricked for the slightest sound, but that was why the cave had been such a great hideout. The depths and heights played tricks with noise.

I couldn't pinpoint any exact sounds. Surprisingly, I thought I heard a heartbeat as I drew nearer, but maybe it was just my own pounding. When I touched the outer entrance of the cave, I felt the energy inside. Vampire power, vibrating the air. Oh God.

Right before I ducked under the threshold, I pressed a button on my watch. Countdown, thirty minutes exactly, had just begun.

Both my hands held wicked-looking silver daggers in them, and I was weighted down with my throwing knives. I'd even brought a gun and tucked it inside my pants, the clip filled with silver bullets. Being prepared to kill cost a small fortune.

My eyes adjusted to the almost nonexistent lighting. From tiny openings in the rock, the cave wasn't completely black. So far the initial entryway was clear. There were noises deeper inside, and the question I'd refused to consider now loomed in front of me. *Could I kill Bones?* Would I be able to look in his brown eyes, or his green ones, and wield that blow? I didn't know, hence my backup plans of the missile. If I faltered, they wouldn't. They'd be strong should I prove to be weak. Or prove to be dead, whichever came first.

"*Come closer,*" a voice beckoned.

It reverberated with echoes. Was that an English accent? I couldn't be sure. My pulse sped up, and I went farther inside the cave.

There had been some changes since I'd last seen it. The area that once doubled as a living room was trashed. The sofa was in sections, and it hadn't been a sectional. Stuffing from the cushions settled like snow on the floor, the television was smashed in, and the lamps had long since seen their last light. The dressing screen that had guarded my short-lived modesty was in pieces throughout the area. Someone had obviously torn the place apart in a fit of rage. Frankly I was afraid to look in the bedroom, but I peeked inside anyway, and my heart constricted.

The bed was reduced to bits of foam. Wood and springs littered the space and stood inches deep on the ground. Stones in the wall were chipped here and there from a fist or other hard object pummeling them. Anguish welled up in me. This was my doing, as surely as if I'd used my own hands.

A cool current parted the atmosphere behind me. I whirled around with knives at the ready. Staring at me with glowing green eyes was a vampire. Behind him were six more. Their energy thickened the air in the close space, but they were evenly distributed, if you could call it that. Only one of them crackled with an abundance of power, but his face was entirely foreign to me.

"Who in the fuck are you guys?"

"You came. Your old boyfriend wasn't lying. We weren't sure whether to believe him."

This statement was from the vamp in front, the one with the curling brown hair. He looked to be about twenty-five, in human years. From the clout oozing off his body, I judged him to be roughly five hundred or a young Master. Out of the seven, he was the most dangerous, and his previous sentence scared the shit out of me. *Your old boyfriend.* That was how they knew about me. Mother of God, it wasn't Bones who killed those people, but these vampires instead! What they would have done to him to make him talk both sickened and infuriated me.

"Where is he?"

The only question that mattered. If they'd killed Bones, I was going to turn them all into exact replicas of the mattress behind me. Indistinguishable from one particle to the next.

"He's here. Alive still. If you want him to remain that way, you'll do what I tell you."

The other minions began to fan out, trapping me with the bedroom as my only exit. Since it was a closed area, there was no help there.

"Let me see him."

Curly Hair smiled smugly. "No demands, girl. Do you think those knives will really protect you?"

When my grandparents were murdered and I'd rammed a car through a house to rescue my mother, I thought I couldn't get any angrier. How wrong I was. The unadulterated bloodlust pouring through me made me tremble. They took my shaking for fear, and their smiles broadened. Curly stepped forward.

Two of the daggers flew out of my hand before I even articulated the order to my brain. They buried past their hilts in the heart of a vamp to my left, who had been licking his lips. He pitched forward before his tongue finished its insinuating path. More knives replaced those, and once again both my hands were full.

"Now I'm going to ask again, and don't piss me off. I have spent the morning up to my ass in guts and I am low on patience. The next one's aimed for you,

Brownielocks, unless you show me what I want to see.
Your boys might get me in a rush, but you'll be too
dead to care."

My eyes bored into his, and I let him see that I meant
every single word. Unless they showed me Bones, I
was going to assume the worst and go down in flames,
and by God, I'd see they went with me.

There must have been something in my gaze he took
seriously. He jerked his head at two of his stunned lieu-
tenants. They took a last look at their friend, who was
slowly beginning to shrivel, before trotting off. One un-
twisted knife wouldn't have killed the vamp. But two
had done the necessary damage to his heart. In the background, I heard the clanking of irons, and then I knew
where they had Bones. Hell, once I'd been chained there
myself. Now I was sure I could hear a heartbeat. Did
they have a human guard on him?

The leader studied me dispassionately.

"You are the one who's been murdering our kind the
last several years. A human with the strength of an im-
mortal, the one they call the Red Reaper. Do you know
how much money you're worth?"

Holy shit, now *that* was ironic. He was a bounty
hunter, and I was his mark. Well, it was only a matter
of time, I supposed. You can't off a hundred creatures
and expect no one to get cranky.

"A lot, I hope. Hate to be on clearance."

He frowned. "You mock me. I am Lazarus, and you
should quake before me. Remember, I hold the life
of your love. Which means more to you—his fate, or
yours?"

Did I love Bones enough to die for him? Absolutely.

Relief that he wasn't behind this made me almost cheerful about my impending death. Any day of the week I'd rather die than suspect him of such cruelty again.

Sobbing brought my attention back to the situation. What was going on? A glance at my watch showed fifteen minutes before bomb time. Bones would have to get out fast before that missile hit. Lazarus wouldn't be around to collect any cash. Maybe I'd tell him that before the timer ran out.

Something human and weeping was thrown to the surface near my feet. I gave it a disparaging look before turning to Lazarus.

"Quit stalling. I don't need to see one of your chew toys to believe you're all badasses. Really, I'm quaking. Where's Bones?"

"Bones?" Lazarus said, his eyes darting around. "Where?"

Two things occurred to me at nearly the same instant. One, from Lazarus's expression, he had no idea where Bones was. Two, the tear-streaked face turning up at me belonged to the lying little shit who'd seduced and dumped me when I was sixteen.

Six

Danny?" I said in disbelief. "Danny Milton? *You're* the reason I had to drag my ass all the way from Virginia?"

Danny also wasn't happy to see me. "You ruined my life!" he wailed. "First your freak boyfriend crippled my hand, then you're not dead, and now these *creatures* kidnapped me! I hate the day I met you!"

I snorted. "Right back at you, asshole!"

Lazarus regarded me suspiciously. "He said you used to be in love with him. You're just pretending not to care now so I won't kill him."

"You want to kill him?" Perhaps I was crazed with the knowledge that less than fifteen minutes remained, or maybe I was just fed up. "Go ahead! Here, I'll help!"

I pulled the gun from the back of my pants and shot Danny at point-blank range. Lazarus and the other vampires were momentarily stunned at this turn of events, and I took advantage. The next rounds landed full in Lazarus's face. I didn't bother firing into his heart, because I wanted him alive. He had information for me, if I lived, and I emptied the clip into him while my free hand flung knives at the remaining five.

They charged me. Fangs sank in and ripped my flesh before I threw them off. This was a flat-out brawl, rolling around on jagged rocks, pummeling and hacking any flesh that wasn't mine. I was acutely aware of the seconds ticking by as I struggled to keep my knives in my hand and their fangs from my throat. After all, it was one thing to die for Bones, whether he'd gone mental or not. Quite *another* to die for that sniveling prick Danny Milton. You could safely say I still held a grudge.

The last vampire was eliminated with a gouge to his heart, and my watch showed less than thirty seconds. Lazarus, not dead after a face full of silver bullets, crawled toward Danny. Danny, still alive, moaned helplessly and tried to back away. There wasn't enough time to pump Lazarus for information, let alone kill him *and* rescue Danny. Barely enough time to do just one.

Without a moment to think, I grabbed Danny and tossed him over my shoulder, running flat-out for the entrance of the cave. He screamed at the jostling and cursed me between gasps. The timer went to zero just as the sunlit mouth came into view. Behind me I heard Lazarus running also, but too far back. He'd never make it. Neither would I. Time was up.

Instead of the explosion I expected, there were voices.

Movement right outside. Two figures entered the cave as I was almost upon them. It was Tate and Dave. I shouted because I knew they couldn't see me in the dark.

"Don't shoot!"

"Hold fire, it's Cat!" Tate boomed.

What happened next happened almost instantly, though it would be forever slow motion in my mind.

"Hostile coming fast, aim high!" I yelled, and ducked down to clear their line of fire. Tate, who hadn't re-laxed stance, fired blindly into the blackness behind me. Dave, who had lowered his gun to try to locate me in the stygian dark, came throat to face with Lazarus instead.

There was a sickening gurgle as his artery was freed. I screamed, dropping Danny and rushing to him. Laza-rus threw him at me with full force, and Dave's body knocked me flat. Hot blood sprayed my face as I locked my hands around his neck, futilely trying to stem the flow. In the midst of this Tate was still shooting, and Lazarus cracked him against the cave wall and ran out. Outside there was the spattering of more gunfire as the perimeter troops shot at the fleeing vampire.

"Man down, man down!"

Juan sprinted inside the cave, flashlight drawn, fol-lowed closely by Cooper and three others. I tore my shirt off to apply pressure to Dave's neck.

Dave could barely talk, but he was trying. " . . .'on't . . . let me . . .'ie . . ."

There was only one chance. Maybe not even that.

"Hold him," I snapped to Juan. Then I dashed deeper into the cave as rapidly as I'd left it. When I came to the first body, I hoisted it on my shoulders and ran back.

"What are you doing?" Cooper demanded.

I ignored him, taking a knife and slicing deeply into the dead vampire's neck. Blood dripped, but not enough. I hacked the head off completely and flipped the vamp upside down, holding him by his feet. Now a steady stream of purplish liquid trickled directly onto Dave.

"Open his mouth. Make him swallow," I commanded. *God, let it not be too late. Let it not be too late . . . !*

Juan pulled back Dave's lips with tears coursing down his face. He was praying as well, out loud and in Spanish. Ruthlessly I kicked the cadaver to send more blood downward, and Juan forced Dave to swallow.

The skin around Dave's neck reacted to the undead blood, but not quickly enough. The flow from his jugular slowed even as the edges started to close. Soon it stopped. Dave was dead.

I stormed out of the cave, seething with grief. Men were searching the area, and I grabbed the nearest one.

"Where did he go? Did you see which way he went?"

The soldier, Kelso, blanched at seeing me covered in blood. "We couldn't tell. Someone said vampire, but all I saw were trees. We're looking now. He can't be far."

"Like hell he can't," I snarled. A Master vampire at full gallop, even injured, could run upward of sixty miles an hour. No way was Lazarus getting away. No way.

The three men still hovered around Dave's lifeless body. Juan wept unashamedly, and Tate's eyes overflowed with tears.

"The vampire got through the perimeter," I began without preamble. "I'm going after him. Tate, fix me with a transmitter and have the team follow. I'm tell-

ing you right now, I don't give a shit what the rules
are, because I'm changing them. When I get him, only
the ones who do exactly what I say will be with me.
If you don't, you can hang back with the rest of the
crowd. I'm not standing over the body of another man
today, no matter what Don thinks is acceptable. Whoever wants to be there when this vamp gets his, come
with me. Tell the rest of the crew to stay back until we
come out."

Tate and Juan stood immediately. Cooper hesitated. I
stared at him and didn't blink.

"Pussying out, Coop?"

He shot me a measured look. "I'm half Sicilian and
half African. Both sides believe in retribution. The only
pussy here is yours, Commander."

"Then order the rest of the men to stand by and follow me. We'll see what you're made of."

He jerked his head at where Danny lay, still huddled
in shock. "What about him?"

"Hand him over to the medics. He's got a gunshot
wound."

"The vampires shot him?" Tate questioned in surprise. Vampires didn't traditionally use guns. Why
would they, when their teeth were more powerful?

"They didn't. I did. Let's move; every second
counts."

Cooper chucked Danny over his shoulder and headed
out into the light without comment. I heard him direct
the troops to stay back while we checked the cave for
survivors. As he did that, I closed Dave's eyes. When
Cooper returned, I held the flashlight in front of me so
they could see where they were going.

"This way."

When we reached the area where I'd killed the other vampires, I started in.

"All right, men, I'm only going to say this once. Take a knife, grab a vamp, and I don't care if you have to suck the blood off their balls, you're going to get as much of that liquid in you as possible. Humans can drink a pint of blood before the body automatically re-gurgitates. I expect a pint in each of you, and *now*. The vampire who killed Dave was a Master and he's running better than a mile a minute. We don't have time to argue about morality. These bodies are shriveling with every second. You're in or you're out."

So speaking, I led by example and sliced the neck of the corpse in front of me, digging my mouth in like a pit bull. For a second, no one moved. I picked my head up and scorched them with the emerald glare from my eyes.

"Would Dave have shrunk back from avenging any of you out of squeamishness?"

That did the trick. Soon the sounds of sucking and swallowing were heard in the cave. It tasted bad, de-composing as quickly as it was, but even after death, the blood still held power. After several hard pulls, I felt the change begin. The second it started to taste less heinous, I threw the vamp aside, shaking.

"Everyone stop," I ordered.

There was glad compliance. With my mixed lineage, it took much less for me to acquire a liking for it. They weren't in danger of succumbing to the urge to feed like I was.

"Cat?"

Tate reached out to touch me, and I flinched. His heartbeat was louder in my ears, and I smelled blood, sweat, and tears on him. That was the whole point. I could smell him now—and everyone else.

"Don't touch me. Wait." My hands clenched. Dimly I remembered Bones flattening me on the bed, restraining me from chewing his throat open. *Ride it out, Kitten, it will pass . . .*

Several deep breaths later I could think again. Unerringly I went to where Lazarus had lain after I shot him. I took a long, deep whiff of his blood, and then licked it, letting his scent fill my nose. With grim satisfaction I turned to Tate.

"I've got him. Give me the transmitter and follow me by car. When I stop moving, that means he's down. We'll find out what he knows."

"Cat . . ." Tate looked in wonder at his hands and then around the cave. I knew he was experiencing more than he had before. "I feel . . ."

"I know. Let's go."

SEVEN

THE BULLETS SLOWED LAZARUS, SILVER BE-
ing kryptonite for vampires. Lazarus had used his
power to heal himself, but because he hadn't fed yet, he
wasn't running on all cylinders. Most of Dave's blood
had spilled onto the ground, not in his mouth, and he'd
hightailed it into the woods without stopping for another snack. I exceeded my previous maximum speeds
and made up lost ground, his scent pointing the way
like invisible road signs. Furthermore, I knew these
woods. This was where Bones had trained me. Roots
and potholes Lazarus stumbled on, I vaulted over with
ease while the memories came so hard and fast, I could
almost hear his voice behind me, that English accent
mocking.

*Is this the best you can do, Kitten? That all you've
got? You move that slowly and you'll be nothing more
than a flush in some bloke's cheeks . . . come on, Kitten! This is a death match, not a bloody tea party!*

God, how I'd hated him those first few weeks, and oh! how I'd do anything to turn back the clock and be there again. Recollection spurred me on faster. I smelled Lazarus about five miles ahead. He couldn't scent me yet, being upwind, but soon he would hear me. I hoped he was afraid. If he wasn't, he would be.

Lazarus broke through the trees to cross over a road, dodging traffic going both ways. Moments later I followed. Brakes screeched as drivers stopped in confusion with the blurs slicing in front of them. Across backyards and over railroad tracks I chased him, closing the distance between us. I could see him now, barely a mile away and heading for a lake. There was no way I could let him get to it. He'd lose me in the water with my dependency on oxygen. I reached down for something more to inspire me, and once again came up with a pair of dark brown eyes.

Don't fret, luv. I'll be back before you know it.

The last words Bones said to me. The last time I heard his voice. That was all the motivation I needed. Maybe if I ran fast enough, I could take it all back and feel his arms around me one more time . . .

I tackled Lazarus from behind less than twenty yards from the water. The silver knife molded around my hand drove with all my anguish into his heart, but I didn't twist it. Not yet. We had some talking to do first.

"How's that feel, Lazarus? Hurts, doesn't it? You know what *really* hurts? If it moves the slightest bit . . ."

I gave the blade a tiny shift. He got the picture and froze, his silvery eyes bleeding to green.

"Release me at once," he commanded in a resonating voice.

I laughed maliciously at him. "Nice try but no cigar. Vampire mind control doesn't work on me, pal. Know why?"

For the first time, I let him see the flare in my gaze. With all the bullets I'd shot into his face, he'd missed it before.

Lazarus stared at my glowing eyes uncomprehendingly. "It can't be. You breathe, your heart beats . . . it's impossible."

"Yeah, isn't it? Life's a bitch and then one stabs you."

A car screeched to a halt, then running footsteps. I didn't need to look away to know it was Tate, Juan, and Cooper.

"Well, *amigos*, look what the cat dragged in," Juan drawled venomously. Their guns were drawn and pointed. Lazarus tried the mind control once more.

"Shoot her. You want to shoot her. *Kill her*," he ordered, glaring at them.

"We don't want to shoot her," Tate corrected, firing a single round into Lazarus's leg. "We want to shoot *you*."

Lazarus screamed once and then twice when Cooper squeezed a shot off as well, striking him in the thigh.

"Hold your fire . . . for now. I have some questions for him. And I'm hoping he'll be stupid and give me an excuse to carve him up like he did that couple last night."

Lazarus was dumbfounded at his helplessness. "What are you? How are your men not under my control?"

"Because they just drank the juice out of your buddies back there and they have undead blood running in their veins. Like a remote control with low batteries, your signals aren't getting through. Now, enough of this shit. I'm going to ask questions, and my friends here are going to cut something off you every time you don't answer me. Gather 'round, boys. Plenty of flesh for everyone."

They crouched over Lazarus, and every hand gripped a knife. I smiled as I flipped Lazarus over, cradling him on my lap with the silver still imbedded in his back.

"Now tell me, how did you meet Danny Milton . . ."

The helicopter carried away Dave's body, and the three of us watched it disappear into the sky. Our chopper with the rest of the team waited nearby. We were the only ones who hadn't boarded.

"Is this what you feel like every day, Cat? Stronger, faster . . . superior? That's what I feel like with this crap in my body. Superior. It scares the hell out of me."

Tate spoke quietly, no need to shout even with the rotating blades churning up around us. My reply was low as well. For the next few hours, he'd hear the softest whispers from a block away.

"Believe me, Tate, seeing Dave without his throat makes me feel anything but superior. Why didn't you listen to me and deploy that missile? He'd be alive now if you had."

Juan touched my shoulder. "Dave wouldn't do it, *querida*. He said no way was he going to detonate. Said we'd get to drag your ass out for once. Then we went to the cave . . ."

"It's not your fault." My tone was brittle. "It's mine. I told you not to fire. I should have warned you about the vampire first. First, before I said anything else." Abruptly I turned away and walked to the helicopter. I was almost to the door when Cooper spoke. He hadn't said a word to me since the cave.

"Commander."

I stopped and waited. My spine was straight.

"Yes, Cooper?" Any accusation I deserved. I was in charge and a man had died. The buck stopped with me.

"When I first heard what you were, I thought you were a freak." His voice was matter-of-fact. "Or an accident of nature, a mistake—I don't know. But I know this. You lead, and I'll follow. Just like Dave did. He didn't make a mistake by doing that."

Cooper passed by me and climbed into the chopper. Tate and Juan each took my hand, and together we went inside.

Don tapped his pen on the report in front of him, one of several. We were both depressed. Dave's funeral had been earlier today. Before joining us, Dave had been a fireman, so it seemed everyone from his old precinct was there. Seeing Dave's sister crumple as she closed the lid on his coffin would haunt me forever. Two days had passed since we returned from Ohio, and Don was reading the final descriptions of what happened.

"Four years ago, after you rescued your mother when she'd been kidnapped by vampires, stories spread about a redheaded human with incredible abilities. After your years with us, those rumors increased. Lazarus was then subsequently hired to track down and kill this mysterious 'Red Reaper.'" Don sighed. "Which still doesn't explain how he tied Catherine Crawfield to you. You weren't able to make him tell you that?"

"No." My voice was flat. "He struggled as we were questioning him and my knife shredded his heart. How he found out the Red Reaper is really the supposedly dead Catherine Crawfield, I don't know. Maybe it was just a lucky guess, like how he found the cave by reading old police reports that had me pegged in that area of the woods. Danny he found because the jerk apparently liked to brag about how he slept with the infamous governor murderer."

"And the 'here, kitty kitty'?"

"Years ago Hennessey, the vampire who'd been running the old governor's operations, knew me as Cat. He must have repeated it to people."

Don rubbed his forehead, a sign he was tired. We were all tired, but I couldn't sleep, only seeing Dave's throat when I closed my eyes.

"I suppose all that matters is that Lazarus didn't know your current identity. On to the next concern. You were clocked at speeds of up to eighty miles an hour when you chased down Lazarus, and some of the team said that after the three of you left the cave, you came out with blood on your faces. Anything you want to tell me about?"

Don was no fool. He knew my previous best was sixty miles an hour. Add that to the elevated levels of antibody in my bloodstream, and he had every cause to be suspicious. The three men categorically denied any unusual activity, citing Brams as the reason for their pathology results. Who was I to make it easy for him?

"No."

Don sighed and pushed his chair back to stare at the wall for a minute. When he turned around, he'd given up on that line of questioning.

"You shot Danny Milton. Is that a new hostage negotiation tactic I'm not aware of?"

He sounded faintly approving. Danny didn't have many fans, especially after nearly blowing my cover and Dave's subsequent death.

"I wanted to distract the vampires. It worked."

"Yes it did. We have him in witness protection. I don't think he'll be stupid enough to brag about you anymore. Not that there's anything he could tell now. The cleaners have been busy with him."

Cleaners. A nice term for the brainwashers. I wished I'd shot him in the head instead of the side. Then I could have staked Lazarus, and Dave would have been alive. Now I owed Danny for three things—my virginity, ratting me to the police years ago, and Dave.

"Cat." Don stood and I followed suit. "I know you blame yourself. Everyone liked Dave. After reading the reports, it's been determined that it was his own error which led to his death. He should have remained at attention instead of lowering his gun. It was a mistake that cost him his life. I'm giving you the next two weeks off. No training, no recruiting, no checking in. Clear your mind and shake off the guilt. There's something to be said for living instead of just existing."

I gave a humorless laugh. "Living? What a neat idea. I'll try that."

Eight

"CAT, NICE TO SEE YOU AGAIN."

Don's words were pleasant, but his expression told me he was about to piss me off. It was my first day back from a two-week forced vacation, and I was actually glad to get back to work. I spent the time either condemning myself over Dave's death, or brooding over the knowledge that Bones was truly lost to me. Somehow, I'd pictured him still in that cave, waiting should I ever decide to return. Illogical, irrational, and incorrect, as it turned out. The scent of him to my improved nose was so faint as to be almost nonexistent. Bones hadn't been there for years.

So, back to the grind where my life was regularly in peril? Sounded good to me.

"There's something you're not aware of," Don went on. "It was a judgment call not to tell you immediately, but it's time to inform you."

"What?" Ice edged the single word. "What did you in your cleverness decide to hide from me?"

He frowned. "Don't be snide. I made my decision based on the information that was pertinent at the time. Since you're recovering from a poor call yourself, you shouldn't be so quick to cast blame."

Uh oh, he was defensive. That wasn't a good sign. "Okay, lay it out. What don't I know?"

"After Dave died, you were understandably distraught. That's why I gave you time off. Four days into your vacation, I received a phone call from witness protection. Danny Milton had disappeared."

"He *what*?!" I jumped up and pounded my fist against the top of his desk. All his papers and equipment jumped. "How could you not have told me that? I didn't kill Lazarus because of that sniveling shit, and Dave died because of my decision!"

Don regarded me calmly. "I didn't tell you because of how you're reacting now. Dave was a soldier before he met you, Cat. He knew the risks. Don't take that away from him. It would make him a lesser man than he was."

"Save the sermon for Sunday, preacher," I snapped. "Has there been any word of Danny? A body, anything? How the fuck did he vanish four days after we left Ohio? Wasn't he moved to a safe location like I instructed?"

"We flew him to Chicago and had him in the hospital under guard. Frankly we don't know what happened. Tate went to the scene himself after it happened. He saw nothing. Danny Milton hasn't been seen or heard from since."

"It was a vampire." My reply was immediate. "Only a vampire could move in and out that easily without being noticed or alarming the guards. Probably mind-fucked them into forgetting they even saw him. Something had to be left at the scene. Vampires always leave a clue—it's like their calling card! I'm going to that hospital."

"No you're not. The scene was checked and photographed, but that isn't the issue now. The issue is whether Danny is still alive, and if so, whether he's a security risk. Is there *anything* you said in front of him that could be used against you? Even though he had his memory altered, is there any risk you can think of?"

My mind was too fixated on the sly way Danny was taken. There had to be a clue. Tate just hadn't found it.

"Let me see the pictures. Then I'll think about your issue."

He grunted in annoyance. "I'll give you the pictures. I'll even do you one better. We have all of the items here at the compound, down to the last piece of lint. I'll have them delivered to your office and you can waste your time, but when you're done, you tell me if there's anything Danny could repeat that should worry us."

I snorted rudely. "I'll do that, Don."

Thirty minutes later I flipped through the photos of the hospital room. Don was correct. Everything looked as tidy as could be. Even the IV needle that had been pulled from Danny's arm rested innocently on the bed, as if waiting for its next vein. No footprints, no fingerprints, no blood, no bodily fluid, not even a frigging sheet out of place. Molecular transportation couldn't have been neater. Maybe that was it. Maybe Danny had been beamed right the fuck out of there. It would almost be worth telling that to Don just to see the look on his face.

After I examined the pictures for an hour, I moved on to the personal and medical paraphernalia that were tucked in another medium-sized box. A pair of shoes, the tread not even worn. Clothes, underwear, socks, shaving cream (I poured some onto my desk. Yep, plain old shaving cream), cotton swabs, bandages, hypodermic needles carefully capped, wadded-up paper towels, a watch . . .

Spots danced in front of my vision. The hand I extended to pick up the watch shook so, I missed it twice. My heart pounded, and I felt like I was going to faint. I knew that watch. After all—it used to be mine.

To anyone else, it was a plain old watch. Nothing fancy, no pricey brand, just an ordinary watch that could be a man's or a woman's. The lack of flash had been deliberate so as not to draw attention, but it had an extra feature that didn't come standard. Push a button barely visible on its side and a page went off. A page that was short-range and only connected to one beeper. That button had saved my life once, and the last time I'd seen this watch was when I took it off my wrist and left it on top of the goodbye note I'd written Bones.

If I'd been the one to go to Chicago, I would have found the watch. Had Don not kept me out of the loop this *one* time, it would have been me who went there. Me, not Tate, and Bones had all but left me his goddamn phone number. The pager was only good for a radius of five miles. He would have been that close, waiting to see if I came and pressed that button.

I held the watch so hard, it cut into my skin. How Bones had heard about Danny or what happened I had no idea, but he'd been quick. After all these years, he'd reached out to me. I just hadn't gotten the message in time.

The sheer irony of it all made me laugh. That's how Don found me, on the floor and chortling in mirthless laughter. He eyed me with caution but stayed near the door.

"Do you mind telling me what's so funny?"

"Oh, you were right," I gasped. "There's nothing here. No clues whatsoever. But you can rest your mind about Danny Milton. Believe me when I tell you, that man is *dead*."

"What kind of vampire are we talking about?" I asked while climbing in the van. Normally the guys didn't pick me up at home unless one was still at the scene. When Tate called to say he was on his way, I apologized to Noah, who I'd had dinner plans with, and left. Another night interrupted. Why Noah was still around, I had no idea.

"Probably a young one, maybe two," Tate answered.

He'd been stiff with me ever since my relationship with Noah began. I had no idea what prompted his attitude, but two could play cold shoulder.

We didn't talk again until we parked at the club. Even over the pounding of the music, I heard the heartbeats inside. Lots of them.

"Why hasn't the club been evacuated?"

"No bodies, Commander," Cooper said. "Just some-one saying they saw a woman struggling with some blood on her neck. Then the woman disappeared. Don didn't want to make the vamp suspicious if he's still here."

Cooper had exceeded my expectations of him. Since that horrible afternoon at the cave, he never ques-tioned my orders again. He still called me a freak to my face, but that didn't bother me. Now it was more like, "You're a freak, Commander. Come on, men, you heard the bitch! Move! Move!" He could call me any name in the book as long as he showed that same dedi-cation.

"And the rest of the team is standing by?"

This was the most half-assed approach to a potential murder we'd ever taken. The guys weren't even prop-erly suited up. They probably figured this was bullshit since the 911 caller had sounded drunk. It wouldn't be the first false alarm we'd received. Or the fiftieth.

"*Querida*, let's just go inside and check it out," Juan said, impatient. "If it's nothing, drinks are on me."

Sold. Without further complaint I pulled my coat on and we headed for the door. The May evening wasn't cold, but the trench coat concealed my weapons. The guys let me enter first as always, and as soon as I crossed the doorway, I knew it was a trap.

"Surprise!" Denise screamed.

The word was repeated by several members of my team as well as the two dozen male employees of what was clearly a strip club.

I blinked stupidly. "My birthday was last week."

She laughed. "I know that, Cat! That's why your party is a surprise. You can thank Tate; he's the one who planned the fake job as a setup to get you here."

I was overwhelmed. "Is Noah here?"

Denise snorted. "At a strip club? No. You can bet I didn't invite your mother, either!"

The very thought of my mother inside a male strip club made me laugh. She would have run screaming out the door.

Tate came up behind me and kissed me lightly on the cheek. "Happy birthday, Cat," he said softly.

I hugged him. Only then did I realize how much our recent estrangement had upset me. He and Juan were like the brothers I never had.

Juan pulled me into his arms from behind. "Denise hired me to be your gigolo for the night. You tell me how many orgasms you want, and I promise to deliver. I'll give you a whole new definition of the term *smooth criminal, querida*. Mmm, your ass feels like a round piece of—ooof!"

Tate's elbow in his rib cage cut him off. I rolled my eyes.

"I'm still armed, Juan. And you still have time left on your sentence for chopping cars. You might want to remember that." Then I looked over some of the heads and spotted another familiar face. "Is that Don? How did you get him to come to a place like this?"

Don approached me, looking about as comfortable as my mother would have.

"Happy belated birthday, Cat," he said, giving me a self-deprecating smile. "Aren't you glad Juan picked the place and not me? We would have had lattes and hors d'oeuvres instead of liquor and G-strings. Anyone get you a gin yet?"

"Here," Denise chirped, handing me a tall glass. She smiled at Don. "You must be her boss. You look just like I pictured you."

"You must be Denise. My name is Don, but don't remember it. You're not supposed to know about this."

She waived an airy hand. "If it makes you feel better, I'm going to get so drunk that I won't even remember my *own* name later. How's that for security?"

He gave me a wintry smile. "I can see why the two of you get along."

"Where's the birthday girl?" a buff young man in a leopard thong cooed as he approached.

"Right here!" Denise said immediately. "And she needs a lap dance, stat!"

"Don't worry, Daddy, I'll take good care of your girl." The stripper grinned at Don.

I almost choked on my gin. "He's *not* my father," I corrected at once.

"No? You have the same look, sugar. All stiff shoulders and sharp eyes. I'll fix you up, gorgeous, but *you*"—he winked at Don—"I'll send Chip over to fix you."

Denise started to laugh. Don looked even more ill than he did when he'd been mistaken for my father.

"If you need me, Cat," he grated, "I'll be in the corner. Hiding."

The club closed at three A.M. Don had kindly arranged for the carpooling for the rest of my team, but even with the drum of gin I'd consumed, I was still sober enough to take Denise, Juan, and Tate home.

Since Tate was the closest to my house, he was my last stop. He gamely tried to walk to his door, but his feet kept getting away from him. Out of amused frustration, I ended up carrying him inside. Thankfully he'd taken his key out so I didn't have to frisk him to find it.

For all the times he'd been to my house, I'd never been in his. The interior of the single-story home was clean enough to make a drill sergeant happy. He didn't have any pets, not even a goldfish, and his walls were bare of any artwork. When I got to his bedroom, it was more of the same. No decorations, just a single TV, and I could have bounced a quarter off his bed, but after hefting Tate onto it and tugging his shoes off, I wasn't in the mood.

He had a picture on his nightstand. It was the only one I'd seen in the whole house, so I looked at it curiously. It was of me, to my surprise, and not one I'd posed for. I was half turned away from the camera at a crime scene, of all things. He must have snapped it while he was photographing the bodies.

"Why do you have this?" I wondered out loud, not really expecting an answer.

Tate mumbled something that might have been my name, and with a suddenness I didn't believe him capable of in his condition, grasped me and pulled me down on top of him.

I was so stunned I didn't move. Tate kissed me, his mouth warm and tasting like alcohol while his lips moved over mine hungrily. He pushed past my lips and scoured the inside with his tongue. When he reached for the front of my pants, I finally reacted.

"Stop it," I snapped, and shoved him back so hard, his head bounced off the headboard.

Tate breathed heavily, his dark blue eyes glazed from inebriation and other things.

"You ever wanted something you couldn't have?" he asked roughly.

I was speechless. Over four years of nothing but a platonic relationship, and now here was Tate looking at me in a way that would put Juan's most lustful leer to shame.

He gave a humorless laugh and ran a hand through his short brown hair.

"Shocked? You shouldn't be. I've wanted you from the first time I saw you in that hospital bed, looking like a goddamn angel with your red hair and your big gray eyes. Yeah, I'm drunk, but it's true anyway. Maybe I won't even remember this in the morning. You don't have to worry. I can handle things the way they are. I just had to kiss you tonight, no matter what happened afterward."

"Tate, I . . . I'm sorry." What else could I say? I must have had *way* too much to drink, too, because he had never looked as attractive as he did now, with that almost dangerous glint in his eyes. Denise had always said he was a dead ringer for Brad Pitt in *Mr. and Mrs. Smith.*

He smiled wryly. "You can hear my heart pounding, can't you? When I drank that blood in Ohio, I could hear yours. I could smell you on my hands."

"You're my friend." My voice quavered a bit, because the rawness in his face alarmed and—on a baser level—aroused me. "But we *work* together. I can't give you more than that."

He blew out a sigh through his nose and nodded shortly. "I know you don't feel the same way about me. *Yet*."

That single word made me draw back and head toward the door. It was too loaded with meaning for me to stay another minute.

"Answer me one thing before you go. One thing, and tell me the truth. Have you ever been in love?"

This stumbled me and I sputtered my reply. "Tate, I—I don't think this is something we should discuss—"

"Bullshit," he cut me off. "I just laid myself open here. Answer the question."

Perhaps I also thought he might not remember this conversation in the morning, or maybe it was just his honesty. Either way, I answered him with the truth.

"Once. Years ago, before I met you."

Tate didn't blink, and his eyes bored into mine. "Who was he? What happened?"

I turned away, because now I was going to lie. When I answered him, it was as I walked out the door.

"You know who he was. He was the vampire I'd been sleeping with who wrecked your car the day we met. So you also know what happened to him. I killed him."

Nine

WORK HAD BEEN HECTIC. IN SOME WAYS that was good. The frantic schedule over the last two weeks kept the awkwardness with Tate and me down to a minimum. It was hard to be gawky when your lives were constantly on the line.

Things with Noah weren't rosy, either. Despite his best efforts, my frequent absences strained our already tenuous dating relationship. And lately he'd started to drop hints about wanting to "deepen" things between us. Not that I blamed him for trying—we'd been going out for over two months, but it wasn't going to happen.

I already knew we wouldn't work, no matter how great of a person Noah was. There were too many lies between us, all mine, of course, and the bottom line appeared to be that I still wasn't ready to let go of my former doomed relationship. Hey, at least I'd tried. Now I had to let Noah down gently. I'd already told him I understood if my schedule was too difficult for him to handle. Either Noah was stubborn or he wasn't taking the hint. I had to start employing more concise methods, but I wasn't about to just say, *We're through!* and hang up on him. I liked Noah, and I hated the thought of hurting him.

Then on a Tuesday, abysmally early, my phone rang. I vaulted up to answer it, already looking for clothes and cursing whatever pulseless creature was causing trouble before eight in the morning, when I heard Denise's voice.

"What's wrong?" I asked immediately.

"Nothing! I'm sorry to call so early, but I couldn't wait to tell you. Oh, Cat, I'm so happy. I'm getting married!"

I didn't go through any of the "Are you sure? It's so sudden!" objections with Denise. She'd only been dating her new boyfriend, Randy, for two weeks, but Denise wasn't normally impulsive and she'd said that she knew she loved Randy and he felt the same way about her. Seeing the bowled-over look in her eyes, I knew anything I said about rushing, waiting, or caution would fall on deaf ears, anyway. Besides, she had enough to deal with. Denise's parents refused to even meet Randy, since he was Catholic and they were Jewish. His parents weren't wild about their extremely short courtship, either. Who said falling in love was easy? Certainly not me.

I was planning a little chat with her parents. For years I'd been trying to harness the power in my eyes. They weren't as potent as a vampire's, but I was going to give it my best shot. Denise deserved a happy wedding, and I would do my damnedest to give it to her. What could go wrong? They couldn't be more opposed to the wedding than they already were.

I insisted on buying the flowers, the photographer, and the cake. They were taking on the expense for the rest of it. Denise tried to decline, but I threatened her with my knives and my PMS. In my nonworking hours, we scrambled to pick out her dress, the bridesmaids' dresses, the flowers, and the invitations. It wasn't until four days before the wedding that I met Randy. To my selfish relief, he was moving into her house, not the other way around. Denise said he was an independent software consultant—a computer *genius*, she'd gushed—and therefore it was easier for him to relocate than her with her local nine to five job.

Denise enlisted me to help unpack, and when Randy pulled up in a U-Haul, I got my first look at him. He was five-ten with light brown hair, rimless glasses, and a slim athletic build. He was handsome in an easygoing way, but I liked his eyes the most. They lit up when he looked at her.

Randy held out a hand after kissing Denise hello. "You must be Cat. Denise can't stop talking about you. Thank you for all of your help with the wedding."

I ignored his hand and hugged him instead. "I'm so glad to finally meet you! And don't worry about the help. I'll probably never get married, so I'm living vicariously through her. Let's get you unloaded. Denise has her final fitting tonight, and she can't be late for it."

Randy coughed. "Um, honey, didn't you say we'd have enough help? There's just the three of us."

Denise laughed. "Don't worry. Cat comes from a long line of farmers. Believe me, we could sit and watch, but that wouldn't be polite."

Randy looked doubtfully at me. Denise, true to her word, hadn't told him a thing about my bloodline. He thought I just worked for the government.

Randy followed me to the back of the truck. "Are you sure about this? I'm meeting my friend tonight, one of the groomsmen, and he offered to help. I told him we didn't need it because of what Denise said, but I could call him. You don't want to strain yourself."

"Randy, that's sweet, but don't worry. We'll be done in no time."

Half an hour later, Randy gaped at his furniture neatly arranged in Denise's pretty two-story home. Sometimes being half dead didn't all suck.

"Farmers?" he asked in disbelief, looking at me.

I smiled. "Farmers. Back five generations."

"Right," he said. Denise hid her giggle.

"Go shower," I urged her. "We have to leave."

"Randy, what time will you be back tonight? Should Cat and I grab dinner?"

"Yeah. I'm meeting my friend, so I'll be a while."

I cleared my throat with mock menace. "Okay, I'm going!" she relented.

"Thank you for all of your help," Randy said again. "Not just the moving today. Or the wedding. Denise told me how you've always been there for her. It's rare to have a friend like that."

He stared at me without pretense, and I knew why Denise felt a connection with him. There was something very direct in his gaze.

"You're welcome." I didn't say more than that. Somehow, I didn't need to.

"I'm ready," Denise chirped several minutes later.

I gave Randy one last hug goodbye. "It was great to finally meet you."

"Likewise. Take care of my girl."

"Oh, she does," Denise assured him. "She does."

Four hours later, after Denise's fitting and then an uninterrupted—for once!—dinner, I dropped her off at home and arrived back at my house. It was nearly one A.M. Almost an early night for me.

I froze as I got out of the car and felt a faint charge in the air outside. There were no unusual sounds, just the background noises of people in the surrounding houses, and I didn't sense anyone. Still, I stretched my hands and felt the empty air of the driveway like it had form. There was the barest impression of inhuman energy, not strong enough for the source to still be there, but something had been. Maybe it was just some creature who'd passed by. It wouldn't be the first time. Something about the residual aura didn't feel threatening. Vampires or ghouls gave off a different vibe when they were hunting to kill.

Mentally I shrugged. If some evil dead thing had found me and had malicious intent, they would be waiting inside. To be safe, I entered cautiously, then checked all the rooms. Nothing.

I took a shower and climbed into bed. No monster was under it—I'd checked as a stupid precaution—but still, that odd feeling lingered. I could have sworn it felt like someone had been in my house. But that was stupid. Jeez, I was getting as paranoid as Don.

I closed my eyes with finality, trying to shut out the memory of that old childhood bedtime prayer . . . *If I should die before I wake . . .*

I slept with one of my knives under my bed, telling myself I wasn't being paranoid. I was just being cautious.

Yeah, right. I didn't believe it, either.

Ten

"**D**enise, it's almost time."

We were sequestered in our own private room of the country club to avoid running into the groom. The ceremony and reception would be held on site. Denise beamed at me as I adjusted her veil.

"I don't know *what* you said to my parents. You must have drugged them, but I don't care!"

In all innocence I hugged her. No need to tell her I *had* drugged them, with the essence of vampire hallucinogenic in their iced tea, then practiced mind control with my eyes. It had worked, to my astonishment. While they still were dismayed over the religious differences, they were here.

Felicity sauntered into the room. I didn't like her, but she was Denise's cousin and one of the bridesmaids, so pleasantness was required. While I'd been helping Denise get ready, she'd been scouting out the guests for any single males. The woman was perpetually in heat.

"That last groomsman finally showed up," she remarked.

I sighed in relief. Now we wouldn't have to delay the
wedding.

"He's yummy," she continued. She thought anyone
able-bodied with a dick was yummy, but I kept that to
myself. "I only saw him from behind for a second, but
what an ass."

"Um, Felicity, could you get the flowers?" I suggested,
rolling my eyes at Denise.

Denise grinned. "Good news, Felicity. He's the one
you're paired with tonight. I've never met him, but
Randy said he's single."

Denise had segregated the bridal party to a long
rectangular table with every seat boy-girl-boy-girl. I
thought it was a bit odd to have the bridal party segregated like that, but this was her show, not mine.

"Yummy," Felicity purred again.

I pitied the man. She'd probably feel him up under
the table before the toasts even began.

Randy's brother Philip poked his head in. "Are you
ready, Denise?"

She turned to me with barely contained excitement.

"Let's go get me married!"

I smiled at Philip. "We'll meet you in front."

Denise eschewed the traditional wedding march for
a lovely instrumental ballad. Instead of the ushers es-
corting each bridesmaid down the aisle, Randy and the
groomsmen were waiting in front. The bridesmaids
would walk down one at a time in pecking order. As
the maid of honor, I was last before Denise. I fluffed

the train of her dress one final time before taking my place in the entranceway.

As I stepped into the room where the forty-five family and friends were gathered, I felt a wave of pure inhuman power. *Motherfucker, one of the guests was a vampire.* They'd better be planning on only eating cake, or I would have to get real frisky with the silverware. That would be a neat trick, slaughtering a guest at the reception without anyone noticing. My eyes swept the crowd from right to left, seeking out the source.

My mother sat next to Noah, whom Denise had invited before I could tell her that I was trying to break things off between us. Noah smiled at me as I walked down the narrow aisle. I smiled back and took inventory in a military manner. *Bride's side of the room, clear. Groom's side of the room, clear.* For some reason, it didn't occur to me to look at the front where the wedding party stood. Even when I did, it took a second for recognition to register in my suddenly paralyzed mind.

His hair was different. Honey-brown instead of the platinum blond from my memory. It was also longer than before, curling over his ears instead of hugging his head like a sleek helmet. Pale skin glittered against the ebony fabric of his tuxedo, such a creamy breathtaking contrast. Eyes so deep brown they were nearly black bored into mine with none of the shock I felt.

Objects in motion stay in motion with the same speed and in the same direction unless acted upon by an unbalanced force. I proved Newton's Law of Inertia, because even though my breath caught and my heart skipped a beat, I somehow managed to keep walking down the aisle.

Bones's gaze devoured mine. Inside me a completely unfamiliar sensation exploded, taking my lagging mind a second to diagnose it. *Joy*. Pure, unadulterated joy flooded me. I was actually about to spring forward and hurtle myself in his arms, when I stopped myself.

What was Bones doing here? And why *didn't he look surprised to see me?*

That froze me from any craziness, like flinging myself at him as I'd been tempted to do. If Bones wasn't surprised to see me, then he knew I'd be here. But *how* did he know that? And the most important questions— *How did he find me? What did he want?*

Now wasn't the time to find out. This was Denise's wedding. I wouldn't ruin it by causing a scene. *Thank God and all his saints*, I thought, *that my mother isn't looking closely at the groomsmen.* She'd have no hesitation about ruining Denise's day in a spectacular way. Whatever Bones had in mind, I'd deal with him after the wedding.

Or I'd pass out. Whichever came first.

Without further drama, I took my place by Felicity. She leaned over and hissed in my ear as Denise began her walk down the aisle.

"Don't even think about the hottie; I call dibs."

"Shut up," I replied, too low for the guests to overhear. My palms were sweating and my knees felt like jelly. How was I ever going to make it through this wedding? Bones's nearness was unbelievable. For four and a half years I had dreamed about him, and now I could reach out and touch him. It didn't even seem real.

Randy took Denise from her father's arm, and they

held hands. The appointed justice began the modified version of the wedding vows sans religious references. Bones turned and faced the man when the rest of the groomsmen did.

The ceremony was a blur. I had to be nudged by Felicity to accept Denise's bouquet when it was time for the ring exchange. When the justice finally pronounced them man and wife, I was relieved. How terrible of me. This was my best friend's wedding, and all I wanted was for it to be over so I could have a moment to pull myself together.

Denise and Randy ascended back up the aisle, and I nearly ran when it was my turn to follow them. Philip tried to restrain me to a sedate walk, but I yanked on his arm to speed him up.

"I have to go to the bathroom," I lied in desperation. What I had to do was take a moment alone to recover my blasted equilibrium. "Tell Noah not to wait for me; I'll go straight to do the pictures afterward."

As soon as we left the sanctuary, I bolted for the ladies' room, my flower bouquet forgotten on the ground where I'd dropped it.

The bathroom was on the other side of the club. Once inside, I sank to the floor by the sink. Oh God, oh God, seeing him made every emotion I'd tried to forget come roaring back with pitiless intensity. I had to get control of myself. Fast. My head fell onto my bent knees.

"Hallo, Kitten."

I was so preoccupied with my breakdown that I didn't hear Bones come in. His voice was as smooth as I'd remembered, that English accent just as enticing. I snapped my head up, and in the midst of my carefully constructed life crashing around me, found the most absurd thing to worry about.

"God, Bones, this is the ladies' room! What if someone sees?"

He laughed, a low, seductive ripple of the air. Noah had kissed me with less effect.

"Still a prude? Don't fret—I locked the door behind me."

If that was supposed to ease my tension, it had the opposite result. I sprang to my feet, but there was nowhere to run. He blocked the only exit.

"Look at you, luv. Can't say I prefer the brown hair, but as for the rest of you . . . you're luscious."

Bones traced the inside of his lower lip with his tongue as his eyes slid all over me. Their heat seemed to rub my skin. When he took a step closer, I flattened back against the wall.

"Stay where you are."

He leaned nonchalantly against the countertop. "What are you all lathered about? Think I'm here to kill you?"

"No. If you were going to kill me, you wouldn't have bothered with the altar ambush. You obviously know what name I'm going under, so you would have just gone for me one night when I came home."

He whistled appreciatively. "That's right, pet. You haven't forgotten how I work. Do you know I was offered a contract on the mysterious Red Reaper at least three times before? One bloke had half-a-million bounty for your dead body."

Well, not a surprise. After all, Lazarus had tried to

cash a check on my ass for the same reason. "What did you say, since you've just confirmed you're not here for that?"

Bones straightened, and the bantering went out of him. "Oh, I said yes, of course. Then I hunted the sods down and played ball with their heads. The calls quit coming after that."

I swallowed at the image he described. Knowing him, it was exactly what he'd done.

"So, then, why *are* you here?"

He smiled and came nearer, ignoring my previous order.

"Not happy to see me after all these years? Do you know why I wanted to catch you unawares? So I could see your eyes, and know what you felt in that very instant."

Danger. Danger. Less than a foot separated us. I'd never been able to resist him touching me, and I wasn't about to test my willpower now. Frantically I tried to think of a way to distract him.

"Have you met my boyfriend?"

There. That was a doozy. His eyes narrowed, and his lips thinned into a tight line. Yep, Noah was a mood kill for both of us.

I pressed my advantage. Peril before passion; it was safer. "Just how did you weasel into Randy's life to become a groomsman in this wedding, anyhow? Find out my best friend was marrying him? You must have mind-fucked him quick. They were only engaged a month."

He pointed a finger near my face. "Your man Randy

I've known for six months. Long before Denise met him. Unusual bloke, don't you agree? You know what his first words were to me, after we sat side by side for an hour in a bar? He said, 'I hope this won't be engraved on my headstone, but you haven't breathed this whole time. Care to tell me how you do that?'"

I blinked. Denise had once said Randy thought outside the box. Way outside the box, it appeared. And I'd underestimated the size of his balls.

"He knows what you are?"

Bones nodded. "I gave him a peep of the eyes, you know, with the green lights on, and told him he hadn't seen anything. He blinked at me the same way you just did and asked me if that was supposed to work."

Now I was *really* impressed. Randy had a natural immunity to vampire power, even from someone as strong as Bones.

"Obviously that was unexpected. I struck up a conversation with him and we became chummy. It wasn't until this week, *after* I'd accepted my position in his wedding, that he met me at a bar with your scent all over him. You'd helped him move furniture that day."

I was relieved, yet at the same time hurt to think seeing Bones was only due to happenstance.

"So running into you is just a coincidence? You've, ah, gotten over what happened before?"

He locked his eyes with mine. "Wouldn't you like to know? But I don't believe I'm going to tell you. You can stew about it, like I've had to stew ever since I got your bloody Dear John note. I will tell you this, though—we have unfinished business between us. And we're damn sure going to sort it out no matter how much you'd rather avoid it."

Oh *shit*. I'd left him with a note before because I knew I couldn't face him and tell him goodbye. Now four years later, I still didn't think I was strong enough.

"Cather—, er, Cristine! Are you in there?"

My mother knocked loudly on the door, and I sagged in relief. For once I was glad she was there.

Bones's mouth twitched. "I think I'll just pay my respects to your mum, Kitten. Been a while."

"Don't you—!"

The threat I'd been about to utter died on my lips as he opened the door. She looked at him in bewilderment for a second before recognition dawned. Then her face went purple.

"*You! You!*"

"Lovely to see you again, Justina," Bones said devilishly. "You look very fetching in that shade."

"You filthy *animal*!" she raged. "Every night I prayed that you were dead and rotting in hell!"

"Mother!" I said curtly. Absence hadn't made her heart grow fonder.

Bones shrugged. "You should have spoken up a bit. The Almighty must not have heard you."

I pointed a finger at the door. "Bones, whatever you want to say to me can wait until this wedding is over. That's my friend and yours out there, waiting for us to get pictures with them, and that's what we're going to do. Mother, you make one fucking peep to trash Denise's wedding, and I swear to God I'll let him bite you."

"Happy to oblige, Kitten," he assured me.

I jerked my head at the door again. "Out!"

"Ladies." He nodded and sauntered off.

I watched him leave before going to the sink and splashing water onto my face. After all, I had to look pretty for the pictures.

ELEVEN

MY MOTHER NEEDED SEVERAL MORE DIRE warnings before she agreed not to do anything to disrupt the reception. Or notify my work about Bones. I had flatly promised to change myself into a vampire on the spot if she did either.

"That's what he wants from you, Catherine. He wants to steal your soul and turn you into a beast," she said for the third time as she escorted me into the hall.

"Well, then, you'll bear that in mind and keep your mouth shut, won't you? And for God's sake, call me Cristine. Can you *be* more obvious?"

We reached the door. Denise abandoned the pose she had with Randy and met us at the entrance.

"Oh, Cat, I didn't know that Randy's friend was . . ." She lowered her voice. "A vampire! But don't worry. I talked to Randy. He was amazed I knew they existed, too! We have so much in common. Anyhow, Randy swears he's harmless. Says he's known him for months."

My mother looked at Denise like she'd grown three heads.

"*Harmless?!* We aren't talking about a dog that may or may not bite! We are talking about a *murderer*—"

"Ahem," I interrupted, stroking my neck for emphasis. She closed her mouth and stalked off. Farther away I heard Bones snort with laughter. He'd been listening.

"It's okay, Denise," I reassured her. "He knows as long as he keeps his fangs clean, we won't have any problems."

"How does he know that?" she asked practically. "Did you talk to him? You were in the bathroom awhile and I didn't see him. Did you corner him?"

The other way around. "Um, well, kind of . . . er," I stammered, something I hadn't done in years. "I know him. I mean, I've seen him around before. Around Virginia, that is. He, uh, he and I have an understanding. He doesn't mess with me and I don't mess with him."

Denise accepted it at face value. "Well, then let's go get pictures. I'm glad you two aren't going to fight. Tell him not to mention anything about you to Randy, okay? Your boss would lose all the hairs off his balls if he found out how many people knew about you."

"Well put." Well put, indeed.

Bones was Felicity's mysterious wedding partner. She was delighted, managing to squeeze herself indecently next to him in every shot. To make matters worse, he was being charming. I could have cheerfully killed them both after the pictures.

But I couldn't show how much it bothered me for the same reason I hadn't run into Bones's arms when I first saw him. No matter what my feelings were, nothing about our circumstances had changed. So I couldn't afford to let him know how much I still cared. All I could do was play it cool—and hope Bones bought the act enough to leave *me* this time.

I made a beeline for the bar right after the last click of the camera. There was only one thing that could help with tonight, and that was gin. Lots of gin. I downed the first glass without budging in front of the bartender.

"Another one."

The bartender made an inquiring face but poured another gin and tonic. I eyed the level he selected and gave him a dirty look.

"More alcohol," I said succinctly.

"Drowning your sorrows?" a familiar voice behind me mocked.

"None of your business," I replied, straightening.

"There you are, darling!"

Noah came over and gave me a peck on the cheek. Bones tightened his lips into a grim line as he watched.

"Um, Noah . . . I'll show you to your table." I wanted to get him away from Bones, who was looking at Noah like he'd rather drink from his neck than what the bar had to offer.

I saw Noah to his seat, since I was sitting separately at the head table with the rest of the bridal party. My mother pulled me aside as soon as I left Noah. Her face was florid.

"Do you know what that beast did when you walked away from him at the bar? He *winked* at me!"

Caught off guard, I laughed. God, that was priceless. She must have had steam coming out of her ears.

"You think that's funny?" she irrationally demanded.

"Well, Mom, he risked his life for you, and then you tried your damnedest to have him killed. He may not like you."

I spoke low but flippantly, not concerned over Bones's actions with her. He would never hurt her, I knew, but she definitely had some needling coming. God only knew what I had coming.

There were place cards at the head table, which was one long, rectangular thing that would have everyone facing the reception room. I sat at the one marked Cristine Russell. Randy sat to my left, with Denise to his right. To my right read Chris Pin. Who . . . ?

"You've got to be kidding me," I said aloud. Why didn't I just shoot myself and get it over with?

"Justina, we meet again." Bones appeared and took his seat next to me as I vaulted out of my chair. "Wouldn't want to be rude, but I believe your table is over *there*."

He inclined his head to where Noah sat, oblivious to the drama.

"There you are!" Felicity squealed. She grabbed Bones by the arm and smiled at him. "You and I are paired together for the night, so no more running off! I hope you dance as great as you look."

"Slut," I muttered, but not softly enough.

"What was that?" she asked, still blinking coyly up at Bones.

"Er, good luck." My voice rose to a normal level and I backed away.

Felicity looked smug. "I don't need luck."

I downed my gin and then headed, again, for the bar. My mother glared at Bones as she followed after me.

"Oh, Ms. *Russell*," Bones called out. I froze. His emphasis on my fake last name was deliberate. Then again, what had I expected? I'd taken Bones's real surname as my alias; did I think he wouldn't notice? Or comment? "Would you be a luv and get me a drink? You remember my preference, I'm sure."

A slew of curses went through my mind, but I took a deep breath and reminded myself to stay calm. Denise was my best friend. She deserved a lovely reception, not a bloodbath.

"That filthy, lecherous—" my mother began.

"Stuff it." We reached the bar. I gave the poor attendant behind it a murderous look. "Tall glass. All gin. Don't even think about commenting."

His face blanched but he poured to my specifications. I took a long swallow before adding, "Oh yeah. And a fucking whiskey, neat."

TWELVE

FELICITY TOOK ONE LOOK AT THE HALF-EMPTY
pilsner glass of gin I returned with and gasped.

"Cristine, can't you keep a lid on your drinking? This is my cousin's wedding, for heaven's sake!"

Her prim tone made me squeeze my glass so hard to avoid slamming it over her head that it shattered. Gin spilled on the front of me, and my palm started to bleed.

"Motherfucker!" I shouted.

Every head turned. Bones smothered a laugh by faking a sudden cough.

"Are you okay?" Randy looked worriedly at me and wrapped his napkin around my hand. He glanced at Bones, who gave him an innocent shrug.

"I'm all right, Randy," I yelped, mortified.

Denise poked her head around her new husband. "Do you want us to switch the seats?" she asked quietly.

They thought I was rattled because Bones was a

vampire. That was the least of my concerns. His nearness was shredding my control, and the reception had barely started.

"Cristine!" Noah came to the table and took the napkin off my hand. "Is it bad?"

"I'm fine," I snapped harshly. His hurt face made me cringe with guilt. "Just embarrassed," I covered. "I'll be okay. Go back to your seat. Let's not make it worse."

Noah looked mollified and he went back to his table. I smiled to mask my treacherous thoughts. "Really," I added for Denise's benefit.

I gathered the shards of glass and began to pile them into the bloody napkin. "I'm going to the ladies' room to wash this off and throw away the glass."

"I'll go with you," Denise offered.

"No!" She looked startled by my abrupt reply. I gave a glance to my right at Bones and then back to her again. Her eyes widened, and she got the picture. Part of it, anyway.

"Cris," she addressed him. "Would you mind going with Cristine and seeing if they have any bandages? Randy says . . ." She paused and then continued wickedly, "Randy says you have a great deal of experience with bleeding wounds."

"Ooh, are you a doctor?" Felicity cooed.

Bones stood and gave Denise an appreciative grin at her choice of words.

"Back in London I was many things," he answered Felicity evasively.

I made a stop at the bar first. The bartender gave a wide-eyed look at my red-stained napkin.

"Gin. No glass, just the bottle," I said bluntly.

"Um, miss, maybe you should—"

"Give the lady the bottle, mate," Bones interjected, his eyes flashing green.

Without delay an unopened gin was thrust in my still-bleeding hand. I twisted the top off, threw away the glass and my bloody napkin, and took a long swallow. Then I led Bones out to the far corner of the parking lot, where there were the fewest cars. He waited patiently while I drank again. I was smearing blood all over the outside of the bottle, but I didn't care.

"Better?" he asked when I came up for air. His lips twitched with amusement.

"Not hardly," I countered. "Look, I don't know how long my mother will keep quiet, but in case you didn't notice, she hates you. She'll call in the troops and try to have you skewered over an open flame with a silver stick. You have to leave."

"No."

"Dammit, Bones!" My temper exploded. Why did he have to be so gorgeous, why did he have to stand so close, and *why* did I still love him so much? "Are you *trying* to get killed? One call to my boss, that's all it'll take, and believe me, my mother's probably caressing her cell phone and fantasizing about it now."

Bones rolled his eyes.

"Sods like your boss have chased me most of my undead life, yet I'm still here while they're not. Neither your mum nor your boss scares me, Kitten. Unless you'd like to choose now for us to have our long-overdue talk, I suggest we return to the festivities. But you can forget about me leaving—or you, either, for that matter. I found you days ago. There's a reason you didn't know about that until now. You try to vanish into the smoke again and it'll be a short flight, I assure you. Plus, then we'll be having our chat under much different conditions. Like with you chained up somewhere so you can't try to sneak off again. You pick your circumstances, luv, but I have damn well waited long enough to have this out with you."

Uh oh. I already knew Bones never bluffed, but even if I hadn't, the look in his eyes said he meant every word.

"It was you I felt outside my house the other night, wasn't it?" I asked accusingly. Had to be. That was the same night Bones had met Randy at the bar.

A small smile touched his mouth. The breeze ruffled his darker curls, and in his tux with the moonlight caressing the chiseled planes of his face, he looked positively devastating.

"So you felt me. I wondered if you would."

I couldn't keep staring at him. I might be immune to vampire powers, but Bones had always been my kryptonite.

"We have to get back to the reception," was all I said, looking away.

He held out his hand. "Mind if I have a drop from your bottle first?"

I handed over the gin, careful not to let my fingers graze his. Instead of drinking from it, however, Bones grasped the bottle and stared into my eyes as he licked my blood off the slick glass surface. His tongue curved around every contour of the bottle, and heat flared through me as I watched, mesmerized. When there was not a red drop left on it, he passed it back into my suddenly shaking hand.

Think about work! my brain screamed. *Think about anything but what that tongue felt like on your skin!*

I went to step by him, but he grabbed my hand. I yanked, but it was like pulling against welded steel.

"Quit that," Bones said mildly, pulling out a knife. My eyes widened, but he just nicked the side of the same hand gripping mine, and then pressed his blood to my cut. It tingled as it healed on contact.

I drew back my hand. This time, he let me, but the swirling green in his gaze said he'd been just as affected by touching me as I had by feeling his skin on mine.

Yeah, I had to leave. *Right. Now.*

I turned and walked away quickly, somehow managing not to look back.

The reception was a living hell. Felicity started up a steady stream of suggestive chatter as soon as Bones returned, and he did nothing to discourage it. Grimly I stayed, drinking with the single-mindedness of the condemned as I watched them.

Noah, tonight of all nights, got paged by the animal hospital. He apologized profusely to Denise before he left, but I hardly noticed he was gone.

Denise and Randy were almost the last to leave. They would depart for their honeymoon two days from now, and were going back to her house tonight. I kissed them and wished them every happiness while I was fixated on the fact that it had been five minutes since I'd seen Felicity and Bones. They were still here, to my knowledge.

Unable to help myself, I searched for them, following the trail of invisible energy that wafted off him. When I found them, I stopped short.

They were in the corner of the patio off the main reception room. It was pitch dark, but I saw everything all too easily. Felicity's back was to me and her arms were around him. The moonlight glowed off his skin, highlighting his face when he leaned down and kissed her.

I have been stabbed, shot, burned, bitten, beaten unconscious too many times to count, and even staked. None of those held a candle to the pain I felt at seeing his mouth on hers. A soft sound escaped me, barely a disturbance of the air, but it was a sound of pure agony.

At that instant, Bones lifted his eyes to stare directly at me. His gaze seemed to be shouting, *Don't like it? What are you going to do about it?*

I fled as fast as I could, running to my car and practically slamming it into gear. The territorialism all vampires had was seething inside me. I had to leave or I was going to kill Felicity, and technically she hadn't done anything wrong. No, I was the one with the problem. She was just kissing the man I loved—and had given away.

Thirteen

I WAS IN SUCH TURMOIL THAT I HAD TO DO something. Tomorrow night we were supposed to investigate the GiGi Club, a place where two girls had disappeared. Their bodies hadn't been found, but something about the way the police dismissed any connection to the club smacked of vampire influence. Fortunately it was local. Only an hour away. Still in my bridesmaid gown, I strapped knives to my legs and drove straight there. Fuck backup. Tate and the boys could have tomorrow night off. I was going vampire hunting and I was doing it alone.

Fifty minutes later I got out of the car, still stomping pissed, and was halfway across the parking lot when a scream whipped my head around. There was a young man, blood on his neck, waving his arms and yelling for help near the entrance to the club. No one looked up. Everyone went right by him. It was only when someone went right *through* him that I understood.

"Hey buddy!" I yelled, striding forward. "Over here!"

Several heads turned. The bouncer gave me a very strange glance, no doubt wondering exactly how much booze I'd already consumed. The bloody guy got an immense look of relief on his face and whizzed toward me in a hazy streak.

"Thank God! No one's listening to me, and my girl-friend is *dying*! I don't know why everyone's ignoring me . . ."

Damn. The only other sentient ghost I'd met had been very aware that he was dead. Most ghosts were just fragments of an image, replaying themselves over and over in a mindless repetition of some long-past event. Not scared and confused and having no idea why suddenly no one paid attention to them.

"Where is she?"

Maybe this was useless. His girlfriend could have died years ago, but he was dressed in contemporary clothes, complete with an eyebrow ring and a pierced tongue. Imagine taking *that* with you to eternity.

"In here!" He sped right through the door while I settled for pushing my way past the people in line.

"Looking for my boyfriend," I said by way of expla-nation to several hostile glances. "I know he's in here with that tramp I work with."

That got the women on my side. They hustled me forward with a few "Go get him, honeys!" The bouncer didn't even card me when I stepped through the doors. Guess I looked over twenty-one.

The dead guy led me to a door on the far side of the club by the bathrooms. It was locked, but I gave it a good yank and it broke open. It revealed a narrow unlit hall that I followed to another locked door. Ah, a private room complete with soundproofing. The pumping noise from the music was almost inaudible in here.

I didn't see the ghost anymore. There was only a girl in a leather chair facing the doorway, and she clearly wasn't in mortal danger, unless you count painting her toenails. Her eyes widened when she saw me.

"How did you get in here? This is a members-only area!"

I smiled and extended my badge, one of the many I carried. "Police, sugar. That makes me a member everywhere," I responded, heading for the only other door behind her.

She shook her head and resumed painting her nails.

"You don't want to go in there, but hey. Your funeral."

With that questionable display of concern, she applied another pink coat to the toe in front of her while I opened the door.

The ghost of the young man was inside, and he gestured to an unconscious girl in a vampire's arms. "Help her, please!"

There were about half a dozen vampires inside. None felt older than I was in undead years. On the floor were two bodies. One of them was my ghost's, who hovered frantically near the equally young girl being snacked on. She was still alive, but not for long judging from her pulse. The vampire hadn't even paused to look at the ghost, even though I knew the undead schmuck could see him. Me, I'd have felt awkward when the specter of someone I'd just killed was whizzing by me while I ate, but this creep seemed blasé about it. The other body was also of a young woman, and there was a third girl cling-

ing to life on another vampire's lap. Her eyes fluttered
and then closed when I flicked my gaze to her.

"You should have listened to Brandy," one of the vampires purred at me in a bad imitation of a sinister voice.

"Miss Pink Toenails?" I asked as I hitched up my
dress.

They watched with interest as my hem climbed higher
up my legs. My hiking it up wasn't for distraction, although that was a secondary benefit. It was to access
the knives I'd strapped to my legs. When they were revealed, the mood in the room shifted from hungry and
lustful to wary.

"Now, you fuckers," I said as I rolled my head around
my shoulders and palmed some knives. "Let me introduce myself."

"You forgot one."

I was just about to fling more knives when his voice
stopped me. Bones came in and cast a thorough look
around at the carnage. Most of the vampires I'd dispatched with my blades, but the ones who'd killed the
kids I'd torn apart with my bare hands. It was the least
I could do.

"Who?"

His smile was pleasant. "The little bitch who was
sneaking around for a gun, but she's not doing that any
longer."

Must have been Brandy with the pink toenails. His
benign expression didn't fool me. Knowing him, she'd
be wearing that shade in hell.

"Two of these girls are still alive. Give them blood.
Yours will work faster than what I have to offer."

Bones took the knife I handed him and sliced his palm, going to each girl and making them swallow his blood.

"Will she be okay?" the ghost asked, hovering over his girlfriend.

Gradually I heard her pulse return to a slow but steady rhythm as Bones's blood went to work in her, offsetting her injuries. After a moment, I smiled. "Yeah. She will be now."

He smiled back, showing that in life, he'd had dimples. God, he was so young! Then he frowned.

"They're not all here. There were three more of those creatures. They said they'd be back."

Probably went out to rustle up more dinner. Bastards. "I'll get them," I promised. "Don't worry. It's my job."

He smiled again . . . and then started to fade at the edges, growing fainter, until there was nothing left of him.

I stared in silence. Then, "Is he gone?"

Bones knew what I meant. "I expect so. He accomplished what he wanted to, so he's moved on. Sometimes a few stubborn people hang on long enough to do one last thing."

And he'd trusted me to take care of that last thing for him. There might not be much I could say I was good for, but avenging people who'd had their lives stolen from them was definitely my specialty.

I headed for the door.

"What do you think you're doing?" Bones asked.

"Grabbing Miss Pink Toenails and piling her in here with the rest of them," I threw over my shoulder. "Then

I'm going to wait until their friends come back, and kill the hell out of them."

Bones came after me. "Sounds like fun."

We were on the dance floor nearest to the bathrooms. Anyone looking to access that grisly private room would have to pass by us first. I'd objected to dancing with him, even though it was our best cover option, but Bones just dragged me onto the floor in much the same way he had on our first date.

"You are a *professional* killer, aren't you?" he asked. "You can't hover around that hallway with blood spattered on you and expect to look inconspicuous."

My lavender dress did have red streaks on it. I'd washed the blood off my hands in the bathroom, but there was no fixing that. Bones was right—I'd stick out like a sore thumb loitering in the hallway, or even at the bar. Pressed against him on the dance floor, however, no one would see it.

Except that being pressed against Bones on the dance floor was playing hell on my self-control. The last time I'd held him this way had been the morning I left him. I remembered it like yesterday: me fighting back tears and reminding myself that leaving him was the only option.

Yeah, some things hadn't changed.

I sought around for a distraction. Anything other than focusing on how much I'd missed being in his arms.

"Why are you here anyway? I thought you'd be busy with Felicity, what with how the two of you looked."

His brow rose. "Did seeing me kiss her bother you?

I can't imagine why. Didn't you tell me in your note to move on with my life?"

A low blow. I started to pull away, but he just tightened his grip. It was either stay put or cause a scene and possibly miss catching the killers.

Grimly I began to dance again, hating that I still cared so much when it seemed Bones only had anger left in him.

"They knew what I was, Bones. The men who came to the hospital that day, they knew everything from my pathology reports. And they knew about vampires. The one in charge—"

"Don?" he supplied.

Oh, so he'd done his homework. "Yes, Don. He said he'd been looking his whole life for someone strong enough to fight vampires who wasn't one of them. He offered me a deal. He'd relocate us, and I'd lead his team. In return he promised to leave you alone. We couldn't have all survived any other way. We would have been hunted like animals, and you know my mother would have rather died than gone with you. She'd also rather see me killed than changed into a vampire, and let's face it, that's what you would have eventually wanted me to do!"

Bones let out a bitter snort, twirling me a little too hard.

"Is that what this whole bleedin' thing was about? You believing I'd turn you into a vampire? Bloody hell, Kitten, did it ever occur to you to *talk* to me instead of just running off?"

"It wouldn't have mattered. You would have insisted on it eventually," I replied stubbornly.

"You should have trusted me," he muttered. "When did I ever lie to you?"

"When have you lied to me?" I pounced. "How about when you kidnapped and murdered Danny Milton? You swore to me you'd never touch Danny, but I don't suppose he's off in Mexico sipping margaritas, is he?"

"You made me swear not to kill, cripple, maim, dismember, blind, torture, bleed, or inflict any injury on Danny Milton. *Or* stand by while someone else did. You should save your concern for someone worthy; Danny gave you up like a bad habit straightaway. You know that brainwashing rot doesn't hold up under a Master vampire's eyes. At least the bugger was finally useful. He told me where you lived. Virginia. I had you narrowed down to three states, and Danny saved me some time. That's why I told Rodney to kill him fast and painless—and I didn't stay to watch."

"You bastard," I managed.

Bones shrugged. "Since the day I was born."

We danced in silence for a few minutes. I kept looking around for any telltale crystal skin on the patrons, but so far Bones and I were the only nonhumans. *Where are you, bloodsuckers? Here, fangy, fangy, fangy . . .*

"So, how long have you been dating the pet vet?" Bones asked.

The derisiveness in his tone stiffened my spine. "None of your business."

He gave a short laugh. "Indeed? You looked like you were about to ram a stake through Felicity's heart earlier, yet you begrudge me a simple question?"

The music changed to something slower. I cursed it, Bones, and the killers who'd put me in this situation.

"I wanted to ram a stake through her heart because she's a shallow bitch who pisses me off. It had nothing to do with you."

Bones's laugh became softer. "Liar."

He moved closer, his body dipping into mine in time with the music. The feel of his muscles moving in sinuous ripples under his clothes made my hands clench. Now I was fighting back something other than tears as I reminded myself it could never work between us.

His nostrils flared. Inwardly I cursed. I could fake cool all I wanted, but Bones was a vampire. He'd be able to tell from one whiff how he was affecting me.

"Perhaps you did miss me after all," he said low, flecks of green appearing in his eyes.

I pretended to be blasé. "Don't get flattered; you're just a good dancer. Felicity seemed to think so, too."

"Seeing me with Felicity was the least you deserved after I had to watch that human teddy bear fawn all over you," Bones replied curtly. "Really, Kitten, what were you thinking? Your mum has bigger balls than Noah."

"His balls are fine!" I snapped, then flushed. Hell if I knew, and God, did I just say that?

Bones snorted and twirled me in a circle before yanking me close. "Right. No wonder you're so hot around me. I reckon you've had a better time shagging yourself than him. Must be frustrating."

His hips were brushing mine as he taunted me. Anger flared in me, covering my lust. No way was I going to admit that I hadn't slept with Noah or, hell, anyone since Bones. Frustrating? That didn't even begin to describe what I was feeling.

But two could play the taunting game. I hitched a leg up, curling it around Bones's hip, and gave a hard circular twist against him that had his gaze turning flat green.

"Looks like I'm not the only one who's frustrated, Mr. Optical Hard-on. Might want to tone your eyes down. People will notice."

Bones closed his eyes, then he locked his hands around my waist and bent until his mouth touched my ear.

"Careful, luv. I might be angry with you, but that doesn't mean I don't still want you. So if you do that again, I'll shag you right here, right now, and sod anyone who wants to watch."

His sudden hardness below emphasized that he wasn't making an idle threat. That scared me—and turned me on in ways I didn't even want to contemplate.

Bones took in a long breath. I shivered, knowing since vampires didn't need to breathe, he was inhaling the traitorous scent of my desire.

"Oh, Kitten . . ." His voice deepened. "Now you're just daring me, aren't you?"

I was saved from a reply—or worse—when the energy in the room shifted. Bones felt it, too, a lot clearer than I did. He tensed and his eyes snapped open, no longer green, but hard brown orbs.

"They're here."

FOURTEEN

THE VAMPIRES CONSISTED OF TWO MEN AND a woman. They moved through the bar with a lethal, sensuous grace no living person could duplicate. Pity the living people around them couldn't sense the danger, however. No, they were vying and jockeying to catch the beautiful predators' attention instead.

Then they did something that made me groan out loud. They split up. Dammit. I'd hoped they would all head en masse to their secret break room, leaving Bones and me to block their exit and kill them at our leisure. But of course that would have been too easy.

"I'm going to have to call in my team," I said low to Bones. "Have the perimeter secured."

He gave a disparaging snort. "Right. Your toy soldiers are well over an hour away, and I can practically feel the bloodlust pouring off these sods. They're going to feed soon. You wait, and someone will die."

He was right. Already the three seemed to be picking out their entrées. If one of them headed back to the very messy members-only area and then sounded the alarm, the other two might get away. Furthermore, I couldn't just do my regular act of offering myself up as a test bite. The blood on my dress ruined my innocent-snack look.

"Got any ideas?" I asked.

Bones smiled. "I do."

He surprised me by grabbing the girl nearest to him and yanking her close. His hands cupped her head as he brought their faces right up next to each other. I was about to ask him what the hell he thought he was doing when his eyes glowed, partially concealed by his hands. It only took a moment. Bones's eyes returned to their normal brown, and she stared ahead with a very obedient expression.

"Go to the ladies' room," Bones told her, "and switch your dress with this woman."

I was shaking my head in admiration when a thought occurred to me.

"You could have done that *before*; then we wouldn't have needed to dance together!"

Bones only smiled. "So I could have."

I gave him a single glare before I led the girl into the bathroom. We received a few odd looks when we both went into the same stall, but now wasn't the time to worry about winks and nudges. Quickly I stripped off my dress and she did the same, just as she'd been instructed. Hers was a little tight and a lot smuttier than my bridesmaid's dress. It was also backless, so I had to take off my bra. When we got out of the stall, I caught a glance of myself in the mirror. My boobs were bulging out from the low-scooped neckline, and anybody could tell I wasn't wearing a bra.

Just like old times, I thought ironically. *I look like a slut, and Bones is my backup while I go after murdering fang-bangers. The only thing that would make this complete would be to take off my underwear.*

Then I smiled. And went back in the stall.

When I came up to the vampire that looked the closest to taking his companion on a one-way stroll, I didn't even bother with small talk. I just elbowed the pretty blonde he'd been speaking to aside and slapped my panties on his chest.

"As soon as I saw you," I purred, "I knew I wouldn't be needing these."

That got his attention. He glanced down at my panties, then put them to his nose and took in a deep breath. *Eww*, I thought, but my smile never faltered. Then he shoved his protesting companion aside.

"Never mind," he told her.

"Bitch!" she hissed at me before stomping off.

Jeez. I'd just saved her life, and that was the thanks I got?

I linked my arm in his, being sure to rub my breast against him. "You're not the conversationalist type, I hope?"

His reply was to begin propelling me through the throngs of people. I didn't see Bones, but that didn't concern me. If I didn't see him, then neither would the other vampires. I might not trust my emotions with him, but I had no hesitation about trusting him with my life.

We were down the hall and almost to the first hidden room when my companion stopped and took in a questioning sniff.

"What the—?" he began.

I didn't let him finish. My hand whipped down the front of my dress and I rammed a silver blade into his heart before he had the chance to form another word. It was simple, really. He'd had his back to me, never suspecting the danger.

Then I dragged him quickly inside the room, muttering and trying not to leave a blood smear. Thank God vampires didn't spurt blood like in the movies, but even a few drops outside would be too much with their sense of smell.

While in there, I checked on the other two girls. They were still passed out, but Bones had said their pulses were steady enough that we could attempt our sting operation. I noted how pale they were and frowned. The last two vamps had to be taken care of quickly. Those girls needed to be in a hospital, not lying in this horror movie of a room with bodies everywhere.

A shocked gasp whipped my head up. In the doorway, the female vampire stood perfectly still, but her human male companion didn't. He gasped again, then started to scream.

"Aw, shit," I sighed.

She swatted him across the head so hard, he was unconscious before he hit the floor. Then she sprang at me with blurring speed, her fangs extended murderously.

I let her come, rolling back at the last second and then kicking out with my legs. Her momentum plus my maneuver had her smashing into the wall behind me. I leapt onto her before she had a chance to regroup, driving my knife into her heart and giving it two rough, satisfying twists.

"Kitten, outside!"

I was out the door and down the hall moments after hearing Bones's yell, but still barely in time to see him chasing after the last vampire, who was hightailing it out of the club. So much for a nice, stealthy execution of the trio.

I shoved past people with nearly the same blurring speed he had. Once in the parking lot, I only paused long enough to snatch a cell phone away from a person unlucky enough to have one pressed to his head while I galloped by.

"Thanks!" I called out, then said, "He'll call you back!" and hung up on whoever was on the other end. I dialed while keeping one eye on Bones as he zigzagged after our last perpetrator. He was about fifty yards ahead of me and gaining. Goddamn, but I'd forgotten how fast he was.

"Tate," I gasped as soon as he answered. "Can't talk, but we need a containment group at the GiGi Club, stat. Got vamp bodies, human bodies, three victims still breathing, and a hell of a lot of witnesses."

"What are you doing at the GiGi Club?" Tate barked. "That was supposed to be with us, tomorrow night!"

I jumped over a fence, ripping my borrowed dress, and played a brief game of speed Frogger as I darted across a busy street.

"Can't talk now," I repeated breathlessly. "I'm chasing down a vamp; I'll call you later!"

Then I threw the phone aside and pulled out one of my knives instead.

I couldn't see Bones anymore. He'd dashed out of my line of vision while I was concentrating on not getting hit by oncoming traffic. I kept running full out in the same direction, however, cursing my heels and debating whether it was faster to stop and take them off—damn ankle straps!—or keep running with the potential neck breakers. Wouldn't that make a charming epitaph? *Here lies Cat. Killed not by fang, but Ferragamos.*

I was half through an empty soccer field, about to say screw it and take off the shoes, since heels plus running in grass equaled very unstable footing, when I saw a flash of green up in the distance. Vampire eyes, glowing in the dark. Screw the heels, full speed ahead!

I saw them just as Bones jerked his blade out of the vampire's chest. They were on the ground inside a fenced new construction site. Mentally I let out a sigh of relief. At this hour, the crews were long gone. Good. No witnesses to worry about.

I came to a halt by Bones once I vaulted over the fence, my heart racing from adrenaline and the run. He gave the body a final kick and then turned to face me.

"You and I need to talk, Kitten."

"*Now?*" I asked in disbelief, gesturing to the dead vampire near his feet.

"It's not like he's going anywhere, so yeah. Now."

At once I began to back away. I'd been so caught up the past hour catching the killers that I'd forgotten things were very different between Bones and me.

How stupid. I'd felt so comfortable in our routine of hunting down the bad guys that I'd let myself end up in a deserted construction site with nowhere to flee. If I were smart, I'd have stayed back at the GiGi Club and let Bones chase down this last jerk himself.

Bones watched me edge backward, and his eyes narrowed. "Don't you move another step."

"I—I have to go back to the club, my team's on the way . . ." I hedged.

"Do you still love me?"

The blunt question almost made me trip. I looked away, biting my lip and hating myself for the lie I was about to tell.

"No."

He didn't say anything for so long, I dared a peek at him. Bones was staring at me hard enough to make me wonder if he was able to see through to the back of my head.

"If you don't love me, then why didn't you kill Ian? You had a knife in his heart. All you had to do was twist. Your job is to kill vampires, after all, but you let him live. It was if you were sending me a bloomin' valentine."

"Sentimentality." I grasped at straws. "For old time's sake."

His mouth twisted. "Well, luv, as the saying goes, no good deed goes unpunished. You *should* have killed him, because now he's looking for you. You made quite an impression. While I would never force you to do anything against your will, Ian wants to find you to do just that."

"What are you talking about?"

Bones smiled, but it wasn't pleasant. "He's enamored, of course. Ian's a collector of rare things, and there's no one rarer than you, my beautiful half-breed. You're in danger. Ian doesn't know I've found you, but he'll track you himself soon enough."

I mulled this over, and then shrugged. "It doesn't matter. I beat Ian before and I can do it again."

"Not the way he'll play it." There was something in his voice that made me look sharply at him. "I know my sire. Ian won't just come at you one night and try to take you on in a fair fight. He'll grab everyone you love first and then strike a deal with you, his terms. Believe me, you won't like them. Now, your one advantage is me. Because of your clever little description of our relationship, Ian believes you hate me and vice versa. Nice touch, that. Especially the money part. Still want a check?"

"I'll write *you* one if you leave," I muttered.

Bones ignored that. "Furthermore, you still have a price on your head. I told you in the loo that I'd been offered contracts on you before that I traced to their source, but I don't know who's behind this last one. He or she is being very discreet. So you have another threat hanging over you that's even more dangerous than Ian, and like it or not, you're going to need my help."

"Vampires and ghouls come after me all the time," I said dismissively. "If I need help, I have my team."

"Humans?" Scorn dripped from his tone. "The only way they'll be able to protect you is if they incapacitate the hitter by making him eat too much!"

"You are *so* arrogant."

Bones came closer until only a few feet separated

us. "I'm powerful. More than you're aware of. That is truth, not arrogance. Every member of your team combined couldn't protect you as well as I can, and you know it. Now isn't the time for your stubborn insistence on going everything alone, Kitten. Whether you want my help or not, you're getting it."

"Dammit, Bones, how many times do I have to tell you that the biggest way you could help is to *leave*? I appreciate the warning about Ian, but if you stay around me, *you're* the one who'll be in danger. Don't worry about me, I can take care of myself."

His brow arched insolently. "And right back at you, pet. I'm not the least bit afraid of your boss or your band of merry men. You want to get rid of me? Then you'll have to kill me."

Oh shit. I couldn't do that. Hell, I hadn't known how I could kill him when I thought he'd slaughtered an innocent family!

"Then *I'll* leave," I said, frustration making me reckless. "I ran away once; I can do it again!"

I was suddenly gripped in Bones's arms with my head tilted back, without seeing him so much as twitch for warning. Maybe that was my own fault and not just due to his speed. I'd been so busy keeping up my emotional shields, I'd pretty much forgotten about my physical ones. And truth be told, I never expected him to bite me.

Yeah, I'd let my usual vampire guards down all the way with Bones.

His fangs buried deep into my neck. Just like that one time years before when he'd bitten me, what logic told me should hurt only felt good instead. Really, *really* good, and increasing with each strong pull from his mouth. The strangest kind of heat flooded all through me, even though with my blood spilling into Bones, I should be feeling colder, not warmer.

Stop it, I wanted to say, but couldn't seem to form the words. What came out was a primitive groan instead. Bones tightened his arms around me, tilting me back, and licking my neck before sinking his teeth in again.

I jerked in pleasure even as a warning shot through me. *Was he going to kill me? Change me into a vampire?* Neither possibility appealed to me. Spots began to appear in my vision, assuming my eyes were even still open. Add that to the roaring in my ears, which was either my heartbeat or the noise one hears right before passing out.

My fists thumped on his back. It was all I was capable of doing to tell him to stop, since my mouth only seemed good for making little ecstatic noises. That's when I realized I *could* stop him, if I really wanted to. My silver knife was still in my hand. I could feel the cold metal of it in my fingers.

Bones must have felt it, too. He pulled back for an instant, drops of my blood staining his mouth like rubies, and then slowly, deliberately, bent to my neck again. The subsequent long, deep suction weakened my knees and sent such a rapturous shudder through me that I found myself thinking if I were going to die, at least I'd die happy.

But I didn't have to die. All I had to do was angle that blade and give it one good push to live. Bones wasn't restraining my arms. They were loosely around his back while one of his hands tangled in my hair and the other supported me. The gray encompassing my vision became thicker, the noise in my ears was almost deafening. It was him or me, because it was clear he wasn't going to stop.

My fingers gripped around the knife to thrust . . . and then relaxed. It slipped from my hand, which I used to press Bones closer instead. *I can't do it*, was my last thought. *Besides*, *there are far worse ways to die.*

Fifteen

AWARENESS RETURNED A PIECE AT A TIME.
First and foremost, I realized my heart was still
beating. *Okay, I'm not dead or changed into a vampire.
Always a plus.* Then I discovered I had a pillow under
my head. More alertness revealed that I was stretched
on my side covered by a blanket. The room was dark,
drapes were shut. Arms encircled me from behind,
nearly the color of my own.

That's when I woke all the way up.

"Where are we?"

Who I was with wasn't in question, even though my
head still felt a little cottony.

"In the house I'm renting, in Richmond."

"How long have I been out?" Silly details seemed
important; why I didn't know.

"Four hours, give or take. Long enough for you to
steal all the covers. I've been listening to you snore and
watching you cocoon into the bedspread, and I real-

ized I've missed this the most. Holding you while you sleep."

I sat up, my hand going at once to my throat. As expected, it was smooth. No punctures or bumps left to show what had happened. Bones had closed the holes with a drop of his blood, erasing any marks of what had happened.

"You bit me," I said accusingly, but with a lot less anger than I intended. It was either the combination of the juice in his fangs or blood loss that made everything seem not as . . . stressful. And I should be stressed. Even though we were still both dressed, I was in a bed with Bones, and that wasn't a good idea if I wanted to keep my emotional distance.

"Yes," was all he said. He didn't even bother to sit up, but stayed stretched out on the pillows.

"Why?"

"Many reasons. Do you want me to list them all?"

"Yeah." An edge crept into my tone. He looked too damn unconcerned for my liking.

"Primarily to prove a point," he said, finally sitting up. "You could have killed me. By rights, you *should* have killed me. You had a vampire sucking the life-blood out of you and a silver knife in your hand. Only a fool wouldn't have wielded that blade . . . or someone who cares far more than she's admitting to."

"You bastard, you bit me to *test* me?" I exclaimed, getting out of bed and then staggering at the sudden wave of dizziness. Looked like Bones had cleaned his plate. "Bet you'd have been pretty fucking sorry if I *would* have sliced up your heart. How could you be so stupid; you could have gotten killed!"

"And so could you," he flared right back. "Frankly after years of wondering how you felt about me, it was worth risking my life to find out. Admit it, Kitten. You haven't gotten over me any more than I've gotten over you, and all your denial, lies, or the moron you're dating won't change that."

I had to look away. Hearing him say he hadn't gotten over me was like a velvet-covered hammer to my heart. I barely even registered the insult to Noah.

"It doesn't matter," I said at last. "It can't work between us, Bones. Nothing can change what you are, and I *won't* change what I am."

"Answer me this, Kitten. When it is just you and me, no one else, does it bother you that I'm not human? I know what the rest of them think—your mother, your work, your friends, but do *you* care that I'm a vampire?"

Actually, I hadn't thought about it under those terms. There were always other things to consider. Stripped of that, however, there wasn't any pause in my response.

"No. I don't care."

His eyes closed for a second. Then they opened with a blaze of intensity. "I know you left me because you thought you had to protect me, that I couldn't handle the obstacles before us. So you tried to get on with your life because you believed it would never work between us. But you see, I couldn't get on with my life because I knew we *could* work. I've been looking for you every day since you left me, Kitten, and I'm sick of being without you. You've had your shot at things, now let me have mine."

"What are you talking about?"

"I'm talking about trusting me, which is what you

should have done over four years ago. I'm strong enough to handle whatever your job or your mum could throw at me. You still care about me, and I certainly haven't given up on you. We can beat the odds against us, if you'd give us a chance to."

Oh, if only. God, if *only* it were that simple!

"Even if you take out my job and my mother, we're still doomed, Bones. You're a vampire. I meant it when I said I didn't care, but you will! What are you going to do when I grow old, just hand me some Ben-Gay for my arthritis? You'll want me to change. You'll resent me when I refuse, and it will destroy us."

He stared at me without blinking.

"For the record: I will never force you to become a vampire. I won't pressure you, coerce you, trick you, or guilt you. Is that clear enough?"

"So you're fine with me getting wrinkled, gray, decrepit, and then dead?" I asked harshly. "Is that what you're saying?"

Something that might have been pity flashed across his face.

"Kitten, sit down."

"No." A chill ran up my spine. Whatever it was, for him to look so compassionate all of a sudden, it must be bad. I'd take it on my feet. "You tell me. What don't I know? Am I dying or something?" That would explain his lack of apprehension over my growing old.

Bones got up and stood in front of me. "Haven't you ever wondered how long you would live? Ever truly pondered it?"

"No." I laughed bitterly. "I thought I would get killed pretty quick with my job."

"Think past that," he went on. My heart began to pound. "You're half vampire. You've never been sick, your body heals at an inhuman rate, and you can't catch any of the diseases that afflict the living population. Even poisons or drugs need to be administered in massive doses before they affect you, so *what makes you think you would only live to an average age?*"

My mouth opened to argue, but then hung loosely. In a way, it felt similar to the night my mother told me what I was, because denial was my first response.

"You're trying to trick me. I have a heartbeat, I breathe, get my period, shave my legs . . . I'm *alive.* I had a childhood!"

"You told me once your differences emerged most notably in puberty. Probably it was the hormonal surge, the same thing which can trigger congenital defects in humans that increased your nosferatu traits, and they've grown ever since. Your pulse and breathing only make you easier to kill, but you're not human. You never have been. You just mimic them better than vampires do."

"Liar!" I shouted.

He didn't flinch. "Your skin hasn't aged a day since you left me. Not one line, not one furrow. Granted, you're only twenty-seven and wouldn't be showing most signs of it until later, but still. There should be some difference in the pores, the texture . . ." He traced a finger down my cheek for emphasis. "But there's not. Then there's the blood."

My mind reeled. "What blood?"

"Mine. Didn't have a chance to tell you this before, because you left two days later. Probably doesn't make a difference in the big picture, but here it is. The night we rescued your mum, you drank my blood. Not just a few drops for healing, but a good two pints. That alone would add fifty years to a normal human's lifespan. To yours, who knows? Double, easily."

I reared my hand back, but he grabbed it before I could slap him. "You bastard! You didn't tell me that. You didn't *warn* me!"

"Would it have changed your decision? You thought we were both going to die that night, if you recall, not to mention you would have done anything to save your mum. And truthfully, you could live to be as old as I am without it. Don't take my word for it. Go see your boss. Look him in the eye and ask what he already knows. All the pathology they must have done on you over the years, I'm *damn* sure he knows. That's why I don't have to pressure you into becoming a vampire. With your mixed heritage and the occasional consumption of my blood, you'll live as long as you want to, just as you are."

This couldn't be happening. The walls felt like they were collapsing on top of me. All I wanted to do was run from the truth and be alone, even from Bones. Especially from Bones.

Numbly I walked toward the door, but he blocked me. "Where do you think you're going?"

I shoved him. "Out. I can't look at you right now."

He didn't budge. "You're in no condition to drive."

I let out a bitter laugh. "Why don't you just open a vein for me, then? What's another fifty years, right?"

Bones reached out, but I jerked back.

"Don't touch me."

I knew some of what I was feeling was irrational backlash anger. The proverbial shooting of the messenger and all that. But I couldn't help it.

Bones dropped his hand. "Fine. Where do you want to go? I'll drive you."

"Take me home."

He held open the door. "After you."

Bones dropped me off at my house with a parting comment that he'd see me the following night. I didn't reply to that. It caused too many mixed emotions, and I had enough to think about already.

Once I got inside, I called Don to tell him I was okay. As expected, there had been numerous messages on my machine from both him and Tate. I could understand their concern—my last call had been hours ago to say I was chasing after a vampire. Then there'd been no trace of me.

I fabricated a story about an hours-long chase that had ended at the construction site, coincidentally not that far from the GiGi Club. Here's hoping Bones had left the vamp's body there, because if not, I'd have to come up with an alternate web of lies. Then I told Don that I was beat from chasing down the vamp and wouldn't be in to work until tomorrow. He didn't question my recounting of the events. Why would he? I'd never lied to him before.

On the plus side, Don informed me that the two victims were at a hospital and were expected to make a full recovery. Little did he know it had taken a vampire's intervention to save them from a vampire's attack. Far be it from me to explain that irony to my boss.

Then I took a hot shower, washing all the remaining blood off me. If only it were so easy to get the mistakes from my life cleaned off. Bones's voice kept echoing in my head. *I've been looking for you every day since you left me . . . You'll live as long as you want to, just as you are . . . You've had your shot at things, now let me have mine . . .*

Yesterday, everything had made sense to me. I knew what I had to do, didn't question my decisions—though some had hurt me unbearably—and I knew the direction my life was headed in. Today, all that had changed. I had far more questions than convictions, didn't know what the hell I was doing, and had found out I might have far longer to fuck up my life than I'd previously imagined.

I wished I could talk to Denise. She had a way of cutting through the bullshit to find wisdom in chaos. But last night had been her wedding. Yeah, to say she was unavailable was to put it mildly.

I'd only call my mother if I wanted last-minute motivation to jump off a bridge. She was full of blind prejudice, not wisdom, and a call to her might make me seriously tempted to end it all. Though I had to admit, I was rather shocked that Don's first words to me earlier hadn't been "So where's the vampire from the wedding?" My mother hadn't tattled about Bones . . . yet. For her, that was showing remarkable restraint.

There was no one from my team I could discuss my personal upheaval with. Even those I counted as friends, Tate, Juan, and Cooper, couldn't be trusted with this.

Noah, well . . . I had to talk to him, all right, but it

wouldn't be to confide my deepest secrets. It would be to tell him it was over between us. I'd let things go on too long, and that wasn't right. Already I was a shit; letting more time drag by just made me a bigger one.

I paced around the house for another hour, tired but knowing I'd never sleep. My cat got bored of chasing my ankles as I attempted to wear holes in the carpet, and went upstairs. Still I paced, Bones's words haunting me. *I've been looking for you every day since you left me . . . You'll live as long as you want to, just as you are . . . You've had your shot at things, now let me have mine . . .*

"Who am I kidding?" I finally asked out loud in frustration. I was less concerned about Ian's intentions to track me down, the contract on my life, or anything else, than about this: Did Bones and I actually have a chance together? With finding out about my longevity, the single biggest obstacle to our relationship had been removed. Sure, I worked for the government version of Graveslayers Inc. and my mother would rather poke needles in her eyes than see me date a vampire . . . but what if Bones was right? What if the two of us *weren't* hopeless together? God, after all these years, I could hardly believe I had a chance to ponder that again.

Now the question was, *What was I willing to risk to find out?*

Sixteen

Don regarded me with tempered curiosity when I walked into his office later that day. It changed to suspicion when I shut the door and locked it behind me. Normally I had to be reminded to even close it.

"What's going on, Cat? You said it was urgent."

Yeah, I had. I'd thought about Bones saying Don knew the secret of my longevity, and it had gotten me good and mad. Time to rock the boat.

"See, Don, I have this question, and I hope you'll be honest with me."

He pulled at the end of his eyebrow. "I think you know you can count on my honesty."

"Can I?" I asked with an edge. "All right, then tell me: How long have you been fucking me?"

That caused him to stop tugging his brow. "I don't know what you're saying—"

"Because if I was going to fuck *you*," I interrupted,

"I'd get a bottle of gin, some Frank Sinatra music . . . and a crash cart for the heart attack you'd have. But you, Don, you've been fucking me for years now, and I haven't gotten any liquor, music, flowers, candy, or anything!"

"Cat . . ." He sounded wary. "If you have a point, then get to it. This analogy is wearing thin."

"How old am I?"

"You just had a birthday; you know how old you are. You're twenty-seven—"

His desk crashed to the far side of the room, splintering in shards of mahogany. Papers flew, and his computer thumped to the carpet. It happened in less time than his shocked blink.

"*How old am I?*"

Don glanced at his demolished furniture before straightening and regarding me across the now-empty space between us.

"Nineteen or twenty, if you judge from your bone density and pathology reports. Your teeth match up to that as well."

The end of puberty, when my body apparently decided it was done aging. I gave a harsh chuckle.

"Guess I won't need to stock up on any Oil of Olay, will I? You ruthless motherfucker, were you ever going to tell me? Or were you just waiting to see if I lived long enough to notice?"

The pretense was gone from him, and if I didn't know better, I'd say he looked relieved.

"Eventually I was going to inform you, of course. When the time was right."

"Yeah, and you knew you had lots of it, didn't you?

Who else knows?" I paced, keeping an eye on him as he sat calmly amid the ruins of his office.

"Tate, and the head pathologist here, Dr. Lang. His assistant, Brad Parker, probably."

"Did you tell Tate about the added decades to his own life? Or were you waiting for an 'opportune time' for that as well?"

Don changed from composed to uncomfortable in the space of those sentences. When he hesitated, I pounced.

"Don't even try to say you don't know what I'm talking about! You tested all of us that night in Ohio, and every fucking week after that as always. You didn't tell them?"

"I wasn't sure," he hedged.

"Well, let me assure you then! They had about a pint each of decently aged vampire blood. That'll give them, what? Another twenty years at least? You know, I always thought you forbade us from drinking straight blood because you worried we'd grow a taste for it, me especially, but you were concerned with more than that, weren't you? You already knew what it would do! How did you find that out?"

His tone was cold. "Someone I knew many years ago started out fighting on the right side like I did, then ended up liking the enemy more. He didn't age in decades. That's when I knew what vampire blood could do, and it's why the Brams is so minutely screened and filtered. It carries none of that dangerous poison in it."

"That poison you're referring to runs in half my DNA," I snapped. "Is that why you don't give a shit every time I go on an assignment that could get me killed? Because it's just one less snake to worry about?"

"At first it was," he brusquely rejoined, standing now also. He spread his arms in an encompassing gesture. "Look at you. You're like a time bomb covered in skin. All that power, all that inhuman ability . . . I used to believe you'd get bored with your limitations and shirk them off. Cross over completely. That's why I told Tate when you signed on to be prepared to kill you. But you never faltered, and you didn't succumb to the urge for more power. Frankly . . . it was inspirational."

Don smiled in a self-deprecating way. "Five years ago, I was quite disillusioned about the human character when exposed to supernatural influence. When I discovered you, I thought you'd crumble all the faster for what was in your blood. Yes, I sent you out on the riskiest missions first, in order to maximize your usefulness until you turned and had to be put down. That didn't happen, however. You, who carry in your genetic makeup the same corruption which has stumbled so many before you, proved to be the finest of us all. In short, and not to overdramatize, you made me hope again."

I stared at him. He didn't drop his eyes from my hard gaze. Finally I shrugged.

"I believe in what I'm doing, whether you believe in me or not. I'm taking a week off to contemplate this and figure out my next step. When I come back, we're having another talk, and this one will include Tate, Juan, and Cooper. You're going to tell them about the consequences of the blood they drank. And you're wrong about something, Don. It's not vampire blood that corrupts—it's whether the person who drinks it is corrupted to begin with. Hey, don't take my word for it, look at the guys. They felt that same power, felt how different it could make them . . . and yet they didn't turn evil. It doesn't twist who you are, it only increases it, for better or worse. Remember that, but I have a feeling I'll have to remind you."

"Cat."

Don stopped me as I kicked back the rubble to open the door.

"You *are* coming back, aren't you?"

I paused with a hand on the frame. "Oh, I'll be back. Whether you like it or not."

It didn't surprise me to feel the change of energy in my house later that night. I was in the kitchen, heating up a frozen dinner in the microwave, when suddenly I knew I wasn't alone.

"It's polite to knock," I said without turning around. "My front door's not broken, you know."

That feeling of power intensified as Bones walked in the kitchen.

"Yes, but this is more dramatic, don't you agree?"

My dinner beeped. I took it out of the microwave, grabbed a fork, and sat down at the dinette table. Bones took the seat opposite me, watching me with tempered wariness.

"I'm not bothering to offer you any," I said flippantly. "My neck and I both know you already ate."

A hint of a frown touched his mouth. "I told you that wasn't about feeding."

"No, it was about you making your point." I skewered a bite and chewed. "Next time, maybe use something *other* than my jugular as your Exhibit A?"

"It wasn't your jugular. That would have made you pass out too quickly, and I wanted you to have time to make your decision to kill me or not," Bones replied, holding my stare. "So I bit around your jugular. That's why it took longer . . . and why I could enjoy drawing your blood into me instead of just swallowing a gushing arterial flow."

That made me hesitate on my own swallow. Bones's eyes were swirling with green from the memory, like mint in chocolate, and if I were honest, I'd admit to an internal ripple of pleasure as well at the recollection. His bite could have passed for foreplay, it had felt that good.

But there were more important things to get down to, even though my libido certainly didn't agree.

"So," I said after I'd finished chewing. "You're hell-bent on not going away until this danger with Ian has passed *and* you've neutralized whoever's waving a check around for my corpse, right?"

Bones nodded. "That's right."

"And you probably followed me earlier when I went into work, just waiting to see if I'd try to fly the coop?"

A shrug. "Let's just say no plane would have made it off the ground there today."

My gaze hardened. "Then I suppose you followed me to Noah's afterward, and eavesdropped on that as well?"

Bones leaned forward with complete coldness on his face. "I normally would never harm someone innocent, but I admit to a certain lack of rationality when it comes to you. You saved that man's life by breaking up with him today, because if I'd have listened to anything else going on at his house, I would have snapped him in half."

"You would have tried," I ground out. "Noah doesn't believe in vampires, ghouls, or anything more supernatural than Santa Claus. You'd better not hurt him."

"Kitten, if I intended to kill Noah, I'd have done it before you even knew I was in town. But you could hardly expect me to twiddle my thumbs and listen to you shag him. Remember your response last night when I kissed Felicity?"

Yes, there had been that whole urge to rip her limb from limb. Vampire territorialism. It really didn't care who was innocent or not.

"Fine," I acknowledged. "We both still have feelings for each other. You think it can work despite my job and my mother's virulent hatred of vampires. Since you're refusing to leave anyway because of Ian and the contract out on me . . ."

He started to smile. "Are you waving the white flag?"

"Not so fast. I'm saying we can take things slow. See if it blows up in our faces. I'm *not* saying declare eternal love for each other while I fall back with my legs open."

His smile deepened. "There are alternate positions."

Those words—and the look in his eyes—rubbed me like a physical caress. I drew in a deep breath. That's why I'd decided on a celibacy mandate. No way could I keep a leash on my emotions if I threw sex into the mix. I'd be screaming out my undying love for Bones in five seconds flat.

"Take it or leave it."

"Done."

I blinked, part of me not believing what was happening. Was this real? Or just another crazy dream, one of thousands I'd had about Bones?

"Okay."

I didn't know what to say. Or do. Shake hands? Seal it with a kiss? Shout "Celibacy sucks!" and rip his clothes off? There should be an undead dating manual—I was lost here.

Bones cocked his head to the side, and then he let out a resigned noise.

"Kitten . . . your resolve is about to be put to the test sooner than you expected."

Huh? "What are you talking about?"

He stood up. "Your mum's here."

Seventeen

I LEAPT TO MY FEET. "OH *SHIT*!"

Panic made me try to walk without fully pulling my chair out, and I promptly tripped. So much for half-dead reflexes. Then I caught Bones out of the corner of my eye. "Er, what are you doing?"

He had calmly gone into the next room to sit on the couch.

"Staying right here. You just agreed to give us a chance, and I refuse to be shoved into a closet this time. You're going to have to come out of the coffin with your mum about me. I should have forced this issue before. Instead, she found out about our relationship only after vampires murdered her parents in front of her. Little wonder she took it poorly."

"Took it *poorly*?" The memory of my grandparents' death scalded my tone. "She tried to have you killed!"

A knock boomed on the door. My mother had never been delicate.

Bones arched a brow. "Will you get it, or shall I?"

This had disaster written all over it. But from the set of his jaw, I wasn't going to talk him into hiding. And he really was too strong for me to shove in a closet again.

"Just a second, Mom!" I hollered. Then I rummaged around for a bottle of gin. Boy, was I going to need it.

"She'll go straight to Don," I muttered.

"Let her," Bones countered. "I'm staying."

I gave him one last ill-tempered look before I went to the door. So much for slowly wading into this relationship—looked like I was about to swan dive right into the deep end. Guess there was no time like the present to see if Bones was right about overcoming our obstacles. This particular obstacle was more formidable than Don ever could be.

My mother swept into my house as soon as I opened the door. She was already bitching.

"—called Noah's cell earlier looking for you, and he told me you broke up with him! Don't think I don't know why, Catherine, and I'm here to tell you that it will stop. This *instant*. You threw away that piece of murdering trash years ago, and you will do it again! I will *not* sit back and watch you turn into the same kind of hell demon that spawned you . . ."

Her voice trailed off into a hiss when she spied Bones on the couch, watching her with what could only be called amusement.

"Hallo, Justina," he drawled. "Lovely to see you again. Won't you have a seat?"

For effect, he patted the empty space next to him.

She went from white to crimson in one glance flat.

I closed the door and took a swig of my drink. Let the hysterics begin.

She turned to me in a fit of wrath. "For *God's sake*, Catherine! What is *wrong* with you? Did he put you under a spell again?"

That drew outright laughter from Bones. He uncoiled himself from the sofa with effortless grace, walking to her as she stepped back several paces.

"If anyone's under a spell, Justina, it's me. Your daughter put one on me five years ago, and I haven't broken free of it yet. Oh, and you'll be delighted to know, we've decided to resume our relationship. Don't bother with congratulations—trust me, your expression is congratulations enough."

I took a longer drink from the bottle. Bones had obviously decided against killing my mother with kindness and was going right for the throat instead. Typical vampire.

My mother's tone was acid. "I thought you'd gotten over your whoring when you left him, Catherine, but it seems you only postponed it."

Bones's face turned to stone, and he answered her even before I could snap out an indignant response.

"Don't you ever speak to her that way again." There was pure warning in the whip of his words. "You can call me any name you like and more, but I will *not* stand by while you slander her out of your own ignorance."

She backed up another step, and something in her expression changed. As though she finally realized she'd have to contend directly with him and not just through me.

"Are you going to just stand there and let him threaten me?" she demanded to me next, switching tactics. "I suppose you'd just sit back and let him suck the life out of me, too?"

"Oh stuff it, Mom," I barked. "He wouldn't hurt you, which is a damn sight more than you'd do to *him* given the chance. Excuse me if I don't defend you when you're pissed that he doesn't want you calling me nasty names. Must be that flaw in my character."

She shook a finger at me. "Blood will out, my father always said, and he was right! Look at you! You have debased yourself, leaving a good man for a filthy animal, and a thing not even an animal! *Lower!*"

"I'm standing right here, Justina, and you'd better get used to it. You want to call me an animal? Turn your eyes this way then."

Bones moved in front of me until she either had to look at him or look away. My mother fixed her attention to him for the first time, looking straight in his eyes. To her credit, she didn't back down under his stern gaze. She was many things, but a coward wasn't one of them.

"You. What's your name again?"

Her taunting allusion to his lack of importance made me hide a smile behind his back. She knew damn well what his name was.

"It's Bones. Can't say it's a pleasure to be properly introduced, but it's about time, don't you agree?"

I could see her to the side of his shoulder. She let her belittling gaze take him in from top to bottom, and finally she gave a dismissive shrug.

"I don't agree, in fact. Well. Aren't you pretty." It

wasn't a compliment from the way it fell from her lips. "Her father was pretty also, just gorgeous. Of course you should know—she looks just like him. Sometimes I could barely stand to look at her for their resemblance."

A jab of pain sliced in me, because I'd felt that all my life. She might love me, but she didn't accept me. Maybe she never would.

"She might look like him; I can't say," Bones replied steadily. "Never met the bloke. But let me assure you, she has a great deal of you in her. Stubbornness, for one thing. Courage. A nasty temper when she's upset. She can also hold a grudge quite well, but you've got her beat there. Over twenty-seven years later, you're *still* punishing her for what happened to you."

That made her advance until she pointed a finger an inch from his chest. "How dare you! You have the nerve to throw up to me what one of your kind did, what you have no doubt done yourself, to my very face, you dirty, murdering *fiend*!"

Bones stepped right up also. They were toe to toe.

"If I were merely a murdering fiend, then I would have punched your ticket years ago. Would have made *my* life a measure easier, I assure you. You had her in shambles when those wolves came with their greedy little offer, and we all know why she took it, don't we? It doesn't bother you a bit that she's been as miserable as I've been these past years, or that she's had more near-death experiences than bloody Houdini. No, you sit back on your satisfaction that she's out killing vampires instead of shagging one! Well, Justina, I hope you enjoyed your interlude, because it's over. I'm back and I'm staying."

She gave me a fraught look over his shoulder. "Catherine! You can't mean to stay with this creature! He'll take your soul, he'll change you—"

"My soul is mine and God's, Mom. Bones couldn't take it if he tried." I moved out to face her and took in a deep breath. *Stand your ground. Now or never.* "But I'm not going to let you or anyone else decide what I do with my personal life anymore. You don't have to like Bones. Hell, you can hate his guts for all I care, but as long as I'm with him, you *will* have to tolerate him. So will Don and the others, or . . . or I'll leave and never come back."

She just blankly regarded me, passing her gaze over each of us in turn. Then a gleam appeared in her eye. I laughed bitterly.

"Just try it, Mom. Try to call my work and have him killed. You saw what he did to them years ago on the highway, and that's when he wasn't even mad! Furthermore, if anyone comes for him, I'll kill them myself. No matter who it is." I let her see from my gaze that I meant it. I might do anything I could to avoid that—but ultimately, I meant it. "Then afterward, Bones and I will disappear. Permanently. You really want that? After all, if I stay here with you and them, I have much less of a chance to want to change into a vampire. Take me away from all of my human support and . . . well, you never know."

I was shamelessly playing on her greatest fear, but she'd earned that. Bones's lips twitched.

"Look at the bright side," he urged my mother with devilish intent. "If you let us be, she could grow tired of me in time. But forcing us to run gives me few other alternatives . . ." He dangled the sentence.

"Like I'd believe anything you'd say," she shot back. "It would be better for everyone if you'd just stake yourself and die for good. If you really loved her, you'd do that."

Bones gave her a jaded look and then let it rip. "You know what your problem is, Justina? You're in desperate need of a good shag."

I downed a gulp of gin to cover the laugh that forced its way out. God, if I'd thought that once, I'd thought it a thousand times!

She let out an outraged huff. Bones ignored it.

"Not that I'm offering you one myself, mind. My days as a whore ended back in the seventeen hundreds."

The gin was abruptly sucked back into my lungs as I gasped. He did *not* just tell my mother about his former profession; sweet Jesus, let me have heard incorrectly!

I hadn't, and Bones went right on. " . . . but I have a friend who owes me a favor and he could be persuaded to . . . Kitten, are you all right?"

I'd stopped breathing as soon as he casually admitted to his prior occupation. Add that to the liquid stuck in my lungs, and no, I wasn't all right.

My mother was oblivious. A torrent of insults erupted from her throat.

"Filthy, degenerate, molesting *sodomite*—"

"Isn't this a proper flashback to her childhood? You're more concerned with yourself than your daughter, bloody woman; can't you see she's choking?"

Bones pounded me on my back as I coughed to expel the gin from my windpipe. The first breath seared me when it came. My eyes watered profusely, but at least I was able to take in another painful one, and then another.

Reassured that I was breathing again, Bones picked up where my mother left off.

"Sodomite's incorrect, Justina. Women were my clients, not men. Just wanted to clear that up; I'd hate to have you think something false of me. 'Course, if you don't trust my recommendation for a shag, I reckon your daughter's friend Juan might be up for the arduous task of—"

"That's *it*!" she shrieked, snatching the front door open.

"Come back soon," he called after her as she slammed it behind her hard enough to shake the windows.

"She'll go straight to Don," I got out, voice hoarse from my accidental attempt to breathe gin.

Bones only grinned. "No she won't. She's riled, but she's crafty. It threw her a good one to see you stand up to her. She'll stew for a while, and then wait for an opportunity. Despite whatever she's told you, she'll never risk you leaving her. She has no one else, and she knows it."

I wasn't convinced. "You should still watch your back. They could send a team after you."

Bones laughed. "To what end? It would take a small army to corner me, and I'd hear that coming. Don't fret, luv. I'm not so easy to kill. Now, do you want to wear that? Or do you want to put something else on?"

"For what?" I asked suspiciously.

"I'm taking you out to dinner," he replied. "That *is* a traditional dating activity, isn't it? Besides, your previous entrée is cold, and it looked none too appetizing when it was hot."

"But what if—" I began, then stopped.

From his expression, Bones knew I'd been about to say, *But what if we're seen together?* If I really meant what I said about giving this relationship a shot, then I'd have to reconcile Bones and my job. More specifically, I'd have to reconcile Don with Bones. Or quit—and hope like hell I wasn't the team's next elimination assignment.

Now or never. "I'll go change; wait for me."

Bones gave me an ironic smile. "I'm rather used to that."

EIGHTEEN

DESPITE MY FEARS, THREE DAYS PASSED WITH-
out a hint of my mother or my work. I was
amazed that Bones seemed to be right and my mother
hadn't run to Don screaming, "Nosferatu, arrgh!" or
some variance. Did she really fear losing me as much
as Bones said? After my whole life of feeling like my
mother would be happier without me, it was very unusual to think she'd sacrifice some of her raging prejudice to have a relationship.

Or she was just biding her time. That was the more
likely scenario.

Bones took me out every night. We went to dinner,
movies, bars, or simply walked around Richmond. If
I was honest, I'd admit I had never been happier in
my life. Every time I opened the door and saw him
standing there, my heart did a crazy little pitter-patter.
He had to hear it, of course, but he never commented.

Bones was staying within the "take it slow" mandate I'd set, waiting for me to make the first move.

Which was getting harder and harder not to do. Sure, I'd said to take it slow, but the more time I spent around Bones, the less I remembered why I'd thought taking it slow was a good idea. Every time he held my hand, every time our bodies brushed, damn, every night he left me on my porch and walked away without so much as a good-night kiss, I ached with longing. I couldn't bear to take it slow much longer. I'd end up assaulting him.

On the fourth night, Bones said he wanted to cook me dinner instead of going out. I agreed, wondering if this was his way of setting up a more romantic evening—and not objecting. If my body had its way, dessert wouldn't be a food item.

Since I didn't have anything in my house other than microwave-ready meals, he went to the store first. I came out on the porch to let him in, smiling at his multiple bags of groceries, and then was puzzled to see his expression harden.

"We're being watched."

Bones didn't turn around as he said it. Years of practice made me resist the urge to look about myself. I took some bags from him and asked a soft question.

"Ian?"

"No. It's your bloke, the same one in Ohio. He's down the street in his car, and from the way his pulse just shot up, you've been found out. He can tell what I am."

"Tate?" He was the only person Bones had seen back in Ohio when Don used his "join me or die" recruiting tactic. "Do you think my mother called him?"

Bones used his body to propel me inside.

"From his heart rate, he's shocked. No, he had no idea. Probably thought to offer you some company in hopes you'd break down and shag him. Wanker."

I began to pace. Bones put away the groceries as if undisturbed. Practicality was definitely his strong suit. *That's what I get for training the guys to notice those slight nuances in appearance and movement that separates a vampire from the rest of the population*, I thought. Apparently I'd done my job too well, since Tate had picked up on what Bones was from down the block. I listened hard, sending my senses outward. In a second I, too, heard Tate's accelerated breathing and heart rate. Yeah, he was shaken, you could safely say.

In the next instant, his car revved up. He was driving away in the opposite direction of his home, and it was no great stretch to guess where he was headed.

"I wanted more time," I said with mild despair.

Bones just mixed a gin and tonic and gave it to me. It was gone before the ice chilled it.

"Better, luv?" His lips curled. "Like your bloomin' security blanket, that stuff is."

"I like the taste. That's what all the drunks say, isn't it?" In sudden weariness I sighed.

"Do you want me to leave, or wait to see what they'll do? I told you, if they come with force, we'll hear them long before they arrive. It's your call."

After a minute of quiet contemplation, I looked up at him. "Well, they were going to find out soon anyway, I suppose. It'll take Tate half an hour to get to the compound, another thirty minutes at least for Don to decide on their course of action, and then another thirty to send a team back here, if that's what they decide. Tate doesn't know we saw him, so he won't think there's a rush. You may as well stay. If I could tell my mother, Don should be a cakewalk."

I attempted humor to cover the lurch of my stomach, but Bones knew I felt far less confident than I sounded.

"It will be all right, Kitten. You'll see."

Exactly one hour later, my cell phone rang. I nearly broke it in my haste to answer it.

"Hello?" To my credit, there was not a trace of apprehension in my tone. On the other end of the line, Don sounded less urbane.

"Cat? Is that you?"

"It's my cell, who else would it be?"

There was a moment of silence, and then he guardedly asked, "Is everything okay there?"

Oh, so he thought perhaps I'd lured a vamp back to my house for some lethal stake and shake. Well, score one for him giving me the benefit of the doubt. Tate hadn't.

"Fine. Why? What's going on?"

There was another hush, and then Don said, "There's an emergency. How soon can you get here?"

I glanced at Bones. He shrugged. "Give me an hour."

"An hour. I'll be waiting." *Oh, I didn't doubt it.*

After I hung up, I burst out, "I'm not giving you up!"

As soon as the words were out of my mouth, I realized I meant them. The past few days had reminded me exactly how miserable I'd been without Bones. Return to my empty life just so everyone around me could feel more comfortable? No thank you.

Bones laughed grimly. "Too bloody right. I'm not going away just because they might not give us their blessing."

"I'm not just going to quit, though." Subconsciously I'd already made that decision, too, but I hadn't voiced it until now. "This is more than a job to me. I'm able to make a difference in people's lives who don't have anywhere else to turn, Bones. I know I need to deal with Don and the guys, but I'm not leaving unless they force me to."

"Bloody hell." Bones sighed. "If you want to continue your crusade to rid the world of undead murderers, you can do that with me. You don't need them."

"But they need me. If they leave me no other choice, I'll go, but I will fight to make them reconsider."

He stared at me with a mixture of frustration and resignation. Finally he threw up his hands.

"All right. I'll have to think on what to do about that, and Ian as well, though we have a little time with him. Perhaps a month, if luck holds. Don't tell your boss who I really am yet, if your bloke hasn't figured it out. There are some details I need to settle first before they realize you didn't kill me in Ohio after all."

"What details? With Ian?"

"Not Ian. Don. Interesting bloke. Been doing a bit of research on him the last several months. I'm waiting to confirm some information, and I'll tell you when I have it."

Don? "What information?"

"I'll tell you when I have it," he repeated. Then he changed the subject. "You know I'll follow you over there, but how secure is this building of yours? If they tried to force you to leave, where would they take you? The airstrip?"

"Yes, they'd try to fly me out, if they were going to get rough. Planes don't normally take off there, so if you see one taxiing, chances are I'm on it."

"You don't have to go in, but I can see you have your mind set to it. Think for a bit, though. If they can't persuade you to relinquish me and they reckon you'll try to escape if they hold you, what's to stop them from simply killing you? I can guarantee that no plane will take off with you on it, but I don't fancy you walking into what could be a trap. How certain are you of these men?"

I did think about it, coldly and impersonally. Then I shook my head.

"Unless they've exhausted all other options, they won't pull that trigger. They'd try to salvage me first. If I started killing people, then they'd try to take me out, but otherwise . . . no. That's not Don's style."

I met his eyes, because I wanted him to see mine when I spoke this next part.

"When I left you, I thought it was the only way to save you and my mother. Really I did. But over the years, I've gotten to know Don. He can be a callous son of a bitch, but he's not the cold-blooded creature I first thought him to be. Don wouldn't leave my mother defenseless if I took off with you, no matter that he threatened to do that when we first met. Yes, he'd kill me if I thought I would destroy his operation, but he'd only do it as a last resort. I'm not afraid of going in, but as I said, I'm not going to give you up just because Don won't like that you're a vampire and I'm dating you."

Bones came over to me. Very gently, he caressed my face. Then his hand slid into my hair and he leaned down. When his lips closed over mine, I let out a soft moan.

The instant jolt going through me could have been from his power, since my lips tingled on contact with his. But I thought it had to do with something else, especially when I felt a stronger surge as his tongue rubbed along mine. I pulled him closer, until our bodies were pressed together as tightly as our mouths. All at once, the need I'd suppressed for years came roaring to the surface. My hands tightened on his shoulders, and then raced around with a sudden frantic urge to feel more of him.

Bones's arms moved to my back to crush me almost bruisingly against him. His mouth ravaged mine with a hunger that made my pulse skyrocket and a ravenous throb erupt below. He must have heard it, smelled it, because he rubbed his groin into mine with a hard, friction-filled stroke that almost had me climaxing where I stood.

I tore away from him. Either I did it right then, or I was never going to. Bones held on to my arms while the bright green blaze of his eyes seared into mine. His hands were flexing on my skin, like he was fighting whether to yank me back or let me go.

"If I kiss you again, I'm not going to stop," he said roughly.

The warning was an echo of my own thoughts. I breathed in short little pants that seemed to mock me with their excited rhythm. *Stay*, they said. *It'll take Don at least an hour to show up with reinforcements . . .*

"We can't, not now," I groaned. "Or it'll be pretty easy for the guys to kill you, since I'll already have you pinned underneath me."

Bones laughed, but it sounded more like a low growl. "I'm happy to risk it."

I backed away, literally uncurling his fingers from my arms.

"Not now," I said again, even though what I really wanted to do was scream, *Yes, now, and hurry!* "I have to take care of this. It's overdue, don't you think?"

He cast a frustrated look at the bulge in his pants.

"*Very* overdue."

I laughed. "Not that; you know what I meant."

Bones ran a hand through his hair, giving me a look that said he still was debating whether to throw me to the carpet. I had to glance away, afraid that what he'd see in my eyes would only encourage him.

"Right," he said at last. "Your work. Let's go over possibilities if they take the news badly. I want you to be prepared to escape if need be."

"Oh, don't worry about that," I replied, with an inward jaded smile. "I've had an escape route planned for years."

Nineteen

THE GUARD AT THE ENTRANCE DIDN'T WAVE
me through as usual.

"Sorry, but . . . um, we have to check your vehicle."

I hid a smile behind my hand. So Don was feeling edgy. "What's up, Manny? New rules?"

"Yep, that's it," he agreed instantly.

Three more armed men came around my Volvo. They explored my interior, the undercarriage, and even the engine. Finally Manny straightened and nodded.

"Carry on."

I was stopped at the second gate and the third one as well, the same procedure repeated. It took me over twenty minutes just to pull inside the four-mile stretch that wound around the main building. Not since my first year with Don had I been so thoroughly screened. Little did he know Bones had no need of piggybacking with me. He'd driven himself over on his snazzy new motorcycle, waiting out of sight near the airstrip. Just in case.

Once inside, the interior guards were less diligent. I passed through the normal checkpoints with ease. Apparently they were only concerned with me bringing an unwanted visitor. When I entered Don's office, I saw that Juan and Tate were there as well. Oh goody, it was an intervention.

"Hello guys," I addressed them.

Juan nodded, but Tate didn't even acknowledge me. Don rose from his desk.

"Cat. You're twenty minutes late."

"I was tied up." I couldn't resist. "Then the guards almost strip-searched me on my way in the compound."

"Shut the door, Juan," Don directed coolly. With a gesture, he indicated my usual seat.

I took it, and promptly put my foot on his new desk.

"Nice color," I commented. "Looks better than the old one. What's the emergency?" *As if I didn't know*.

"You are," Tate snapped.

Don waved him silent and gave him a look. So he was playing Papa Bear, and Tate and Juan were backup support.

"Cat, just the other day, I told you how amazing it was you'd never faltered in your tenure here. It seems I spoke too soon. We know about the vampire. What do you have to say for yourself?"

I gave him a frosty smile. Bones had said not to reveal who he really was, and that was fine by me for now. God knew they were rattled enough already.

"Spying on me? I thought you gave that up a long time ago. You nosy bastard, what business is it of yours who I date as long as I do my job?"

That answer he wasn't expecting. Don obviously

thought I'd shrink under his withering stare. But if my mother couldn't cower me, then he had no chance.

"You're dating a vampire! You just admitted it!" Tate burst out.

I shrugged. "You know the old saying. Once you go dead, no one's better in bed."

"*Christos*," Juan muttered.

"I hadn't heard that one," Don stonily replied. "You fail to see the enormity of what you're admitting to? You are fraternizing with the enemy in the most compromising way possible, jeopardizing the lives of all you command. This creature is no doubt using you to infiltrate our operation."

That made me snort rudely. "He couldn't give a rat's ass about your operation, Don. Believe it or not, he cares more about me than what goes on here."

"I fail to see how that's possible," Don barked, his composure slipping. "Look at the influence he already has over you, making you risk your life for sex. And I seem to remember that personal association with vampires was expressly forbidden in our agreement when you signed on."

I wasn't about to correct Don's misassumption of my relationship, and besides, I'd already decided on changing our celibate status. Plus, clearly Tate hadn't recognized Bones from before, or this whole thing would be going down far differently. Well, who could blame him? He'd only seen him for a split second—right before Bones demolished his car, drank him, and chucked him through the air. That, and his hair was different.

"Yes, well, a lot of things have changed since then, haven't they?" I observed mildly. "Take for example the invention of Brams. Or the caged vampires on the premises. Oh, and don't forget, the added years to their lives."

I jerked my head in Juan and Tate's direction. Don's expression confirmed that he hadn't told them. There was nothing like clouding the issue to redirect the heat.

"That's not relevant now," Don grated.

I raised a mocking brow. "Let's ask them, shall we? Tate, Juan, did you both know if you drank vampire blood, it would add at least twenty years to your natural lives? *I* didn't know that, but old Don here sure did. He knew what went on in Ohio, but didn't figure on telling you. Guess he thought you wouldn't be interested."

"*Madre de Dios*, is that true?" Juan blurted. Tate looked a bit dazed as well, and I pounced on him.

"It's not nice when someone knows how long you might live and keeps it to themselves, is it? At least *I* told Don you had to be informed, whereas *you* didn't give me the same courtesy!"

"Is this some sort of payback?" he asked low.

The pain in his eyes had little to do with this latest revelation and everything to do with my previous admission. Right then I saw what I'd been blind to before. God, Tate was in love with me. It was so clear, even I couldn't fail to notice.

"No, it has nothing to do with that." No need to lie there. "It has nothing to do with *any* of you, and that's the way it stays."

"There is no way I will allow this behavior to continue," Don stated flatly. "Too many lives are at risk, and I care about that even if you don't."

I stood and loomed over him. "Fuck you, *boss*. I

care about each and every man in my unit, and I've proved that countless times. You don't believe me? Then fire me."

"*Querida*, don't be so hasty," Juan implored. Don hadn't moved. "We're concerned for you; what if this vamp finds out what you are—"

"He knows," I interrupted.

Don cursed freely. That made me blink. He never lost his cool.

"How does he know that, Cat? You told him? Did you draw him a fucking map of our location and numbers as well? I hope he's amazing in bed, because you've just ruined everything we've worked for!"

"No, I didn't tell him." As I spoke, I improvised. "I met him years ago. He knew what I was from back then, and he left Ohio before all that shit went down. I hadn't seen him until a month ago when I ran into him around here. He's only a hundred and I'm stronger than he is, so he knows to keep his trap shut or I'll kill him. There you have it."

"How could you do it?" This from Tate, who gave me a faintly disgusted glare. "How could you fuck a corpse? You really went from one extreme to the other. First Noah, then right to necrophilia!"

That pissed me off. "Does everybody forget I'm half vampire? When you say shit about the undead, you're also talking about me! It's like skinheads trying to convince Halle Berry to march in their neo-nazi parade! How could I do it? Why don't you tell me, Tate? Or you, Juan? Both of you have tried to fuck me. Guess that makes you necrophiliacs as well."

It was a low blow, but one that was deliberate. They

had to stop seeing all vampires as evil, and God knew that was a tough habit to break. After all, it had taken me years to be less narrow-minded, and I'd been in love with one.

Don coughed, not liking the direction of the conversation. "No one forgets what you are. However, it doesn't change what your mission is. You kill the undead. All of you do. This is a momentous task with great responsibility. What's to stop your lover from doing his kind a favor by informing them where the elusive Red Reaper lives? After all, if you're dead, then you can hardly threaten him."

"Juan, how many different women have you slept with in the past four years?" I abruptly asked.

He scratched his chin. "*Yo no se*, *querida*, perhaps . . . about one a week?" he answered before Don gave him a censuring glare.

"That's not necessary!"

"I think it is," I said sharply. "One a week, give or take. That's over two hundred different women in the past four years he's worked here, and on a side note: Juan, you're a *slut*. But how many of them were carefully screened to ensure they weren't a Renfield, or some ghoul's underling? You sexist bastards, I'm the only one called on the carpet for who I date! Well, I've had enough of this little chastity session. Don, it comes down to this. You either trust me or you don't. I've never let you down, and I won't walk away unless you make me. Period. Now, unless you have a *real* emergency, I'd like to get back to my vacation. And my corpse, thanks."

I marched to the door, but Tate didn't move from in front of it.

"Get out of my way," I said with an undertone of menace.

"Cat." Don got up and lightly took my elbow. "If we have nothing to fear from your association with this vampire, then you won't mind stopping by the lab for a blood sample. You haven't been indiscriminately drinking blood, have you?"

I snorted. "Not my beverage of choice, sorry. But if it'll make you feel better to check my lab work, fine. Lead the way."

"I'll be frank with you," Don said as we walked to the second level, Tate and Juan following. "I don't know what I'm going to do about this. I have the team to consider. I'm not comfortable risking their lives on only your word that this creature isn't dangerous."

"That's where the trust part comes in. Besides, if he wanted to hurt the team, he could have done that last weekend at the GiGi Club. Don't fuck up a good thing because of blind prejudice, Don. We both know you need me."

He regarded me as I stepped into the lab. "I want to believe you can't be turned against us. But I don't know if I can."

Later, after a spot processing proved I wasn't hyped full of nosferatu juice, Tate walked me to my car. He hadn't said a word since Don's office, and I didn't speak, either. They were letting me go, but I knew nothing had really been settled. That was okay—I had nothing to hide now. Well, almost nothing.

Tate opened my door out of polite habit. I slid inside but didn't shut it. His fingers tapped on my roof.

"I bet you thought that was poetic justice, me not knowing about how much longer I could live. I told Don to tell you about your aging three years ago, when they were sure. He disagreed, and he's the boss. Sometimes you just have to follow orders, even if you don't want to."

"Sometimes." I stared at him without blinking. "Not always. Not when it affects your friends, but we have different opinions about that."

"Yeah, well, we have different opinions about a lot of things." Dark blue eyes met mine. "You really handed me my ass in there. First you casually admit to having a vampire boyfriend, then you tell everyone I tried to fuck you. What's next? You going to whip out a dick and say you're really a man?"

His sour tone didn't lend to humor, but I smiled slightly. "Back me into a corner and I come out clawing. You know that. I wish all of you would just have a little faith. I care about my team and the job I do. If I didn't, why would I put up with this shit?"

His mouth twisted. "You might have Don fooled, Cat, but not me. I saw your face tonight. You've never smiled at anyone the way you smiled at that vampire. That's why I don't trust you not to get in over your head. You already are."

Twenty

Bones showed up promptly at seven the next night. We had plans to have an early dinner and then escape—until the following morning, anyway. As soon as I'd left the compound the previous evening, Don put round-the-clock surveillance on me. That had been a mood kill, to say the least. They probably had microphones pointed at my house, too, for maximum spying potential.

It pissed me off no end. What did Don think, that if left unsupervised, I'd hold undead rallies to give every pulseless person within a hundred miles a blueprint of his compound? If Don didn't have such a strong "greater good" agenda, I might have quit my job right then and there.

I was still scowling over it all when I opened the door to let Bones in . . . and then I stopped and gawked at him.

He wore tailored black pants and a dark blue shirt, his skin radiating against the deep-colored fabric. A black leather jacket was slung loosely over his shoulders and complemented his ensemble. It was the jacket itself that held my attention. It was long, trailing almost down to his calves.

"Holy shit, is that what I think it is?" I blurted.

Bones grinned and did a circle. "You like? After all, you kept *your* Christmas present"—he nodded to the Volvo in my driveway—"so it only seemed fair to retrieve mine, especially since you took my other jacket."

The jacket I'd bought him for Christmas years ago fit him perfectly. I'd never had the chance to give it to him, since Don had swooped me up before the holidays. Bones must have pried it out from its hiding place under the loose board of the kitchen cabinet in my old apartment. I'd told him where it was the day before I left him. The thought of Bones going back to get it made me almost burst into tears.

Some of that must have shown on my face, because his expression softened.

"Sorry, luv," he said, pulling me into his arms. I could almost hear cameras snapping as Don's spies zoomed in on us. "Didn't think it would make you sad."

I put a rein on my emotions. "I'm fine," I said briskly, giving the leather a light rub. "You look great in it. Just like I pictured you would—except your hair's different, of course."

Bones shook his head, making his honey-brown curls sway. "This is my natural color. Didn't really care about coloring it much lately, and the platinum did stand out more, don't you agree? Why, which do you prefer?"

I considered it. "Since I met you as a blond, that's just what feels right to me. But don't worry. I won't break out the peroxide later."

He chuckled low. "Whatever turns you on."

His eyes roamed over me as he said it, making me feel warm everywhere he looked. I had on a simple, short black sheath that was sleeveless, with a front and back V-neck. Light makeup, no jewelry, *definitely* no perfume. Every vampire I knew hated that. With their sense of smell, it was always too heavy, no matter how sparingly applied.

"Ready to go?" he asked softly.

"Um hmm." Somehow I couldn't come up with a more articulate response. God, I'd wanted nothing more than to spend the night in his arms for literally years now, and very soon I'd get my wish. So why was I so nervous all of a sudden? You'd think I'd somehow morphed into a teenager on prom night.

Bones climbed onto his bike, a snazzy new Ducati. He'd always liked motorcycles, even though they weren't my favorite method of transportation. Still, the bike was the obvious choice for our plans to lose Don's tail on us later. For one, I wouldn't have been surprised if Don had ordered my car bugged while I met with him yesterday, and for another, *nobody* could catch a vampire on a motorcycle.

Bones gave me an amused look as I put my helmet on and climbed onto the back of the bike.

"I can hear them; they're scurrying like rats now.

Let's see how well they can keep up. I'll take it easy on them to start."

And he gunned the bike, shooting down the street with no regard for the speed limit.

I tightened my arms around his waist. Yeah, this definitely reminded me of old times.

The restaurant Bones took me to was called Skylines. It sat at the top of a twenty-story building overlooking the city. Glass made up the exterior walls for an unobstructed view, and our table was right up against the window. The red and white lights of the cars crawling along the street below us held my gaze, and idly I wondered which contained Don's men. With all the noise of surrounding traffic and the building's occupants, it was hard to tell. They were out there, though, I knew it. It was all I could do not to wave at them from my window perch.

"Showing them we haven't tried to escape?" I commented after the waiter took our wine and appetizer order.

He gave me a smile. "Didn't want them to come barreling up here and ruin our dinner. Come now, you haven't even looked at the menu."

I scanned the food options in front of me, but kept returning my gaze to Bones. I wasn't alone in admiring him. Bones's perfectly etched features, matched with that prowling grace, had turned every female head when he walked in. His darker hair contrasted against the smooth brilliance of his skin, and I wondered how its longer length would feel in my hands. The top button was open on his shirt, giving me the faintest peek of his chest, which I knew was as hard as the table we were sitting at. I remembered how erotic it felt to slide my nails down his back and pull him closer. How his power pulsed against my skin when our flesh merged. How green his eyes were when he was inside me. And how his vampiric ability to control where the blood went in his body meant he could make love to me until I was beyond sated.

No wonder I couldn't concentrate on the menu. Food? Who needed it? All of a sudden, I wasn't the least bit nervous about later. In fact, I wanted later to be a damn sight sooner.

Bones must have picked up on that, because his eyes began to glint with green flecks.

"Stop it, luv. You're making it very difficult for me to behave."

"I don't know what you mean," I said as I recrossed my legs, letting him hear the rub of skin on skin since I was sans hose.

Our wine came. I sipped it while shifting in my seat and casually stroking my cleavage. After years of practice, one thing I'd honed to precision was how to make a vampire hot. It was practically my livelihood, only in this case, there would be no silver stake at the end. How refreshing.

Bones leaned forward. "Do you know how beautiful you are?" There was a gravelly edge to his voice. "Absolutely ravishing. I'm going to spend hours reacquainting my mouth with every inch of your body, and I can barely wait to see if you taste as good as I remember."

The wine lingered in my mouth a moment before I swallowed. This was the part that wasn't normal for me.

My previous targets had never evoked such a heated response.

"Do we really have to stay for the whole meal?" My eyes locked with his, and I stroked his hand with one finger. "Let's just take it to go, hmm?"

He opened his mouth to reply—and suddenly I was rolling underneath the neighboring tables with him on top of me. There was the sound of glass shattering and shrill screams. Tables crumpled and people were knocked from their chairs while I wondered what the hell had happened and why my forehead was burning.

I must have instinctively shut my eyes, because when they snapped open, I cried out. Bones's face was right next to mine, and a blood-smeared hole was staining his hair red before it began to close on itself.

"You've been shot!" I gasped. "Someone tried to kill you!"

It took a moment for the facts to register. We were on the floor. He'd rolled me away from our table, but I could still see where we'd been. Three holes punctured the glass, and none of them were by his seat.

Bones pulled me to my feet with his back to the window, and the truth hit me even as he answered.

"Not me, Kitten. You."

Twenty-one

I DIDN'T HAVE TIME TO DIGEST THE NEWS. "Hold on to my neck and don't let go," Bones said next with seething ferocity. "We're getting the sod."

He wrapped both arms around me the same instant I clung to his neck, and then he vaulted himself backward straight through the windowed wall behind us.

The thunderous noise of glass crashing outward drowned out my screams at suddenly free-falling from a twenty-story building. My legs flailed helplessly and my stomach lurched upward with a nauseating lift. Wind stung my eyes, which were fixed in horror at the rapidly approaching ground. The grip I had around his neck stiffened into the hold of the damned, and then an incredible thing happened. We started slowing down.

Incredulous, I looked up to see if a parachute had miraculously appeared, but there was nothing beyond the lights of the building. Before I could even wrap my mind around that, however, I felt a *whoosh*, and then we weren't falling anymore. We were sailing diagonally through the air toward a black van that had just sped into traffic. My screams died in my throat, choked off by astonishment.

Cars screeched, either from the erratically driving van or the people who'd hit their brakes in disbelief at seeing a dark form streak above them. The van was speeding, but we were faster. Bones caught up to it in seconds and grasped the rear bumper, flipping the vehicle without even letting go of me with his other hand.

It upended with a spectacular crash. Oncoming cars swerved and more brakes squealed. Bones flew upward in a single spurt that bore us clear of the traffic melee and set me down on the sidewalk with a short directive.

"Stay here."

He streaked back toward the wrecked van before I could even croak out a reply. There was a crack of gunshots, more screams from onlookers, and then moments later he reappeared with a man flung over his shoulder.

"Let's go."

Bones grasped me firmly once more, and then the ground left our feet. My eyes bugged. Mother of God, we were going so *fast*. To keep my feet from swinging crazily, like my mind was doing, I tangled my legs in his and held on, almost afraid to look down to see how high up we were.

Ten minutes later, Bones set us down in a warehouse alley as neatly as if he'd hopped off a curb. I was panting in amazement and staring at him like I'd never seen him before.

"You can fly?" I gasped out the obvious.

He glanced over at me while shaking the hapless assassin like a rag doll.

"Told you I was more powerful than you were aware of."

I kept staring. Bones would have seemed nonchalant—if he wasn't shaking the living hell out of the man in his hands.

"But you can *fly*?" I finally repeated, struck into stupidity.

"I'm a Master vampire. If a Master gets to be powerful enough and old enough, this is one of the perks. There are others, but we can get into those later," Bones said as the man's eyes fluttered open, focused on him, and then bulged. He was awake now, and he looked like I'd felt when Bones had catapulted us out of that window. Scared shitless.

Bones dropped him to the ground and knelt in front of him. A flash of emerald spilled out of his eyes, and after a harsh command, the man quit struggling and sat still.

"This woman," Bones said, indicating me with a jerk of his head. "Why did you try to kill her?"

"Business," the man replied in a monotone, mesmerized by the glowing orbs fixated on him. "I was hired to."

Another hit man. Guess Bones hadn't been wrong about that contract out on me.

"Who hired you?" Bones asked immediately.

"Don't know. The contract came in, instructions were enclosed, and the money was to be wired on completion. Sometimes I get jobs through referrals, but not this time."

"Kitten." Bones didn't break eye contact. "Write this down."

He withdrew his wallet. A tiny pen was clipped to it. I used the first piece of paper I found, which was money.

"Name."

"Ellis Pierson."

Such a normal-sounding name, and it went with his appearance. Aside from his fresh bloody nose and bruises, he looked about as threatening as Mickey Mouse. Ellis had black hair neatly trimmed, a paunch, and round baby cheeks. The prick was obviously good with a rifle and a scope, though. I'd be missing several choice pieces of my brain now if it weren't for Bones tackling me. How he'd known about the shots was still beyond me.

"Alias, all of them."

There were several. I was going to need more money.

One by one, Bones asked Ellis questions about the contract out on me, and he knew better than anyone which ones they were. *Tricks of the trade*, I thought sardonically as I wrote. *It takes a hit man to interrogate one.*

My jaw clenched when Ellis outlined in a dull voice how he'd been given very special instructions regarding my dispatch. It was to be a head shot only, a minimum of three bullets, and at a range no closer than a hundred yards. No car bombs, poison, physical confrontation, or any contact near my car or residence. Ellis didn't know what I was, but whoever had hired him must have had a frigging good idea. These stipulations were too specific to be coincidental.

By the end, I'd written on over a dozen different bills, and my hand was cramped from the minuscule pen. Considering the alternative, however, I wasn't going to complain. Finally Bones sat back on his haunches and asked if there was anything else Ellis hadn't mentioned.

"The client got anxious in the last e-mail and moved up the time frame. Said new circumstances mandated immediate results. My price was increased by twenty percent if the job was done tonight. I followed her from her house to the restaurant. Easier to escape in the confusion there."

Motherfucker. Someone wanted me dead in a hurry, and whoever that was also knew where I lived. A sick feeling swept over me, because there were only a select number of people who knew that.

I didn't think we were going to turn him over to the police, but the swiftness with which Bones yanked Ellis to him and latched his mouth onto his throat still startled me. This wasn't the first time I'd witnessed death by fang, but it was the first time I did nothing and just watched. Ellis's heartbeat raced at first, then slowed, and finally stopped.

"Does that hurt?" I coldly wondered when Bones released him, letting him fall to the ground.

He wiped his lips with the back of his hand. "Not nearly as much as he deserved, but we don't have time for that."

With a touch now gentle enough to soothe a baby, he traced his fingers along the scratch on my temple. I knew what it was. The graze from a bullet.

"So bloody close to losing you," he whispered. "I wouldn't have been able to stand it, Kitten."

He pulled me to him, hard, and a delayed reaction to my near-death experience set in. I'd had people try to kill me before, sure. Too many times to count, but a gunshot at far range seemed so . . . mean. I shivered.

"Cold? Want my jacket?" He began to shrug off his leather coat when I stopped him.

"You're warm. I've never felt you this warm before."

The reason for his new temperature was ten feet from us, but I didn't care. I held him and savored his unusual heat. Then I tugged at his shirt collar, popping loose a button, just so I could feel his heated skin next to my cheek.

"Don't, luv," Bones said in a strained voice. "I have very little control left in me."

Except I didn't want his control right now. Or mine. Back at that restaurant, I'd been nanoseconds from being blown to kingdom come, but here I was. Alive, unhurt . . . and unwilling to waste another moment.

I kissed his collarbone, sacrificing another button to better access it. Bones's hands tightened on my back. The waves of leashed power emanating from him excited me. Under my mouth, his skin seemed to crawl with voltage begging to be let free. My tongue flicked out, sliding lower on his chest to follow the hard grooves—until Bones yanked my head up and slanted his mouth across mine.

There was a metallic taste to his mouth, but it didn't

repel me. Instead I kissed him like I was trying to devour him, sucking on his tongue while tearing at his shirt. Bones picked me up and walked swiftly to the end of the parking lot, where there were more shadows. Something hard and uneven touched my back, but I didn't turn around to see what it was. I was too busy running my hands over the warm flesh that his torn shirt had revealed.

There was a yank at my dress and the front split open. Bones's mouth left a hot trail down my neck to my breast, his fangs deliciously grazing my skin. A strangled moan tore out of me when he pushed my bra down and sucked hard on my nipple. Throbs of desire so acute they were almost painful burned in me.

I moved my hand between our tightly molded bodies with the single-minded intent of destroying his pants. Then all thought fled as his fingers slid under my panties to push into me. I arched back hard enough to hit my head on whatever I was propped against, harsh cries of need spilling from me. My loins twisted in pleasure with each new rub, the intensity inside me building— until his hand was gone, leaving me wet and aching.

"I can't wait," Bones muttered fiercely.

If speaking was still in my control, I would have immediately agreed. But all my vocal abilities were used on gasping at the unbelievable sensations his fingers caused. Bones shifted, I heard another rip, and then he thrust deeply inside me. His mouth claimed mine at the same instant, muffling my cry at the ecstasy of his hard flesh filling me. Then there was the sweetest edge of pain as he began to move rhythmically, almost roughly, inside me.

My mind was seized with a single jumbled rant: *Harder-faster-more-yes!* It was all I could think as I clawed at his back, desperate to somehow get closer. Bones's arm was under my hips, holding me tighter even as the solidness at my back rocked with our movements. Between his kiss, my grip, and that unknown brace, I could barely breathe, but I didn't care. All that mattered was the escalating passion within that had my nerve endings contracting and twisting in a frenzy.

"Don't stop, don't stop!" I cried, but it came out as only a garbled shout against his mouth. Bones must have translated, however, because he ramped up his speed until I wasn't even sure I was still conscious. Spasms began to shake me from the inside out as my body convulsed with the overload of pleasure. I heard Bones groan, barely audible above the thundering of my heartbeat, and then moments later felt the wetness of his release inside me.

It took a few minutes before I could speak. "Something's jabbing me . . . in the back."

I was still panting. Bones wasn't, of course, that whole not needing to breathe thing. He pulled me away and then glanced at the offending object.

"Twig."

Finally I looked behind me. Yes, there was a tree. With a very smashed twig on the front of it.

My legs slid down from his waist until I was standing once again. I glanced at my dress. Ruined. Guess I couldn't complain, not with how Bones's shirt was in strips. Then I looked—belatedly—around the parking lot to see if we'd just given anyone a free show. No one was nearby gawking, thank God. Good thing this store closed early and Bones had chosen a tree in an unlit area.

"That took the edge off years of deprivation," I murmured, still basking in the residual tingles.

Bones had been kissing my neck. At my words, he stopped. "Years?" he asked quietly.

I felt inexplicably shy all of a sudden. Yeah, with what just happened, shyness didn't make sense, but it was true. It was one thing to risk getting caught with my pants down—literally—in public during the heat of the moment. Quite another to get caught with my previous celibacy swinging in the breeze.

Still, it was too late to take it back. I took in a deep breath. "Yes. Noah was the first guy I dated since you, and we didn't . . . well. We didn't. Enough said."

Bones slid his hands up my arms in a slow caress. "It wouldn't have mattered if there'd been other men since me, Kitten. Oh, I'd have cared, make no mistake, but in the end, it wouldn't have mattered. Yet you'll forgive me if I confess to being very, very glad that there weren't."

He kissed me, long and searching. Then he pulled away with a noise of resignation. "We need to get out of here, luv. Soon someone will stumble across us."

Yeah, and with a dead body across the parking lot, if it was a police officer, we'd get charged with a whole lot more than indecent exposure.

"Bones." I paused. Okay, I had no right to ask, since I'd dumped him and given him written instructions to get on with his life. But I couldn't stop myself. "I'll say the same thing, it doesn't matter, but . . . what about you? I'd rather know than wonder."

He met my eyes squarely. "Once. Close enough to count. I'm not going to be all Clinton about it and call it by a different name. After Chicago, when I left you that watch but you didn't come to me, I was very out of sorts. Thought perhaps you'd truly forgotten me, or didn't care. At the same time, an old lover of mine was in town. She invited me to her room, and I went."

He stopped at that, but I couldn't let it go. How typical of me.

"And then?"

Even though his gaze didn't waver, his expression tightened. "She and I were in bed, I'd tasted her, and then I stopped before it went further. I'd been imagining she was you, and I couldn't pretend any longer. So I apologized and left."

Tasted her. I knew he wasn't referring to feeding. Scalding jealousy filled me, and I closed my eyes against the mental image of his mouth on another woman in *that* way.

"It doesn't matter," I managed to say, and I meant it. But, oh God, it still hurt.

"I'm sorry," he said. I could hear the remorse staining his voice. "I should have never allowed it to go that far. I was angry, lonely, and feeling rather entitled. Not an honorable combination."

I opened my eyes. The moon was in white relief against the night sky, and its rays seemed to make Bones's skin glow.

"It doesn't matter," I said again, with more strength

this time. "And for the record, I didn't find out about that watch until after the fact. I'm not saying I would have run off with you had I found it sooner, but—I would have pressed that button. I wouldn't have been able to stop myself."

He smiled. Seeing it eased some of the hurt from his earlier confession. "I've never been able to stop myself either when it comes to you, Kitten. But we really do need to leave now."

I cleared my throat. "Um, on foot?"

"No," he snorted as he pulled up his pants. "The faster way."

"I still can't believe you didn't tell me you could fly," I complained. "I can think of a few times back in Ohio when it would have saved me some gas money!"

"I didn't tell you about it back then because I was afraid to show you even more ways that I wasn't like a normal man."

Considering my many prejudices at the time, it was hard for me to blame him for such caution. "Can you also leap tall buildings in a single bound?" I asked after a pause.

He enfolded his arms around me, breath from his laughter tickling my neck. "We'll try that tomorrow night."

I nodded at the dead hit man across the parking lot. "What are we doing with him?"

"Leaving him. I'm sure your blokes will come along soon enough, so he's their problem. We're going back to my house to find out who employed the late Ellis Pierson."

His arms tightened, and there was expulsion of air as he vaulted upward like his feet had invisible rockets. This time I didn't squeeze my eyes shut, but I welded myself to him as the distance grew between us and the streets below.

"You don't ever crash, do you?" I managed to ask breathlessly.

He chuckled, the sound snatched away by the wind.

"Not lately."

Twenty-two

Bones had left his laptop and other possible incriminating information back at the house he was renting, which is where we went. For another piece of luck, his cell phone was safely inside the leather coat he still wore. We wouldn't go back to my house anymore, for obvious reasons. With how much of a rush the mysterious source behind the attempt on my life was in, there could be another hit man waiting for me. I'd have to send someone else over to feed my cat for the next day or so.

Once we were safely inside the house and I could concentrate on more than "Eek, too high, too fast!" my mind spun with possibilities.

"Do you think Ian was behind the hit man?"

"Not a chance," Bones said without hesitation. "Ian wants you alive so he can add you to his collection. Be a bit hard to do that if your head was in pieces."

I remembered those three tight-knit holes in the window. "How did you know to knock me out of the way?"

"I heard the shots go off. He didn't use a silencer."

My head had been less than four feet away from the window at the time. Holy shit, he'd moved *fast*.

He read my look. "Not fast enough. One touched your skin. That's far too slow for me."

I gave a humorless chuckle. "That's faster than I even knew was possible. And the flying trick blew me away as well. Still, we can never go back to *that* restaurant again. You destroyed the place and didn't even pay for our wine."

"We both know what it has to be, Kitten," Bones said, ignoring that. "Obviously Don decided not to trust you."

I thought it over, and then shook my head.

"It's not Don. It doesn't make sense. Ellis said that he had originally been given the contract a week ago. That means the hit was planned *before* anyone knew you came into my life. Don had no reason to want me dead then. I was playing by all his rules."

Bones got up and began to pace. "You're right. I'm still so bloomin' unsettled about almost wearing your brains, I'm not thinking clearly. Right then, Don looks clean. *Perhaps*. But then that means that there's a traitor at your compound. This isn't just some random contract by an undead bloke who wants the mysterious Red Reaper eliminated. *This* is someone who's privy to who you are, what you are, and your whereabouts. How many people does that equate to?"

Reflectively, I rubbed the wound near my hairline. "My entire unit, Don's scientists, some of the guards . . . about a hundred people."

He frowned. "That's a large number of suspects, and that means it won't take Ian long to pick up on you, either. I'll have to pay a visit to your work. Sniff out the potential Judases one by one."

"Bones." I marched over to him. "You don't understand. That place is heavily armed and heavily guarded. I should know, I helped design the security! There are only two ways a vampire can get inside the compound without a massive bloodbath. One way is shriveled. They store those vampires on ice for study. The other way is nearly as unpleasant—pronged with silver near the heart and transported inside our capsule. We keep those vampires alive for their blood to supply the Brams. That's it. End of story."

Instead of being discouraged, he tapped his finger on his chin and then picked up his cell and dialed.

"Yes, thank you, I'll hold . . . Right, one large pizza, extra cheese, pepperoni, mushrooms. Two liters of Coke also. Um hmm, cash. Forty minutes? Here's the address . . ."

When he hung up, I blinked at him in confusion. "Is that code for something?"

He laughed. "Yeah, it's code. For a large pizza and soda. You never did have a bite to eat, and we can't have you starving on me. Don't fret; it's all for you. As you know, I'm full. Now tell me about this capsule."

"This is the worst idea you've ever had."

My jaw ached from grinding my teeth. I was practically hoarse from arguing, but Bones was unperturbed.

"This is the only way I can get within sniffing distance of whoever's trying to take you out. If they're a vampire or ghoul's lackey, I'll smell it on them. Or they'll try to run, or stink like fear. Either way, we'll know."

"Or you'll be packed on ice next to Switch."

"Not going to happen, pet. Make the call."

Bones handed me his phone for the fifth time. With a withering glare, I finally took it and dialed. Here went nothing.

"Don, it's me," I said when he answered.

"Cat, are you hurt?" To his credit, he sounded genuinely concerned.

"No, but someone's trying to change that. Look, I'm coming in; I'll see you in an hour. Don't let anyone, and I mean *any*one, leave until I get there. Call in whoever's out. We have a rat."

"Of course, come in at once. We'll discuss it when you get here. But no one here could possibly be involved—"

"Do you want me to come in or not? These are my terms, and I'm pretty goddamn inflexible about them, since my head nearly parted company with my shoulders last night."

He paused and then sighed. "If that's what makes you feel safe. Where is, ah, your companion?"

"He went out, I don't know where. Right now I'm more worried about my own ass."

"Hurry in. I'll recall the teams, but if you don't arrive in an hour, I'm sending them back out."

I hung up and almost flung the phone at Bones. "Happy now?"

He pressed his lips over the scab on my temple. "Not

yet, but I will be. Go straight there; don't stop for anything."

I started to leave, but then paused.

"Bones, before we do this, I have to tell you something. You know I still care about you, obviously, but it's more than that. I'm . . . I still love you. I've never stopped, actually, even though I tried to snap out of it over the years. I don't expect you to feel the same way, but—"

"I've never stopped loving you," he cut me off, coming over to take me in his arms. "Not for an instant. Even when I was so angry at you for leaving me, I've always loved you, Kitten."

He kissed me, a slow, deep kiss, like we had all the time in the world. I wished we did, but right now, I was afraid I might never see him again.

With a shuddering sigh, I pushed him back. "I'll give you another kiss later. Right now I'm too scared about what you're doing."

Bones smiled, undisturbed, and traced my lower lip with his finger. "I'll look forward to it. There's one more thing, and you must swear to do exactly as I tell you. Take this." He placed a sealed envelope in my hand. "Hide this in your clothes and don't open it until I tell you. This is the information I'd been waiting for, and I need to be there when you see it. Swear to me you'll wait."

"Quit being melodramatic." I thrust the envelope down the front of my shirt, tucking it in my bra. "Scout's honor, okay?"

"I love you." He made it difficult to stay mad at him.

That stopped me by the door, my hand on the knob. "Don't get killed. No matter what."

From the look in my eyes, he knew what I meant.

"It shouldn't come to that, but if it does, I'll try not to kill any of them."

"Right." My tone was brittle. "I don't know if they'll show you the same courtesy."

This time, when I drove up to the guard gates on a motorcycle and took off my helmet, I was rushed through without hesitation. After all, I couldn't exactly hide a vampire on the handlebars, could I? I rode straight through to the entrance, literally leaving the bike by the door, and was met by Tate and Juan. They both looked awful.

"*Christos, querida*, we thought the worst," Juan exclaimed. Tate was less expressive, but he stared at the scratch on my forehead as if transfixed.

"Jesus. Is that from the bullet?"

"Sure is." Flippantly. "Were you one of my spies last night? Or did you get the report secondhand?"

We headed for Don's office. To my relief, I saw the building's doors seal promptly behind me. Good, Don was keeping everyone inside.

Tate still looked rattled. "Actually, I saw it on video. You were being recorded. Don has the tapes."

"At least I'll get to see how my dress looked, even though it's toast now."

"You looked beautiful, *querida*." Trust Juan never to miss an opportunity, no matter the circumstances. "Throw away that pulseless pale man and I'll take care of you."

"That 'pulseless pale man' saved my life, Juan," I bleakly reminded him. "I wouldn't be pretty with three holes plugged in my head, would I?"

Don stood when we entered, a rarity. He stared at me for a moment, and something flashed across his face I couldn't name.

"Let me see it," I began without pleasantries.

He knew what I was referring to, and clicked a button that flicked on the plasma screen as Tate shut the door.

Whoever had been filming me had a better vantage point than my would-be assassin. This looked to be from a neighboring building, since the slant was less steep. Dispassionately I watched the silent footage of Bones and me at our seats, the waiter bringing us the wine, him leaning forward, and me stroking his hand. The next scene was a blur of volatile movement that defied tracking with the naked eye. Then there was the unbelievable sight of the window exploding outward and a black-draped form free-falling with me before zooming off to wreck the van below.

The cameraman had apparently stopped filming and started moving, because the next footage was far more mundane. It showed the dead body of Ellis Pierson, and a close-up on the puncture wounds in the throat. Bones hadn't bothered to heal them. He knew my team would scoop up the evidence.

Don clicked off the film and regarded me with guarded expectancy.

"I take it that was the hired gun?"

"Yeah. My date wasn't happy at his dinner being interrupted."

"Oh, your date got his dinner, all right," Tate muttered sarcastically.

"You know, Tate, I can't say I minded much at the time. After all, I'd just listened to a detailed description of how he was paid to blow my head off."

"Cat." Don rested his hands on his desk as he sat down. "You need to tell us about this vampire you're with. You start dating the undead, and suddenly you're targeted for assassination? From someone who knew exactly where you'd be? It's too coincidental."

"Did you just miss what you saw?" Exasperation filled my tone. "That vampire took a fucking bullet in the head for me! Explain to me how that's hostile!"

"I've studied this recording frame by frame, Cat," Tate answered flatly. "He moved faster than a speeding bullet, literally, and then he jumped from a building and *flew*! So not only does he have to be a Master vampire, but he also has to be the most powerful fucking Master we've ever encountered."

Good thing Tate still hadn't recognized Bones from Ohio, even though he'd studied the film footage from last night. Maybe it was like the old prejudiced saying went, except for Tate, it was all vampires who looked the same. Still, that was an issue for another time. Let them keep thinking Bones was just some new vamp I'd met. Later they'd learn the truth, but for now, it fit the plan to keep them ignorant of who he was.

"I'm not an idiot, Tate. I realized the same thing after he was finished with the hit man, but as I said, *he* obviously doesn't want me dead. He thinks someone close to me does, though, just from a different angle. He thinks it's someone here, and that Don is the key."

"What? Huh? *Que?*"

They spoke at once, and I waved a hand.

"He wouldn't tell me much, but said he had to con-firm it. I have his cell—he'll call when he's finished. But he did mention a name, and said this person was connected. Maybe you'll recognize it, Don, because it doesn't ring a bell with me."

This part Bones had been very specific about. I didn't blink as my eyes met the older man's. "Maximillian. Ever heard of him?"

Something happened to Don's face I'd never seen. He blanched and almost looked like he'd faint. Mother-fucker. For Don to look that sick, he recognized the name, all right.

"Why, boss, you look like someone just walked over your grave," I said softly.

Tate and Juan cast interested glances in his direction as well, but their faces were blank. Maybe Don was the only one in on the secret.

Don opened his mouth to speak, but was saved when his cell phone rang. He glanced at the number, an-swered it, and then shot me a guarded look and covered the phone.

"I, ah, have to go in the hall where there's better re-ception."

"Is something wrong?" I asked at once.

"No, no," he assured me while backing away. "Give me a moment."

Don left the office, and from the sounds of it, the entire sublevel as well, since I couldn't hear anything from him anymore.

Tate used the interruption to start on me. "Cat, you

need to tell us who this vampire is that you're consort-ing with, and anything else you know about him, be-cause he knows far more than he's letting on."

I bristled at being spoken to like a junior officer. "His name is Crispin, he's lived in and around Virginia for the last ten years, and he can go all night in bed." *There. Take that and shove it.*

Tate shot me an angry look. "That's nice for him, but it still doesn't tell us anything useful."

I shrugged. "Isn't the bigger problem who this Maxi-millian is, or how he's connected here? Don't you know the name?"

"No." His denial was immediate. From his expres-sion, I didn't think he was lying, but I wouldn't have sworn to it.

Then Tate's cell rang. He glanced at it and frowned.

"Yeah . . . *what?* Okay, on my way." Tate hung up and then rose. "I have to go, Don needs me for some-thing. Juan, he wants you to wait in here with Cat—and he says neither of you are to leave this room until he gets back."

Tate left. It was just Juan and I.

"Between Tate's jealousy and Don's paranoia, they're probably on a three-way call with my mother to dis-cuss my lack of brains," I said bitterly. "After over four years and all the times I've risked my life, this is the payback I get. Cooling my heels with you babysitting me. What a joke."

Juan didn't reply, but his silence said it all.

"Juan." I swiveled to face him. "You're the only one who isn't operating with clouded judgment. There's more to a person than their temperature. You've seen enough to know that. Don't let them fuck everything up because of prejudice. Just look at all the facts before rushing to condemn anyone, that's all I ask."

"I owe you, *querida*. You've saved my life many times." Juan's normal playfulness was gone, and he was equally somber. "I will give you the benefit of the doubt, but your lover . . . I owe him nothing."

I took his hand and squeezed it. "Then do it for me. *Please*. For me."

The door swung open as Don and Tate returned. Don was the first to speak.

"Cat, I'm sending some men to escort your mother here, where she'll be safe until we've determined who's behind the threat on your life. It's just precautionary. I have some calls to make and a few other employees to round up, so you can wait in your office. The compound will be locked down when they leave, as you requested. We'll speak when they return."

My stomach twisted with anxiety but I squelched it. Bones had told me to trust him. This time, I'd do just that.

"Fine. Go ahead. Get my mom."

Tate grabbed Juan's arm and almost yanked him out the door. "We're on our way."

Twenty-three

Time limped along. It was well over
three hours before I heard activity at the far end of
the compound. Several of my team were there, talking
in loud, excited voices. That was the only way in from
the exterior to the fourth sub-level, where we housed
the vampires. I strained my ears, then heard the unmis-
takable alarm bells for the reinforced elevator that was
only used for transporting the capsule inside.

I barged straight into Don's office. He'd been on the
phone, and with a supremely confident air, he set it
down.

"They're back, and they've got the capsule with
them. What the fuck is going on, Don?"

"Sit down." He inclined his head toward the chair,
and with a huff I sat. "I'm afraid I have some disturbing
news, Cat. I didn't tell you before because I couldn't
risk you endangering yourself by leaving. Your mother

called me earlier because she was afraid. Apparently your new vampire boyfriend phoned her to say he was coming over. Once he got there, he attacked her. She's okay, just cuts and bruises. After we arrived, he, ah, surrendered and was brought here. Already he's implied that he knows who's after you and that he's in on it. The men are securing him now, and then they will question him in detail."

"I want to see him," I said at once.

Don shook his head. "Not a chance. You're too emotionally involved, and it's clouded your objectivity. As of an hour ago, your access to the lower levels is restricted. You are to have no contact with any of the vampires. I'm sorry, but your actions have determined my response. Don't be too harsh on yourself. Many others have also fallen prey to their influence. Let this be a lesson to you, and I'll keep you informed."

He was dismissing me. I jumped to my feet, pissed.

"Fine, if you want to be all brass balls about it, then let me talk to Tate before he questions him. You can at least do that. Bring Tate up here if you're so goddamn worried I'll cause a scene downstairs. He can meet me in my office."

Don gave me a look of thinly veiled annoyance, but picked up his phone and placed the call.

"He'll be here in fifteen minutes."

I slammed the door behind me.

If Tate expected me to be quivering on my couch when he opened my door, he was disappointed. Coolly I sat behind my desk and waved a hand at the door.

"Shut it."

Tate closed it and then folded his arms across his chest.

"I came like you asked, but you can save your breath, Cat. Nothing you say will change anything. We caught him red-handed at your mother's. She's lucky to be alive, if you can see past your concern over your lover to be bothered with that."

He looked mildly disgusted with me, yet his heart-beat still accelerated when I went to stand near him.

"Oh, I care more than you imagine, Tate. Not just about him, but about you as well. That's why I'm going to ask you this first, and hope you do the right thing. Take Juan with you and let him out. Then we're lock-ing down the building in emergency mode and finding out who our mole is. We can do this two ways, but it *will* get done."

His nostrils flared as he shook his head. "You've lost your mind, Cat. Just absolutely lost it! God, no fuck can be worth throwing your life away for—"

"I love him," I interrupted.

He cursed viciously before finishing with "Now I *know* you're crazy! You've only been seeing him a couple weeks and you think you're in love? That's fucking nuts!"

He grasped my shoulders and gave me a hard shake. I just closed my hands over his.

"Tate, once you accused me of not trusting anyone. You were right—I haven't. I'm going to trust you now, though, and I hope you'll trust me. When you saw him today, when you looked in his eyes and *really* saw him . . . didn't he look familiar?"

"Of course he did. I've been over that goddamn video

for hours! And I'm the one who spotted him outside your house the other night."

I tightened my hands. "Not from last night or the video. Further back. To be fair, you only saw him for a second, but it was a memorable one. After all, you shot him. Right before the car plowed into him."

"That's—"

Tate stopped. A growing look of awareness dawned on his features. He stared at me with widening eyes, and then his mouth tightened in a thin, hard line.

"*Well.*" The word was soft. "Didn't you play us all for fools, Catherine Crawfield?"

I took in a deep breath. "It's Bones, the vampire I told you I'd loved and killed in Ohio, but I didn't kill him. I left him and passed another body off as his. I hadn't seen him until recently, when he was at Denise's wedding. This was all a setup today to get Bones in here so he could find the turncoat. He knew if he went to my mother's that she'd call in the troops, and I'd told him the only way in was that capsule or dead. Bones chose the capsule, despite the risk that he might be killed once he was strapped inside."

Tate still looked shell-shocked. "I almost did kill him. I had him in those restraints, and I knew all I had to do was shake him and those spikes would shred his heart. Juan stopped me. He told me we were questioning him first before condemning him. It's been over four years. You haven't seen this vampire until recently, but you've been in love with him this whole time?"

"Yes."

Tate laughed, a harsh little bark. "Of course you have. But that doesn't mean I'm breaking every rule ever implemented about vampires to let him out."

"He *is* getting out." My fingers cut into his hands. "The only question is, will you be conscious when he does? You're my friend, Tate. In many ways, my best friend, but I want to be very clear—I'll get him out and destroy anyone in my way to do it. You. Juan. Don. Anyone. I want you with me, as my partner and my friend, but I *will* do it alone if I have no other choice."

He looked like he wanted to slap me. "Goddamn you, Cat. Goddamn you! You've been with him a total of what? Six months? You've been by my side for over four fucking years! Is he worth that much to you? More than all you've fought for and all you've done? Think, for Christ's sake!"

I stared straight into his eyes and didn't hesitate. "Yes, he is. Maybe you don't understand. Have you ever owed someone everything? All your strengths, all your victories, every last thing that's meant anything in your life . . . and it can be traced back to one single person? That's what Bones is to me."

Tate suddenly yanked me closer. "You bitch, I do understand, because that's what you are to me."

I didn't shove him back, but let him stand with only an inch between us. "If I passed on anything of value, it's because I first learned it from him. So then you owe him, too."

Something sparked in his midnight gaze even as his shoulders slumped. "I don't owe him shit. But yeah . . . I owe you. Is this your price?"

"If that's what you want to call it." Better to negotiate than beat him senseless.

"There's more to it than opening that capsule, Cat.

There are four levels of highly trained guards, and there will be an automatic lockdown as soon as someone spots a prisoner strolling the halls. He can't green-eye all of them into submission; *some*one will trigger the alarm. You know this, you designed it!"

"That's why you're going down there nice and casual with Juan, and I'm going to stay up here and override the security."

Tate moved away from me and started to pace. "Don changed your computer clearance as soon as he found out about you and the vampire. Your codes won't work anymore. Even mine only go so far."

Ignoring that, I pulled out my cell phone and dialed.

"Randy, we're on schedule. In exactly ten minutes pull the plug. All levels except four and the connecting elevator back up to one. Full shutoff, prehistoric. Kiss Denise for me. I owe you."

I hung up and gazed at Tate. "Go down now. In ten minutes, all the power will shut off and this place will be a tomb. Appropriate, don't you think, since we *are* letting out a dead man. The only things that will work will be the ones I want to work. Did you really think after all these years I wouldn't have left myself with some back-door passwords in case Don turned on me?"

He stood up with a look of disbelief.

"If you could do all of that, why did you bother to ask me for help?"

"You're my friend," I repeated, pulling open a desk drawer and then tucking the gun it held into my pants. "And I still want to lead this team, although none of you seem to believe that. Hurry, you only have nine minutes now . . ."

* * *

Denise had been correct about Randy. He was indeed a genius with computers. With the passwords I gave him, he'd hacked into the mainframe and dropped a virus that he remotely controlled. It froze out everything. Even the phones didn't work. The neighboring cell phone tower, which intercepted our wireless signals, had also just experienced a power failure. My phone was satellite and still operated, and when the lights went out, I was the only one who didn't gasp at the sudden dark. I just went to the elevator and waited.

When the doors slid open, Bones was right in front of me. I threw my arms around him even as I gave directions to Tate and Juan, who were backed warily into the far corner.

"Guard this door. No one gets close, not even Don."

"What are you doing?" Tate asked as they stepped past us out of the elevator.

"Giving him blood. That box drained him. He needs a refill."

"Cat, Jesus—"

I hit the manual button and the elevator doors closed, effectively cutting off Tate's protests.

"I knew you'd come through, luv," Bones said.

I hugged him hard. "God, I've been worried sick these past few hours!"

He kissed me, gently exploring every crevice of my mouth while running his hands over me. I clutched him, feeling sick over the multiple holes in his clothes where the silver prongs from the capsule had pierced him.

"No need for foreplay," I whispered, breaking the kiss. "Just bite me already."

Bones laughed low. "You are ever impatient."

Then his lips trailed to my neck as he pushed my hair back. His tongue circled the hollow in my throat for a moment before his fangs sank into me.

I shivered, instinctively clutching him tighter at those twin stabs of sensation. This felt different from the other two times he'd bitten me. Less erotic and more predatory. Still, my heart raced, my knees went deliciously weak, and that same strange warmth crept over me.

The elevator doors opened right as Bones lifted his head. There was an ominous sound of a gun cocking as I pulled mine out of my pants at the same time.

"Back off, Tate! You shoot and I fire back."

We must have looked quite the sight, Bones licking the last drops of my blood off his fangs and me with my gun pointed at everyone but the vampire drinking me. Hell, I could understand Tate's reaction, but that didn't mean I was letting him shoot Bones. Juan also had his gun drawn but at least it was lowered. Smart man.

Bones eyed Tate and didn't bother to sheathe his fangs. "Don't fret over her safety, mate. I'd never hurt her, but I've seen the way you look at her, so you don't have that same pass."

"Tate," I said warningly. "Drop the gun."

Tate stared at me. "Goddamn, Cat. I hope you know what you're doing."

"It's all right, Kitten," Bones said. "He won't shoot."

Tate lowered his gun even as the sudden dizziness from blood loss made me sway. Bones took my gun and casually handed it to Juan, who gaped at him in amazement.

"You called her Kitten? And she let you? She put me in a *coma* for three *day*s when I called her that! My balls never recovered from her smashing them into my *spine*!"

"And well she should have," Bones agreed. "She's my Kitten, and no one else's."

I poked him in the chest. "Do you mind? I'm a little woozy here."

"Apologies, luv."

He lifted me off my feet as his fangs cut into his tongue with a snap of his jaws. There were so many other ways for me to get blood from him, but I was figuring he'd chosen this one because of his comment to Tate. I kissed him back while swallowing those needed drops. How like Bones to kill two birds with one stone—both staking his claim and replenishing my strength at the same time.

Don picked that moment to come striding through the throngs of stunned spectators just in time to see me curled inside a vampire's arms with my feet dangling off the ground.

"What the *hell* is going on?"

Bones set me down and went to my boss in a blink of speed. To Don's credit, he didn't try to run.

"You must be very determined to kill me to go to such lengths," he flatly commented, squaring his shoulders.

"I'm not here for you, old chap," Bones said, looking him up and down thoroughly. "I'm here to find out what rat you've got in your garden. But first we're going to have a chat, the three of us. You've kept her in the dark long enough."

"Tate, Juan, make sure no one comes through that

door and no one tries to get frisky. The place is secured, but someone could pull a weapon. Keep sharp."

I inclined my head toward Don's office. "After you, boss."

Don took his seat like it was any other visit and not a hostage situation, and we sat across from him.

"Don, I'd like to introduce you to Bones. The real Bones, not the impostor on ice in the fridge. You'll remember him from Ohio, where he gave the highway a whole new look."

"All these years, Cat," Don said with sadness. "You've been working the other side this whole time. Bravo, I was totally fooled."

My mouth opened in outrage, but Bones beat me to it. "You ungrateful sod, the only reason I'm not picking you out of my teeth now is because of her. She fancies you a decent man, not that I agree, and has in no way betrayed your trust. *You* can hardly say the same."

I rolled my eyes. A death threat, gee, great way to start out a talk.

"I haven't played you at all, Don," I said. "When I left Ohio, I thought I was leaving Bones behind for good. He tracked me down and found me only two weeks ago, and I have never done anything to betray this operation."

Don shook his head in self-rebuke. "I should have sensed a trap. No vampire ever surrenders. How did you get your mother to play along?"

"She didn't," I said grimly. "Bones told her he wanted to meet without my knowledge. We knew what she'd do."

Bones snorted. "When I got to her house, she'd already blacked both her eyes and knocked over every stick of furniture in the place. But back to you, Don. For most of my years, I've had a trade. I find people, and I'm right good at it. So imagine my surprise when I had such a devil of a time tracking her, and then also my inability to find much out about her father. Now, failure to locate one I could see, but two? Both hidden so carefully, it was almost as if they were concealed . . . by the same person."

A foreboding sensation crept up my spine. Bones squeezed my hand.

"Two things always struck me as strange when she disappeared into the smoke. The first was how you found her so quickly. You showed up with all of her facts and figures the day she was arrested. Too pat, that. Such research takes time. You'd have to have been keeping tabs on her for a while, and how would you have known to do that? Only one way. You already knew what she was."

"What?" I shot out of my seat with a shout. "Don, what have you been hiding?"

"Sit down, luv." Bones gripped me when I would have sprinted across the desk to throttle Don. For his part, Don had turned a fine shade of parchment.

"The second thing that stumped me was how there were no records of any recent deaths matching her father's description at the time her mother was raped. Not even any John Does. Ian's the one who solved that riddle. You know him as Liam Flannery, Don, and you sent her after him, but he wasn't her usual target, was he?"

"No," I answered for Don, whose mouth was sealed in a tight line. "He wasn't. Get to the point, Bones."

"I'd rather hoped Don would step up and finish it for me, but he's staying quiet. Probably hoping like blazes I'm only fishing, aren't you?"

Don didn't reply. Bones made a regretful noise. "Open that envelope I gave you earlier, Kitten."

With trembling fingers I drew the paper out of my shirt, ripping open the seal and unfolding the single page inside. It was an article with a photo, but the caption underneath blurred into nothingness because all I'd needed to do was look at the face.

The man standing with a grin had red hair, high cheekbones, a straight nose, a jaw that was masculine but eerily similar, and I couldn't tell, but I'd bet those were gray eyes. Even faded, the likeness was unbelievable. Finally I had a face to put to my hate, and it was a mirror of my own. No wonder my mother had such issues.

As absorbed as I was in devouring the image of my father, it took me a minute to look at the other person in the photo. The one with an arm around my father's shoulders. "Family Celebrates Commendation of Federal Officer," the title read.

The years hadn't been kind, but I recognized him at once. A furious chuckle escaped me, and I flung the page at Don.

"Well, isn't life just one big joke? One *huge* cosmic one-liner! I now know just how Luke Skywalker felt when Darth Vader told him who he was, only you're not my father. But you're his brother."

†WENTY-FOUR

I GLARED AT MY BOSS. "SHOULD I CALL YOU Uncle Don? You son of a bitch, you sent me out on *how* many suicide missions when you knew I was your niece? You and my mother have a lot in common—the two of *you* should be related!"

Don finally broke his silence. "Why would I think you'd be any different? Thirty-five years ago my older brother was investigating Liam Flannery, and then he disappeared. Years passed. We thought he was dead, and no one would tell us about the last case he'd been on. I joined the FBI myself to find out what had happened to him. Over time, I also found out what my brother had really been chasing. I vowed I'd continue his hunt and give him justice, but then one day out of the blue, he came to me. He told me to forget about Liam and the underworld I was tracking or he'd kill me. My own brother. I couldn't believe it.

"Six months later, your mother was attacked in the

same city in Ohio I'd followed him to. When I read the description of her rapist, I knew it was him, and I knew that he'd finally crossed over. Then five months later, she gave birth to a child. One with a genetic anomaly documented at birth. Yes, I suspected all along, and made it a point to check up on you periodically while I created this department. Years went by, nothing happened, and I began to forget about you. Then your name came up in connection with a series of strange murders and grave robberies. I was already on my way back to Ohio when your grandparents were killed."

Don smiled but it wasn't happy. "I also believe that life is a comic accident. Here God had given me the one thing strong enough to stop my brother and his kind, and it was his own daughter. Yes, I used you while waiting for the day when you'd turn as he did, but that didn't happen. When I finally believed you were different, I sent you to capture Flannery so I could use him to draw Max out. But as fate would have it, Liam got away. I'm guessing he's the one who sent the shooter after you last night."

My mind reeled with this latest bombshell. *Ian* had made my father? The same man who'd turned Bones had also been the one who sired Max? That made Ian partly responsible for my half-dead existence. Unbelievable.

"It's not Flannery who hired that gunman," Bones stated. "He wants her alive. No, it has to be someone else who's trying to kill her. Someone affiliated here."

Don made a derisive noise. "How are you going to find out who this mythical traitor is? Torture all the staff?"

Bones glowered at him. "For someone who's studied vampires for years, you certainly don't give them much credit. Forgetting these?"

He flashed green into his eyes, and their light hit Don's face. He looked away.

"The spellbinding eyes of the nosferatu. Many days I'd wished I had the ability to glare the truth out of people, but without all the other consequences."

"Yes, well, there's a price for power and it always gets paid. Shall I let you go, Kitten, so you can bash his head in?"

Bones didn't sound troubled at the notion. I stared at Don. We had the same eyes, I realized. How had I never noticed that before?

"I should kill you for what you did to me, but I won't. I happen to understand wanting vengeance better than most people. It can make you do rash things, like sending your niece out to get killed so one day you can try to trap your brother. Besides"—a shrug—"aside from my mother, you're the only real family I have left. You can come with us or stay, I don't care, but if you come, don't interfere. Think you can handle that?"

Don rose. "I can handle it."

Tate and Juan still stood outside the door.

"Are we good, Cat?" Tate inquired. He glanced at Bones, who was appraising the openmouthed employees with a practiced eye.

"For now. Tate, you and Don can help. Let's start with the obvious. Where's the team? They know both what I am and where I live. After this room, they're our first stop."

"We called in all thirty of them, they're in the training room, but they're armed in there, Cat. We'll have to bring them out in groups so they don't stake Mr. Pointy Teeth on sight." Tate threw a disparaging look at Bones, who had vamped out to the horror of the staff and was sniffing each of them.

"Think I'd fret over a room full of humans?" Bones retorted. "Let them keep their toys; it'll teach them a valuable lesson. No matter how well she's trained them, they're not her."

Juan blinked. "He can take on all of them when they have silver?"

As much as I wanted to dispute it, since I'd worked hard on training them, the simple truth was, they'd never come across a vampire as strong as Bones before. Especially one in a closed space, football-sized or no.

"Yeah. Is that necessary, though, Bones? Time-wise? And you don't get to kill any of them; they're my men."

"Time-wise it's more efficient. All in one place is faster than group by group. Your culprit will be the one trying hardest to kill me. Or wetting himself, whichever. This room is clear—none of these people are your turncoat. Don't fret about your merry men, Robin Hood; they'll live to die another day."

"I want to be there." Don looked professionally intrigued. "I don't get to see a Master vampire in action. I only see their messy end results."

"That's where you're wrong again," Bones stated. "You've seen her fight for years, so you've seen a Master vampire in action. She just also has a heartbeat."

Our training room was more than a gym. It was an extravaganza of an obstacle course complete with swinging ropes, falling debris, shifting ground, water hazards, and lots of room to run. The dim emergency lights in there served to Bones's advantage, providing only subtle illumination. Bones had insisted we wait in Don's box overlooking the area. He didn't want me to get stabbed or shot in the melee.

It was something to watch, all right. There were shouts when his pale face became visible in the intermittent lights, and then a frenzy of motion even I couldn't fully follow.

"*Christos,*" Juan breathed in awe. "Look at him *fly.*"

Bones was surging around in gravity-defying bounds as he picked apart the careful formation I'd taught the men, bowling into them with his body and scattering them like pins. Tate shook his head in disgust.

"Years of work, right down the fucking drain. Makes me want to beat them myself."

"Cooper's trying to rally them," I observed. "Oops, down he goes. Goddamn, Bones can really hit like a sonofabitch. I'll need a pint of his blood after this to heal them all."

"What makes you think he'll do that?" Don asked skeptically.

"Because I'll *ask* him to, that's why. You really are thick. He climbed into our hell capsule for me earlier, yet you think he'll refuse to donate a little blood to make me happy? Dumb ass."

My boss—or should I say *uncle*—didn't respond.

"All right, Kitten," Bones called out. "They're clean. Not a bad bunch of blokes."

Almost offhandedly, he kicked one of the fallen

forms, eliciting a groan in return. I shook my head at Tate's expression.

"I told you he taught me everything I know. Kick 'em when they're down. That was his favorite rule. You're familiar with the rest of them."

"Goddammit, Cat, he's been in there less than ten minutes. How can he tell that none of them are involved? Most of them aren't even conscious now!"

"I trust him," I answered simply. "Bones wouldn't say it unless he was sure, and that's enough for me."

Juan had a dazed look on his face as he studied the remains of our team. Then a smile tugged his lips.

"That," he said emphatically, "was cool!"

It wasn't until we approached the pathology floor that Bones quickened his step. His eyes went green as soon as the elevator doors opened, and he gave me a quick, hard kiss before shoving me back inside it.

"Stay here," he said briskly. "I smell something."

Bones walked away with Juan and Don following. Tate hung back with me.

"This is a wild fucking goose chase," he muttered. "Smells something? What can he smell—"

"Shh!" I said, honing my ears to pick up every nuance of sound in the next room. There was a scrambling noise that was very short-lived, a squawk, and then a mocking deadly sneer.

"Well, now, what do we have here? No, you're not turning away, look right here at me . . ."

"He's got someone," I said for Tate's benefit, and brushed by him.

In the lab, Bones had our pathologist's assistant, Brad Parker, pinned to the wall by one pale hand. The glow from his gaze lit the room with an eerie green luminance.

"Right then, where were we? Tell me all about what you've been up to, and be specific. You can start with any partners."

"One," Brad mumbled. "He looks just like her."

I froze. Don's gaze met mine as a chill went through me. There was no doubt who Brad had to be referring to.

Bones glanced at me once and then turned his attention back to the man in front of him.

"Indeed? Now, tell me everything else . . ."

This time, Juan and Tate took dictation and I merely listened for the second time in as many days as a plot to kill me was outlined. Brad called him by a different name, but the perpetrator was clearly my father. Apparently after Ian pieced together the family resemblance between the Red Reaper he'd tangled with and his own lackey Max, my father had decided he didn't want to be a dad. He traced me by tracking Don, knowing he had to be the one backing me. Find one and the other wasn't far, he'd assumed correctly. With his inside knowledge of both the Bureau and his brother, Max had progressed with remarkable swiftness. Then he found what he was looking for in Brad Parker, a man whose loyalty could be bought and who knew enough to make it worth the payment.

It had almost worked. If not for my being on a date with a vampire, my head would have been blown off.

When Bones was finished, he arched a brow at Don. "You have any more questions for him?"

Don looked stunned. "No, I can safely say you covered it. Tate? Juan? Anything else?"

Mutely they shook their heads. Tate was more grudging in his silent response, his lips thinned to a straight line, but Juan looked at Bones with a flash of admiration. A start.

"Fancy locking him up?"

The question was again addressed to Don. I appreciated the gesture behind it. Bones was deferring Brad's fate. To my surprise, Don waved a hand.

"You know we're not letting him live, not with what he knows. Just don't make a mess."

Tate was incensed. "For Christ's sake, we can take him below and shoot him!"

"Don't be childish, Tate," Don snapped. "Bullet or bite, the end's the same, and it's his right. He found him; we didn't. Cat would be dead soon if he hadn't, and despite what she thinks of me, I don't want that to happen."

Don looked straight at me when he said that last part, and understanding dawned as to what this was. He was giving a peace offering in the form of Brad Parker's jugular. It wasn't pretty, but again, it was a start.

"Make it fast," I said to Bones. "I know you want to take your time, but don't. He's not worth it."

I didn't leave the room, but Tate did, in a huff. Juan shuffled but stayed, and Don remained where he was.

Bones didn't mind the audience. He bit into Brad's neck with his fangs fully extended, swallowing deeply and repeatedly. No one except me heard the inevitable sound of death as it occurred, and true to my request, it was fast.

"There you are, old chap," Bones said a minute later as he let Brad fall limply to the tile. "Not a drop spilled."

I went to him, stepping over Brad, who was sprawled by his feet. Bones kissed my forehead with warm lips. Two kills in two days; he was probably stuffed. Then again, his dinner last night had drained into the capsule.

"You know I'm going after him, Don." There was no need to say the name, and somehow, I didn't want to.

"Yes, I know." He appraised the two of us together and tugged his eyebrow. "I want to speak in private with you, Cat. There are some things we need to discuss."

"We can speak, but Bones is coming. Really, even if he couldn't hear us, which he can, I'd just tell him later."

Bones gave Don a smug smile. Well, he'd earned a little gloating.

Don coughed. "If you insist. Juan, would you remove . . . ?" He gestured vaguely at Brad's body as we followed him back to his office.

Twenty-five

"**A**RE YOU LEAVING US?" DON BEGAN WITHOUT preamble when I shut the door.

It was a good question, since I now knew what he'd hidden from me these past years.

I looked around Don's office and then back at the man himself. Don and I didn't have similar features, but he was my blood, as surely as my mother was. After several quiet moments, I realized I didn't hate him for his lies, both outright and of omission. Who was I to judge him so harshly for his mistakes? After all, I'd made an exceptional number of my own.

"No."

Don let out a sigh that might have been relieved, but Bones ran a hand through his hair in frustration.

"Bloody hell. You just won't take the easy road."

"I need to do this."

Bones stared at me for a long moment, then turned to Don.

"The only way you're keeping her is if I'm with her. Consider it a two-for-one deal. I won't stop her from doing what she considers her job, but I will *not* see her die for it. None of those men are strong enough to back her up, but I am. You want her? Then you'll get me also."

This I hadn't expected. Clearly neither had Don. He gaped.

"You can't expect me to allow a vampire inside an operation designed to *kill* vampires! That's not even lunacy—it's suicide!"

Bones smiled a very patient smile and sat down, tapping his fingers on Don's desk.

"Look, mate, I could give a rot about your operation, but do happen to care a great deal about her life, so I'm going to make you an offer, and you're going to accept it."

Don blinked at the baldness of the statement. I was curious myself to hear what this offer was, because it was news to me, too.

"Why does the success of your missions hinge on her?" Bones went on. "Because she's your strongest fighter. Without her, you have a group of men who might do jolly well in a regular war, but against ghouls and vampires, they're roadkill. You know it, too. That's why you got your knickers in a twist when you discovered how lethal she was at twenty-two. And don't think I've forgotten that it was *your* manipulating that kept me alone the past several years. Just for that, I'd fancy peeling your skin off like an orange while you were alive and screaming, but that's off topic."

"Quite," I said edgily.

Bones continued as if I hadn't spoken. "But since she insists on still working here, we have to come to an arrangement. As skilled as she is in battle, no one is infallible. If she went down in a fight right now, your operation would be finished, since you have no one strong enough to replace her. This is the first part of what I'm offering. You will never have to fret about her coming back from a job, because unless I'm shriveled on the ground, she will."

"You want to work for me?" Don asked in astonishment.

Bones laughed. "Not for you, old chap. For her. She's the only one I'd listen to, anyway."

My expression must have been as astonished as Don's, because Bones paused and took my hand.

"I'm not fretting over control with you. You can have all of the command you desire as long as we're together. I'll just save my demands for the bedroom."

I flushed. Bones just chuckled and brought my hand to his lips.

Don also looked as though a change in subject were in order. "What's the second part of your offer?"

Bones straightened but still grasped my hand. "Ah, the second part, and this is why you won't refuse me. I can give you what you've been secretly itching for ever since you started your little science project here."

"And what do you think that is?" Don asked, openly skeptical.

"Vampires," Bones responded. "You want to make your own vampires."

"No he doesn't!" I immediately denied.

Except Don wasn't jumping to his own defense. Instead he stared at Bones in a very odd way. Like he'd just found him interesting.

Bones settled back into his chair. "You want what every commander of troops wants—loyal soldiers who are stronger than your enemy. How many times have you wished more of your team had her powers? How often have you longed for soldiers blessed with the same advantages your enemies had? This is a onetime offer, mate. You choose your best, and I'll make them better."

Stunned, I watched Don consider the offer, then he set his hands on the desk.

"What if after they crossed over, they turned on us? That happens, as I know, and then I'd have unleashed mayhem on myself and my remaining team."

"Simple. They threaten you, then they threaten her and I kill them. I wouldn't hesitate for a moment to eliminate a danger to her, and you already have two bodies to prove that. However, a period of apprenticeship might rest your mind. Pick your potentials and give them raw blood. See how they handle the new power. If they can't control a little, then they can't control the rest of it. But if they can . . ." Bones let the sentence dangle.

"Let me get this straight," Don said briskly. "You'll accompany Cat on missions in order to minimize her risk. You'd also agree to change selected soldiers into vampires. They would be under your supervision, terminated if necessary, and directed by me via her. Do I have this right?"

"Yes." No hesitation in Bones's reply. I was still dumbfounded over the entire negotiation.

"Anything else?"

"I have some conditions," I interrupted, seizing the opportunity. "My schedule changes. Your operation just got seriously upgraded, Don, so I don't want to hear any complaints. First, no more surveillance. I better not see *or* hear any of my team spying on me anymore, because after tonight, my location's going to be secret. That way, no one can torture or green-eye the information out of them, or have them just give it up for money, like Brad Parker did. And everything else waits until my father is taken care of. Your brother takes priority, don't you agree, *Uncle*?"

Don was silent for several moments. At last he gave a sardonic smile.

"Well, Cat, Bones . . . I guess we have an agreement."

Parley completed, there were some loose ends before we could leave. "Is my mother still here?"

"She's in one of the bunkers. You want to see her?"

"No. But keep her here. If my father knew where to find me, then she's not safe at her house."

"We also can't have your team wandering around for Max to snatch them up and discover I'm involved, Kitten," Bones stated. "As for the rest of your employees, round them up. They won't remember seeing me."

"What about Noah?" This from Don, and I winced.

"He doesn't know anything."

"That's not what he means," Bones stated in an even way. "Noah would make right good bait for you, whether or not he knows why. Max might reckon you still hold feelings for him."

I hadn't thought of that. "Then put a watch on Noah, Don, work and home. Any sign of the supernatural, and we move in. Maybe we can catch Max at his own trap."

"I'll make the call now," Don promised.

We stood. It had been a long day, and it wasn't over.

"Bones, while you and Don play Bright Eyes with the other staff, I'm going to talk to the team about your new status."

Bones grinned. "Give your bloke my regards, Kitten. Can't wait to start working on him."

I knew who he meant. "*With* Tate, Bones. Not on him."

His smile broadened. "Right."

An hour later, my temples pounded with a nasty headache. Tate, as I expected, had hit the roof. Juan had been unexpectedly blasé after I answered some of his concerns, and since Cooper was the third captain, he'd been roused from his concussion and informed that the cause of it was now officially joining our team. Tate had expected Cooper to back him up, but he'd actually taken it better than Juan had.

"He whipped our asses, Commander. If he wanted us dead, I guess we would be."

"He's the same vampire who trained me, Coop. Oh, and I'm sleeping with him, to save Tate the trouble of announcing it next. Got a problem with any of that?"

Cooper didn't flinch. "You're a freak. Why wouldn't you want a freak also?"

"I don't fucking believe this," Tate said in disgust.

Bones strode into the room. Tate glared at him as Bones put his arm around me.

"Feeling better, mate?" he inquired of Cooper. "If not, you will soon. Don drained a pint out of me just now, Kitten," he said with a grin. "Seems the head pathologist didn't want to stick me himself. Poor bloke was quite jittery, though I can't imagine why."

"Could be because you made dinner out of his assistant, *amigo*," Juan dryly commented.

Cooper hadn't heard that. He swung his gaze to me.

"We're letting him eat people?"

"Apparently," Tate snarled.

"Brad Parker plotted with another vampire to put me out of my misery, Cooper." I shot Tate a dirty look. "You heard about last night? Well, you can thank the late Mr. Parker for giving away my location and my weaknesses."

Cooper eyed Bones, and then shrugged. "So he deserved it. Too quick, though. He should have been hurt first."

Bones smothered a laugh against my temple. "You and I will get along famously, soldier."

Tate muttered something profane, and I'd had enough.

"I want you with me on this, Tate, but I can't force you. Are you in or are you out? Decide now."

Tate folded his arms across his chest. "I'm in, Cat. I'd never leave you. Especially when you've got death breathing down your neck."

"Very funny," I retorted, since Bones was inches from my throat. "And as you know, he doesn't breathe. Now that details about our new team member are settled, I'm leaving. I've got a family reunion to plan."

Twenty-six

WE PULLED AROUND THE SOUTH SIDE OF THE Virginia Tech campus. Bones shut off his motorcycle and left it leaning against a tree. I gave a look around at its stone-front buildings and cobbled streets, students still milling about even though it was eleven at night, and cleared my throat.

"I thought you said we were meeting some big important vampire. Did you just stop here because you wanted to grab a bite to eat first?"

Bones chuckled. "No, luv. This is where we're meeting him. Well, under here, as it were."

My brows rose. "*Under* here?"

He took my arm. "Follow me."

We went across the campus to Derring Hall. Seeing all the young faces milling around reminded me of my own college days. I hadn't graduated—that whole murdering the governor and being scooped up by Don interfered with my diploma plans. Still, I'd more than gotten my chance to get out of my small town and travel. Who knew it would be my skills with a silver knife, instead of graduating with honors, that would be my ticket to a new life?

Once inside Derring Hall, we went down. After several turns and then a long corridor, we were at the basement. There was a guard there, and Bones walked right up to him with a genial smile—and then hit him with his gaze.

"Let us pass, and we were never here," he said. The guard nodded and let us by him without losing the glazed look on his face.

There weren't any other people in the basement. Bones took me past several storage rooms until we came to a small, locked gate. He casually ripped the bolt away from the gate and held it open for me.

"After you, Kitten."

I went inside and waited at the entrance of the narrow, tight tunnel that led into darkness. There were WARNING, ASBESTOS! and other such signs on the walls heralding danger.

"We couldn't have just met at a Starbucks?" I remarked.

Bones shut the grille behind him. "Less chance of anyone seeing or overhearing us down here. No one knows Mencheres is even in the States yet."

"And you said Mencheres is the same vampire who made Ian," I commented thoughtfully. "So that makes him, like, your fang granddaddy."

After a short walk, the tunnel broadened in size. Tubes and wires were all along the wall, and the temperature kept rapidly changing from normal to hot. Once past this section, there were multiple passageways to choose from. It was like a labyrinth down here.

Bones began to walk to the tunnel on the right. "He's my grandsire, yes, but more importantly, he's a very powerful vampire who Ian wouldn't want to cross. Since your father, Max, is a member of Ian's line and still under his protection, any attack against Max would be the same as an attack against Ian in the vampire world."

"But the fact that Max tried to have my head blown off is okay?" I asked irritably.

"You have no Master claiming you under their line," Bones replied in an even tone. "You remember I told you vampires operated under a form of feudalism? When one vampire changes another, they take that person under their protection, and conversely, so does the head Master. But you weren't changed—you were born, so no vampire's ever claimed responsibility for you. That makes you without a Master to defend you against any outside attack."

"So just killing Max once I find him could set off a full-out war with Ian's people, like there aren't already enough problems with your horny sire to begin with."

Bones nodded. "Which is why I'm going to change your status in the vampire world. I'll claim you under my protection, but first I'll need to break free from Ian's line. Otherwise, anything I claim as mine is also his, since he's head of our line. That's why we're meeting with Mencheres. Ian would be a damn sight less likely to retaliate against me if Mencheres chooses to ally himself to my side."

"Did Ian know you were looking for me . . . before?"

"After your run-in with him, yes. I told him I'd been

hunting you to limit the damage you'd do to the undead world. When he expressed his desire for you and fed me your description of our former relationship, I said a few ungentlemanly things to try to discourage him from his pursuit."

"Like what?"

"Let's see . . . I told him that you whined ceaselessly, snored with abominable loudness, and were terrible at shagging. Oh, and that you lacked desirable hygiene."

"You *what*?"

He chuckled. "Now, Kitten, I had your best interest at heart. After all, *you* called me a welsher and said I refused to pay you for your work. Weren't worried about my reputation, were you?"

"I was trying to protect you, not slander you!"

"As was I. But Ian didn't fall for my description and still obsessed over you. Not as much as I did, of course, but he didn't know that."

I'd address his way of trying to discourage Ian later. After all, he could have come up with *something* other than saying I was a whiny, smelly, trumpeting-snoring bad lay.

We reached a fork in the tunnel. Bones went to the left this time, and we ventured farther into the campus's underbelly. *Talk about private*, I thought. We had to be at least fifty feet underground here.

"How about you just kill Ian and I kill Max?" I muttered. "That would solve a lot of undead political hassle, if you ask me."

Bones stopped. He grasped my shoulders, and his face was very serious.

"If it came to a choice between you or Ian, Kitten, yes,

I would cut him down. But despite our many feuds over the years, or the fact that he's being a ruthless sod in his pursuit of you . . ." Bones closed his eyes for a moment. "We have a bond," he said at last. "Ian changed me into what I am, and he's been a part of my life for well over two centuries. If there's a way to solve this without killing him, then that's the route I'll seek."

A wave of shame swept over me. *Idiot*, I lashed myself. *You should have known that.*

"I'm sorry. Of course you couldn't just kill him. I couldn't, either, when I knew who he was."

Bones smiled a trifle grimly. "I may well have to kill him before this is over. But if I do, at least I'll know it was my only choice."

We started walking again. Occasionally I saw graffiti along the walls, showing that these tunnels weren't always kept free of visitors.

"Why is all this down here, anyway?"

"Used to be primarily steam tunnels," Bones replied. "It was how they heated the university above. Now it's also used for phone, computer, and electric wires as well. Some parts of these tunnels run all the way to the power plant. It's right easy to get lost in here, if you don't know where you're going."

Finally we reached another apex, and there, to my amazement, was an underground stream.

Bones stopped. "This is where we meet Mencheres."

"No way," I snorted.

After a minute, there was a grating noise. Then, just like something out of an old Dracula movie, a crypt-like door slowly opened in one of the walls and a dark-haired vampire came out of it. *All he needs is a cape*, I thought irreverently. *Then it would be perfect.*

The vampire didn't have a cape, though, and I felt power slide all over my skin, sharp as an electric shock. *Whoa. Whoever he is, he's packing some* serious *voltage.*

"Grandsire," Bones said, stepping forward. "Thank you for coming."

Mencheres looked no older than thirty. He had long black hair, charcoal-colored eyes, and a hawkishness to his nose that, combined with his finely tinted skin, suggested Middle Eastern ethnicity. But it was his power level that flabbergasted me. His crackling aura was like nothing I'd ever felt before. No wonder Bones had said Ian wouldn't want Mencheres as his enemy. Feeling the power surging off him, neither did I.

"Bones," he said, hugging my lover. "It has been too long."

Okay, at least he sounded friendly.

Bones turned to me. "This is Cat."

I came forward and stuck out my hand, unsure of what the proper protocol was. Mencheres gave me a slight smile and took it.

As soon as his fingers closed over mine, I wanted to jerk my hand back. *Zing!* I might as well have jammed my wet finger in a light socket. I managed to give him the barest shake, then I let go, using all my control not to rub my hand to try and get the numbness out of it. Later I'd have to ask Bones exactly how old Mencheres was. I was betting he measured birthdays by millennia, not centuries.

Once proper greetings were exchanged, Bones dove right in.

"I'm leaving Ian's line," he announced. "Ian wants her, and she wants to murder one of his people, so you can see why I need to shirk my loyalties to him and be head of my own line."

Mencheres flicked his gaze to me. "Do you really think killing your father will make anything in your life better?"

I wasn't prepared for that question, so my reply was a little stuttered.

"Uh, yeah. *Hell* yeah, in fact. For starters, I wouldn't have to worry about hit men sighting my head in their scopes, and for another, I think it would be really, *really* satisfying."

"Vengeance is the emptiest of emotions," Mencheres said dismissively.

"Beats suppressed rage," I shot back.

"I didn't say it was her father she wanted to kill," Bones interjected in a smooth voice. "How did you know that, Grandsire?"

How indeed? My brows lifted. Mencheres shrugged.

"You already know how."

Bones seemed to accept that. I didn't. "*And?*" I prodded.

"Mencheres sees things," Bones replied. "Visions, glimpses of the future, that sort. It's one of his powers."

Great. We had to convince a vampire swami to take our side. Guess if he could see the future, he'd already know whether or not that was a good idea.

"Got any stock tips?" I couldn't help but ask. "The government doesn't pay shit for salary."

"Are you going to claim her as one of yours?" Mencheres asked Bones, ignoring me. "Is that why you wanted to meet with me in secret? To ask for my support should you go to war with Ian over her?"

"Yes," Bones said without blinking, while it was all I could do not to snap, *Shouldn't you already know that, Miss Cleo?*

Mencheres gave me such a look that I shifted uncomfortably. Jeez, I hadn't said it out loud.

Bones sighed. "Kitten, I'm guessing I need to inform you that Mencheres can also read humans' minds, and from his expression, half-breeds, too."

Uh oh. I was *so* busted. "Whoops," I said. Then my eyes narrowed. "Not vampires' minds, I take it, or you wouldn't have phrased it that way."

"No, not vampires' minds," Bones acknowledged. His mouth quirked. "Unless you've been hiding something, Grandsire."

Mencheres also had a ghost of a smile. "If I did have that power, it would have saved me from many wrong decisions. No, just humans. And half-breeds. Have you told her under what pretext you'd claim her as yours, Bones?"

From the way Bones suddenly tensed, I didn't need mind-reading skills to know there was indeed some information he'd left out.

"Fess up," I said warningly.

Bones met my eyes. "Every vampire is territorial. You know that. I found you, I bit you, and I shagged you. All before Ian ever laid eyes on you. In the vampire world, that makes you my . . . my property, unless I willingly relinquished my rights to—"

"Son of a *bitch*!" I burst out. "Bones! Tell me you did *not* intend to growl over me like I was some slab of meat you didn't want to share!"

"I don't see you that way, so why does it matter what loophole I utilized?" Bones flared back. "I frankly don't see why Mencheres even had to bring it up."

"Because I refuse to side with you unless she is aware of all the ramifications," Mencheres replied coolly.

I huffed. "And he didn't need special powers to figure out I'd be pissed. Neither did you, obviously, because you sure left *that* detail out. No way, Bones. No. Way. Go ahead, declare your independence from Ian and be Master of your own line. But you can forget about calling yourself *my* Master, loophole or no loophole."

"You do realize you're being a hypocrite?" he asked in a scalding tone. "Just the day before yesterday, I told Don truthfully that I'd take your orders on missions, but here you refuse to let strangers even *think* you'd heed mine?"

I opened my mouth—and had nothing to refute that with. Damn people who argued using logic. Talk about unfair.

"There has to be another way" was what I settled on in a more rational tone. "Instead of skirting around Ian with sexist loopholes, there's got to be something we can do to make him agree to leave me alone."

"It's not sexist," Mencheres said with a shrug. "If Bones was a woman and you were a man, he'd still have the same claim over you. Vampires don't discriminate by gender. That's a human failing."

"Whatever," I snapped, not interested in comparing the fairness of human versus nosferatu culture.

Then something began to form in my mind. Maybe there *was* a way to use undead societal structure to my advantage . . .

I gave Bones a wide smile. "You're going to tell Ian you found me. And you're going to offer to bring me to him."

†WEПTY-SEVEП

CAT." DON LOOKED UP FROM HIS PAPERWORK. "Come in. I'm just going over the pathology reports from the other day." He looked almost gleeful as he flicked his gaze to Bones. "You have quite a massive component in your blood. We could practically get rid of our other in-house vampires if we siphon a pint a week from you."

"Going to tap me like a tree?" Bones asked in amusement. "Bit of a greedy bloodsucker yourself, aren't you?"

"We came for a reason, Don. You may as well call in Juan, Tate, and Cooper. Then we'll only have to go over this once."

Don, curious, made the call. The three other men filed into the room after several minutes, and when the door shut, I began without preamble.

"You all know I'm a half-breed. What you don't

know, and what I didn't until recently, was that the vampire who raped my mother is Don's brother."

Don looked markedly displeased at being exposed, but I ignored that.

"You remember Liam Flannery from New York? His real name is Ian, and he's the vampire who made Bones. Ian's also the vampire who made my father, Max. Don's known *that* one, too, for years—it's the real reason why we were sent to bring him in. So after we tangled, Ian got all excited over my being a half-breed and decided he wanted me as his new flavor of the week. According to Bones, Ian's the type who won't hesitate to use people I care about to ensure my compliance. There's a way to get him off my back without an all-out bloodbath, but it's dangerous."

This was the difficult part. My plan had been just to challenge Ian to a fight myself, winner takes all, but Bones pointed out that Ian would likely refuse. No, Ian had to feel that he was in control, and there was only one way to ensure that.

Bones made an exasperated noise and plowed ahead. "Look, in order for her to turn the tables on Ian, he needs to be confident that he's got something over her. A valuable hostage, more specifically. Now, Ian's a smart bloke who likely wouldn't kill someone who's a useful bargaining tool, but there are no guarantees. She intends to rescue whoever's bait, then use Ian's guards as bargaining chips to force him to swear to leave her alone. If Ian makes a blood oath promising that, he'll be bound by it in the vampire world, and he would be looked on very shoddily if he refused to bargain for his people out of mere lust. But until she gets there . . .

there will be no one to ensure the safety of whoever volunteers."

There was a hush when Bones finished. Tate was the first to break it.

"This'll keep a vampire from hunting you, Cat? Then count me in."

Don coughed a trifle unsteadily. "There must be a different approach we could take . . ."

"Me, too, *querida*," Juan added. "That *pendaho* can have two worms on the hook instead of one; it will look better."

"I'm in," Cooper said. "Who wants to live forever?"

Jesus, Mary, and Joseph, I was going to squirt tears. How unprofessional.

Bones overrode Don's instant objections with a curt interruption.

"Save it, old chap. They're grown men, and it's not like they've been gardening these past years, is it? Besides, I knew they'd all offer, and here I've only just met them. How could you expect any differently?"

"Cat, you can't take the three top members of my team into a hostile nest the likes of which they've never seen! If they all died, it would destroy this operation, utterly *finish* it!"

Don pounded his fist on the desk for emphasis. Bones leveled him with a look devoid of green.

"Here and now, decide which is more important to you. Your niece . . . or the risk to these men and your operation. We all make choices we have to live with. This is yours."

"And it's not like they're docile lambs," I added. "They're not just bait—they're Trojan horses. Whoever

Ian picks to guard them will never expect how tough they are. They've been fighting vampires for a long time, Don. If I didn't think they could handle it, I'd never let them volunteer."

Don glared at me. I held his gaze, not blinking. Bones had made a prediction on this outcome also.

Don was the first to look away. When he spoke, his voice was rough.

"I pray to God you're not wrong to trust this creature, Cat. If he's played you, we'll all go down in flames for it. He'd better be as good as he is arrogant."

Four out of four. Bones smiled triumphantly. "Don't fret, mate. I'm not playing her, and I *am* as good as I am arrogant. After all, I had you pegged. She was sure you'd refuse. I told her you wouldn't."

Don looked as worried as I felt, but he didn't object further.

"It will take a few weeks to assemble everything," Bones said, "and the three of you will be busy until then. If things go south, you'll need to react quickly. You all know the price behind drinking vampire blood, right?"

Cooper didn't. In a few minutes, he was informed about the ramifications of his actions in the cave. He took it far better than I had. He simply snorted once in disbelief.

"Welcome to the freak club," I sympathized. "All of you will need to be immune to vampire mind control, and blood's the only way to do that. Anyone who refuses will stay back. I won't risk your lives, or the lives of those around you, by letting some vamp green-eye you into submission."

"I'm up for juicing," Tate said, again being the first to offer. "But you won't mind if I refuse to suck blood off his tongue like you did?"

Bones let out a bark of amusement. "Don't fret; you're not my type. Anyone else have a concern?"

There were no other voices of dissent. Bones rose.

"Right then. Let's go to the lab, so Don can put my vein on tap again. Really, old chap, you're as excited over my blood as any vamp is over a juicy artery. Sure you're not hiding some family traits?"

"That's not funny," Don brusquely responded, but he also stood, and we proceeded to the lab. The path leading to it had been cleared of other employees, minimizing Bones's exposure on the premises. The same was done to the pathology unit. Once we got there, Bones gave Tate a calculating look.

"Ready for an upgrade? After your first dose, I'm going to beat the seven shades of shit out of you to see how much you can take."

"Bring it on" was Tate's reply. "Cat's been pounding on me for years. *Years*. How long have you spent with her, combined? Only six months?"

Bones grabbed him, intending to do something painful, no doubt, but I hauled on his arm.

"Quit it! Tate, enough of the taunts, and Bones, *how* old are you? Why don't I just give you a pair of my panties to hang around your neck? Then whenever you feel jealous, you can wave them at whoever's pissing you off."

"Like you wear panties," Tate muttered.

I punched him. "Not that it's *any* of your business, but I only go without when I'm on a job!"

Instead of being incensed by Tate's knowledge of my underwear, Bones gave me an odd look as he sat in the chair Don indicated. Don set up a line and a bag and inserted the needle, since Dr. Lang, the head pathologist, still didn't want to stick Bones himself.

"Kitten, are you still hunting vampires without your knickers on?" he asked with that same strange countenance.

"If I'm playing the bait, yes, but if it's a search-and-destroy, no. Why?"

His lips twitched. "We'll talk about it later," he demurred.

I pounced. For him to look so peculiar, there had to be something to it.

"Tell me *now*."

Five sets of eyes regarded him expectantly. Only Don didn't look intrigued at this exchange. His eyes were glued to the IV bag filling with red liquid.

Bones's lips twitched more. "It's just that you can expand your wardrobe, luv. Not that I'm advocating it, of course, but then I'm biased. That thing I told you about no knickers making a difference when it came to luring vampires . . . well. I might have stretched the truth a bit."

"You *what*?" My mouth dropped open in incredulity.

Juan gave Bones the most admiring look he'd bestowed on him yet.

"You talked her into going without panties all these years? *Madre de Dios*, now that's impressive. I could learn a great deal from you, *amigo*."

"You *lied* to me."

I ignored Juan's praise and advanced until I pointed

a finger in Bones's chest, which shook with suppressed laughter.

"Now, Kitten, it wasn't exactly a lie. Merely an embellishment of the truth. I told you vampires found that right irresistible, and some do. Myself, for one, whenever I'm around you. And do you remember how you were back then? So uptight and prissy, I couldn't resist needling you. Really, in all fairness, I never intended to let it go on this long—"

My voice trembled with wrath. "You perverted, depraved bastard, how could you!"

"What a mean trick," Tate agreed instantly.

Bones reached out to me, chuckling, but I slapped his hand.

"Don't touch me. You're a dead man."

"Since before you met me," he agreed, still grinning. "I love you, Kitten."

"Don't try to get out of this. We'll see if you love me when I pay you back."

"Even then I will love you," Bones called out as I stomped away. "Even then."

I watched with empathy as the tremors ripped through Tate. The white cup that had held half a pint of Bones's blood fell from his trembling hand. Bones gripped him by the shoulders until the glaze faded from Tate's eyes, he stopped shaking, and he breathed without sounding like he was choking.

"Let go of me," Tate snarled as soon as he could talk.

Bones released him. Tate inhaled several deep breaths, and his widened gaze met mine.

"Jesus, Cat. This isn't like before at the cave. What the hell is in that asshole's blood?"

I didn't respond to the insult but only to the question. "Power. The blood you had before was from a weaker, shriveling vampire, so it doesn't compare. Are you okay now?"

"Everything is so loud, and so clear." He shook himself like a dog flinging off water. "And the smell! Goddamn, Juan, you stink! Didn't you shower today?"

"Fuck off," Juan growled, looking sheepish. "I showered, but I ran out of soap. Didn't know we were getting sniff tested."

I knew to suddenly have a vampire's sense of smell was an incredible thing. It was like being born blind and then later recovering your sight. You couldn't believe how much you'd missed.

"All right, Juan, you're next."

After all three men had been given blood, we proceeded to the training room. It went well, though I'm sure my guys had other views over their treatment at Bones's hands. Don was nervous, but he visibly relaxed when Bones revived Tate after their bout and sent him on his way with constructive criticism and even praise. Tate took his place by my side and made one statement about the experience.

"Bastard hits harder than a fucking freight train."

I just smiled. "I know."

"You've schooled them brilliantly, Kitten."

Cooper had just been perked up with a blood chaser, and Bones glided over to me.

"They are without a doubt the toughest humans I've

come across," he said to Don next. "With the additional strength of blood, they'll be equal to a young vampire."

Bones kissed me on the forehead as he spoke. That single touch, combined with the past couple of hours of watching his shirtless predatory ballet, made me react in a purely instinctual manner. My loins clenched, greedily demanding attention.

Uh oh. I had to get out of here. Fast. Before the boys picked up on the fragrance of my lust.

"I'm off to clean up; I'm sweaty. I'll, ah, see you all later," I said, and practically ran out of the room in my attempt to salvage my dignity.

"Where do you think you're going?" I heard Tate ask, with an edge to his voice. "Wrong way, Bones. The men's showers are in the opposite direction."

"I'll file that away with all the other information that doesn't pertain to me" was Bones's mocking reply.

I ignored them and kept going, reaching my locker room, shutting the door, and stripping off my clothes in a blur. A cold shower, that's what I needed.

Tate's voice still reached me through the door. "Got something you're embarrassed to show us, vampire?" he taunted.

Bones merely laughed. From the sound of it, he was almost at the door.

"Just not stupid. Where would *you* rather be?"

"Don't answer that," I heard Juan caution Tate, and then Bones came inside my locker room.

I was already under the cold spray of water. When Bones turned his eyes to me, I shivered, but it had nothing to do with the chilly liquid.

"Not here. It's . . . inappropriate."

Bones removed his pants and kicked off his shoes in a single motion that made my breath catch. He came toward me, reaching behind me to turn the water from cold to hot.

"Sod 'em," he responded, kneeling in front of me. His mouth caressed my stomach. "I want you, Kitten, and you want me." His tongue snaked out and moved lower with relentless accuracy. "That's all I care about."

I clutched his shoulders as my knees went weak and my worries over propriety went out the metaphorical window. The hot water poured over us in much the same manner as the blood now racing through me.

"I'm going to fall," I warned him with a gasp.

"I'll hold you," he promised throatily.

I believed him.

When we emerged an hour later, my face was flushed from sex, the heat of the shower, and the look Tate gave me when I walked into my office. He was waiting for me there. Bones had stopped by the lab again for more blood extraction, per Don's request.

"Christ, Cat, you couldn't even wait until later to crawl into the coffin with him?" Tate asked, giving his head a disgusted shake.

That succeeded in dampening my good spirits. "First of all, none of your business, and second, how do you know we weren't just talking?" We weren't, but that wasn't the point.

Tate snorted rudely. "My senses just got put on steroids, remember? Not only could I hear you—now I can smell it on you. You reek of it, even after your shower."

God, how could I be so *stupid*? Frankly, I was used to being the only one with extra perceptions.

"Then I switch to my first point, which is that it's none of your business." No way was I going to cringe under his gaze.

Another snort, but with bitterness this time. "Yeah, you've made that crystal-clear."

The pain on his face stopped my next spiteful remark. "Tate. I'm not trying to hurt you or prove anything. What happens between him and me doesn't have anything to do with you."

As if mentally summoned, Bones appeared in the doorway. Tate brushed by him without acknowledging his presence, throwing a last parting comment to me as he went.

"You might not be out to prove anything, but he sure as hell is. Forget him wearing your panties around his neck—he just smothered himself in your scent."

"Ready, luv?" Bones asked, ignoring Tate.

"Is he right?" I didn't let it drop, even though I could already guess the answer.

Bones regarded me with all seriousness. "Partially. I always want you, and you know how fighting gets my blood up, but did it cross my mind that I'd be literally rubbing his nose in it? Yes. Better he lose his illusions, fast, when it comes to you. But would I have acted any differently if we were alone? Of course not. I can't get enough of you."

"This isn't going to be easy," I grumbled as we headed toward the exit.

Bones shrugged. "Nothing worthwhile ever is."

Twenty-eight

Bones was very busy the next day, pulling in hispeople from around the nation and even across the globe. He wanted them nearby when he told Ian that he'd found me and had hostages. Bones made me stay put while he went to my house and fetched my cat, who hadn't been happy to be left alone for two-plus days. Then the next morning we woke up at ten, frightfully early for us both, and headed straight to the compound.

"You said you had captive vampires here, right, Kitten?" he asked after we arrived.

"Yeah, three of them, why?"

Bones clucked his tongue in contemplation. "They might be useful. Let me see them."

Tate, Juan, and Cooper accompanied us down to the lower level where the vampires were housed. The guards averted their eyes when Bones walked past, having been instructed by Don not to interfere, but they had never seen a vampire unfettered and strolling about. Their obvious discomfort filled the air.

"In this pen we have Grumpy," I narrated, flipping up the concealing liner that hid the vampire in his prison. It was only raised when the other guards were safely out of eyesight. Since Tate, Juan, and Cooper were juiced with Bones's blood, they could look at him and not worry. "His real name is Dillon, or so he told us. He's about thirty, I guess, in grave years."

Dillon's blue eyes widened when they met the cool, appraising brown ones. Bones nodded, indicating he was done viewing him.

"Next is Jack, but he's known as Chirpy. He's got a real high-pitched voice, hence the nickname. I'd say sixty? Seventy? We snagged him at a baseball game. He liked to drink the beer vendor girls."

Sixty or seventy again referred to his undead years, but the living ones didn't seem far off from that number, either. Jack was small, wrinkled, and frail-appearing. Right up until he'd try to rip your throat out.

"And this"—I raised the last shield to reveal the blond vampire I'd captured months ago—"is Sunshine. We don't know her real name; she never told us."

As soon as Sunshine looked up, she vaulted off her cot in a blur of speed to press herself against the glass.

"*Bones!* How did you get here? Never mind, just kill them and let me *out*!"

"Belinda, fancy seeing you here," Bones chuckled. "Sorry to disappoint, but I'm not here to rescue you."

"You know her?" I asked foolishly, since it was obvious.

She touched the glass. "How can you say that, after what we meant to each other?"

I stiffened, but Tate jumped right in. "You fucked Sunshine?"

I was waiting for his reply as well, with a pointed glare.

"We didn't mean anything to each other aside from a few shags, Belinda," Bones answered the question bluntly with his rejoinder.

My hands clenched. Now I wished I'd killed her instead of capturing her.

Juan said something in Spanish I couldn't follow, and to my added amazement, Bones replied in the same language. Juan's forehead crinkled as he laughed at whatever the exchange was.

"That's rude," I snapped, not amused in the slightest. Somehow I knew they weren't discussing Sunshine's— or Belinda's—teeth.

For the first time, I looked her over as a woman, and I didn't like what I saw. Belinda was very pretty, even without a smidgen of makeup. She had long blond hair, hence the nickname we'd given her, big breasts, and a small waist on top of curvy hips. Her cornflower-blue eyes complemented her full pink lips. *All the better to kiss Bones with . . .*

"Sorry, Kitten," Bones apologized, switching back to English.

Juan clapped me on the back. "He speaks better Spanish than I do, *querida*."

"Apparently there are a *lot* of things I don't know about him," I purred dangerously.

Tate hid a smile behind a sudden cough.

Bones turned back to Belinda. "Quit batting your lashes at me. If you're in there, then you tried to hurt her." He nodded at me. "So you could shrivel to dust for all I bother. However, your stay here could be more pleasant if two things happen. The first involves the lovely lady at my side. She would have to agree. The second pertains to your total cooperation or, failing that, your gruesome, prolonged death. Are we clear?"

Belinda nodded and stepped back from the glass. I shut the obscuring screen, since her face was more than I wanted to see anymore.

"I for one vote for her gruesome, prolonged death," I said as I stomped away. When we were out of the holding level for the vampires, I rounded on Bones.

"You and her? *Eww.*"

My three captains hung back, but with their new hearing abilities, it didn't matter. Bones crossed his arms and let out a resigned noise.

"Kitten, this was before you. It didn't mean anything."

I understood that, but still. This felt worse than when I'd met another of Bones's previous girlfriends, Francesca. At least *she'd* been helping us track down a scumbag who used to run a Meals on Wheels with humans as his main course. Belinda, who I'd met when her roommate brought me home thinking I'd make a nice dinner for two, had no such saving attributes.

"Clearly it meant something to *her.*"

Bones shrugged. "Then kill her, if it makes you feel

better. Can't say I'd blame you, and I truly don't care. If you like, I'll do it myself."

That stopped me in my tracks. By his face, Bones was serious. He really would kill her, or just stand by and watch while I did.

"I don't murder people just because I'm jealous." *Not yet, anyhow.* "Fine. I'll be adult, even though the thought of you with her makes me want to hurl. So, then. What's your idea?"

Tate, Juan, and Cooper filed into the training room. They weren't wearing full battle gear, which would have been a bulletproof vest, a flexible silver-lined neck protector (which I designed after Dave's death), or automatic and semi-automatic guns complete with silver cartridges. No, they were each wearing just the usual cotton pants with crewneck T-shirt that all our team wore while training.

Except this was no ordinary training operation, even by our standards. Next to me, Bones held Belinda in an iron grip. Don, safe in his overlook box above us, looked decidedly bleak. He hadn't liked this idea. Neither had I, but that didn't mean I couldn't see the merit of it.

"Are you guys ready?" I asked.

My tone was calm, belying my inner churning stomach. All three men nodded.

"Then take a knife, each of you. Just one."

They complied, going over to the container where we had knives piled up like so much garbage. I glanced at Bones. He nodded once and then bent to Belinda's ear.

"Remember what I told you," he said very softly, yet his voice dripped with ice.

Then he released her, and she charged like a blond Tasmanian devil at my men.

They scattered, moving with a speed that would have been impossible for them a week ago. Pumped full of Bones's blood, however, they managed to avoid her first grab. Tate spun behind Belinda, flinging his single knife at her back, and it lodged to the hilt right where her heart would be.

She swung around, reaching behind her while I barked out a reprimand.

"That's great if you're intending to kill her, but I told you to treat this situation like a test run for Ian's guards. If they're *dead*, what hostages am I supposed to bargain with?"

A fleeting look of sheepishness crossed Tate's face. "Sorry," he muttered. "Just knee-jerk reaction, I guess."

Belinda snatched the knife out of her back and flung it at Tate's feet.

"Asshole," she growled at him.

Bones gave me a knowing look. "See why I insisted on steel knives instead of silver? I reckoned one of them might panic and go for the kill instead of the capture."

I knew it was more than nerve-wracking to face a vampire with nothing more than a single weapon, but Tate and the others had to master their emotions. Not only would it be bad for bargaining purposes to be without hostages, but if we slaughtered Ian's men, I was guessing he'd be even more unreasonable to deal with.

"Your objective is to restrain Belinda with nonlethal

means," I said sharply. "If you can't manage to do that, then you're off this mission. Period."

"And if after an hour you haven't restrained me," Belinda purred, "I get to taste one of you. Mmm, fresh blood. I haven't had *that* in over a year."

She licked her lips as she said it, eyeing them with a lustfulness that had nothing to do with sex. Juan swallowed. Tate backed away. Even the normally stoic Cooper looked uneasy. This was news to them.

"For motivation," I said coolly. "Now, who's going to be happy in an hour? You guys, or her?"

Belinda bared her fangs and leapt at them again. This time, she picked just one and dove low, knocking Juan's legs out from under him. Juan scrambled, but Belinda was faster. She had her fangs near his throat before he could push her away.

I tensed, ready to hurl myself into the action, but Bones grasped my arm. At that same moment, Cooper and Tate jumped on Belinda. Cooper yanked her head back by her hair, and Tate gave her a roundhouse kick to the face that would have snapped the neck of a normal person.

Belinda was dazed for a moment. Only a moment. Then she reached behind her and flung Cooper over her head so hard, he landed a dozen feet away.

"Let them handle it," Bones said low. "You can't always be there to protect them."

I set my jaw. Sure, Bones had threatened Belinda with truly horrible punishment if she got out of line and killed one of them, but that wouldn't make the unlucky one any less dead. Bones didn't think she was dumb enough to try it. I wasn't so confident. Still, his logic had been undeniable. Belinda was an average-strength vampire, and if my guys couldn't handle her, then they couldn't be counted on with Ian's men. *Nothing like trial by fang*, I thought grimly. *Come on, guys, make me proud. Take the blond bimbo down.*

Tate and Juan circled around Belinda while Cooper got up and shook himself. His forehead was bleeding. Belinda's nostrils flared with hunger. She glanced at Juan, smiled, and then ripped her top open. Her full, bra-less breasts bounced into view.

Juan stared, faltering for an instant. It was all the time Belinda needed. She lunged, slamming her fist into his head. Juan's eyes rolled up, and he dropped to the floor. Tate chased her, but she'd already reached Cooper. A hard blow to his abdomen had him instinctively hunching, and her tongue snaked out to lick the red trail dripping from his forehead.

"An appetizer," she murmured, then lifted Cooper like he was a toy and threw him at Tate, who was almost on them. The two men went sprawling with a jumble of limbs.

I gritted my teeth. Bones reached down and gave my hand a squeeze. I knew what he was thinking. We'd have to come up with a Plan B for capturing Ian's men, because Betty Boop here was whipping their asses even though the odds were three against one. Well, two against one now, since Juan was solidly passed out. Wait until I got ahold of him, letting a pair of tits distract him like that. Juan would wish he hadn't woken up.

Fifty minutes later, Tate and Cooper were soaked with sweat, Juan was just coming to, and Belinda hadn't been successfully restrained. Oh, Tate and Cooper had come close a few times, but they hadn't managed to hold on to her long enough to hand her back to Bones, which had been their objective. My stomach seemed to drop. If it had just been a matter of taking a kill shot, they would have succeeded several times over. But they couldn't subdue her without resorting to unacceptable means. Motherfucker. That was going to have two bad consequences, the first of which would start now.

Belinda smiled with her fangs fully extended. "I won, so I want my victory spoils. Unless you're a liar, Bones."

Bones crossed his arms, giving her a hard stare. "I said you'd get your prize. I didn't specify *when*, however."

Belinda began to curse him when, amazingly, Tate interrupted her.

"Let's get this over with," he said shortly, and walked—or rather limped—up to her.

My gaze widened. "Tate—" I began.

"Save it," he cut me off. "We failed you, Cat. You think her biting me is gonna hurt more than that?"

The rawness in his tone made me blink and turn away. I wanted to tell him it wasn't his fault, that even with the added strength from Bones's blood, he was still human and Belinda was still *not*. It was a lot easier to kill than to capture a vampire, even for me, or Don would've had more sets of fangs in his undead stable. But I knew my sympathy would only make Tate feel worse, so I didn't say anything. I pretended to be fascinated by the wall in the opposite direction from where he was.

"Who says you're the one I want?" Belinda asked dismissively.

"Doesn't matter; I'm the one you're gonna *get*," Tate replied, his tone hardening. "You understand chain of command, suck head? Out of the three of us, I'm the top of the chain, so you're getting my vein and no one else's."

That made me blink more rapidly. God, how like Tate to insist on taking the bullet, or in this case, the bite. It was what made him such a great leader. He never shirked from his duty to his men.

I felt rather than saw Belinda smile. "I guess you'll do, then. Come here."

"Not so fast," Bones said, even as I composed myself and turned around. "Wrist only, Belinda. Not his neck."

She gave a pout that was both menacing and sultry at the same time. "But I like the throat better."

"Too bloody bad," Bones said coldly. "Argue again and you'll get nothing."

I'd been about to insist on the same thing. A ripped-up arm was a damn sight less lethal than a ripped-up jugular, just in case Belinda thought about reneging on her promise to behave. Still, she seemed afraid enough of Bones to believe that he'd make her more than sorry if she did, which I guess stemmed from her knowing his reputation. That's why Bones picked Belinda versus our other two caged vamps to test the guys, he'd explained. They hadn't known him, so they didn't know that he would follow through with exactly what he said. Belinda did know him. Too much of him for my liking, but there was nothing I could do about that.

She smiled as she reached out to Tate. Her shirt was still hanging open, leaving her breasts bare, and she cradled his arm next to her. Tate's heart rate was way above normal and increasing, but I thought that had to do more with the anxiousness over being bitten versus excitement over Belinda's tits.

"Don't worry, gorgeous, you'll like it," she purred, giving her fangs a last lick.

Tate grunted. "Not on your afterlife, bitch."

Belinda just laughed. Low, throaty, and knowing. "Yes you will." Then she sank her sharp incisors into Tate's forearm.

I saw the tremor go through him even as his heart began to beat faster. He thinned his lips, but not before a soft sound, almost like surprise, slipped from them. When Belinda swallowed and drew deeper, sucking on his arm, Tate's eyes fluttered closed for a second before he snapped them open. And stared at me.

It was only a few moments, but it seemed to stretch much longer. Tate's indigo gaze took on that same heated intensity it had the night he'd gotten drunk and confessed how he felt about me. I knew he'd be feeling that intoxicating warmth slipping through his veins. That heady, seductive rush that belied all logic. It didn't happen every time a vampire bit someone, of course. I knew from experience after some nasty fights with them that a bite could hurt like hell. But when a vamp didn't want it to hurt—it *didn't*. Not even in the slightest way.

"That's enough," Bones said in a clipped tone.

Belinda slowly drew back, licking the drops of blood from her fangs. Tate didn't move. He just kept staring at me like I'd somehow grown undead powers and mesmerized him.

"Close the holes," Bones directed Belinda. Tate hadn't

even bothered to wipe the blood leaking out in a slow drip from his arm.

Belinda scored her thumb on a fang and held it over the punctures. They vanished in seconds.

"Is this why you can't stay away from him, Cat?" Tate finally asked, ignoring everyone else around him.

I was stunned at the question, but Bones only smiled, showing a hint of his own fangs.

"You'd like to believe that, wouldn't you, mate?"

"Tate, why would you even *think* such a thing?" I managed.

"Don't bother, luv," Bones said lightly, still showing that same toothsome smile. "I don't care what lies he uses to comfort himself with when he's alone at night and you're with me. Belinda, your time-out's over. Back to your cell."

We left without another word, Belinda still licking her lips as we corralled her back to the lower level and her confinement.

Twenty-nine

WE BROUGHT BELINDA OUT EVERY DAY TO
train with Tate, Juan, and Cooper. This was at
their insistence, not mine. They refused to accept that
they couldn't rise to the challenge of pinning her, and
were determined to still play an active role in capturing
Ian's men. I didn't like it, but Tate had been as adamant
as I'd ever seen him. Belinda didn't seem to mind. Although she didn't get her prize of fresh blood anymore,
she did get to leave her small cell and also had an extra
bag of plasma daily for cooperating. Plus I think she
liked how frustrated they were by their inability to pin
her—at least at first.

After four days of humiliation, the guys started getting better at it. They managed a few times to plug Belinda's chest at just the right angle so one twist would
have ended her, if the knife had been silver.

And that, I knew, was enough to make any vampire
suddenly become really, *really* cooperative. With an-

other week or so of practice, they might be ready for Bones to make that call to Ian saying he'd found me and had hostages. Then I could put into action my *other* plan. The one regarding my father that I hadn't told Bones about. Oh yeah. I was looking forward to that.

On Thursday we went to pick up one of Bones's people from the airport. This person was flying in from London, and was apparently the first vampire Bones had ever made. Some days, vampire hierarchy felt like *The Godfather* to me. On acid.

"You haven't asked and there's been little time, but you need to know who it is we're getting, Kitten."

We'd just reached the section of the airport where the rest of the nonflying public waited for arriving passengers. With today's airline security, it was as far as we were allowed to go, unless Bones turned on his optical headlights.

"Another old flame?" I joked.

Bones didn't laugh. "You could call her that, yes."

I needed a gin for this crap. "Great, can't wait to meet her."

"You remember I told you when I was human, one of my clients saved my life by convincing the judge to ship me to Australia instead of hanging me for pick-pocketing? Well, that was Annette. After I returned to London as a vampire, I looked for the people who'd shown me kindness. Madame Lucille, the bordello owner who helped raise me, was dead by then, as were many of the prostitutes I'd lived with, but Annette was still there. I offered her this life, and she accepted. She's who we're picking up now."

Shit. I hated her already, and we hadn't even met. That was a new low for me.

"And she'll be staying with us tonight. How cozy."

Bones took my hand. "Don't let it trouble you. You're the only woman for me, Kitten. Believe that."

There was a whoosh of charged air moments later. "She's here," he said unnecessarily.

A woman walked toward us with the unmatched grace only a vampire could harness. Her cool, patrician features screamed aristocracy, and her lightly lined skin had that trademark glowing luminescence. *Why couldn't she be ugly?* was my first thought. *She looks like a cross between Marilyn Monroe and Susan Sarandon!*

Her champagne-colored eyes fixed immediately on mine, and right away, I knew we had something in common. She already didn't like me, either.

"Crispin, can I have a kiss after my long flight?"

Her accent was pure British upper-crust. She was also chicly dressed in a navy jacket with matching pants, and I'd bet her shoes cost as much as my last paycheck. Just looking at her, I felt like I had a smear of something on my face, or food in my teeth.

"Of course," Bones replied, brushing his lips across each of her cheeks. She returned the gesture while giving me a once-over that made me feel as insignificant as her smirk judged me to be.

He turned to me. "This is Cat," he introduced me.

I held out my hand. She shook it with ladylike graciousness, only tightening her pale, delicate-looking paw for an instant.

Oh, she had power as well. Not a Master, but a nice, steady level of torque.

"Delighted to finally meet you, darling. I so hoped Crispin would be able to locate you." She traced a finger down his face as if in solace. "Poor sweet dear, he was positively wretched with worry that something ill had befallen you."

It was official. I hated her. How gracious of her to remind me that I'd made him miserable for several years. Where was a nice silver dagger when I needed one?

"As you can see, Annette, he found me safe and sound." For effect, I brought his clasped hand to my lips and kissed it.

Her smile grew frosty. "My bags should be arriving momentarily. Crispin, why don't you fetch the car whilst Cat and I collect my things?"

It was a toss-up which I didn't like more—being alone with her, or offering to get the car so he would be. I chose the first, since it was more bearable, and Bones left us to get our ride.

Annette had a lot of things, which she helpfully loaded onto me like I was a pack mule while making conversation zinging with underlying hostility.

"Don't you have lovely skin? All that fresh country air no doubt played a part. Didn't Crispin tell me you came from a farm?" *Like the animals*, her smug smile implied.

I hoisted a heavy suitcase over my shoulder before I replied. God, what had she packed, bricks?

"A cherry orchard. But that hardly affected my complexion. The vampire who raped my mother gave me that."

She clucked her tongue. "Faith, I had difficulty believing Crispin when he told me what you were, but after two hundred years together, you take someone at their word."

Nicely done. Throw in how long you've had him, like I don't already know. But two could play at low blows.

"I can't wait to hear all about you, Annette. Bones barely mentioned you at all, just something about how you used to pay him to have sex with you when he was human."

She gave an arch little curve of her lips. "How charming that you call him by his acquired name. All his newer acquaintances do that."

Acquaintances? My teeth ground. "That was the name he gave me when we first met. We are who we become, not who we start out as." *He's not your boy toy anymore, got it?*

"Indeed? Here I've always believed people truly never change from what they were to begin with."

"We'll see about that," I muttered.

With her numerous items weighing me down, we proceeded to the exit. As I followed behind her, I took the opportunity to study her. Her hair was shoulder-length and pale strawberry-blond, just lovely next to her peaches-and-cream skin. She was far more voluptuous than I, and about three inches shorter than my five-eight height. If she were human, I'd judge her to be in her mid-forties. That didn't sit in a negative column with her, though, because she gave off a smoldering, ripe sensuality that made youth look like a boring waste of time.

Bones took one look at me buried under all her luggage and vaulted over to assist. "Blimey, Annette. You should have told me how many bags you had!"

"Oh, forgive me, Cat," Annette chuckled in false apology. "I'm accustomed to having an underling travel with me."

"Don't mention it." Tightly. *Underling! Who the hell did she think she was?*

Luggage finally stored in the trunk, we drove off.

"When are the rest of our people arriving?" she queried, settling back in her seat. We drove a new vehicle, as my Volvo was known to Max. This was a loaded BMW. I'd ask Bones later where he got it.

"Today and tomorrow. By Friday, I reckon we'll all be in place."

Annette sniffed, though it wasn't like she needed to clear her nose. "I say, Crispin, how did Belinda get herself in Cat's little snare? I haven't seen her since your birthday six years ago, or was it five?"

"She got caught because she started running with a group who liked to bring home live meals."

There was something cold in his tone that perked my ears up even as Annette's smile grew sly.

"Terrible. She must have really changed. Wasn't it only five years ago that we three got together?"

Bones glared at her in the rearview mirror right as I translated "We three got together." I was betting it hadn't been for tea. And five years ago, Bones had been with me.

"Answer the question, *honey*. Was it six or five years ago that the three of you all fucked? See, Bones already told me that he'd screwed Belinda, Annette, but thank you for letting me know you participated also."

Bones pulled the car to the shoulder of the road.

"I won't tolerate such rudeness, Annette," he said, pivoting to face her. "She knows bloody well what you're implying, as you can see, and I don't know why you feel the need to throw that up at her. You also know that it was eight years ago, before I met her, and I'll thank you not to entertain her with any more recollections."

He sounded as pissed as I felt. Annette glanced at me before raising her brows in feigned innocence.

"I apologize. Perhaps it was the long flight which made me forget myself."

"Kitten." Bones looked at me. "Is that sufficient?"

No, it wasn't, and I'd have cheerfully thrown Her Majesty *and* her hundred pounds of baggage to the curb, but that wasn't mature.

"I think I can handle a little ménage à trois reminiscing, but just for the record, Annette, you can forget any repeats involving the three of us."

"Wouldn't dream of it," she assured me with a gleam I caught from the rearview mirror. Oh, she and I weren't through. I'd bet my life on it.

The rest of the drive passed without incident. Annette made arrangements for alternate accommodations after tonight, to my relief. Bones planned to tell Ian next week that he'd found me, and he'd pretend to capture my three captains the following week. And somewhere in the midst of worrying about Ian, the safety of my men, my father actively trying to kill me, and Bones successfully winning his freedom, I had the image of Annette, Belinda, and Bones doing the naked pretzel in my mind. Goddamn her. That was the last thing I needed to think about.

When Annette heard the part of the plan involving my men, she was fascinated.

"Mere humans? Willingly walking into Ian's den as his collateral? Oh, Crispin, you must let me meet them. Can we have them for supper tonight?"

"She better mean to dinner with real food on the table," I muttered.

"Why, Cat, that's precisely what I meant. Can't have me eating the bait, now can we?" She chuckled.

Bones glanced at me. I shrugged. "It's not such a bad idea to have them meet first. Maybe it will make them less jittery about this whole Army of Darkness thing." Or more so, depending on Annette.

"Whatever you like. I don't care. If they agree, I'll pick them up when I get Rodney. He's our other guest tonight."

"Rodney the ghoul?" How low I had slipped on the Humanity Totem Pole to be so excited about seeing a flesh-eater again, although *that* would complicate my menu. "Oh, I liked him. He didn't get angry no matter how many times my mother insulted him."

Bones gave me a sideways smile. He'd just finished taking Annette's bags to her room. She was sitting at the kitchen table, sipping tea. I sat on the couch with a tall glass of gin and tonic that was almost empty.

"Wait." I hated saying this in front of Queen Bitch,

but whispering was redundant. "Is he . . . I mean, because of the last time we met . . . does he hate me?"

It was Rodney's house we'd been staying at years ago when I left Bones. The two of them had gone out on an errand, and there had no doubt been an unpleasant scene when they returned to find it empty.

Bones sat next me, setting my glass down.

"Of course he doesn't hate you. He was right sore at Don for threatening you, although we didn't know who'd done it then. As far as your mother—well. She didn't make a friend."

I gave a watery laugh. "She seldom does."

He leaned closer. "Actually, he's a bit unsettled himself about seeing you again, but not for that reason. Rodney thought perhaps you'd be upset with him over Danny."

Ah. I'd forgotten about that. The murder of my ex-boyfriend hadn't ranked high on my current list of worries. Poor Danny. He'd certainly regretted seducing me in a permanent way.

"That was more your doing than his, Bones. We've already been over that. Besides, he's coming to help."

"That's what I told him you'd say."

Miffed, I poked him in the chest. "You think you know everything?"

His hands caressed my back. "Not everything, but some things. I knew without a doubt I'd fallen in love when we met. Then I knew I'd do anything to make you feel the same way."

Annette's cup clattered to the table. "I'll take myself off to shower now."

Bones didn't even glance up. "Do that."

The bathroom door closed decisively behind her.

"You keep saying you fell in love right away, but you beat me unconscious, and you were so surly with me those first few weeks."

Bones chuckled. "You asked for that beating, and you'd have stomped me into submission if I'd shown you any weakness. Of course I didn't let on how I felt about you. You hated the very sight of me."

"I don't hate you *now*."

To prove the point, I gave a long, slow lick to his neck. He responded by gathering me up in his arms and heading toward the stairs.

I gasped at his clear intent. "Wait, I was teasing! We can't, she'd hear us!" Even with the shower running, we might as well have invited her to join us after all.

Bones kept going, climbing the steps three at a time, and then depositing me on the bed.

"*I* wasn't teasing, and I don't care." He kissed me thoroughly, tugging off my clothes. "We only have an hour. Let's not waste it."

Thirty

"I t'll take me about two hours to fetch Rodney and pick up your blokes, Kitten. Are you going to be all right with Annette until then?"

Bones was already running late. I was the reason for his tardiness, and I couldn't bring myself to care.

"Don't worry about it. If she gets really lippy, I have my silver." For emphasis, I glanced at the stack of weapons in the closet.

He snorted in laughter. "If it's all the same to you, I'd rather come back to both of you the way I left you."

"If you insist. Go on, I'll be waiting for you."

It was said automatically, but his eyes clouded. With a sigh, I flung myself out of bed and hugged him.

"You can tell Rodney to bet his ass I'll be here this time."

Bones pressed his lips to my forehead and smiled, chipper again.

"Too right you will. Call your men and have them ready; I'll see you shortly."

"Don't smack Tate on the way over."

He snorted. "We'll see."

After he was gone, I made the invite to dinner, then listened for five minutes as Don argued about the men leaving the compound with Max on the loose.

"Two vamps and a ghoul, Don, plus me. Who's gonna take that on? It's only dinner, for God's sake. I swear they're not on the menu. They may as well meet one of the people they'll be trusting their lives to."

He finally gave the phone to Tate and relayed the offer. Tate accepted at once. He wanted to check out every deadhead he could, as he so nicely put it. There was no food in the house and not enough time to cook, so I showered and went to the kitchen to find the phone book. Rodney would be shit out of luck, because no delivery place I saw advertised raw meat or body parts. I settled on Italian, and ordered different dishes for everyone. Delivery would be in an hour, right about when they'd arrive.

Annette glided into the room twenty minutes later, dressed in a long, flowing skirt with a pale peach top. She looked like a million bucks, but as soon as I felt her vibe, I knew she was itching for trouble.

"Well, my dear, you must be feeling quite smug after that scene in the car, but let me remind you that I have been with Crispin for over two hundred years, and I will last the next two hundred. You, on the other hand, will astonish me if you last out the month."

I shut the Yellow Pages with a bang. Oh, so the gloves were off, were they?

"I can see why you feel threatened, Annette. When the person you love falls in love with someone else, that's a real bad day, isn't it? Look, I'm willing to overlook your previous relationship and be friendly, but piss me off and you'll regret it."

She smiled, a nasty little curl of the lips. "You silly girl, I've weathered thousands of dreamers like you. Tens of thousands, as it were. Crispin always comes back to me, and do you know why? Because I give him what he really wants. He didn't mention the rest of the story about his birthday years ago, did he? It wasn't just the three of us—it was the *five* of us. Two human girls plus Belinda and I, all shagging together. I picked the humans out myself. Crispin just adores warm living flesh, and besides, we had to eat something. Well, something else, that is."

Mother*fucker.* Annette chuckled at my livid expression, her goal scored. "Oh, my sweet, I can't count all of the times there were at least two of us with him. Crispin's so bloody insatiable. He always was, even as a human. And you're not that sacred to him, darling. Did he tell you about the two of us just a couple months ago? You're nothing more to him than a mere bump in a long, winding road. Best you realize that now."

A couple months ago. So she was the "almost" from Chicago. My knuckles went white on the table.

"In fact Bones did tell me about that, Annette, but you didn't get your usual service, did you? Bones told me he gave you a tongue lashing and then left you high and dry. That must have stung a bit, hmm? All fired up and no cock to ride?" If she wanted to play dirty, I was ready to roll. Let's see who got covered in the most sludge.

Both impeccably plucked brows arched. "You haven't had much experience with men, have you? He might have left me high, but it was in no ways dry. Crispin can do more with his mouth than most men can accomplish with their entire bodies. I was well satisfied, I assure you, before he left. Not what I would have preferred, certainly, but vampires are a patient lot. He'll be back, and I'll be waiting."

That was it. "Do you know what you've done?" I asked in a bland tone. Annette gave me an inquiring look. "You've gotten on my last nerve."

The table went crashing into her before she could blink, and then my fist found a home in her perfectly arranged hair. She sprawled on the tile floor before leaping up with nosferatu quickness. My cat decided to run up the stairs, apparently not interested in who won this battle.

"Fast little child, aren't you?" Annette mocked. "You'd have to be, to still be alive. Oh dear, did I upset you? Listening to you two in bed earlier almost lulled me to sleep. I've never heard Crispin sound so bored."

"I am going to knock the slut out of you, Annette," I gritted between clenched teeth. "And *that* should take some doing, you uppity English tramp!"

"I am not so easily—oof!"

The chair cracked over her head, smashing into pieces, and then I threw her bodily into the next room. She wasn't a shrinking violet, however. Annette came at me with her eyes lit up and her fangs pointed, splinters decorating her from the ruined dinette chair. Instead of waiting for her to make a move, I charged and knocked her to the floor. She snapped her jaws with purpose, but I held her by the neck, landing brutal blows with my legs and free fist. We rolled around on the floor in a blur of limbs, but the bitch never stopped speaking the whole time.

"You've never had him the way I have, you puritan baby. Leaving Crispin was the cleverest thing you could have done, because it only inflamed his interest. He'd have tossed you away long ago if you hadn't. I can't imagine why he endures the monotony of shagging you at all, since you couldn't handle him without his leash on. Oh, and Crispin telling you he loves you? I've heard that from him a thousand times as well, but in *my* case, time has borne the truth of it. You may as well pack up and leave now; you're already through."

I bashed her head into the floor to shut her up, smiling when I heard a crack as something fractured. Annette was strong, but not strong enough. I jabbed my knee into her spine until it snapped. She howled as her body bent at a wrong angle. While she was temporarily immobilized, I dashed up the stairs to the bedroom, grabbing a curved silver knife.

Annette was still on the floor when I ran back down, and a bark of grim amusement escaped me.

"By God, you think I'd fall for that? The first thing Bones taught me was to kick someone when they were down."

I drew back my foot to slam it into her ribs when she moved faster than I'd given her credit for, sweeping my other leg out from under me.

"I know that, you insolent half-breed, but you clearly didn't listen to him instruct how to *block* it!"

Back on the carpet we rolled, furniture flying in our

wake. For a solid ten minutes, we grappled with each other. Annette scored several blows, but in the end, I plunged that silver blade through her chest.

She froze. Her eyes went from emerald back to champagne at once, and a single ragged breath escaped her.

"At least you lived up to your billing, but you missed. Not close enough."

I straddled her, holding the knife still. "I didn't miss, bitch. One flick of my wrist and you're a bad memory and an even worse smell. I think we need to have a little talk, woman to skank. I know why you're doing this. You want me to leave him again, but I can save you the oxygen in your words, because it won't happen. Bones forgave me for deserting him and running off for years, so you can bet your overused, group-orgy twat that I will forgive him for one bad mouthful of you. Now, are we very clear on that?"

Annette glared up at me with pain in her expression. That silver hurt, I knew from experience. "You don't deserve him."

I almost laughed. "You're right. That's his issue, though, not yours. Here's *your* issue—are you going to accept things the way they are, or are you exiting his life? See, I'm not plugging your ticker now because Bones really does care for you. Poor bastard doesn't have any sense when it comes to women, does he? If you can handle being around him in a platonic way, I'll deal with not slicing up your heart even though I really, *really* want to. What do you say? Do we have a deal?"

Suddenly her eyes widened in alarm. "Do get off, he's almost here! Faith, he'll be so cross with me!"

In wonder I blinked down at her. Here I sat with a

knife in her chest, and she was more worried about a berating from Bones? Her priorities were way out of whack.

"Deal?" I persisted.

She shot me an annoyed glance. "Heavens yes, now let me up! I have to put the house to right. Blast it, he just sped up!"

I rolled my eyes and carefully took the knife from her chest. She sprang up at once, but not in hostility. On the contrary, she became a blur of cleaning motion, like Martha Stewart on crack cocaine.

The car door slammed a moment later, and then the front door flung open. Bones glared at Annette with an expression so infuriated, I actually pitied her.

"And *that*, Annette, is called Pilates," I said, giving an exaggerated stretch.

"*Very* entertaining," she hastened to agree, turning blameless eyes to him. "Why, Crispin, you're back early—"

"Save it," he cut her off. With a raised brow, he went to me, reached inside the back of my pants, and withdrew the bloody knife I'd hastily shoved there. He then prowled over to Annette and dangled it in front of her stricken face.

"Unless Pilates has become downright lethal, I'd say the two of you were fighting. Fighting so loudly, in fact, that I could hear you miles away."

There was simmering menace in his tone. The tension thickened. Behind him, a face peeked in the doorway.

"Rodney!"

I threw my arms around the surprised ghoul, who looked like he hadn't expected such a warm welcome.

Tate, Juan, and Cooper hung back by the car, but I waved them in. Anything to defuse the ticking bomb of a scene I didn't want to get into. At the same time, another vehicle pulled up in the driveway with an Italian logo on its door.

"Look." Broad, false smile. "The food's here! Who's hungry?"

†HiRTY-OΠE

Aппεττε ρoιïτειγ εχcuseδ herself το change clothes, and I did the same. Rodney picked up the broken fixtures without comment while Bones followed me into the bedroom.

"Not now," I began before he opened his mouth. "We settled it. The guys are here and so is dinner. Let's sit down on whatever furniture is left and eat. The rest can wait."

His lips thinned. "All right. But this isn't settled. You're still seething mad, I can smell it, and we're dealing with this after supper."

Bones threw his coat on the bed and then gave one last parting comment over his shoulder as he left.

"Best put on something with sleeves; your arms are covered in scratches."

Dinner was an exercise in endurance. Annette was effortlessly charming with my three men. No awkward chagrin for her. Butter wouldn't melt in her mouth, but then again, she was room temperature. Juan flirted with her outrageously, and she even got a few smiles out of Tate. Bones, meanwhile, sat and brooded with a quietness that bordered on rudeness.

I engaged Rodney in conversation and tried to ignore those brown eyes burning into my side. Was Bones angry that I'd stabbed Annette? God, she was still talking and taking up space! Furthermore, in spite of my denials, what she'd said was festering. *Multiple women at once. Warm living flesh. Tens of* thousands.

Was it true? Sure, I knew Bones hadn't been a monk before me—duh, former gigolo, so I'd expected some promiscuity—but *that* kind of history staggered me. Yes, I'd known there would be exes. Probably a lot of exes, but I hadn't expected that the notches on Bones's belt would have a similar number to the miles on my car's odometer! Just thinking about it made me want to kill him and crawl into an insecure ball at the same time. When the plates were finally cleared away, I was a mass of conflicted emotions.

"Cards, gentlemen?" Annette asked. She pulled out a deck from one of her many bags and shuffled them with practiced hands. Tate and Juan's eyes gleamed. There were few things they loved more than a good game of poker.

Bones stood at once. "Not for the two of us. Enjoy your game, Annette, by all means. Then you can take her friends back. Rodney will accompany you and show you the way. After that, your luck will have run out."

The four men weren't fools. Everyone knew there had been a brawl, and it was an easy guess as to what it was about. Hell, Rodney had probably heard it also. He gave a sympathetic glance at Annette.

"That was hardly polite," I hissed as we went upstairs, Bones shutting the bedroom door behind us. "You may as well leave it open; they can still hear us."

"Anyone ill-mannered enough to eavesdrop when they can choose to ignore us listens at their own peril," Bones replied in clear warning to those below. He leaned back against the door. "Dinner was a waste of time; you barely ate. Now, tell me what happened."

Frankly I was trying to forget, because maggots of doubt were worming inside me. No wonder I'd had no appetite.

"A catfight, no pun intended. Annette said some nasty things and so did I, and then I stabbed her to make a point. Now that was a pun."

Bones wasn't amused. "So that's it, then? All's well and no hard feelings?"

I nodded without conviction.

He moved suddenly, just inches away in a blink. When he lowered his head to kiss me, I flinched.

He straightened. "Right. There are two ways I'm going to hear every blasted word Annette said to you. One is from you by request. The other is after I beat it out of her. Now, the selfish part of me hopes you'll stay silent, but then that would defeat the greater good. You can tell me anything, Kitten, as I've often said. Anything at all. The question is, will you?"

There was a quarter of a bottle of gin on the nightstand. I sat on the bed and drained it before replying.

"Fine. Here goes. Annette said you were basically a

raging pervert who liked your women in minimums of twos, humans especially because of their warm bodies, you've fucked more women than the population of this state, I'd never hold your interest . . ." I paused to take another breath. "You sounded bored in bed with me earlier, I'd never be able to handle what you *really* liked to do, you tell half the women you fuck that you're in love with them, you'd have tossed me out years ago if I hadn't left you first . . . oh, and that she was the one you munched on a couple months ago."

"I am going to flog Annette fleshless for this." Bones's voice was low and furious. "If I were you, I'd have killed her. Bloody *hell*."

He snatched open the door. "Rodney, take them back and leave Annette here!"

He didn't bother waiting for a response before slamming it closed again. I heard Rodney's mumbled acceptance and then the sounds of them leaving.

"Is it true?" I asked. "You're pissed at her, but is that because she lied to me? Or because she told me the truth?"

His eyes closed for a second. "I'm sorry to be having this conversation under these circumstances, Kitten, but I had no intention of concealing my past from you. The short answer to what Annette told you is *yes*, I have been with many women. Many. Human and otherwise."

Many. Again, that wasn't unexpected considering his age, former profession, and drop-dead gorgeous— literally!—looks. But I needed a little more clarification than the word *many*.

"Usually in bunches? Thousands? *Tens* of thousands?"

Bones came to the bed and knelt next to where I sat.

"Let me explain how I was after I was changed into a vampire. For a few years, I brooded over the fate Ian forced on me, but eventually I figured I may as well have a grand time being dead. Back then I had a talent for exactly one thing, and that was shagging. If the girl fancied feminine company also while we were in bed, I certainly didn't object. Then as the years passed, I began meting out death to those I thought deserved it. Later I started making an income from it. Soon killing became the other thing I excelled at, and between the two, I thought I was as happy as I had any right to be.

"My life went on like this, and yes, Annette was frequently one of the women I shagged, either alone or accompanied. Then one day a friend of mine asked me to find his daughter's murderer, and I traced her killer and his operation to a bar in Ohio. There I met you, and I fell in love. You can't imagine what that was like after centuries of . . . emptiness. I hadn't thought I was *capable* of falling in love, but at last I felt like I had something to give other than a good shag or killing a bloke for someone. And now my trusted friend Annette has sought to rip that away from me by taunting you with things in my past, hoping it would destroy your feelings for me."

We had never discussed how Bones became a hit man, or very much at all about his early years. Despite our months together, I realized we'd spent most of our time chasing the bad guys and very little time talking about who we were, or who we had been. It wasn't hard to imagine the type of life Bones had described, either. I couldn't relate to all the sex, but for the past four and a half years, I'd had little to offer people but my ability to kill as well. And at the end of the day, that was a very lonely feeling.

"Don't judge her so harshly, Bones. Annette loves you; that's why she did what she did. I don't like your extensive sexual history, but I can handle it—if it's in your past. But I will never participate in a threesome, foursome, fivesome, whatever. If that's what you're hoping I'll eventually get into . . . then we have a problem."

"Except for that one instance I truly regret with Annette, I didn't touch another woman while we were apart, because I don't want anyone but you. And as far as telling other women I loved them, when I was a whore, I used to tell all my clients I loved them. Almost part of the job, as it were. That's why I'd said it before to Annette, but not since I was human have I said it to anyone but you."

The truth was in his eyes, and it took the sting out of discovering everything, and everyone, that had come before me.

"Well, then . . . okay."

"Okay?" Bones pulled me onto the floor with him until our faces were level.

"Yeah," I said softly, touching his face. "Okay."

When he kissed me this time, I didn't flinch. I coiled myself around him.

Bones drew back after a long moment. "I still have to deal with Annette. You might look leniently on her, but she violated my trust, and I cannot dismiss that. Annette!" he suddenly called out. "Get up here!"

I shrugged, an idea I normally wouldn't have considered threading its way into my head.

"Do it your way, but I suggest another one. You could go ahead and beat her bloody, or . . . you could give me such loud, screaming orgasms that the sound of them blisters her ears. If you have any former-whore-turned-promiscuous-vampire tricks you've been holding back, well, bring them on. I only have one stipulation: You'd better outperform any service you gave to her *or* anyone else, because if I don't wake up tomorrow red in the face from embarrassment at what you did to me, I'll be disappointed."

Annette opened the door without knocking. Bones rose and gave her a frightening look.

"We have business to sort out, you and I," he said with silky threat. Then he glanced back at me. "*Later.*"

And he slammed the door in her face.

"Trying to hang my knickers around your neck?"

The look in his eyes, already marbled with green, made my reply unsteady. "You don't wear any."

He glided over and drew me to my feet. "I should assure you that in bed you have nothing to prove to me, or that I've never enjoyed making love to anyone more, but only a fool passes up what you just offered me. Now, I am short on some props, and there isn't nearly enough time in one night to run through all the ways I've fantasized about taking you, but I promise you this . . ." His voice deepened. "You'll be scandalized in the morning when you can think again."

Thirty-two

With deliberate slowness, Bones began unbuttoning his shirt. I watched his creamy skin revealed with each unfastened clasp. When he was finished, he pulled it off, and then ripped each sleeve free with a tug. The reason for that strange action was revealed when he tied the fabric around my eyes, blindfolding me.

My nails dug into my palms as everything went black. He'd done a good job with it. The next thing I felt were his hands pushing me back onto the bed, and then easing off my clothes until I was naked.

Something was secured around my wrist, stretching my arm out lengthwise and then restraining it, presumably to the bed frame. The same action was repeated with my other arm.

"Don't fight them," Bones whispered. "They're not strong enough to hold you. Relax." A low chuckle. "Let me work."

Thus shackled, I could only listen as he moved around. It sounded like he was in the bathroom rummaging through the cabinets, for what I had no idea. Being blindfolded and tied naked to a bed was disconcerting, to say the least, but he didn't take long before he returned.

Hands trailed over my shoulders and moved lower to cup my breasts. A mouth closed over my nipple, fangs already extended. He laved the peak with his tongue, and then the flatness of his human teeth nibbled it to hardness.

I inhaled sharply when he carefully dug his incisors in next, just short of breaking the skin. He drew stronger on my nipple until ribbons of raw desire shot through me.

"I want to touch you," I moaned, pulling on the bonds that prevented me.

He clamped his hands over my wrists without breaking contact with his mouth.

"Later."

His English accent was thicker, and I knew from the brush of his hip that he was naked now as well. Below us the TV switched on, Annette pointedly turning up the volume, but it barely registered to me. Not with Bones increasing the pressure until my nipple felt seared, and there was a sharp stab when his fangs pierced it.

A cry wrenched from me, but not of pain. He made a hoarse noise and began to suck harder, pulling my blood into his mouth. As before when he drank from me, I started to feel warm all over. My breast was positively burning, but I also felt a thrill of apprehension. I'd said anything goes, and Bones wasn't wasting time.

"Your heart is thundering in my ears, but you won't

fret long," he murmured, switching to my other breast. "I'm going to knock the fear right out of you."

I gasped and arched underneath him when he bit me again in the same way. Now both my nipples were sizzled and each breast throbbed with heat. His lips slithered up my arm as he shifted higher in bed, moving off me.

I felt the probe of his tongue on my wrist below where those unseen bonds held me. His mouth covered the spot in the next instant, fangs puncturing so quickly I didn't even have time to tense.

That same throb from my breasts was now duplicated in my wrist. Hot, pulsing waves beat in accordance with my pulse. *If heroin addicts feel anything like this*, I thought dizzily as it spread like warm caramel down my arm, *then I completely understand why they do it.*

"That's the juice from my fangs you're feeling," Bones said throatily. "It's moving through your veins with every heartbeat. If you were human, I wouldn't dare bite you more. Too much would drug you, but you're not human. So I can do this . . ."

I moaned out loud when he bit my other wrist. Now that sweet unbelievable heat was covering my entire upper body. Good *God*, but I hadn't known vampire bites could feel like this, or I might have demanded he drink from me every day.

Bones squeezed my wrists, and I jumped. The pressure seemed to push that warmth deeper in me.

"Don't move, luv."

Easier said than done. I wanted to pull on the bonds to have their tautness drive that heat further into me.

His skin brushing against my mouth distracted me from that, however, as he slid his body down the length of me and then firmly pinched my nipples. That sudden jab of double fire had me twisting toward him with a cry.

"*More!*"

He laughed softly. "Oh yes. Much more."

Anticipation heightened within me when Bones parted my legs and moved between them, one arm underneath my hips. His mouth was so close, but he didn't do what I wanted him to. Instead he started nuzzling my thigh.

"Bones, please." The request was ragged. I needed to feel his tongue inside me. Probing me. Licking me.

"Not yet."

The breath from his words teased me, causing the ache to expand. I gritted my teeth, mentally cursing him.

"Yes. Now."

"Not yet."

I was actually going to argue, caught up in a whirlwind of lust from the heat running through me, when Bones bit into my thigh.

My whole body arched, and I inadvertently pulled on the bonds holding me. More liquid fire cascaded in me, tripled by the new flames in my leg, and I came with an internal spasm that left me trembling. Holy shit! He hadn't even *touched* me between my legs, and here I was shaking from a 9.0 on the orgasm scale.

Bones's mouth left my thigh, which was throbbing so hard, it felt like my artery was trying to *shove* his juices through my veins. I didn't even have time to catch my breath when a dominating lick deep within me took it away. With his arm under my hips, he pressed me closer, his mouth greedily ravishing my pink flesh. My head fell back while my moans got even louder. Another climax drew near, accelerated by his tongue swirling and stabbing inside me, and then he abruptly stopped.

"Not yet!" I cried in blind need.

"Hold still."

Bones's arms hardened around me until I was immobilized from the waist down. A rasp of his mouth against my flesh made me tremble, and then he sealed it over my clitoris and sucked slowly. Deliberately. Even through the numbing ecstasy, something about the way he did it darted trepidation inside me. He couldn't mean to . . . ?

There was a split second of clarity when I felt his fangs penetrate, and then nothing but white-hot fire. Dimly I felt more suction and heard ear-splitting shrieks, but couldn't register who made them. One after the other the orgasms convulsed me, shattering me from the inside out. Everything burned and then exploded, only to burn again. Eventually I fell back into awareness, and found the frenzied cries to be coming from me.

My blindfold was off. The strips of his shirt that had held me to the bed frame were severed, and apparently I had torn up the sheets around us. Bones had me pinned underneath him, restrained by his body. The last haze lifted, and his face came into focus.

He wore a purely masculine smile that had passed smug and hovered near conceited. I couldn't stop shaking, especially when he kissed me and I tasted blood and other things on his tongue.

"Oh, Kitten," he growled. "You have no idea how

much I enjoyed that. I've already spilled myself inside you, bloody hell, I thought you'd castrate me with your pleasure. Do you know how long you've been whipping around from the effects of my bite?"

Not a clue. "Five minutes?"

To my shock, my voice was hoarse and nearly unrecognizable. He chuckled.

"Try twenty, give or take a few. The police have already come and gone; Annette sent them away. I think the neighbors thought someone was being murdered."

"Huh?" I croaked, and then gasped when he moved lower and thrust fully inside me with one stroke. That gasp turned into a cry when his pelvis ground into my bitten, throbbing clitoris. It felt like lightning just struck me below the waist.

He groaned in satisfaction. "Feels hot, doesn't it?"

That didn't even begin to describe it. "It burns. Burns. God, Bones, *it feels so good!*" My vehemence surprised me on an internal level, but skin-deep, I wanted more. *Needed* more, and wasn't shy about telling him.

"Don't stop, don't stop!"

Bones moved harder, faster, and I reveled in his fierceness. Every thrust sent new heat blasting into me, making me almost insane with desire. His chest flattened my breasts, pressing on my nipples, and he clamped his hands around my wrists. The combined pressures sent me spinning into another orgasm, and yet it still wasn't enough. I urged him on in between shouts, crying out for more until I couldn't speak, and when he came, I joined him with a scream that took most of my voice with it.

Bones pulled out of me and left the bed, but I hardly noticed. I couldn't move, and my heart was beating so rapidly, I felt certain it was dangerous.

He came back moments later, turning me until I lay on my side. His fingers slid between my thighs with something liquid but thicker coating them. He kissed my neck, and then smeared the substance into the crease of my buttocks.

I trembled. *Oh God.* I knew what he intended.

Bones curled his body along the length of mine, positioning. "It's all right, Kitten, don't fret. Relax . . ."

Wordless grunts emerged from my throat when he spread my cheeks and I felt the first start of penetration. A soft cry escaped me, almost a wheeze. Bones moaned, grasping my hips. His next thrust breached me and the tip of him slid inside.

He throbbed, or perhaps it was me. Either way, the new sensation was strange and almost disturbing. Bones reached down, rubbing my clit to quickly reignite that heat in me. Then he slowly invaded further into the depths that had never before been crossed.

Another jagged noise left my throat. Bones stopped at once.

"Does this hurt?"

His voice was thick with lust, but he didn't move as he waited for my response. The fullness inside me wasn't pain in the strictest sense, but it was indescribably intense. I wasn't sure if it hurt me, or I liked it, or both.

When I didn't respond in the affirmative, he asked another question. "Do you want me to stop?"

My voice, when it came, was scratchy and very soft. "No."

Bones craned his neck to kiss me. His fingers bombarded my flesh while he began to move in and out, slowly, a little deeper each time. I didn't know if it was the passion in his kiss, his fingers stoking the fire in me, or something else, but when my back arched, I was shocked to find myself moving with him.

"Yes," he groaned. "*Yes . . .*"

My mind might still be objecting to this new activity, but my body had no morality. Bones increased the motion by infinitesimal degrees, building a gentle rhythm I couldn't help responding to, while rubbing my clit with every stroke. I dug my nails into his arm, moaning into his mouth, and let a hidden instinct take over.

I didn't think it was possible. It probably *wouldn't* have been possible if I'd been thinking at all, but eventually my release hit me as surely as the astonishment over what caused it.

Bones growled deeply in his throat and abruptly pulled out. A warm wetness spilled onto my thigh moments later.

"Don't move, luv," he whispered, voice still vibrating with his climax. "I'll clean us up."

Seconds after the unnecessary command, because I didn't think I could move anything, he drew out a sudsy towel from a nearby bowl and ran it over my thigh. With half-closed eyes, I watched him wipe himself with another cloth after I'd been attended to. Then he threw the rags to the floor and took me in his arms.

He kissed me, biting his tongue so his mouth was flavored with drops of blood that I swallowed as if I were thirsty. That soreness in my throat vanished, which was a plus, but then that flaring heat in me also ebbed. I broke the kiss to look down at my breasts. The puncture marks in my nipples vanished before my eyes. Bones's blood had healed more than my voice, of course, and I couldn't help feeling the tiniest bit disappointed.

He smiled when he saw where I was looking. "Oh, Kitten, I'm not nearly done feasting on your flesh. I can't get enough of that *pop* when your skin breaks, or the taste of your luscious blood filling my mouth . . ."

He proved his statement by biting me in every place he had before, until I was in danger of damaging my voice once again. Not that I cared while I was on top of him, each rock of my body shooting exquisite pleasure into me. Vocal cords? Who needed 'em?

Bones sat up, brought me closer, and sank his fangs into my neck. God, if he didn't kill me before dawn, I'd be amazed. He drew on the punctures while shifting me on his lap until my legs wrapped around his waist. His thrust brought on another shallow suction, and another, and another, while vaguely I wondered why my skin wasn't smoking, because it felt like I had to be on fire.

"Bite me, Kitten. Drink me as I drink you."

I buried my teeth into his neck with far more roughness than he'd shown. There was a giving way of skin—yes, a *pop*—and then blood filled my mouth. It was warm, heated from being in my body minutes before, but irrevocably altered after being in his. We drank from each other, me more deeply, and nothing seemed separate anymore. His body was my body, his blood my blood, *our* blood, and it flowed back and forth between us with every swallow.

Scent began to fill my nose. Colors sharpened, becoming clearer. My heartbeat, which had sounded loud before, now practically deafened me. Just as an over-whelming hunger hit, Bones wrenched me away.

"No more."

In fury I clawed him to get to his throat. He slammed me back on the mattress, tearing into me with an un-bridled vehemence that still wasn't enough. There was a creak as the bed broke under us.

"Goddammit, Bones, give me *more*!" I roared, and didn't know if I called out for blood, or sex, or both.

"Is that all the fight you've got?" he taunted me.

I laid open his back with my nails, trying to lick his blood off my hands from the scratches. He held my wrists together and plunged repeatedly inside me, his throat tantalizingly near. I wanted that throat in my mouth. Wanted to tear it and feel his blood spilling into me, overflowing me, covering me. Something had taken over inside me, and it was clawing to get out.

"You'd better not stop fucking me," I snarled, and a decadent grin lit his face. "Because if you do, I'll drain you dry."

Bones laughed, savage and exultant. "You'll drain me dry, but not my neck, and you'll beg me to stop before I'm finished," he promised before abandoning himself to the battle.

Thirty-three

"**W**AKE UP, LUV. IT'S NEARLY NOON."
My lashes fluttered open to meet a pair of dark brown eyes. Bones sat on the bed. Or the remains of it.

Lucidity returned with a vengeance. He laughed at the color that immediately scalded my face.

"And there is my payment, the rubies in your cheeks. Are you properly scandalized by your wicked behavior? If you were Catholic, you'd singe the ears of the priest you confessed to. Do you remember making me swear to repeat all those naughty actions again, no matter what you said this morning?"

Now that he brought it up, I *did* recall saying that. Great. Betrayed by my own immorality.

"God, Bones . . . some of that was depraved."

"I'll take that as a compliment." He closed the distance between us. "I love you. Don't be ashamed of anything we did, even if your prudery is on life support."

I studied his neck where I'd bitten him. There were no marks, of course, and none on my own throat. With all the blood I'd drunk from him, I'd probably heal as fast as he did for the next few days.

"I'll never look at your fangs the same way after last night. A part of me wants to apologize for holding you back before, and the other part wants *you* to apologize to *me* because you knew better!"

He laughed again. "I still have more to show you, trust me, but there isn't time now. We're behind schedule as it is since I let you sleep."

I threw the covers off me and headed to the bathroom. Behind schedule or not, I was taking a shower. Bones was already washed and dressed. His hair was still slightly damp.

"There's something you should know," he called after me. "Tate's here. He spent the night."

The shampoo squirted across the wall instead of in my hand. For the first time, I noticed the heartbeat downstairs. "Why?"

There was tempered deliberation in Bones's words as he entered the bathroom. "He convinced Rodney to drop the others off and bring him back here, out of misguided concern for you. When he arrived, you and I were well occupied. Annette invited him to stay and entertain her. He accepted."

The shower rod came off when I yanked the curtain back too hard to look at him. Bones caught it and hung it back without comment.

"Tate and Annette? Not playing poker, were they?"

"No, why, are you jealous?" he bluntly asked.

"No, are *you?*"

"Not at all. Just annoyed at her spite toward you, but that's been dealt with."

"Tate called me a necrophiliac once." There was an edge to my voice. "I'll have to return the compliment."

"You just did. He's listening, I can feel it."

Was he? Nosy prick. He knew I didn't like Annette. She wasn't the only one being spiteful. Another thought registered. "You knew last night, didn't you?"

Bones inclined his head in acknowledgment. "You can forget asking me why I didn't tell you. Not for worlds would I have interrupted us, and if he chose to stay, that was his prerogative. Never fear—I forgot about him at once, because you demanded all my attention."

As I lathered my hair, I decided I wasn't upset at Bones. After all, it was pretty damn difficult to even shower and not throw him back on the bed. My modesty might still be outraged, but the rest of me wasn't.

Bones inhaled, his eyes glinting as he caught my scent. "I'm going downstairs. I can't be so close to you without wanting you, and there's no time."

He left in a swish of motion, making me smile as I resumed washing.

Four heads swiveled in my direction when I came down. The kitchen table was full. Since most of the chairs were broken from yesterday, we were short a seat. Bones pulled me onto his lap without pausing in his conversation with Rodney, tapping the plate of food in front of him.

"Eat something. Can't have you getting faint because you keep skipping meals."

"I'm amazed she can even walk," Tate griped without looking up. "You must have given her a gallon of blood after what I heard last night."

"Is that any concern of yours?" Bones coolly inquired, tightening his grip when I would have risen to smack Tate. "At work you have your seniority, Kitten, but he's on personal ground now, so those rules don't apply."

"I'd keep a lid on it if I were you, Tate," I warned. "Nice to see you walking without a limp, too, or are you? You're seated so I can't tell."

Tate didn't back down. "You're the one who said once you go dead, no one's better in bed. Thought I'd see if you were right."

Rodney laughed. "You said that, Cat?"

Bones gave me a sideways smirk. "Happy to represent my kind," he assured me.

I glared at Tate, but then my mouth twitched. His did, too, and he grunted once in bemusement. "Christ, Cat, can you imagine Dave looking down on us now? He probably doesn't believe his eyes. Breakfast with a table of vampires."

Tears clouded my eyes at the mention of Dave. Tate glanced away in embarrassment at the sudden moisture in his own gaze.

"Wish we would have had you with us that day, deadhead," Tate said gruffly to Bones. "At least you could have probably saved him with that turbo blood of yours. Cat couldn't get enough in him, even when she squeezed the other vamp like a sponge. If you can keep that from happening again, maybe it's worth having you on the team. Even though I can't stand you."

Instead of being offended, Bones tapped his chin

thoughtfully. He exchanged a glance with Rodney, and then turned me around more fully in his lap.

"Kitten, you didn't tell me you poured vampire blood on your friend as he died. Did he swallow any of it?"

"Juan made him swallow a little, but God, Bones, Dave had been missing almost half his throat. He bled to death before it could heal all the way."

"Tricky," Rodney stated.

I shot him a look. "A lot more than tricky. He was a friend."

The ghoul started to open his mouth when Bones cut him off.

"Not now, mate. Kitten, the timetable's been moved up. While you were sleeping, Ian called me and said he'd gotten information on your location. We knew it was only a matter of time, though I would have preferred another week or two to get everything in place. No matter, the die is cast. I told Ian I'd found you myself just last night, and that I'd have hostages for him later today. Ian was overjoyed, and he's assembling a welcoming party. Bloody bloke always did like things flashy."

I stiffened. "Okay, well, then we do this tonight. I'll tell Don, we'll get the rest of the guys assembled, and . . . we'll settle things."

"Actually, luv, there are a few problems. Ian wasn't satisfied when I told him I had three of your men as collateral. He wants more, and he's dispatched someone to get it."

A chill ran up my spine. "What's more?"

"Noah," Tate bluntly supplied. "And that's not even the punch line."

"Do you mind?" Bones glared at Tate before continuing. "Your rash bloke is correct, Kitten, and that's the second problem. Ian figures he'll kill one of your men in front of you, both as incentive for you to heed his demands, and as payback for you slaying his butler Magnus. Ian intends to save Noah for the coup de grâce, however, because whoever gave him information about you didn't know you'd broken up with Noah. Furthermore, he sent your father, Max, to get Noah, since apparently Max offered to do it."

I shoved the plate away and vaulted off his lap. "Don's watching Noah's place, right? We'll catch Max, that piece of shit, and I'll kill him. It'll make my whole existence."

Bones shook his head. "We can't, luv. If we do that, Ian will know we're playing him false. How else would you have a team of vampire killers there at the ready? We'll lose our advantage of surprise, and I'm not endangering you that way. Why do you think Max offered to go? He's probably intending to set Noah up as his own blackmail and then kill you on sight! Ian doesn't know that, but we do. Don't fret; I'm sending Rodney to ensure Noah's safety. He'll grab him first and beat Max to it. Ian's not going to kill Noah—he thinks he's too valuable. Max, on the other hand, would do just that to enrage you into coming after him."

"You go," I said at once. "Rodney, it's nothing against you, but if something goes wrong . . . if Max shows up sooner than you expect, I want someone there who'll scare my father into not pulling any tricks. That's you, Bones. You're not just an old vampire with a badass hit man reputation, you're higher up in Ian's line and Max knows it. He wouldn't dare try shit with you around, and without you, I have visions of Noah's tombstone dancing in my head."

"No," Bones said inflexibly. "I'm going to be with you, helping to capture Ian's guards. Annette can accompany Rodney to get Noah, if you're concerned about Max."

"Please," I scoffed. "Like Annette would care if things went wrong with Noah. It would hardly break her heart if Noah died, or *yours*, for that matter, but it means something to me!"

It was a low thing to say, but still true. Bones lifted a shoulder in admission.

"Left to myself, I couldn't give a rot if Noah dies. I won't deny that. But you'd suffer for it, and that I do bother about."

"I'll take Annette." The words flew out without much forethought. "She can come with me as backup to help with Ian's guards, then you can be with Rodney to get Noah."

Bones gave me a look like I'd gone crazy, which wasn't a far trip for me. "You think I'd let you attack a group of vampires—a group you're not even intending to kill, which as we all know makes it bloody harder— while I'm off securing your pet vet?"

His scathing delivery on those last two words made me even more determined to ensure Noah's protection. Rodney would know Bones wouldn't *really* be upset if anything happened to Noah. Annette would know it, too. But if Bones went himself . . . then he'd feel honorbound to make sure Noah was kept safe. No matter how much he didn't like him.

"Actually, it would work better this way," I said, improvising. "We can assume two things: one, the guards won't know who I am at first, thanks to my brown hair, and two, once they *do* realize who I am, they'll try not to kill me. Ian would be pissed at being denied his prize, right? They'd know that. I'm safer with them than anyone else."

"It may indeed work better, Crispin," Annette offered. "They'd be less likely to suspect an ambush if they thought we were there for their . . . entertainment."

Bones didn't respond for a long moment, then he turned to Annette and smiled coldly at her.

"After yesterday, I have cause to wonder if you're offering with ulterior motives, so let me tell you what will happen if any harm comes to her. I'll cut you off from my line." Bones took a knife out of his pocket and sliced it across his palm, his eyes never leaving Annette's. "On my blood, I swear I'll cut you off. And then I'll offer a standing reward to anyone who makes your life an unbearable hell, do you understand me?"

Annette actually gulped. I couldn't help but wince in empathy for her. What Bones had just promised her was worse than a death sentence. Annette would be open game for anyone undead and uncaring, and she wasn't strong enough to protect herself. Throw in some cash prizes to any interested Dead Depraved, and she'd be truly screwed.

Bones arched a brow at me. "*Now* you can have Annette accompany you, and I'll go after Noah."

Poor Noah. The only reason he was involved in this to begin with was that he'd had the misfortune to date me. In fact, out of everyone, I was the only truly safe one in this whole messed-up scenario. Annette would

protect me with her whole afterlife now, and Ian's men
would probably risk getting killed themselves rather
than hurt their sire's coveted new toy. That left Bones
at risk trying to keep Noah safe, not to mention if Annette and I couldn't beat Ian's men, my three guys were
in the most danger of all. Ian had said he'd kill one of
them, for revenge and to prove a point. Tonight would
decide everything, and suddenly I couldn't bear to just
gamble that we'd be all strong enough or smart enough
to pull it off. What if we *weren't*? Why should any of
them have to risk dying to save me? After all, there was
another way out. It only required my sacrifice, and I
made the decision in a split second.

"Bones." I came over and grasped his hand. "None of
this has to happen at all. Ian only wants me because being a half-breed makes me rare, but if I'm a full-blown
vampire, then I'm nothing special. So do it. Change me
over. Make me a vampire."

The howl of protest I expected from Tate, but the
most emphatic refusal came much softer.

"No."

I blinked in surprised anger. "Come on, dammit, do
it! Or was Annette right? Does my body temperature
mean that much to you?"

Cheap shot number two. Bones tightened his grip
when I tried to tug free.

"You're not leaping before you look on this one.
Balls before brains won't do it." His refusal finally penetrated the rampage by Tate, who shut up and stared at
Bones with disbelief. "You don't want this, luv," Bones
continued. "You think you have no choice, but I've
told you time and again, there is *always* another way.

If you truly desired me to change you, then I would. You know that. But not like this. There's no going back from this decision, and then even the most poignant regret is wasted."

He pulled me to him, and his next words fell softly near my ear.

"And if I were *really* just so fond of your flesh being warm, I'd throw you in a hot tub each time before I shagged you. You'd be ninety-eight degrees in twenty minutes, vampire or no, so sod Annette and her nasty little comments."

"Something could happen to you with Max," I muttered.

Bones let out a snort. "Not a chance. You're right—Max is too much of a coward to take me on, and if he did, I'd bend him in half the wrong way and deliver him to you in a box."

"That leaves my guys. If Annette and I fail, I can't just stand there and watch Ian kill one of them."

Bones sat back, but still didn't let go of my hand.

"There's another way around that as well, if it comes to it. Once I'm free of Ian's line, then I'm free to take my people—and my possessions—with me. You don't like it, but the fact remains that in vampire culture, you're considered mine by right of blood and bed. I'll claim your men as mine, too. Ian couldn't kill them then, not without risking war with me."

"But you haven't fed from *or* fucked any of them!" I burst. "And unless things are going to get downright freaky, that isn't going to change!"

"I for one would rather die," Tate muttered.

"You're already covered, you sod," Bones said curtly.

"Annette is under my line, so when she shagged you, that gave her the ability to call you hers. Which then makes you mine by default, though I won't be proud to say it."

"What?" Tate asked, incensed. "I'm not some fang boy toy!"

Annette chuckled throatily. "But according to vampire laws, darling, you're *my* fang boy toy if I say so."

"You should've read the fine print before hopping into bed with her, Tate," I said pitilessly. "You'll be lucky if I don't pay you back for what you did to me, and tattle to Don about it. Still, right now we've got bigger issues. Okay, Bones, if you or Annette bite Cooper and Juan, we're covered if things go south with Ian?"

"Yes," he said, ignoring Tate's glare.

That worked for me. I didn't want to announce myself as property to a room full of vamps, but if it was that or watch one of my men die . . . fuck my pride. Theirs, too. Life was more important than bruised egos.

"All right," I said, standing. "We'll go to the compound so one of you can bite Juan and Cooper, then Annette and I will take the guys to play bait and switch with Ian's men, you and Rodney will get Noah . . . when are we all supposed to meet up later with Ian?"

"'Round midnight, Kitten, which gives you time, because between capturing Ian's blokes and going to see Ian, you need to go to a spa."

"A *spa*?" I repeated, like I'd never heard the word before. "Why on earth would I do that?"

"Because you need at least an hour in a steam room to sweat my scent from your pores," Bones replied calmly. "If you go to Ian as you are now, he'll know from one sniff that we've double-crossed him, and then we may as well just start the mayhem. Don't fret, everything's been arranged."

"A spa," I repeated again, shaking my head. That would have made my top ten of things I did *not* count on doing today, but looks like I had a date with a steam room. And Ian's men. And Ian. And my father.

Tonight was going to be a busy night, no doubt about that.

†HiRTy-FOUR

†ATE, ĴUAN, AND COOPER WERE iN THE BACK of the van, handcuffed, with duct tape over their mouths and three unused rolls of it near their feet. This van wasn't the luxury kind with the DVD player, surround sound, or heated seats, either. There weren't any seats in the back, actually, and aside from the metal grille separating the two front seats from the rest of the vehicle cabin, the interior was as stripped as could be. Rodney had supplied the van, and from the looks of it, my guys weren't the only people who'd ever been restrained in the back of it.

Annette drove. I didn't complain about that, since it made sense, appearance-wise. Bones had told Ian he was sending Annette to deliver the hostages to his men, and Ian would have relayed that. I was supposed to be the bisexual fang groupie who was Annette's date for later. The really *horny* bisexual fang groupie, since I was also supposed to suggest to the guards that they blow off a little steam with us. Neither Annette nor Bones thought they'd be hard to convince, since what danger would leaving three trussed-up humans alone for a bit pose to a group of vampires? None that they were aware of, which was the point.

"We're almost there," Annette said, her first words this whole trip. The hour-long silence had suited me just fine. Chatting with Annette wasn't high on my list of priorities.

A new waft of scent from the back coincided with an increase in my guy's pulses. The news that we were almost there was kicking their adrenaline into gear. Since we hadn't had more time for them to practice with Belinda, I didn't expect them to be able to pin Ian's men long enough for Annette and me to secure them. But we were hoping Tate, Juan, and Cooper would prove to be enough of a distraction to make it easier on Annette and me. And for them not to get killed in the process, of course.

I inhaled again. It was such a unique thing to be able to discern emotions by scent. I'd inherited a lot from my undead father, but a heightened sense of smell hadn't been one of those upgraded senses. Maybe when I saw him tonight, I'd thank him for my other abilities. Right before I killed him.

Then I took another deep breath and frowned. Bones's scent still clung to me, of course, even after my shower this morning. Hence his whole spa idea later, but that wouldn't do me any good now, ten minutes away from facing Ian's men.

"I still smell like Bones," I said to Annette. "Won't

smelling him on me cause suspicion when we play our little act with Ian's guards?"

Annette's mouth curled. "They think you're just another pretty girl, not the Red Reaper Ian's after, so it would make perfect sense that you'd smell like Crispin. The two of us supposedly just came from picking up prisoners from him, remember? Crispin does have a reputation. In fact, you really should smell more like me as well, for things to be truly believable."

My teeth ground, which only made Annette's smirk broaden. "When hell freezes," I said evenly.

She clucked her tongue. "Pity." And she gave me a slow once-over that reminded me loud and clear that Annette found women just as enticing as men. Guess since she hadn't succeeded at pulling me away from Bones, she thought she'd try a "can't beat 'em, join 'em" approach.

I drummed my nails on the van door, biting back the urge to groan, "Are we there yet?" Fighting vampires held a much stronger appeal than getting hit on by Bones's former main squeeze. Especially since she only wanted to get me in bed so that Bones could join us.

About five minutes later, Annette pulled into the parking lot for a strip of warehouses. I glanced around. It was after six in the evening on a Friday, so most of the working world had left, assuming any of these warehouses were owned by the average company with average employees. Annette pulled out her cell and dialed.

"Open the bay door," she said by way of greeting. "We're here."

* * *

Annette backed the van up into a bay door, which closed as soon as we were inside. I'd wondered how we were supposed to hand over three handcuffed and gagged men without attracting attention. I gave a quick glance around what I could see of the warehouse from my vantage point in the van. Aside from the six vampires approaching us, there didn't appear to be anyone else in the immediate vicinity. That was a plus.

The fact that the warehouse consisted of one open, big-ass room was a definite negative, however. The van was the only thing that interrupted the space in here. Mentally I cursed. So much for bringing the vamps back into a room two at a time so no one else could see what was going on. I caught Annette's eye and nodded at the open area around us. She just shrugged and got out of the van.

Bitch.

" 'Allo, my beauty," one of the vampires greeted Annette in an accented voice. He had a patch over his right eye, and a crooked nose that, when he was human, must have been broken repeatedly. Still, those defects somehow worked with the rest of him, giving him a roguish air that complemented his dark looks.

Annette gave the man a kiss on the mouth. A long one. My brows shot up. *Well.* Annette was either *very* friendly when meeting people, or he wasn't a stranger.

"Francois," she murmured. "It's been too long."

He said something in French that I couldn't translate, but Annette did, because she laughed and replied in the same language. It was irritating not knowing what they were saying. *Note to self: Expand linguistic skills.*

Whatever their exchange was, it had Francois looking over at me with a glint in his, er, *eye*. Suddenly I wasn't so sure about my bright idea of having Annette back me up instead of Bones. She didn't like me; that had been firmly established. What if she was telling the other vampire that this was a trap? What if Bones's warning of horrible punishment didn't scare her as much as it should? Jealousy *was* an irrational emotion, and Annette might figure that she could come up with a whopper of a story afterward to deflect Bones's anger. I shifted uneasily in my seat, casting a quick look toward the back at my three bound guys. Things could get very ugly, very fast.

Francois stroked a strawberry-blond lock of hair from Annette's face before turning on his heel and coming over to my side of the van. I tensed, my hand sliding down to my thigh-high boots. I had silver knives tucked away in those. Maybe there wouldn't be any hostages for me to use as leverage against Ian after all.

Francois opened my door and I smiled, pretending to play with the tops of my boots in girlish flirtation while in reality, I was fingering the hilt of one of my blades.

"I have not had the pleasure of meeting you," Francois said. "I am Francois, and my friend Annette tells me you are Selena."

I let him take my hand and kiss it, even though it meant being farther away from my knives. Behind Francois's shoulder I saw Annette saying hello to the other guards. She knew all their names, I realized with an inner wince. If she wasn't backstabbing me, then she was about to do it in a big way to these people. Finally I realized the magnitude of what Bones was doing. These were Ian's people; therefore, Bones probably knew them residually, if not quite well. And for me, he was double-crossing them. Sure, it wasn't like they were innocents, since they'd agreed to be guards and potential executioners for my men, but still. It was so much easier to betray strangers than friends.

"Selena, my pet, come here," Annette said, waving me over.

I smiled at Francois once more and excused myself. Francois nonchalantly went around the back of the van, out of my sight, as I met Annette by the cluster of five vampires. *If she's going to turn on me*, I thought grimly, *now would be the perfect time to do it.*

But all Annette did was pull me close and kiss my neck while casually stroking my arm. Behind us, in the back of the van, it sounded like Francois was unloading Tate, Juan, and Cooper. Their hearts were beating faster, but nothing that made me think they were in imminent danger.

"Selena, meet my friends," Annette said.

I was quickly enveloped in warm hello kisses, as if this was a swingers' bar instead of a warehouse hostage transfer. Annette laughed when one of the men, Hatchet I think he'd said his name was, gave me a kiss heavy with tongue and decided to feel all the contours of my ass.

"Enough of that, Hatchet," Annette said, playfully pulling me back. "Selena likes to get warmed up first, but by the feminine persuasion. Isn't that right, darling?"

Bitch, I thought again, seeing the dare in her eyes, but I smiled and let Annette fold me in her arms. At least she wasn't grabbing my ass. Yet.

"That's right," I said breathily. "Still, it's nice to have something more substantial than a tongue to finish me off. Are you men going to be very busy here? Or do you get to take, um, breaks?"

I licked my fingers as I spoke. Annette was behind me, caressing my sides suggestively, and it was almost funny to see five sets of gazes all of a sudden turn streetlight green.

"When are we supposed to be at Ian's?" one of them asked.

Francois's voice came from the other side of the van. "Not until eleven, over four hours from now."

Annette's mouth ran along the line of my neck to my shoulder, and I shivered pleasantly without faking it. The way her teeth grazed my skin had made little goose bumps appear. Then she followed the line with her tongue, rubbing along the back of me with a slow, voluptuous slide.

Hatchet began taking off his clothes. I blinked. Apparently that was enough incentive for him.

Francois came around the van and put his arms around Annette. She purred and snake-hipped against him, which had me moving in the same way, too, since her hands still gripped my sides. Then Francois extended his reach and cupped my breasts. The rest of the guys started stripping as well. Pretty soon I'd have visual proof that none of them were packing weapons. So far the only knives I'd seen were carelessly laid several yards away by where the van pulled in. They really hadn't expected a trap.

I bent forward, like I was reveling in the sensations . . . and then I palmed four knives from my boots. Good timing, too. Francois had been about to feel me up, or were those *Annette's* hands starting to get frisky?

"Now!" I shouted, and flung the blades.

Two landed in Hatchet's eyes, and the other two in the eyes of the vampire next to him. They screamed, snatching at the blades while I leapt forward, throwing myself on them and smashing their heads together hard enough to hear crunching sounds.

But not hard enough to kill. Hatchet and his friend were on the ground, writhing and blinded, but they'd heal. The other three vampires had gone for their weapons—and came face to face with Tate, Juan, and Cooper instead.

"Remember those handcuffs?" Tate asked, dangling one. "Fakes."

The vampires didn't bother to attempt to green-eye them into submission. They came tearing toward them with their fangs and fists instead. All this I saw while grappling with the two wounded ones on the floor, trying to get just the right slant with knives on both of them without killing them. Annette had her hands full with Francois, who sounded like he was cursing her up one side and down the other in French.

My three guys had exactly one silver knife apiece, which had been hidden in the soles of their shoes. They were all that stood between the vampires and their own cache of weapons. Right now, watching the vampires charge them as if time had shifted to slow motion, I knew I couldn't intervene. Not unless I killed the two vampires I was wrestling with.

I straddled Hatchet, holding him down, while roughly cutting the other vampire's throat deep enough that it nearly hacked his head off. That kept him occupied for a moment. Long enough for me to seize one of my blades, ignoring the pain as Hatchet landed a brutal blow to my stomach, and ram it into his chest.

He froze. The knife had gone clean through his heart. I leaned over until my hair brushed his face.

"Don't move, and I won't twist this blade. I don't want you dead. I just want you docile."

He stared up at me and spoke one word. "Reaper."

I knew my gaze must have been lit up, which was typical under the circumstance. I nodded.

"That's right. Now, don't fucking move."

I jumped off him, catching the blur of motion to my right as Juan, Tate, and Cooper were involved in the fight of their lives. Cooper already had two wide slashes on his collarbone, but he was holding his own and countering each lightning-fast move. Tate had blood running from his mouth, but he, too, seemed relatively unhurt, and Juan . . . where the hell was Juan?

The vamp beside me was getting up, his throat almost completely healed. I slammed his head into the hard ground, stunning him, and dragged him off several feet from Hatchet. Then I jumped to avoid his leg from swiping my feet out from under me and skewered him in the chest.

"You want to live?" I asked, giving the blade a tiny flick. "Then don't dare so much as twitch."

Annette had Francois on the ground. Neither one of them had weapons, so it looked like they were trying to *chew* each other to death. I glanced at her, and then my guys. Juan still wasn't in sight. He must be on the other side of the van. I paused, then flung a blade as I caught

Hatchet's hand beginning to creep toward the knife in his chest. It landed square in his forehead.

"Next one finishes you," I snarled. "Don't test me again."

Juan went flying over the top of the van. He had gouges all over him, but his heart rate was steady. Elevated as hell, but steady, and I leapt up to catch him before he barreled into the ground.

"Watch where you're going," I said with a quick grin, setting him on his feet and then jumping onto the top of the van. From this higher vantage point, I could see the blond vampire Juan had been battling almost reaching the pile of weapons. I didn't hesitate, but pushed off the side of the van like it was a diving board and hurled myself at him. He went down, hard, with me grabbing his back.

"Juan, make sure those two vamps don't pull out their silver!" I managed to shout before an elbow to my face cut me off. Ow ow oww! My nose broke and I tasted blood. That didn't stop me from returning the favor and slamming the vampire's face into the ground, however, which produced a satisfying crunch.

"Now we're even," I panted, then flicked a knife from my boots and sent it home through his back. "And now I'm ahead."

"Cat, watch out!" Cooper yelled.

My head snapped up to see another vampire flying toward me. I reached in my boots again—and found nothing. I was out of knives, and out of time to get away.

Then suddenly the vampire was knocked to the side. Tate's head appeared in the jumble of flying limbs. He must have barreled into the vamp at the last second. I scrambled forward to the silver knives, scraping the hell out of my knees on the concrete, but came up with several lovely, gleaming blades.

"Heads up!" I called out. My guys ducked immediately, and those blades landed in undead flesh, garnering fresh howls. Tate jumped back on the vampire who'd tried to ambush me, and I tossed him a blade that he caught one-handed before driving it into the vamp's back.

"Don't twist, don't twist!" I reminded him, joining in Cooper's fight.

Five minutes later, it was done. Francois was the last vampire to be taken down, and when I pulled him off Annette, lodging a knife firmly in his back, he was still cursing her.

"Why?" he demanded at last, his accent making the word almost incoherent.

Annette had blood all over her, some of it hers, some of it Francois's. With her unmarked skin and that red gore coating her, she could have passed for a curvy Sissy Spacek at the end of *Carrie*.

"You see who she is?" she asked Francois curtly, jerking her head toward me. "Your sire wants her. *My* sire loves her. I'm sorry, Francois, but my loyalty is to Crispin, not Ian."

I maneuvered Francois over to the van, where Annette began wrapping duct tape around his wrists. It wouldn't be enough to hold a vampire normally, but too much jiggling would drive that knife farther into Francois's heart, and he'd know it.

"You may as well kill me," Francois said bitterly.

'For that is what Ian will do once he discovers we were duped and failed him."

"I don't think so," I replied. "Or I'll tell everyone that Ian fell for the same trick back in February. See, I had *him* in the same position you're in, Francois, and Ian seems the arrogant type who wouldn't want that to become public knowledge. If you guys behave, you'll live to bite another day, I promise."

Tate came over. He took off his shirt and handed it to me.

"Your nose is still bleeding, Cat."

Yeah, I knew that. I could taste it, since it was running in a slow drip into my mouth. I swiped at my face with Tate's shirt. Annette finished with Francois's wrists and then sliced her palm, holding it an inch from me.

I met her eyes . . . and then brought her hand to my mouth. Her cut had been deep, and though the wound healed almost instantly, the blood it drew remained. I sucked on it for a second, noting with detachment that she tasted different from Bones, and felt my nose tingle as it healed.

"Thanks," I said, dropping her hand.

A slight smile curved her mouth. "Wouldn't want to have your lovely face marred, now, would we? After all, you have another party to go to."

†HiR†y-FiVE

An hour later, one would never guess I'd done anything more strenuous today than paint my toenails or shop at the mall. I was relaxing in the steam room, with an attendant rubbing my feet, of all things. I'd tried to politely refuse such pampering, but I was told it was part of my prearranged treatment. And truthfully, it felt so wonderful, my protest was halfhearted at best.

After that, there was the sauna, exfoliating, and an herbal bath with exotic oils and mints. If there was any trace of Bones's scent on me after this, it'd be a frigging miracle. Even my teeth were treated to a bleaching solution that nearly burned my gums off.

When I was done being put through a high-end version of a car wash, the attendant came in and handed me a box.

"Here you go, miss. This is for you."

Inside was a dress, a cell phone, a set of car keys with a vehicle description, and a pair of high-heeled shoes. As soon as I took them out, I smiled. The guys wouldn't be the only ones with dangerous footwear. The heels on these were solid silver, covered with only a layer of black paint.

I got dressed quickly, checking the clock on the wall. Then I looked at my reflection and paused. The dress had Bones written all over it, since it was more like a teddy than evening wear. It had a halter that plunged to my waist in a style that would have made even Jennifer Lopez pause. Double-sided tape held the two black strips of material to my breasts in vertical swaths. The bottom was attached, cut high on the legs front and back, and the only thing that saved the outfit from being obscene were the translucent bits of fabric that ranged from hip to mid-thigh length and swayed when I moved.

One thing was for sure—this dress sure as hell didn't lack for fluidity. There wasn't enough of it to hinder movement.

Once I had my makeup on, the new cell phone from the box rang as if on cue. An unfamiliar voice was on the other end.

"Reaper, meet us at the overpass of Forty-fifth and Wilkes. You'd better be alone. By now you should know that we have four of your people, and we don't need all of them."

How charming. Not even a hello. "I'll play ball, but if you kill any of them, you're next."

I was already on my way to the parking lot, those

new keys in my hand. They went to the blue Explorer parked near the entrance. I fastened my seat belt as I drove off, since going through the windshield wasn't in my plans tonight. At least not that I knew of.

Two cars waited for me at the designated area with four vampires in each of them.

"Let's get this show on the road, boys," I greeted them.

Sixteen pairs of eyes roamed me from head to high-heeled feet. Helpfully I spun in a circle and stretched out my arms.

"You can check me for weapons, but what you see is what you get. Now, if you're finished gaping, I have a date with whoever your boss is."

"Hello there, darling," a voice behind me said, with a pronounced English accent.

I spun around to see a tall vampire with long, spiky black hair lounging by the guardrail. He hadn't been there a moment ago. His aura announced him as the most powerful of the group, a Master vampire, and it wasn't the first time I'd met him.

"Where I come from, it's polite to introduce your-self first before calling someone a sexist demeaning nickname, or maybe you weren't brought up with manners?"

He smiled and straightened from his easy slouch to sweep me a bow that was still the courtliest I'd ever seen.

"Of course. How *rude* of me. My name is Spade."

I controlled my expression to show nothing, but in-wardly I grinned. This was Bones's best friend. Years ago when we met, I'd automatically assumed he was a bad guy and tried to smash his head in with large stones. After Bones arrived and cleared up his identity, Spade had brushed himself off—and then roundly criticized me for my method of introduction.

"Spade. Nice name. Were you forced to pick from a comic book or something?"

I knew why he'd chosen the name, of course. Spade had been a South Wales prisoner along with Bones. The overseer used to call the former Baron Charles DeMortimer by his assigned tool, a spade. He'd kept the name so he wouldn't forget his former helplessness.

His mouth twitched before he stilled it. "I'll ponder my choice later, angel. If you would step this way? I'm going to search you for weapons."

The other eight formed a protective circle around us as Spade ran his hands leisurely and thoroughly over me. When he was finished, he wore a slight grin.

"*Now* it's a pleasure meeting you." He inclined his head toward one of the cars. "After you."

We drove to a deserted road where a helicopter waited. There was no more conversation. I drummed my fingernails on my leg as we took off. The other vampires kept staring at me, but I ignored them. For his part, Spade was silent, but every so often, he'd cast a sideways smirk at me.

We landed just over two hours later. I didn't have a watch, but guessed the time around eleven-thirty. *Soon, then. Very soon.* I said a silent prayer that no one but my father would get killed tonight, and then I got out to start the party.

* * *

Ian certainly liked to entertain in style. This house was even grander than his last one, a virtual mansion. Gardens formed eerie shapes in the moonlight, and torches were decoratively displayed for maximum effect. Sculptures frozen in permanent pose either welcomed or warned, and some of them were downright barbaric. Idly, I wondered if the ancient-looking Greek ones were authentic as we crossed underneath a marble trellis. Knowing Ian's penchant for rare and valuable things, they probably were.

The collective force of supernatural power that hit me when the doors opened made me pause. It was like walking into liquid electrocution with all the inhuman currents buzzing around. Good *God*, what kind of creatures were in here? A twinge of apprehension shot through me. This was the big leagues and I wasn't sure if I was ready to go pro, but it was too late to turn back now.

There was a gauntlet of vampires and ghouls lining the hall we strode through. The weight of their stares was heavy, but I looked straight ahead and forced my legs not to tremble. *Never show fear*. That would be the same as ringing a dinner bell.

A set of impressively carved, giant double doors were pulled open by two attending vampires. Spade motioned for me to go inside. I squared my shoulders and straightened my spine, gliding into the dangerous unknown as casually as if I were Cinderella to the ball.

Thunderdome, was my first thought. Gothic, luxurious Thunderdome. An amphitheater of sumptuous chairs, couches, and pedestals circled an open bare center that could have been an arena. The room was set up stadium style, with each level overlooking the ominous square platform. Since my path took me in a straight line to center stage, that's where I went.

Murmurs broke out at the sight of me, so many it was hard to translate. Apparently I was the main attraction tonight. How flattering. With sheer willpower I refused to search the dozens and dozens of faces for the one I loved. Bones was here. Even in the maelstrom of whirling energies, I could feel him. Hell, I could *smell* him after downing all that blood last night.

Ian was seated front and center like royalty. The lowest balcony was one level up from the platform, so I tilted my head toward him and feigned surprise.

"So *you're* the one who's behind all this? Serves me right for not twisting that knife before. Come on down and I'll fix my oversight."

Ian had dressed up as well, wearing a vintage flowing shirt with ruffles of antique silk. I guessed it was late seventeen hundreds, from the style. Its pearly color nearly matched his skin, and his chestnut hair was tastefully arranged. Turquoise eyes gleamed at me with anticipation.

"Your prissy pants suit didn't begin to do you justice, Catherine. You are simply dazzling."

"Once and for all, and it's good that so many people will hear this so I don't have to repeat it—my name is Cat." Since they'd all seen me, concealing my work name hardly seemed important. "Now, I dragged my ass up here for a reason, and it wasn't to hear that you liked my dress. Where are my men? And what do you want? It must be a real doozy for you to track me down and blackmail me."

Ian had a superior grin when he answered, comfortable in his presumed control. "You can thank your old friend for helping me find you, *Cat*. I have a feeling you'll remember him. Crispin, say hello to your former protégée."

"Hallo, luv. Long time no taste," a voice drifted down to me.

I hid a grin and turned in his direction.

Bones cleaned up better than Ian, in my prejudiced opinion, and I couldn't help the tug of a smile when I saw his hair. Sometime since I'd last seen him, he'd colored it the same shining platinum it had been when we first met. It was newly cut as well, hugging his head in closely cropped curls. His shirt was a full-bodied crimson, contemporary by contrast with Ian's, and his skin glowed like cream-covered diamonds against the vivid fabric. It was time for me to look away. Fast. Before I drooled.

"Bones, what an unexpected revulsion," I said cleanly. "Jeez, you're not dead yet? I'd hoped to see the last of you years ago. Still having that premature ejaculation problem?"

Ian guffawed in amusement. So did the rest of his section. They were segregated by lineage, with the youngest members higher up in the nosebleed seats. Bones sat symbolically on the lower edge of Ian's group, and a snort of laughter accompanied his response.

"Perhaps if your snoring hadn't been so bloody loud

in the interims, I would have been able to concentrate better."

Touché. I turned my back to him. "All right, Ian. Enough of this crap. I'm all decked out in my pretty dress and it's clearly a party. What's the occasion?"

Ian went right for the melodramatic. "Far and wide I've told everyone that the avenging human called the Red Reaper is actually a vampire disguised behind a pounding heart and warm flesh. There isn't another known half-breed in the world. Put simply, I want you with me, Cat, as part of my people. Since I didn't reckon on you being agreeable to the thought after our last meeting, I've taken four of your men to ensure that you're more . . . open-minded when we discuss it now."

Ian didn't know I'd already gotten back three out of those four, and had six of his own men to boot. He probably just thought Francois and the others were running late.

"Uh huh," I said cynically. "I'm guessing this whole being 'part of your people' means I'd have to spend a lot of time with you."

Ian smiled with more than a hint of wickedness. "You would require supervising at first, after all."

"And if I refuse, I suppose you'll kill my men?"

He shrugged. "Really, poppet, would it require me killing all of them before you'd see what I'm offering isn't so repugnant? I think it would only require killing one or two, at most."

You cold bastard, I thought, eyeing Ian. The fact that he was being practical, not maniacal, told me a lot about him. Ian didn't seem like he'd particularly enjoy killing a couple of my men, but he'd do it. Bones had some of that same coldness, I knew. And so did I, if I was honest.

"You told people about me," I said abruptly, changing my tactics. "But I bet they had trouble believing you. Want me to give them a demonstration of what I can do? I mean, you've got all these guests, but so far, they haven't seen anything exciting yet."

An interested look came over Ian's face. Bones had said Ian liked a flashy show. It didn't appear that he was wrong.

"What are you offering for a demonstration, my lovely Red Reaper?"

"Bring out your strongest fighter. I'll beat him or her, and I'll do it with only what I've got on me now."

I spread my hands and twirled to show that I didn't have any weapons, but of course Ian would know that I'd been searched. It wasn't my fault no one had taken a good look at my shoes.

"What do you want if you win?" Ian asked.

"One of my men back unharmed. And I get to pick who."

Ian looked me over for a long moment. I gave him my most innocent expression. "Agreed," he said at last.

"Good," I said instantly. "I'll take Noah."

Shit, if I could win back Noah myself, that was a big load off my mind. Wouldn't Ian be surprised later when he found out he'd bartered his only hostage back to me?

Bones chose that moment to stand up. "Ian, before this circus begins, I have an issue to settle with you.

Frankly I would have skipped this event altogether if you hadn't commanded me to appear. That is the rub, my sire. I wish to be under no one's authority but my own, and it is time. Release me from your line."

Ian looked like he'd been punched in the gut before he shielded his expression.

"We will speak on this later, Crispin, when there aren't so many distractions," he said, struggling to stall without appearing weak.

Bones encompassed the multitudes with a wave of his hand. "There is no better time than now, with all present to observe tradition. I want nothing more when I leave than what is mine by right—the vampires I've created, their possessions, and all my human property. I've waited long enough for this, Ian, and I'm not waiting any longer."

There was an uncompromising edge to his last sentence, and everyone there heard it.

Ian's tone changed from coaxing to curtness on the spot. "And if I refuse? Are you threatening to challenge me to win your freedom?"

"Yes," Bones replied bluntly. "But why the need? Our paths go back to our humanity, and we shouldn't part with one of us destroyed by stubbornness. Release me by your favor and not by a fight, for that is my wish."

I couldn't imagine having a centuries-old history with someone like Bones had with Ian, and one that had literally transcended death to boot. Ian didn't seem like anything special to me, but for Bones to try so hard not to have to kill him, there must be more to him than met the eye. I knew loyalty over Ian changing Bones into a vampire would only go so far. Maybe Ian was a bit like Don. Ruthless and manipulating when it came to what he wanted, but at the core, not an evil person. Otherwise Bones wouldn't bother asking for his freedom, when he could challenge Ian to a duel and kill him for it. Bones could beat Ian if it came to that, and he knew it. The question was, did Ian?

Ian weighed his decision silently for a minute. There was a hushed expectancy. I tensed when he took a knife from his pants and made his way through the guests to Bones.

He looked at the knife, at Bones, and then flipped it until the blade was facing inward instead of pointing out.

"Go then, and be Master of your own line, subject to none but yourself and the laws which govern all of Cain's children. I release you."

Then he handed the knife to Bones, who accepted it respectfully.

"You all bear witness," Bones called out, to various audible acknowledgments.

Wow, that was short and sweet. I'd expected something more bloody or ceremonial.

Ian let out a resigned noise. "We've been together a long time, Crispin. It will feel odd not having you as one of my people. What are your plans?"

"The same as any new Master of a line, I suspect," Bones said lightly, though his expression hardened. "I'll protect those who belong to me at all costs."

I knew what he meant by that, even if his deeper meaning flew by Ian.

"You're under no more obligation to stay; will you be leaving, then? Or will you wait to see if your former protégée wins her challenge?"

Bones smiled, and his eyes flicked to me. "Wouldn't miss this part, mate. I wager she wins, unless she's forgotten everything I taught her."

"I rather doubt that," Ian responded dryly.

"What are the rules for this fight?" I questioned. "Are you judging the winner by who's first to be pinned and helpless?"

Ian returned to his couch and settled comfortably on it. "No, poppet, this isn't a wrestling match. You'll only win back your man if you kill your opponent. Now, your opponent doesn't have the option of killing you, however. But he can deliver you to me in any state, and once he does, then you're mine."

I absorbed that information. With that, I let my own light loose from my eyes. Their glow pierced the air like twin emerald lasers, causing a multitude of voices to speak at once. Ian had told them what I was, but seeing was believing.

"Bring on your best, Ian. I'm ready."

He smiled. "Don't you want to have your former lover wish you luck first?" And he pointed at the ceiling above me.

I looked up—and stared. Son of a *bitch*. Suspended in a cage at the top of the domed ceiling was Noah. Talk about a bird's-eye view. He was even tilted at an angle for perfect scrutiny. What a shitty position to be in, watching your fate played out below you while you were helpless to do anything about it.

The green shine from my gaze fell on Noah's face, who was looking down at me with horror. It was the expression I always knew he'd wear if he found out what I was. Sometimes it truly sucked to be right.

"Grendel," Ian called out. "How would you like to deliver this half-breed to me?"

There was a laugh from the other side of the room. A bald man stood and gave a slow, appreciative whistle.

"I'll bring her to you, Ian. It will be my pleasure to break her."

I looked my challenger up and down. *Uh oh. This* might be a problem.

†hir†y-six

For one, the man standing had to be almost seven feet tall. His arms were thicker than my waist, and he had legs like tree trunks covered in skin. For someone his size, he moved down the aisle with a light, quick grace that gave me a sinking feeling in my stomach. Massive and fast; that wasn't good. But what had me the most concerned was that the man now jumping into the arena wasn't a vampire. He was a ghoul.

I could kick my silver heels through his heart until the cows came home, but it wouldn't kill him. Neither would these heels suitably double as a sword to cleave his head off. Alrighty, then. This would be interesting.

Ian grinned at me with expectant victory. "Do you know who that is, Cat? That's Grendel, the most famous mercenary of the ghouls. He's almost six hundred years old and a former *stradioti* of the Venetian armies. Grendel used to be paid according to the number of heads he lopped off in battle, and that, my dear poppet, was just when he was human."

I caught Bones's eye. He raised a brow. *Did I want him to intervene?* he was asking silently. He could stop all this by pulling the property card, I knew, and Bones's expression told me that Ian wasn't exaggerating a bit in his description of what a badass Grendel was.

I gave the smooth-skulled ghoul another thorough evaluation. Yeah, he looked like a mean motherfucker, no doubt about it. And here I was armed with only a pair of high heels. I glanced up at Noah, who had a resigned expression on his face. Clearly he thought he was a dead man no matter what happened. I could take the easy way out. Call myself Bones's Bite Bitch and walk away with nary a broken fingernail to show for it, but that wasn't my style. No, I'd rather fight this giant and *win* my freedom than get it handed to me by default. But where was a cannon when I needed one?

"Don't bash her about too badly, Grendel; I have plans for her later." Ian smirked.

The ghoul gave an ominous laugh. "She'll be alive. Anything else is up to you to heal."

How comforting. I shook my head ever so slightly at Bones, indicating I didn't want him to intercede. Then I cracked my knuckles with a hint of grimness, watching as Grendel approached. The ghoul looked me over with a professional, callous scrutiny, no doubt deciding which of my bones to break first.

"To show that I have no fear," he said in his deep voice. "I'll let you strike the first blow without defending myself."

"I'm not giving you the same thing," I responded instantly.

A cold smile wreathed his face. "I would hope not. Then this would end too soon and spoil my fun."

Nice. Grendel the Giant was a sadist. Who said anything in life was easy?

I took a deep breath—and then leapt in the air toward him, kicking my feet out with all my strength. My heels landed in his throat and I scissored outward, hoping to sever the spinal column in his neck.

But it didn't. What it did do was tear off two big chunks of his neck and leave me straddling him as we both fell back from the impact. I landed with my knees very indecently around his face, and then I jumped back.

Ian laughed so hard, his eyes turned pink from tears. "You didn't use *that* battle tactic with me before, Cat. I daresay I feel cheated."

Grendel wasn't in as jolly a mood. He got to his feet, rubbed his throat where the skin was healing back into place, and gave me a very unpleasant look.

"You will pay with pain for that."

What was I supposed to say? It wasn't good for me, either?

Grendel's fist shot out. It was almost comical, because I only saw a blur and then *boom*! I flew into the stands behind me. Landed on two well-dressed female vampires who helpfully threw me back into the arena without even a how-do-you-do. As soon as I hit the ground, I rolled, narrowly avoiding a kick that would have landed my intestines into my chest cavity. Then I jumped up to prevent him from crashing down onto me like a WWE wrestler. Fuck me, he was fast! And he wasn't fooling around! Another leap made his balled fist land on my shoulder instead of my ribs. There was a crack as my collarbone broke. Another crack as he feinted left and followed through with an underhanded right, smashing three of my ribs at least. I darted away, gasping, to be hit in the back when I wasn't fast enough. Face-first I sprawled onto the arena floor, scrambling, my heart sinking as I felt an iron fist close over my ankle.

Grendel yanked me closer and drove his fist into my side. I pulled back at the last second, so he didn't take out my entire right rib cage, but he blasted my kidney. I doubled over, coughing up blood in a crimson ribbon, barely able to even breathe. Grendel let go of my ankle. He got to his feet and began to laugh.

"This was the feared Red Reaper? *This?*"

There was an outbreak of applause. I wasn't the crowd favorite, obviously. Grendel took a bow, still laughing, while a cold rage erupted in me. This fucker was *not* going to hand me over to Ian while chuckling at how easy it had been. I would take him down, pain or no pain. *Come on, Cat. You're not done yet.*

"Pussy."

I said it while pushing myself into a half-crouched position. Grendel stopped laughing at once. He loomed over me, drawing back his hand to clock me.

Instead of flinching away, I surged forward. My lower position put me in perfect range to do the most damage I could with my mouth.

Grendel let out a high screech. I didn't bite anymore, because the main purpose was distraction, and there was nothing like a chewed groin to get a guy's full attention focused on that. When he instinctively shielded his crotch, I whipped around him to jump onto his back like a monkey, using my legs to hold on. Then I plunged my fingers into his eyes.

Grendel screamed in earnest at that. I shoved my fingers deeper, ignoring the disgusting squishy sensation. His arms flailed back as he tried to hit any part of me he could. I jumped off, missing those murderous blows, and swept his feet out from under him. Even though my fingers weren't in his eyes anymore, he still couldn't see. They hadn't healed yet. I only had seconds.

I launched myself at him again, using the speed from that charge as leverage while I squeezed his head and yanked it around with everything I had. There was an audible break, but not enough. All my muscles bunched as I pulled with my last spurt of strength, using my legs to brace myself—and then I toppled backward with Grendel's head in my lap, bloody eye sockets staring up at me.

"You forgot . . . to kick me . . . when I was down," I managed to wheeze.

The instant of shocked silence was broken when several voices began to speak at once. I spat some blood out of my mouth, not caring how unladylike that looked, and cradled my aching side. Grendel would have had me if he hadn't been so smug. One more blow like the last one to my side, and I wouldn't have been able to twist the top off a soda bottle. Even now, I felt like I'd been in a car wreck. Make that a train wreck. A big one. Grendel's face looked up at me, his skin beginning to wrinkle, and I shoved his skull away with distaste. Some people liked to keep trophies. I wasn't one of them.

Slowly I pushed myself to my feet and glared at Ian, who was still gaping.

"Lower . . . the cage . . . down."

I still couldn't speak right from the pressure of my broken ribs. Ian nodded, tight-lipped, and with a rasp of metal, Noah was brought to the floor. When he was let out of the cage, he looked at me and the headless ghoul with horror. Then he started to scream.

"Somebody shut him up," Ian ordered, annoyed.

Spade stepped forward immediately, his piercing gaze and order for silence quieting Noah in seconds. Then he led him back up the aisle to the double doors where he'd been watching. I relaxed a tiny bit. It was as safe a place as any for Noah to be.

Ian, surprisingly, began to clap, but his clapping had more of a mocking sound to it than the genuine applause Grendel had briefly garnered.

"Well done, Red Reaper! No one could scoff at that name for you now. I'm more than impressed, as is everyone here. You've proven to be resourceful, strong, and ruthless. You've won your challenge and one of your men back. However . . . I still have three more of them. How much are their lives worth to you, poppet? Join me, swear your loyalty to me, and I'll let them go. Come now, it won't be that unpleasant. Indeed, there are many perks, as you'll discover."

Ian smiled when he said that last sentence, leaving me little doubt as to what he was talking about.

Bones stood. "I've seen enough, Ian. I'm leaving now."

"But this is the best part," Ian said, winking at me.

I held up my middle finger. He laughed. "Now you're reading my mind, Cat."

Bones made his way down the aisle. Over a hundred people also stood and began to follow suit. My eyes bugged. All of those were *his*?

"No need to stay any longer, mate. I bid you good night." He got farther down until he was on the lowest level above the arena, and then he turned and grinned at Ian.

"But before I go, I think I'll pay my respects to your guest of honor."

Ian guffawed. "Be careful. You might end up alongside Grendel."

"I always did like to live dangerously," Bones replied, hopping down into the square space with me. Once there, his grin widened.

"Congratulations on a magnificent display of unsportsmanlike conduct. What a dirty fighter you are. Somebody *really* skilled must have trained you."

I laughed even though it hurt. "Yeah. An arrogant bastard."

"You know what they say about sticks and stones. Come now, pet, how's about a kiss farewell for old time's sake?"

"Want a kiss? Come and get it."

I could see Ian just to the right behind Bones. He chuckled and muttered something to the person next to him about Bones's high chance of getting his lips bitten off. That chuckle turned into a hiss of outrage when Bones took me in his arms and I slanted my mouth over his. I didn't close my eyes as I kissed him, either. The look on Ian's face was too priceless.

"What the hell—?"

Ian stood so abruptly, the couch overturned beneath him. I ignored that, sucking the deep gash on Bones's tongue that he'd given himself in full view of everyone. It healed even as I started to feel better, his blood mending the damage within me.

Ian was livid at this change in the program. He shot Bones a glare sizzling with emerald rage.

"That's enough, Crispin! Cat's mine now, so you can remove your hands and get out."

Bones tightened his grip on me instead. "I'm afraid I must disagree. I rather like my hands where they are."

"Have you gone mad?" Ian jumped down into the arena. If he were human, he'd be having a heart attack. "What *is* this? You'd dare to antagonize me over a woman you barely tolerate? One you haven't even seen in years? That's hardly the behavior a new leader shows his people, unless there's more to it than that? Is this some sort of excuse to start a war with me?"

Bones gave Ian a measured look. "I'm not trying to start a war with you, Ian, but if *you* start one, I'll finish it. It's very simple. I won't let you force her into doing anything, but if she fancies you, I'll walk away. So, luv, who would you rather be with? Me or Ian?"

"You," I said at once, with a sly grin. "Ian, sorry, but you're not my type. Plus kidnapping my friends to try and make me become your arm trophy? *Not* cool."

An angry gleam flashed in Ian's gaze, and when he smiled, it was dangerous.

"You remember slaughtering my friend Magnus, Cat? You've just decided that fate for one of your own friends."

Then Ian pulled out a cell phone, continuing on as he dialed. "If you step away from Crispin right now, I might consider letting you persuade me to allow that person to live. But you'd better come up with a damn enticing offer, because I'm very brassed off. Otherwise, it's the luck of the draw as to who my men execute."

I heard the first ring coming from Ian's cell. Then Tate's voice answered.

"He*llo*," he said cheerfully. "Francois's phone."

"Put Francois on the line," Ian snapped.

"Hi there, buddy," I called out loudly enough for Tate to hear me. "That's Ian you're talking to. Tell him the good news."

Tate's laugh flowed through the phone. "Oh hi, Ian. Francois can't come to the phone right now. He's tied up . . . with a silver stake in his chest."

Ian snapped the phone closed, and his expression turned to pure, livid ice.

"You don't have any of my men hostage, Ian," I said cleanly. "But I have several of yours."

Thirty-seven

I**an stared at Bones, looking like he might** attack him right then and there. "You betrayed me," he said with a growl.

Bones didn't flinch. "I took the steps necessary to make sure you didn't force Cat into making an unwise decision. It's not the eighteenth century, Ian. Manipulating women into bed isn't fashionable anymore."

"If you want your boys back, Ian," I continued, "then you'll agree to leave me—and *my* people—alone. I haven't killed any of your men, and I'll return them all to you unharmed. But first I'll need your word that you won't bother me again. What's it gonna be? Your men, or your hard-on?"

Ian's eyes slid around, taking in the many faces waiting for his decision. Then they paused at Bones, giving him another truly incensed glare, and finally fixed on me.

"Well done, Red Reaper," he said again, but this time

with an edge of bitterness. "It appears once more I underestimated you . . . and your resourcefulness." He lasered Bones with one more sizzling emerald look, and then swept out his hand. "We have an accord. You are free to go."

Bones smiled, taking my arm, but I dug in my heels.

"Not so fast," I said, drawing in a deep breath. "There's one more issue to be settled first."

"Kitten, what are you doing?" Bones asked low.

I didn't look at him, but concentrated on Ian instead. If I'd told Bones in advance what I planned, he would have argued. Said it was too dangerous, maybe even refused to get me in front of Ian. But Bones didn't understand that I couldn't come this far and *not* do what I was about to do.

"I know vampires have the right to challenge their sires to a duel. Well, Ian, I challenge my father, Max. If you're here, then he's here somewhere. Bring him out. I'm claiming my vampire right to duel him."

Bones groaned something that sounded like "Bloody hell, Kitten," and to my surprise, Ian began to laugh. Heartily. Like I'd just told him the funniest joke ever. He actually had pink tears appear at the corners of his eyes, and he wiped them while still overcome with laughter.

"What's so fucking funny?" I demanded.

"Did you all hear that?" Ian asked, controlling his mirth enough to spin in a circle and address our audience. Next to me, Bones's face went to stone.

"You should have talked to me about this, Kitten," he gritted.

"You would have told me to wait," I hissed back, which only made Ian laugh harder.

"Oh, indeed he would have, Cat. You see, you just acknowledged that you consider yourself a vampire. *You* know what that means, Crispin, as does everyone else here. As a vampire, Cat, you are therefore mine, and I'll thank you, Crispin, to get away from one of my people."

"But I challenged *Max*," I said angrily. "So he has to accept. And if I kill him, then I'm my own damn vampire, and *no one* has claim over me!"

Ian laughed more as Bones gave me a look that said he was tempted to throttle me.

"Oh, poppet, you've got a few things wrong. You *could* challenge Max for your freedom—if he was the head of his own line. But he's not. He's still under *my* rule, and you, as a brand-spanking-new member of my line, can't challenge me for a year. That law was put in place to prevent rash baby vampires from taking on more than they could handle in their first year," Ian kindly explained. "So as it turned out, I didn't need to kidnap your men at all, because you've just delivered yourself into my hands. And I'm afraid you've got three hundred and sixty-five more days before you can issue that same challenge to me. I wonder what we'll do to fill the time."

Ian's grin said he had a few choice ideas picked out already. Inwardly I cursed. Goddamn, *why* hadn't I made sure to find out more about lineage and lines before deciding this was a good idea? Why had I let my blinding need for revenge against my father trick me into hiding this from Bones? Mencheres had said revenge was the emptiest of emotions. Apparently it motivated people to do the stupidest things as well.

"Except I'm already Bones's," I said, using the property card as a last resort. "He's bitten me *and* done things in bed with me that are illegal in a few states at least!"

"Lineage trumps property, my dear Reaper," Ian said silkily. "So while Crispin will no doubt have fond memories of your time together . . . memories are all he'll have of you."

"I beg to differ, Ian," Bones replied, straightening. "You're right, lineage does have a higher claim than property. But you have no claim over her if she's my wife."

Ian looked as confused as I felt. "But she isn't," he stated the obvious.

Bones pulled a knife out from his pocket. I tensed, assuming this meant we were starting the free-for-all. But Bones just drew it once across his palm and then clapped his bleeding hand over my own.

"By my blood, you are my wife," he said in a clear voice. Then he said more softly to me, "I rather envisioned something more romantic for this, Kitten, but circumstances don't allow for that."

"You must be *mad*!" Ian raged, snatching his own blade from his pants.

"Do not move!" a voice thundered down at once.

Ian froze, and Bones, in the act of whipping his own knife toward Ian, froze as well. A dark-haired figure glided down the aisle, people moving aside to let him through. I didn't even need to see his face to know it was Mencheres. The unadulterated power washing over me told me that.

"Mencheres," Bones said, with an inclination of his head. "Am I correct in my assumption?"

"In all ways but one" was the vampire's smooth reply.

"You have ever taken his side over mine!" Ian snapped, losing his quiet deference.

Bones rolled his eyes. "Not *this* again."

"It is not a matter of sides," Mencheres stated calmly. "I said Bones was right in all ways but one. Cat has not yet claimed him as her husband."

Ian snatched at that. "You don't know what that means, Cat. This isn't like a human marriage, where divorce is as common as breathing. If you agree to this, you'd be bound to Crispin for the rest of your life. No changing your mind, no release from it, until one of you was truly dead. If you even shagged another man, he'd have the right to kill him for it without retribution."

Mencheres smiled, but it wasn't cheery. "Yes. Once this is declared, it can never be retracted."

Brown eyes met mine when I looked away from Mencheres. Bones arched a brow, waiting.

"Don't you think it's time you met your father?" Ian baited me next.

That got my attention. I swung back in his direction, and my hand clenched over the knife I'd just accepted from Bones.

Ian pressed his advantage. "I'll make you a bargain, Cat. A vastly different one from what I'd first intended. You can leave here tonight with my assurances that I won't press my claim over you, *or* trouble your men again. Furthermore, I'll give you Max, to do with what you will. All I require in return is that you refuse this offer and part company with Crispin permanently. Your word on it."

My mouth hung open, fingers whitening over the handle of the blade.

"Maximillian, come here!" Ian trumpeted.

The doors to the hall opened, and Spade moved out of the way to let a tall man through. Well, well. Apparently that picture had showed only a glimmer of our resemblance. Face to face there was no question. I *did* look just like him.

I pulled my hand free from Bones in a sort of shock. Max went to the edge of the arena and then paused, not coming nearer. I walked the last few steps that separated us.

His hair was crimson, just as bright and thick as my own. God, *those eyes*, silvery gray and exactly like mine. He had high cheekbones, a full mouth, straight nose, strong jawline . . . Everything was identical to me but in masculine proportion. Even the way he stood was similar. It was like looking in a weird gender-bending mirror, and for a minute, all I could do was stare.

For his part, Max didn't say anything. His face flashed defiance and resignation in equal parts as he looked from me to Ian. He didn't ask for mercy, though. Not from either of us. Was that bravery . . . or a simple realization that it wouldn't do him a damn bit of good?

Finally I found my voice. "Do you know what I promised myself when my mother told me what I was, and how it happened?"

I slid as close to him as possible without touching. He held himself stiffly, like one of the statues outside. Only his eyes moved, and they followed me with rapt concentration.

My fingers grazed his shoulders as I circled him. He flinched under their weight, and I laughed low and viciously.

"Oh, Max, I feel your power level, and it's not that high. I'm much stronger than you are, but you must know that, right? It's why you tried to have my head blown off, so I couldn't get to you first. *Do you have any idea how long I've been waiting to kill you?*"

Still he said nothing. Ian gave me a questioning glance, but I ignored him. He didn't know what Max had arranged; it was plain. I paced around my father, getting angrier that he wasn't talking.

"I first heard about you on my sixteenth birthday. Sweet sixteen, and what did I get? The full knowledge about my nightmare of a heritage. So *I swore* to myself that one day, I'd find and kill you for her. That you'd pay for raping my mother with your life. Did you hear what Ian just offered me? Your ass, with all the other parts attached!"

The rage leaked out of my pores, and my eyes blasted him with their glow when I faced him again.

"Come on, Max, whatcha think? What a gift, right? Who could say no to that? I mean, I've wanted to kill you more than I've ever wanted anything in my whole twisted, subnormal, dysfunctional life!"

The knife Bones had given me trembled in my hand with the ache to bury it in his heart. Finally, after another long stare, I chuckled again. Bittersweetly. My need for revenge had almost cost me Bones once tonight. At least I wouldn't let myself make that same mistake twice.

"You worthless piece of shit, you're about to do the

first, last, and only thing you've ever done for me as a father, because there's someone in my life who means more to me than even killing you. Congratulations, scum. You just gave away the bride."

Instead of twisting that knife through my father's heart, I slashed it across my palm and slapped it over the pale hand still outstretched to me.

"Bound together forever, huh? Sounds good to me. By my blood, Bones, you are my husband. Is that what I'm supposed to say? Is that right?"

Bones bent me backward with the force of his kiss, and I assumed that was my answer.

THIRTY-EIGHT

MAX BROKE HIS SILENCE ONLY AFTER BONES let me up from his kiss. He raked me with a glance and then smiled. Chillingly.

"If at first you don't succeed, try, try again. Do you believe that, little girl? I do. You and I will have our day, mark my words."

"Is he threatening her?" Bones asked Ian with a cold pleasantness as I met my father's steely gaze. "Perhaps you need to remind him that anyone who comes after my wife—or anyone belonging to her, such as her uncle—is in fact declaring war on me as well. Is that your position, Ian? Does he speak for you?"

Ian gave Max a truly menacing glare. "No he does not, and he has nothing else to say on the matter. Do you, Max?"

Max gave a glance around at all of Bones's people, who were watching him with threat as well.

"No, I have nothing else to say about that," he replied

in a tone that said he'd have plenty to say under other circumstances. "But I do have something to say about her mother." He fixed his eyes back to me. "You've been misinformed. I fucked her, oh yes. But I didn't rape her."

Bones tightened his grip on me, sensing I was about to explode. Ian saw it as well.

"You gave up your chance, Cat, and it works both ways. Max is mine and under my protection. If you lay a hand on him, it's an act of war."

I got ahold of myself. *Another time, another place.* Not here where it would turn into a bloodbath between Bones and Ian's people.

"You've probably raped so many women that you don't even remember who she was," I settled on evenly.

Max smiled. "You never forget your first, and she *was* my first after I'd been changed. She was a beautiful brunette with big blue eyes and nice round tits. So young and eager. So fresh. I had such a great time fucking her in the backseat of that car, and the only time she objected was after I was done. She opened her eyes, saw mine glowing green, saw my fangs . . . and started to scream her head off. Started to cry, too. Just bawled hysterically and said I was a hell spawn or something like that. It was funny. So funny I didn't bother to deny it. I told her she was right, that I was a demon. That all vampires were demons, and she'd just let herself be fucked by one. Then I drank her blood until she quit screeching and passed out, and that, little girl, is what *really* happened between your mother and me."

"Liar," I spat.

His smile turned cruelly knowing. "Ask her."

Max was obviously capable of lying. Anyone who could conspire to murder his own daughter wouldn't be above lying his ass off if he wanted to, but somehow . . . somehow . . . I wasn't sure if he was lying now. My mother had vehemently stated from as far back as I could remember that all vampires were demons. I'd thought it was just a general term of repugnance, but maybe there was more to it than that. If Max *had* told her he was a demon, that all vampires were, it would certainly explain her mixed feelings toward me as well as her outright refusal to consider vampires as anything but evil.

"You remember her mum that distinctly, do you?" Bones asked in a conversational tone while I wrestled with this.

Max didn't lose that hateful smirk. "Isn't that what I just said?"

"What was her name?" Again, blandly.

"Justina Crawfield!" Max snapped. "Going to ask me what color panties she wore next?"

Bones suddenly smiled, but it was far from pleasant. "When Ian figured out you were her father, I also wager he mentioned that she very much wanted you dead. Scared the stones off you, didn't it? Finding out someone strong enough to get the drop on him was coming after you. You remembered her mum—clearly, as you've proven—and it would have been simplicity itself to look up the name of the child she'd given birth to all those years ago. You gave that information to a hit man named Lazarus, didn't you? Had him murder that couple in her old house to draw her out, yet even when she walked into his trap, he didn't succeed in killing her. You must have been really scared then, so you decided to go after her through the one source you had. Your brother. You knew he'd sent her after Ian, who else would have, and so you dug around until you found a mole in his operation. One who could give another hit man her location and more importantly, her weaknesses. Good plan, mate, but I'm here to inform you that your little rodent and his accomplice have been exterminated."

"You *prick*!" I gasped, seeing it all fall into place.

"What's this?" Ian asked suspiciously.

"Max found her long before I did, but he kept that to himself. He's been going behind your back for months, Ian, trying to murder her to protect his own miserable arse. Not very loyal of him, is it?"

"I don't know what he's talking about!" Max insisted.

I stared at the man who was my father and knew that now, unequivocally, he *was* lying. Ian wore a look on his face that said he knew it, too.

"You have any proof of this, Crispin?"

No one was fooled by his cool demeanor. Ian's eyes had gone flat green.

Bones nodded. "I have copies of bank records and transactions from the most recent attempt. Stupid sod used a personal account to pay the informant at her uncle's operation, and I reckon if you look, you'll find that account can be traced to Max. You'll also no doubt find another large transfer of funds in April, when the people living in her old house were murdered."

Ian whitened around the lips. I grinned maliciously at Max.

"Uh oh. Looks like someone's in trouble."

Granted, it wasn't his head on a stake, but from Ian's expression, Max might soon be wishing I'd chosen to kill him earlier instead.

Ian gave Bones a last, long look, and then he turned away, gesturing curtly for Max to follow him.

"Hey Max," I called out as he stalked after Ian. "Watch your back. You never know when someone might stick a knife in it."

I saw his shoulders tense, but he didn't turn around. He went right through those big double doors and then was gone. *I'll see you again*, I promised him silently. *I know who you are now, and you can run, but you can't hide.*

Perhaps my greatest shock was when the other vampires began to disperse as well, without even so much as a muttered threat among them. Guess they were taking Bones's warning seriously that anyone starting trouble with me would get a piece of him and his people, too.

Spade made his way down to the arena to give Bones an affectionate slap on the back.

"Bloody hell, mate. You a married man? Now I've seen it all."

The tension visibly drained from him as he smiled at his friend. "Charles," he said, calling him by his human name. "I believe we're in need of a lift."

We hitched a ride with Spade, who drove us to the airstrip where the same helicopter that had brought me here would now take all of us back to the warehouse. Once we got there, Bones let Ian's six men loose and told them they were free to go. They looked stunned to e released so easily, but didn't question it, and melted way into the night. Then there was one more stop to et Spade off before we reached the compound. By that ime I was tired, physically and emotionally, but there vere still things to do.

When we arrived, the five of us went straight to Don's office. My uncle's forehead creased in what might have been embarrassment, and he quickly ceased his examination of my attire. Oh yeah. I'd forgotten I was barely dressed.

"Uh, Cat, would you like a lab coat or . . . something?"

Bones took off his jacket. "Here, luv, put this on before your uncle turns red. Best do that anyway, since 'm about to flog Juan for trying to memorize every curve of your arse."

I took the proffered coat and glared at Juan pointedly. He smiled, unrepentant as always.

"What did you expect? You shouldn't have let her walk n front of me, *amigo*, if you didn't want me looking."

"You're all here, so obviously the operation was a uccess." It was straight to business as always for Don. "Cat, you gave instructions to have Noah Rose transferred directly to a hospital? And to have his car wrecked and police reports of a hit-and-run accident filed?"

"That's right. Bones just might put your brainwashers out of a job, Don. Noah has no idea what he saw tonight. All he'll remember is that he was in a car wreck and he has to call his insurance company in the morning. You don't have to worry about him."

"You know, that brings up a very good point." Tate

gave Bones a hostile glance. "How do we know he hasn't been fucking with our minds this whole time? Your decision to make him part of this team could have been planted, Don!"

Bones answered the accusation for him. "He knows it wasn't. For one, this office is being recorded by a battery-powered camera stuck up in the ceiling. I can hear it, old chap," he supplied at Don's flabbergasted expression. "Of course, I could have just made you think you watched what occurred when you hadn't, but you went on alert as soon as you heard your niece was shagging a vampire. You've been tipping the bottle, as it were. Drinking vampire blood to immune yourself to mind control. I can smell it on you."

Don's face confirmed it all. I shook my head.

"You will just never trust me, will you? Look, I'm tired, so let's make this brief. Ian and Max are still alive, but they won't mess with either of us anymore. It's been settled. Under nosferatu laws, Bones kind of . . . um, married me."

Don tugged madly at his eyebrow. "*What?*"

I explained briefly about the laws of binding, and then shrugged.

"Humanly speaking, I'm still single. As far as anyone undead is concerned, however, I'm married to Bones lock, stock, and two smoking barrels. Sorry I couldn't give Max your best, Don, but I'll get him one day. I promise."

Those same steel-gray eyes stared at me. At last, Don smiled faintly.

"I did give Max my best. I sent him you."

A lump rocketed its way up in my throat, and I had to blink.

"There is another matter we need to discuss," Bones said, surprising me.

"Okay, but make it fast. I'm about to fall asleep on my feet."

"Yesterday Tate told me your friend drank vampire blood as he died. That's a rather significant detail."

I frowned wearily. "How so? It couldn't have made him a vampire. He only had a few swallows at most. We buried him three days later, and believe me, he was *dead*."

"Quite so, as far as being a vampire or a human is concerned. But there is another species, isn't there?"

We all looked blankly at him. Bones made a noise of concession.

"Vampires and ghouls are sister races, as I've told you. You know a vampire is born after a human is bled to the point of death and then drinks deeply of vampire blood. Making a ghoul isn't that dissimilar. You first mortally wound a human, then have him drink vampire blood, but *not enough for him to live*. After he dies, a ghoul takes the human's heart and switches it with his own. Ghouls can survive having their heart ripped out, which is why the only way to kill them is decapitation. After the hearts are switched, you pour vampire blood over the transplanted heart. It activates it, for lack of a better term, and then you have the birth of a new ghoul."

His meaning penetrated. Rodney's face flashed in my mind last night when he had glanced at Bones and said,

"Tricky." He hadn't been referring to Dave's murder. He'd been alluding to his possible rebirth.

"Dave's been dead for months, Bones. Planted in the ground after being pumped full of formaldehyde. You're telling me it's possible? Of course you are; why else would you bring this up? Oh God. Oh God."

"It's possible, but do you want that? He'd still be your friend, with all of his memories and personality traits except one: what he eats. Now, ghouls mainly eat just raw meat, but every so often, they have to vary their diet, and you *know* what I'm taking about."

"Jesus," Tate muttered. I seconded that. There went my appetite.

"Get past your instinctive aversion for a moment," Bones went on. "Now, normally I wouldn't even consider participating in changing a person without their consent, but as he's unavailable for comment, I'm asking all of you. You were his friends; what do you think he would choose? To remain dead in the ground . . . or to come out of it?"

The opportunity to have Dave back—walking, talking, cracking jokes, and actually being *here*, was real. Suddenly I wasn't a bit tired.

"Do we have to decide now?" Don asked.

Bones nodded. "Normally rejuvenation is done at the time of death, for obvious reasons. Each day he lingers in the ground, the chance of rousing him diminishes. As it stands, it will take a great deal of power to accomplish it. Rodney has offered to sire him, Kitten, but he wants to leave town because of this business with Ian. He's of his own line, therefore not under my protec-

ion, and he reckons Ian might try to take retribution on
those he can get away with. He leaves tomorrow, so if
it's to be done, it would have to be tonight."

"If your friend is leaving, what would happen with
Dave, if we do this?" Don asked practically. "Would
he leave with him?"

Bones waved away the concern. "Not necessary. I
could handle him. Vampires have been foster parents
to ghouls for millennia and vice versa. As I said, sister
races. After a few weeks of adjustment, you could get
him back better than new, as it were."

"What if we say yes, you do this, and Dave decides
he'd rather be dead than undead? What then?" Tate
looked tormented by the thought. The same one had
occurred to me.

"Then he gets his wish," Bones said softly. "He's
dead as it is, and if he chooses to return to that, he
would. That's why we'll have a sword at the grave. It
would be quick, and he would be as he was."

I wanted to throw up at the mental image. The feeling looked mutual on everyone there. Bones tightened
his hand over mine.

"If none of you can accept him as a ghoul, then don't
expect him to accept himself. He would have to have
your unprejudiced support or this conversation ends
now. Being a ghoul wouldn't change him as a person;
it would only change his abilities. He would be stronger, faster, and with new senses, but still be the same
man. Is that man worth more to all of you than your
squeamishness over what he'd eat?"

"Yes."

It was Juan who spoke. His eyes were bright with unshed tears. "We wake him up and let him choose. I miss my friend. I don't care what he eats."

That lump was back, with reinforcements. Nearby Cooper shrugged. "I didn't know him very well, so my opinion should count the least. However, if Cat can handle being half of a freak, couldn't Dave handle being a whole one? It would seem easier to me."

Tate stared at Bones in a measured, calculating way. "You don't give a shit what the rest of us think. You're only offering to do this for her."

"Absolutely," Bones said at once. "Better for the rest of you as well? That's just your luck."

"Yeah, well, I say go for it, but I think you're full of shit and you can't pull him out from under that headstone. But I'll be sure to apologize if I'm wrong."

Don and I were the only ones not to ante up, and it was betting time. There was almost no hair left at the end of my uncle's eyebrow as he stared at Bones.

"We have a saying in the military: Leave no man behind. We haven't done that on any of our missions yet, and I'm not about to start. Bring him up."

That only left me. I thought of Dave, and the fear of trying to get him back and failing. Or even worse, him coming back and then being repelled into suicide by what he was. Finally I thought of Dave's last garbled comment as he bled to death in my arms: *'on't . . . let me . . .'ie . . .*

That made the decision for me. "Do it."

Thirty-nine

The cemetery was completely quarantined off. Even the airspace above it was closed. My entire team was in place around the perimeter. Farther back, there were more guards. Don wasn't taking any chances on interruption. He was even filming, and one of the dozen men in the immediate vicinity of the grave held a portable camera.

Rodney glanced at all the pomp and shook his head. "You've got to be kidding me. Look at all this shit."

"All this shit" encompassed the hundred-plus military presence. Rodney was camera-shy. He didn't trust the government as far as he could throw them, which, in his case, was actually pretty far, but suffice it to say he didn't like the audience of brass.

Bones didn't care about the onlookers. When it was finally time, he held up three fingers. From the dozen volunteers in our unit, that number stepped forward. We could have used plasma bags, but according to Bones, fresh blood had more kick to it. My three captains and I weren't on the menu tonight, because he wanted us strong in case things went south. Like Dave's head, for example. A sword was at my feet just in case. I'd insisted on being the one to wield it, if it came to that. Dave was my friend. If he wanted to die a second time, it would be from the hand of someone who loved him, although what comfort that might give was questionable.

A medical team stood by, discreetly out of direct eye-sight. After Bones drained them to the point of dizzi-ness, the three men staggered over to the med unit. They would get transfusions on the spot with the handiness of modern science.

The casket had been raised from the dirt. It hurt just to see it. All the clamps and seals were broken, and the spotlights illuminated Dave's face when the lid was flipped back. We were under a tent even though it was well after dark. Don's paranoia that someone would witness this attempt mandated the tent, on top of ev-erything else. A little corpse reanimation made him downright jittery.

Rodney had a special curved knife for the next part. The five of us gathered closer as Dave was lifted from his casket and laid on the ground.

"Jesus," Tate mumbled as he saw Dave fully under the lights.

I gripped his hand and found that it was shaking. So was mine. Even Juan trembled next to me, and I clasped his hand as well. My grip increased when they cut the clothes off him from the waist up.

I smothered a gasp when that wickedly curved blade drove into Dave's breastplate as easily as a knife through cake. Rodney carved out a sizable piece of his rib cage, exposing the heart and surrounding organs. Bones casually placed that piece aside on a waiting tray that now resembled nothing short of a platter.

Who ordered the ribs? the macabre thought raced through my mind.

Rodney doffed his shirt and folded it neatly before placing it well outside the circle. He already had a spare pair of pants there. Then he squatted beside Bones, who was dressed only in a pair of dark shorts. His skin gleamed under the fluorescent lights, but my usual admiration was absent. Must have been the sight of him plunging that same dagger under Rodney's rib cage, wiggling it around, and then drawing out the ghoul's heart.

Two of the waiting blood donors vomited. The rest looked like they wanted to join in. I couldn't blame them, but thankfully, my throat stayed clear. Rodney was amazingly quiet throughout, only grunting a few times and making a comment about paybacks. Bones snorted with grim amusement at that. Rodney's heart was then placed on another waiting tray before they turned their attention back to Dave.

This part was much simpler with his breastplate off. *Swish, swish, swish*, and out came Dave's heart. Rodney unceremoniously shoved it inside his chest cavity while Bones arranged Rodney's former ticker in Dave. Finally satisfied with the placement, he leaned over Dave's torso and dragged the knife deeply across his own throat.

The soft outcry came from me, not him, at the sight of his neck hacked open. Bones had warned me that this would be graphic, but hearing and seeing were two different things. With his power, he forced the blood from his body. It came in crimson streams. He had to cut his neck three more times after it healed, and there were more sounds of indigestion from the troops. When that red flow finally slowed, Bones set the knife down and waved at the remaining donors.

"Move it," I hissed when there was hesitation.

One by one the seven men knelt down, Bones drinking from their necks before they stumbled away. When the last one headed for the medic unit, Bones reopened his artery and the faucet was turned back on.

Something began to happen. I could feel it before seeing anything. The air became charged with energy. My skin crawled as it slipped over me. Blood continued to gush into Dave's chest, overflowing the cavity, and then my own heart stopped for a second when I saw his finger twitch.

"Holy fucking Christ," Tate breathed.

Dave's hand lazily curled, flexing. Next came his feet, toes flinching sporadically even as the torrent of blood from Bones ebbed again.

"He needs more. Get another six men," Rodney barked, since with his throat open, Bones could hardly speak.

I shouted out the order, unable to tear my eyes away. There was scrambling as more donors were rounded up. Rodney helpfully held them in front of Bones long enough for the refills to take place, and then each man was dragged away to the medics. Distantly I hoped they'd brought enough plasma, because this was taking much more blood than we had anticipated.

When Dave's head tilted to the side and his eyes opened, I fell to my knees. Rodney placed his severed rib cage back over Dave's chest like fitting a piece into a puzzle. Bones rubbed the area with the blood pooling around him, and I had to try twice before I could speak.

"Dave?"

His mouth opened and closed before a scratchy reply sent tears coursing down my cheeks.

"Cat? Did . . . the vampire . . . get away?"

God, he thought he was still in the cave in Ohio! That made sense, since it was his last memory. Bones and Rodney moved away. Juan wept, mumbling in Spanish. Tate knelt, shell-shocked, before he touched Dave's hand and broke into tears at the answering squeeze.

"I don't believe it. I do not *fucking believe it!*"

Dave frowned at the three of us.

"What happened? You guys look awful . . . Am I in the hospital?"

I opened my mouth to respond when he reared back suddenly and sat up.

"There's a vampire! What . . ."

He finally noticed the blood. Bones was also covered in it where he sat a few feet away. I held Dave by the shoulders and spoke urgently to him.

"Don't move yet. Your chest hasn't knitted together completely."

"What—?" He looked down at himself, and then around the tented area before his eyes settled on the coffin and the headstone bearing his name.

"Dave, listen to me." My voice was thick. "Don't worry about the vampire; he won't hurt you. Neither will the ghoul next to him. You . . . you weren't hurt in that cave in Ohio. *You were killed.* This is your grave, and that's the coffin you've been inside for the past three months. You died that day, but . . . we brought you back."

He stared at me as though I'd gone crazy, then a heartbreaking smile tugged his lips.

"You're trying to scare me for breaking formation. I knew you'd be mad, but I never thought you'd go *this* far—"

"She's not trying to scare you," Tate croaked through his tears. "You died. We saw you die."

Dave glanced in alarm at Juan, who gulped and hugged him hard, crawling behind him.

"*Mi amigo,* you were dead."

"But what . . . how . . ."

I went to Bones and Rodney, laying a hand on each of them.

"We had a choice, Dave, and now you have to make one, too. These two brought you back, but there's a price. Your humanity died with you, and nothing can change that. You're only with us now . . . because you're a ghoul. I'm so sorry for not warning you in time when that vampire ran out of the cave. He killed you, but you *can* continue on . . . undead."

The denial filled his features as he looked at us, his surroundings, and then the headstone.

"Look, mate, feel your neck," Bones said practically. "You don't have a pulse. Take that knife." He pointed at the instrument that had been busy all evening. "Slice it across your hand. See what happens."

Dave cautiously placed two fingers to his throat,

waited, and then his eyes bugged. He grasped the bloodied blade and drew it swiftly across his forearm. A thin line of blood welled before his flesh neatly closed together, and then he screamed.

I abandoned my previous position and clutched his hands. "Dave, let me tell you from experience that you can overcome an unexpected heritage. We are who we make ourselves to be, no matter what. *No matter what.* You're still you. You'll still laugh, cry, do your job, lose at poker . . . We all love you, *listen* to me. There's more to you than your heartbeat! So much more."

He started to cry, pink tears leaking out of his eyes. Juan, Tate, and I wrapped him in a group hug, covering him as he shook. Finally he pushed us back and wiped his eyes, staring at the blood on his fingers.

"I don't feel dead," he whispered. "I remember . . . hearing you scream, Cat, and seeing your face, but I don't remember dying! And *how* can I go on if I'm dead?"

Tate answered fiercely, "Dead is stuffed inside that box, not what you are now. You're my friend, always will be, no matter what the fuck you eat. I didn't believe that pale prick when he said he could wake you up, but you're here, and don't you dare think of covering yourself back up with dirt. I need you, buddy. It's been hell without you."

"I missed you, *amigo*," Juan said in almost incoherently accented English. "You can't leave me again. Tate's boring and Cooper only wants to train. You stay."

Dave stared at us. "What's been going on that you have a vampire and a ghoul raising the dead for you?"

I clutched his other hand. "Come with us and we'll tell you all of it. You'll be all right, I promise you. You used to trust me before; please, *please* trust me now."

He sat where he was, silently staring at the headstone and the faces close to him. At last a wry smile twisted his lips.

"This is the weirdest thing of all. I feel fine. My mind's cotton candy, but for a dead man, I feel pretty goddamn great. Are we in a cemetery?"

At my nod, he slowly stood up. "I hate cemeteries. Let's get the fuck out of here."

I threw my arms around him and the tears fell again, but this time, I smiled through them.

"I'll be right behind you."

Juan led him out of the tent. Wordlessly, Don clapped a hand on his back, his own gaze shiny as they walked away. Bones still sat on the ground by Rodney.

I flung myself on him so hard it flattened him, heedless of the blood soaking him. With all my joy I kissed him, and when I finally pulled back, he smiled.

"You're welcome."

"Ahem." Rodney grinned. "I helped, too, remember?"

I gave him a fervent lip-lock of gratitude that had Bones snatching me back with a snort of amusement.

"That's thanks enough, luv. You won't be able to get rid of him if you keep it up."

"You look awful, Bones. God, is it always that brutal?"

Rodney answered the question. "No, not normally. Just about a pint usually does the trick, but your boy was cold for a long time. Frankly, I didn't think it would work. You're lucky Bones is strong."

"I am lucky," I agreed, but not only for that reason.

"Hey Crypt Keeper."

It was Tate, and he had a resolute look to his face.

"I keep my word, so I'm here to say I'm sorry for saying you were full of shit, and in this case, I'm fucking thrilled to be wrong. Since vampires are more about actions than words, though, you can have a swig at my expense. You look like shit. Anybody ever told you you're too pale?"

Bones laughed. "Once or twice, and since I'm knackered, I'll take you up on your offer."

He rose to his feet and Tate tilted his head. "Don't kiss me first," he snidely remarked.

Bones didn't reply to that, but just sank his teeth into him. A minute later, his blond head lifted.

"Apology accepted. Kitten, we don't want to keep your friend waiting. He has a lot to learn. Rodney, your assistance was greatly appreciated, but I know you want to go. I'll ring you in a few days."

I gave the ghoul a last hug before he disappeared into the night. Bones walked with his arm around me while Tate kept pace at my side.

"We still have to deal with my mother," I said.

"Indeed, yes. Can't have her trying to kill me all the time, can we? But don't fret. She won't be any harder to manage than raising the dead."

"Don't be so sure." But even my mother couldn't dampen my mood. Not with the empty grave behind me, and its former occupant waiting ahead of us by the car.

Dangerous Liaisons . . .

*W*ho doesn't love a little romance tinged with a sense of danger? In the coming months, meet four heroines who like to live on the edge with their deliciously wicked heroes . . .

Turn the page for a sneak preview of these exciting new romances from bestselling authors Jeaniene Frost, Loretta Chase, and a back-to-back appearance from Suzanne Enoch!

One Foot in the Grave

A Night Huntress Novel
by *New York Times* bestselling author
Jeaniene Frost

It's been four years and Cat is sure she's moved on: there's a new man in her life and her vampire-slaying is now government sanctioned. But it becomes clear that a hit has been taken out on Cat and she must team up again wit h volatile and sexy Bones as they track down the mole inside Cat's organization, prevent her father from killing everyone, and try to resist their white-hot passion for each other.

*L*iam Flannery's house was as quiet as a tomb, apropos as that may be, and it had been a long time since I'd battled with a Master vampire.

"I believe the police told you that the bodies of Thomas Stillwell and Jerome Hawthorn were found with most of their blood missing. And not any visible wounds on them to account for it," I said, jumping right in.

Liam shrugged. "Does the Bureau have a theory?"

Oh, we had more than a theory. I knew Liam would have just closed the telltale holes on Thomas and Jerome's necks with a drop of his own blood before they died. Boom, two bodies drained, no vampire calling card to rally the villagers—unless you knew what tricks to look for.

Flatly I shot back, "*You* do, though, don't you?"

"You know what I have a theory on, Catrina? That you taste as sweet as you look. In fact, I haven't thought about anything else since you walked in."

I didn't resist when Liam closed the distance between us and lifted my chin. After all, this would distract him better than anything I came up with.

His lips were cool on mine and vibrating with energy, giving my mouth pleasant tingles. He was a very good kisser, sensing when to deepen it and when to *really* deepen it. For a minute, I actually allowed myself to enjoy it—God, four years of celibacy must be taking its toll!—and then I got down to business.

My arms went around him, concealing me pulling a dagger from my sleeve. At the same time, he slid his hands down to my hips and felt the hard outlines under my pants.

"What the hell—?" he muttered, pulling back.

I smiled. "Surprise!" And then I struck.

It would have been a killing blow, but Liam was faster than I anticipated. He swept my feet out from under me just as I jabbed, so my silver missed his heart by inches. Instead of attempting to regain my stability, I let myself drop, rolling away from the kick he aimed at my head. Liam moved in a streak to try it again, but then jerked back when three of my throwing knives landed in his chest. Damn it, I'd missed his heart *again*.

"Sweet bleedin' Christ!" Liam exclaimed. He quit pretending to be human and let his eyes turn glowing emerald while fangs popped out in his upper teeth. "*You* must be the fabled Red Reaper. What brings the vampire bogeyman to my home?"

He sounded intrigued, but not afraid. He was more wary, however, and circled around me as I sprang to my feet, throwing off my jacket to better access my weapons.

"The usual," I said. "You murdered humans. I'm here to settle the score."

Liam actually rolled his eyes. "Believe me, poppet, Jerome and Thomas had it coming. Those thieving bastards stole from me. It's so hard to find good help these days."

"Keep talking, pretty boy. I don't care."

I rolled my head around on my shoulders and palmed more knives. Neither of us blinked as we waited for the other to make a move.

Your Scandalous Ways

An eagerly anticipated new novel
by *USA Today* bestselling author Loretta Chase

James Cordier had done a lot of things for his country, and when he's called for one last dangerous mission, saying no is impossible—especially when he sees his target. Francesca Bonnard, a beautiful and powerful courtesan, has many secrets, and how much she knows about a plot against the English government is just one of them. She has always been able to bend any man to her will, but the enigmatic stranger who moves in next door may be more than her match.

James's attention shifted from the golden-haired boy to the harlot beside him. They sat at the front of the box in the theater, Lurenze in the seat of honor at her right. He'd turned in his seat to gaze worshipfully at her. Francesca Bonnard, facing the stage, pretended not to notice the adoration.

From where he stood, James had only the rear view of a smoothly curving neck and shoulders. Her hair, piled with artful carelessness, was a deep chestnut with fiery glints where the light caught it. A few loose tendrils made her seem the slightest degree tousled. The effect created was not of one who'd recently risen from bed, but one who had a moment ago slipped out of a lover's embrace.

Subtle.

And most effective. Even James, jaded as he was, was aware of a stirring-up below the belly, a narrowing of focus, and a softening of brain.

But then she ought to be good at stirring up men, he thought, considering her price.

His gaze drifted lower.

A sapphire and diamond necklace adorned her long, velvety neck. Matching drops hung at her shell-like ears. While Lurenze murmured something in her ear, she let her shawl slip down.

James's jaw dropped.

The dress had almost no back at all! She must have had her corset specially made to accommodate it.

Her shoulder blades were plainly visible. An oddly-shaped birthmark dotted the right one.

He pulled his eyes back into his head and his tongue back into his mouth.

Well, then, she was a fine piece as well as a bold one, no question about that. Someone thought she was worth those sapphires, certainly, and that was saying something. James wasn't sure he'd ever seen their like, and he'd seen—and stolen—heaps of fine jewelry. They surpassed the emeralds he'd reclaimed from Marta Fazi not many months ago.

Bottle in hand, he advanced to fill their glasses.

Lurenze, who'd leaned in so close that his yellow curls were in danger of becoming entangled with her earrings, paused, leaned back a little, and frowned. Then he took out his quizzing glass and studied her half-naked back. "But this is a serpent," he said.

It is?

James, surprised, leaned toward her, too. The prince was right. It wasn't a birthmark but a *tattoo*.

"You, how dare you to stare so obscene at the lady?" Lurenze said. "Impudent person! Put your eyes back in your face. And watch before you spill—"

"Oops," James said under his breath as he let the bottle in his hand tilt downward, splashing wine on the front of his highness's trousers.

Lurenze gazed down in dismay at the dark stain spreading over his crotch.

"*Perdonatemi, perdonatemi,*" James said, all false contrition. "*Mi dispiace, eccellenza.*" He took the towel from his arm and dabbed awkwardly and not gently at the wet spot.

Bonnard's attention remained upon the stage, but her shoulders shook slightly. James heard a suppressed giggle to his left from the only other female in the box. He didn't look that way, but went on vigorously dabbing with the towel.

The red-faced prince pushed his hand away. "Stop! Enough! Go away! Ottar! Where is my servant? *Ottar!*"

Simultaneously, a few hundred heads swiveled their way and a few hundred voices said in angry unison, "*Shh!*"

Ninetta's aria was about to begin.

"*Perdonatemi, perdonatemi,*" James whispered. "*Mi dispiace, mi dispiace.*" Continuing to apologize, he backed away, the picture of servile shame and fear.

La Bonnard turned round then, and looked James full in the face.

He should have been prepared. He should have acted reflexively, but for some reason he didn't. He was half a heartbeat too slow. The look caught him, and the unearthly countenance stopped him dead.

Isis, Lord Byron had dubbed her, after the Egyptian goddess. Now James saw why: the strange, elongated green eyes . . . the wide mouth . . . the exotic lines of nose and cheek and jaw.

James felt it, too, the power of her remarkable face and form, the impact as powerful as a blow. Heat raced through him, top to bottom, bottom to top, at a speed that left him stunned.

It lasted but a heartbeat in time—he was an old hand, after all—and he averted his gaze. Yet he was aware, angrily aware, that he'd been slow.

He was aware, angrily aware, of being thrown off balance.

By a look, a mere look.

And it wasn't over yet.

She looked him up. She looked him down. Then she looked away, her gaze reverting to the stage.

But in the last instant before she turned away, James saw her mouth curve into a long, wicked smile.

After the Kiss

First in The Notorious Gentlemen trilogy
by *New York Times* bestselling author
Suzanne Enoch

The illegitimate son of the Marquis of Dunston, Sullivan Waring has made himself into a respectable gentleman, allowed into the fringes of Society, but never all the way in. If he resented his legitimate half siblings, he never let it show—until they stole what was rightfully his. Now he is determined to exact a little bit of revenge on the ton . . . except Lady Isabel Chalsey was never in his plans.

A woman stood between Sullivan and the morning room. At first he thought he'd fallen asleep outside the house and was dreaming—her long blonde hair, blue-tipped by moonlight, fell around her shoulders like water. Her slender, still figure was silhouetted in the dim light from the front window, her white night rail shimmering and nearly transparent. She might as well have been nude.

If he'd been dreaming, though, she *would* have been naked. Half expecting her to melt away into the moonlight, Sullivan remained motionless. In the thick shadows beneath the stairs he had to be nearly invisible. If she hadn't seen him, then—

"What are you doing in my house?" she asked. Her voice shook; she was mortal, after all.

If he said the wrong thing or moved too abruptly, she would scream. And then he would have a fight on his hands. While he didn't mind that, it might prevent him from leaving with the painting—and that was his major goal. Except that she still looked . . . ethereal in the darkness, and he couldn't shake the sensation that he was caught in a luminous waking dream. "I'm here for a kiss," he said.

She looked from his masked face to the bundle beneath his arm. "Then you have very bad eyesight, because that is not a kiss."

Grudgingly, though occupied with figuring a way to leave with both his skin and the painting, he had to admit that she had her wits about her. Even in the dark, alone, and faced with a masked stranger. "Perhaps I'll have both, then."

"You'll have neither. Put that back and leave, and I shan't call for assistance."

He took a slow step toward her. "You shouldn't warn me of your intentions," he returned, keeping his voice low and not certain why he bothered to banter with her when he could have been past her and back outside by now. "I could be on you before you draw another breath."

Her step backward matched his second one forward. "Now who's warning whom?" she asked. "Get out."

"Very well." He gestured for her to move aside, quelling the baser part of him that wanted her to remove that flimsy, useless night rail from her body and run his hands across her soft skin.

"Without the paintings."

"No."

"They aren't yours. Put them back."

One of them *was* his, but Sullivan wasn't about to say that aloud. "No. Be glad I'm willing to leave without the kiss and step aside."

Actually, the idea of kissing her was beginning to seem less mad than it had at first. Perhaps it was the moonlight, or the late hour, or the buried excitement he always felt at being somewhere in secret, of doing something that a year ago he would never even have contemplated, or the fact that he'd never seen a mouth as tempting as hers.

"Then I'm sorry. I gave you a chance." She drew a breath.

Moving fast, Sullivan closed the distance between them. Grabbing her shoulder with his free hand, he yanked her up against him, then leaned down and covered her mouth with his.

She tasted like surprise and warm chocolate. He'd expected the surprise, counted on it to stop her from yelling. But the shiver running down his spine at the touch of her soft lips to his stunned him. So did the way her hands rose to touch his face in return. Sullivan broke away, offering her a jaunty grin and trying to hide the way he was abruptly out of breath. "I seem to have gotten everything I came for, after all," he murmured, and brushed past her to unlatch and open the front door.

Outside, he collected his hammer and then hurried down the street to where his horse waited. Closing the paintings into the flat leather pouch he'd brought for the purpose, he swung into the saddle. "Let's go, Achilles," he said, and the big black stallion broke into a trot.

After ten thefts, he'd become an expert in anticipating just about anything. That was the first time, though, that he'd stolen a kiss. Belatedly, he reached up to remove his mask. It was gone.

His blood froze. That kiss—that blasted kiss—had distracted him more than he'd realized. And now someone had seen his face. "Damnation."

Before the Scandal

Second in The Notorious Gentlemen trilogy
by *New York Times* bestselling author
Suzanne Enoch

When Phineas Bromley suddenly becomes Viscount
Hamilton, his world is thrown into a tailspin. More
used to battlefields than ballrooms, the adjustment
to town life is not easy. But there's nothing like a
little mystery to liven up what seems like a mundane life. Aware that someone is stealing from the
family coffers, Phineas must come up with a way
to expose the culprits. His plan is risky—but not as
dangerous as his unexpected attraction to Alyse
Donnelly, the young lady next door.

*P*hin Bromley. Alyse Donnelly had never thought
to set eyes on him again. He was undeniably
taller, but he also seemed . . . larger. Not fat, by any
means, because he'd always been lean, but . . . more
commanding. Yes, that's what it was. And—

Richard jabbed her in the shoulder. "Who is he?" her
cousin hissed.

Alyse shook herself. "Their brother," she answered
in the same low tone he'd used. Either the footmen
knew already or they would soon, but if Richard didn't
want to be seen gossiping, she could understand that.
"The middle sibling."

"You never mentioned another brother."

"He's been away for a very long time. Ten years or more." She smiled a little, remembering. "I haven't set eyes on him since I was thirteen."

"Well, this could be an opportunity for you then, cousin, couldn't it?" Richard murmured. "After all, if there are things you don't know about him, then there are bound to be things he doesn't know about you."

Her face heated; she couldn't help it. After four years she should have been used to the insults, direct or implied, but obviously they still had the power to cut her. "Thank you, Richard," she said softly, "but I prefer to make his acquaintance first."

"I suggest you speak to your cousin with less sarcasm, Alyse," her Aunt Ernesta cooed. "You are not who you once were."

And no one in her family ever let her forget that fact. "I remember, Aunt Ernesta."

"Then have someone fetch me a blanket. My legs are cold."

Carefully hiding her annoyance, Alyse motioned to the nearest of the footmen and passed on her aunt's request. Things in the Bromley household might have taken a turn for the unexpected, but her life progressed with the predictability of a clock. An endlessly ticking clock.

The dining room door opened again. Lord Quence entered first, being wheeled in on his chair with a somber look on his pale face. Beth followed a heartbeat later, her expression tense. The door closed again, but Alyse kept her gaze on it.

Phineas Bromley. Phin. The last person she ever would have imagined joining the army, though he obviously had. She didn't know what the insignia on his shoulder meant, but he was clearly an officer.

A moment later he walked into the room, his gaze touch-

ng on the rest of the occupants, then finding her. Alyse
blushed again at those clear hazel eyes, wondering what
she looked like to him. Other than his eyes, she wasn't certain she would have recognized him. His dark brown hair
was a little long, as though he'd been too busy to seek a
barber, and his face leaner than she remembered. And a
narrow scar dissected his right eyebrow, giving his appearance the rakish bent he'd always seemed to have inside.

"Alyse," he said, and took the seat across from her.
"Miss Donnelly. William told me that your parents passed
away. I am truly sorry."

"Thank you. It was . . . unexpected."

Richard leaned over to cover her hand with his. "I'm
only glad that we've been able to give Alyse a place in
our household."

Phineas glanced at her cousin, then back to her again.
"Do you still like to ride?" he asked.

It felt odd to have someone pay attention to her these
days. "I haven't had much opportunity," she hedged. "My
aunt is unwell, and I sit with her a great deal."

"If I stay long enough, we should go riding," he pursued.

Alyse smiled. "I would like that."

"How long *will* you be staying?" Richard cut in again.

This time Phin glanced at his brother. "As long as I'm
needed. I have several months of leave coming, if I require it."

"Where are you serving?" Alyse asked, disliking when
that gaze left her.

"The north of Spain at the moment. I'm with the First
Royal Dragoons."

"A . . . lieutenant, is it?" Richard asked, eyeing the
crimson and blue uniform.

"Lieutenant-Colonel," Elizabeth corrected, pride in her
tone. "Phin's received five field promotions."

"That's extraordinary." Richard lifted a glass, not in Phin's direction, but in the viscount his brother's. "You must be very proud of him."

"Yes," Lord Quence said, returning to his meal. "Very proud."

Clearly all was not entirely well at Quence Park, though Alyse had known that before. But for Richard to poke a stick into the tension—it was so unlike him in public, though in private he did little else. "When we were all children together," she said into the air, "we had the most hair-raising adventures."

Phineas sent her a short smile. "I can face cannons fearlessly after surviving the infamous pond-jump dares."

Alyse snorted, then quickly covered her mouth with one hand and made the sound into a cough. "You were fearless well before then."

THE NIGHT HUNTRESS NOVELS FROM

JEANIENE FROST

✝ HALFWAY TO THE GRAVE ✝

978-0-06-124508-4

Before she can enjoy her newfound status as kick-ass demon hunter, half vampire Cat Crawfield and her sexy mentor, Bones, are pursued by a group of killers. Now Cat will have to choose a side…and Bones is turning out to be as tempting as any man with a heartbeat.

✝ ONE FOOT IN THE GRAVE ✝

978-0-06-124509-1

Cat Crawfield is now a special agent, working for the government to rid the world of the rogue undead. But when she's targeted for assassination she turns to her ex, the sexy and dangerous vampire Bones, to help her.

✝ AT GRAVE'S END ✝

978-0-06-158307-0

Caught in the crosshairs of a vengeful vamp, Cat's about to learn the true meaning of bad blood—just as she and Bones need to stop a lethal magic from being unleashed.

Available wherever books are sold or please call 1-800-331-3761 to order.

JFR 0109